ROMEO SPIKES

BOOK ONE OF THE LoLife TRILOGY

JOANNE REAY

TITAN BOOKS

Lo'Life: Romeo Spikes
Print edition ISBN: 9781781165348
E-book edition ISBN: 9781781165355

Published by Titan Books
A division of Titan Publishing Group Ltd
144 Southwark Street, London SE1 0UP

First edition: October 2012
10 9 8 7 6 5 4 3 2 1

A CIP catalogue record for this title is available from the British Library.

Printed and bound in Great Britain by CPI Group Ltd.

What did you think of this book? We love to hear from our readers. Please email
us at: readerfeedback@titanemail.com, or write to us at the above address.

To receive advance information, news, competitions, and exclusive offers online,
please sign up for the Titan newsletter on our website: www.titanbooks.com

To Emma, Katie, and Georgie

BOOK I

I

"...But I say, life's too short."

She ignores him. Her lacquered fingernails agitate the cashew bowl.

He forges on. "Fifty-five. But firmer than I was at forty. Lotta fruit and fiber. And fish oil."

He moves closer. A blast of breath in her ear. "So what's your secret?"

"I eat six pounds of grapes a day."

"That's a lot of grapes."

"Not when you squeeze them down to wine." She turns to him. "The night is young. Fish elsewhere."

She feels the ripple of his departure. Turns back to the bar and taps the bowl of her wineglass. The young barman responds to her semaphore, picks up a bottle, and approaches with a boyish grin. His hair is surfed into a halo of gold.

"It's the rioja, right?"

He twists the cork, dialing up the volume of his appeal. The woman tilts her chin. Not in answer to his question, but to pull taut a hammock of neck flesh.

She watches as he pours the glass brimful. Pirouettes her fingers about the stem. "Won't you join me?"

"I'm working."

"Join me later?"

"Aren't you waiting for someone?"

Her fur coat swamps the adjacent stool but she wafts a finger in dismissal. "Just company business."

"Well, if you're wanting company, ma'am"—the barman motions a finger between his chest and hers—"that's business too."

Her purse snaps open. She pulls out three twenty-dollar bills. "What does that get me?"

"Fresh nuts."

She withdraws, jaw tight.

"Lady, this is Manhattan." He taps the cash. "And that don't get you a man."

She rolls back her shoulders, hoisting her breasts. "Ten years ago, I would have been your fantasy. I looked very different."

"Did you look like Spider-man?"

She grimaces. Froths her hair with furious fingers. *How young is he… ?*

He moves to take the bottle, but she snatches it by the neck. "I'm not finished. Not yet."

The barman gathers up one of the twenties. "That should cover it." Glances at the bottle. "It's just the dregs."

She watches as he turns and walks away. *His whole life ahead of him.*

And mine? She inhales deeply. All her best years lay behind, spilled like the trail of a dancing drunk.

Squandered. Scattered.

The young Annie Torgus had graduated top of her class with a doctorate in psychiatry. Her specialty was the early diagnosis

 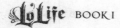

of suicidal tendencies. The perception may be that suicide is a practice of the poor, but evidence shows a life of dull luxury to be the sharper spur.

Renting costly offices on the Upper West side, she imagines a wealthy clientele clamoring for her services. Anxious parents, perhaps, of a teenage girl who festers in her bedroom. To draw her out, Mommy and Daddy have applied a poultice of promises: a new Porsche, a trip to Paris, a pony in the upper field—but nothing has worked. So they urgently call upon Dr. Annie Torgus. And she comes at once, and at quite a price.

Easy money.

But the young doctor is kept awake by the sound of her phone not ringing. Her debts rise and so, to raise her profile, she rushes to publish, submitting a lengthy article to the *New Scientist*. With a racy title, "How the Kids Hang in the Hamptons," the article exposes a culture of self-harm and suicide amongst the wealthy teens of New England. Snatched up by the *New York Times*, her shocking data flies across the Sunday pages. Radio stations ring for interviews and television soon chases after, faster still once it discovers that Dr. Annie Torgus is young and big-breasted. But as the media spotlight intensifies, it becomes an invasive, burning heat, igniting her research and turning it to ashes. Dr. Annie Torgus, it transpires, fabricated the statistics and falsified the teenage testimony. The glitter she saw surrounding her career turns out to be knives, and, blow by blow, amid howls of derision from her peers, her professional reputation is destroyed.

Sliced. Shredded.

Sued by everyone, she struggles on, living off store cards.

Until she's thrown out of her apartment at Broadway and Fourth, landing back in the swamps of Louisiana where she was born. And where the only local employer is Morphic Fields Penitentiary. The black brick structure looms like a mausoleum, and appropriately so, as more prisoners await their execution here than at any other facility.

There is a position available and, faced with little local competition, she secures the job of chief psychiatric officer. Her duty is to monitor suicidal tendencies amongst the inmates. The urge to kill oneself is a prime indicator of insanity, and a suicide attempt is all too often used by appeals lawyers to certify an inmate's unsound mind. A stay of execution frequently follows. The warden of Morphic Fields, who resents any disturbance to the natural delivery of death within his domain, decides to create the post of prison psychiatric officer to stifle this trend. On her first day, walking into the concrete bunker of her office, Annie Torgus assesses her job as this: to stop death-row prisoners from taking their own lives.

The irony is not lost upon her.

Her sense of purpose is lost forever.

She works alone, day after day, year after year, examining the inmates, declaring them sane and signing away their last chance of appeal. Clutching her clipboard and ticking the boxes, she idly imagines that Warden Duggin might eventually decide to extend her responsibilities one degree further, one gesture more—to have her swish her signature and then plunge her pen deep into the inmate's carotid artery, ripping wide a hole, a gushing slash…

She splashes the last of the wine into her glass. Knocks it

 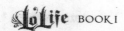

back. Thirty-five years she has been at Morphic Fields. Her whole life… a life sentence.

The glass stem lowers, unleashing her reflection onto the mirror behind the bar. She grimaces at the old woman who stares back at her.

Hair too black, too brittle. Eyes rolled in wrinkles. And those hands, those ancient hands. Spotted, scaly, fatless claws—

The bitter self-attack continues until she slams down her fist and loudly orders another bottle, drags an angry cuff across her eyes. *God, no wonder when people off themselves, they shoot their head.*

She inhales slowly. Eases back a sleeve to expose her watch. It is later than she thought. She pulls her coat from the adjacent stool. He could arrive at any moment. She needs to compose herself. Remember why she is here. Remember at least his name.

She urgently fumbles in her pocket, retrieving a business card. Holds it at arm's length, straining to read the small cursive print.

Christopher Hatchling
Senior Buyer, Phobos Books

On the journey out from Louisiana, idling hours at the airport, she bought a Phobos title: *Pharaohs from a Far-Flung Star*. A brick of a book, it promised to "stun the reader."

If it falls on your skull, then perhaps.

Torgus peeled back the gold-embossed cover and her heart sank as she scanned the trashy text within. But she plowed on, commending herself that she was, at least, doing some research. Then a thought burned her brain: *If I'd done my research thirty-five years ago, I wouldn't now be reduced to this.* Offering a tawdry publishing house what she knows to be an earth-shattering manuscript.

How could they ever appreciate the prophecy it holds? So strange, so obscure...

But this raw material fell into her hands and it will be her salvation.

She pulls her spine straight. Lifts her chin. Reminds herself that Annie is short for Anstice—a Greek name, reflecting her roots. It means "resurrection." She will rise again.

I'm not finished. Not yet.

She pulls a small mirror from her purse. Checks her teeth for lipstick and her lips for teeth marks. Her habit is to bite down hard when nerves attack. The mirror twists in her palm as she searches the bar behind her. She'd like to see Christopher Hatchling before he sees her. She needs that fractional head start, to drop her face into a casual cradle of welcome.

The mirror picks up a man. His hair tumbles in thick curls. Dr. Torgus thins her lips. She had hoped for someone older, as suggested by the epithet *senior* buyer. But *Hatchling* it is. Fresh from the egg of ambition. He strides across the carpet, nose up and neck extended. She recognizes the gander-gait of a man arriving for lunch with a mystery woman. She waves her hand, and, as his eyes connect, his swagger slows.

"Dr. Torgus, I'm sorry I'm late."

I'm sorry I'm old.

She delivers a shallow smile, so as not to ripple more wrinkles. "You're quite on time." She takes a deep swig, fluffs

 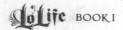

her hair. "I can recommend the rioja, if you would like a glass."

"Too early for me."

Too young, too young…

She tosses her hair and inside her head, the alcohol swills the rim of her skull.

I can do this!

Her voice drops, husky now. Or haggard. She can no longer tell. "So, Christopher… are you ready?"

She lifts her bag between her legs, reaches deep into the old, brown folds. "I have something very special to show you."

And from within, she lifts a tightly bound file.

2

An eagle arcs across the sky. Its head swivels down, drawn by something below.

The glint of a rifle, sliding from the corner of a watchtower.

Down the length of the barrel gazes a prison guard. His head dips, drawn to the exercise yard below.

A flash of metal.

The guard primes his rifle. Then removes his finger from the trigger and waggles it in his ear to pop a wave of atmospheric pressure.

One helluva storm coming.

The finger returns to the trigger and his eye presses against the eyepiece.

Dammit, he saw *something*.

He swivels the rifle sight toward the most likely location of a shank. *Always bet on the Petra Loa.* The shaven-headed Haitian gang members arc across the center of the yard, owning it.

In their midst stands a flat-faced giant of a man, who once went by the name of Little Bit. The heat of the Cajun hip-hop scene kept the rising star's ears and wrists nicely iced—until the Louisiana State Police gave him bracelets on a charge of murder one.

 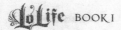

The trial was big news. Little Bit towered in the dock, so warped with muscle that they had to find a fatter chair to take his weight.

But his defense was slim. His prints were on the gun. His legal team argued for accidental shooting—the victim, little LouAnne Titley, was caught in the crossfire of a long-standing feud. *But she isn't standing no more,* said the young district attorney as he brandished a blowup of LouAnne's blasted body. The fine ladies of the jury, with their shoes and totes carefully color-coordinated, wept into white handkerchiefs and, with matching Confederate values, swiftly condemned the black man to death. Little Bit was led from the courtroom, headed for the big chair.

At Morphic Fields, news of his arrival caused a stir amongst the guards. They all wanted the bragging rights to his admission. *Yeah, it was me who stripped that big-ass rapper down.*

Right up to the moment when the bus shuddered to a halt outside the prison gate, elbows were flying amid the guards, each man pushing to the fore. Until Little Bit thuds down from the bus, one giant boot, then another landing in the dust. The guards ghost back toward the gates. Not spooked by his size. But something more. A dark force surrounds him, like invisible fur.

Elbows jostle again, this time forcing one of the guards to the front, allowing the others to shelter behind. The elected officer waggles a hand over his holster and barks an order. *Strip down!*

Garments gather in the dust.

An hour later, steel chains now his sole accessory, Little Bit lumbers to his cell, dripping from the hose-down and greased up from the hand-search. But the guards know that he still carries something. Something hidden deep, where no frisk can ever reach.

Bad voodoo.

The watchtower guard shifts his shoulder against the rifle. Blinks against the eyepiece.

Real bad voodoo.

His thumb flips on a two-way radio. "Molloy, you got your ears on?"

The speaker crackles a confirmation from far below.

"I saw something. Shined like a shank. I wanna see the Petra Loa lay out hands."

Guard Molloy peels his spine from the base of the watchtower ladder. Pokes up his hat. Surveys the gang, who stand with their backs to him. They seem to be chanting.

Molloy cocks his thumb against the two-way. "I don't see nothing." The chant has the raw rhythm of an incantation.

"What's your problem, Molloy? Too chicken 'cause they're toastin'?"

Toasts are dark poems, once composed by prisoners, cursing and celebrating the street life that took them to jail. They are acknowledged as the precursor to rap, but have long since been forgotten. Little Bit decided to use his time on death row to revive this tradition. So he killed off Little Bit and became Kon'Verse. And while Kon'Verse is imprisoned, his albums get released twice a year. *Doin' Time and Makin' Rhyme* just went platinum.

The gang riffs lyrics. With slow, deliberate strokes of a pen, Kon'Verse commits to paper the verses of "Kentucky Fried Suicide." Eyes down, deep in the flow.

 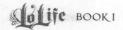

Molloy thrusts the two-way into his belt, readying himself. *Just picking the moment.*

Takes a wary step forward, moving against the tide of the other prisoners, who spread out from the center of the yard, as if the boombox beat of the Petra Loa caused sonic waves.

Only one prisoner dares to wander close to their perimeter. A thin, white man who barely fills his prison blues. Agnus Day staggers in chaotic circles. In his hand is clasped a sheet of paper.

He scrawls furiously with a blunt pencil across the paper, gibbering as he writes one word—the same word—again and again, his fingers too twisted to move at speed.

Molloy halts, observing the old man's perilous path. *Sweet Jesus, no...*

The Petra Loa are dead ahead, but Agnus lurches on, eyes down and unaware. The paper falls to shreds between his fingers, the pencil carving deep. With a howl, he bursts through the muscled gang and stumbles toward Kon'Verse, snatching fresh paper from the black fist. With frenzied strokes, Agnus crosses out the existing lyrics and writes on the reverse his one chosen word, again and again, filling the sheet. Kon'Verse slowly rises. To a boom of thunder.

He unfurls his giant arms and launches forward. Lightning explodes about the yard, and amid a rush of rainfall, Kon'Verse engulfs the tiny man—with tender care, gathering him up against his giant body.

The wind roars, straining to pull the storm closer. Sirens wail. The prisoners respond to the command to break and abandon the yard. Molloy is already by the gate, gun drawn, herding them through the lashing rain, two by two.

And through the deluge comes the last of them. The silhouette of Kon'Verse. And in his arms he cradles the twitching figure of Agnus Day, who still madly scrawls.

Molloy tugs down his hat, emptying a brimful of water onto his shoes. He is determined not to look up.

The boots of Kon'Verse heave up to the gate. They halt and Molloy jerks back as a thin, white hand thrusts out, forcing a scrap of paper beneath his chin.

Molloy's hand stays low, refusing to take the paper. Instead his palm waves an order for Kon'Verse to pass.

But the boots do not move. And so Molloy surrenders an upward glance, to read the silent command in the eyes of Kon'Verse.

Take the paper.

And with a trembling hand, Molloy obeys.

3

ICE CLATTERS in a cocktail shaker. Christopher Hatchling has ordered an extra-dry martini with Carpano Antica vermouth.

His face is turned toward Dr. Torgus but she senses that he awaits the pouring of his drink with more interest than anything that may emerge from her mouth.

She forces a smile. When she rang the New York offices of Phobos—making a cold call, in effect, as she had no introduction there—the flirtation that crackled between them had nudged his agreement to meet her. She watches now as Hatchling sips his freshly decanted drink. His disappointment with her is palpable.

His smile is for the barman. "Perfect."

The boy gathers a generous tip from the counter. Turns to Dr. Torgus. "Another rioja for the lovely lady?"

She inhales deeply, mustering calm.

"Thank you, but no."

She leans back, uncrossing her legs and spreading wide her leather file. Scraps of paper flutter across the bar. Each fragment is covered with what looks like the dense spikes of a seismograph readout. But a closer inspection shows that it is in fact a manic text, written tight and tall to make use of every inch of paper. Hatchling picks up a fragment, flipping it round like a candy wrapper, trying to determine where the text begins.

"Let me first explain." Dr. Torgus nips the paper between her nails with a surgical precision and returns it to the file. "The story I bring to you concerns a patient of mine."

"A patient?"

She concedes a correcting smile. "A *prisoner*."

Hatchling sucks down his olive. "I'm aware that you don't have a practice, Doctor, just a penitentiary. According to the notes I read."

He has notes *on me?* Dr. Torgus hides her unease in the folds of her skirt, which she busily rearranges.

"Prison work is a vocation… a calling."

"The kind you answer when the phone stops ringing." Hatchling bats away his own quip with a raised hand that catches the barman's eye.

"Another martini. And make it dirty."

He knows about my past. My dirty past! Dr. Torgus shakes her head, admonishing herself for hearing innuendo in Hatchling's every comment.

She closes her eyes, finding focus. Opens them to see that now a striking redhead has taken the stool next to Hatchling. Torgus exhales through gritted teeth.

"The prisoner's name is Agnus Day. And his case, without doubt, is the most extraordinary that I have ever seen."

Hatchling flashes a boyish smile at the redhead.

"It begins twenty years ago." *When you were still waiting for your balls to drop.*

 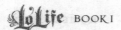

Dr. Torgus thrusts out a photo of a man in a white laboratory coat. It serves to momentarily snap Hatchling back. He glances at the image. "The prisoner was… a scientist?"

"One of the most eminent of his generation. A highly respected neurophysicist. His area of expertise was telomeres."

Hatchling's blank expression confirms a need for further explanation.

"Telomeres are molecular threads, coiled in the center of every living cell. Each time the cell divides, the telomeres shorten in length. When these threads have dwindled to nothing, the cell stops dividing and dies. In short, telomeres control how long we live."

He snatches a glance at his watch. "Will this take long?"

"I'll speed things up." A smile, significant just to her. "Life's too short, right?"

She plucks at the cashews, quickly recalculating a new route through her pitch.

"Agnus was researching ways by which these threads could be controlled, extended even. In short, Agnus was looking to create an ever-extending life span."

The adjacent redhead shimmies out of her coat, revealing legs that define *forever*. Torgus runs a hand through her dry hair, crackling static, then slides closer to Hatchling, determined to keep his attention.

"One factor, however, continually confounded the work of Agnus Day. Each time he found a means to extend the telomeres, the cell would turn cancerous. A likely complication, when one considers that cancer is essentially a human cell refusing to cease reproduction."

Hatchling and his thirty billion sperm are focused on the redhead. His stool swivels away from the doctor, as if her story is concluded.

Torgus slugs the last of her wine, tasting defeat. Then brings down the glass.

I'm not finished. Not yet! She raises her voice and presses on.

"Agnus's mind became locked on resolving this conundrum, an obsession doubtless driven by the death of his daughter. She'd been a troubled teen—"

Hatchling suddenly swivels toward Dr. Torgus. "A *suicidal* teen?"

Torgus is taken aback by his sudden reengagement. "Well... actually, no."

"You sure about that, Doctor?" Hatchling smiles like a paper cut. And now she divines his true intent. He's been waiting for this opportunity. "You were something of an expert in the field of teenage suicide, from what I read."

Torgus twitches her lips. "In your notes."

"I did my research. Quite thoroughly." The deliberate dig strikes her hard between the ribs.

She straightens her spine. Girds the muscles of her abdomen. "It wasn't suicide. At fifteen, his daughter succumbed to a brain tumor. After her death, the papers Agnus submitted for publication rapidly went from groundbreaking to perverse. Telomeres became more than his research. They became his mania. His sanity collapsed. The final paper he submitted, handwritten, sprawled across the page, contained no reference to his study. It was instead an incoherent diatribe against the three Fates—the women of Greek legend who control human

 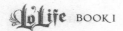

life span by the pulling, spinning, and cutting of thread."

"Yeah… the three Fates. I've heard of them."

Dr. Torgus nods, feigning delight in his familiarity with the fifth-grade element of this story.

"When those close to Agnus tried to intervene, to get him psychiatric help, he disappeared. In his laboratory, there were signs of an attempted suicide and—inexplicably—a burned void in the floor, as if a human body had combusted."

Hatchling's face now betrays a burgeoning interest. Torgus smiles. If this were a bedtime story—*and dammit, I'm old enough to be his mother*—this would be the moment to turn the page and show the child a vivid picture.

She pulls a photo from the file but keeps it face down, not ready to reveal it. Leans in deep. "He was not seen again until the night of the murder."

"What murder?"

Gotcha!

"They called it 'the Slashing at Sulphur.'" Torgus turns the picture over. Hatchling jerks back on his stool, unprepared for what he sees. The naked corpse of a young girl, her flesh torn into long strips that uncoil from her chin to her pelvis.

"Jezebeth Hooger was just fifteen years old, the same age as Agnus's daughter when she died. They found her like this— raped, ripped—in a motel bed in Sulphur City."

Torgus produces a second photo. This one shows a man, covered in blood, lying beside Jezebeth's corpse. His eyes are wide and his jaw is clenched in spasm. Hatchling looks closer at the agonized face.

Agnus Day.

"Wh-what happened to him?"

"They found him in some sort of catatonic coma. The blade was still in his hand."

Hatchling pushes the pictures away, disturbed. But his lingering fingers suggest a tingle to know more. "And he did this?"

"So said a jury of his peers." Now Torgus seizes the moment, her eyes drilling deep into Hatchling's. "Though I would say that Agnus Day has no peers. Not anymore." From the file comes a clutch of crime scene photos. "What he is now is… beyond compare."

From the stack of photographs she pulls a blowup of Jezebeth's torso. On the narrow stretches of flesh that cling between the knife wounds are words, handwritten words, tall and thin and densely scrawled.

Hatchling's fingers trace the text, severed between syllables. "What does it say?" He picks up photo after photo, eyes wide. "And why did he—?"

Each chunk of corpse is overrun by writing, the ink as copious as the blood.

"It's called hypergraphia—a manic imperative to write. And it is a symptom of Geschwind syndrome." She rolls her shoulders, relaxing back. Now she's in charge.

Hatchling waves the barman away when he threatens to approach. He beckons Torgus to continue.

"Those afflicted by the syndrome feel their cognitive powers overwhelmed by visions. Powerful, violent, inhuman visions. The hypergraphia arises from a compulsion to record these visions before they dissipate. Any surface will be

 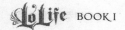

indiscriminately utilized, walls, floors… human skin."

Now it is Torgus who signals to the barman, transmitting with taps to her wineglass the decision to have another.

"Geschwind syndrome is rare, but not so rare that I would pin my hopes of publication upon it. There must be another reason why I traveled all this way." Now she even dares to stroke the back of Hatchling's hand. "So let me tell you what that reason is."

She reaches once more into her bag. "I have copies of all the murder investigation files. Standard practice, because I am Agnus Day's mental health worker." She taps the folder. "And by any standard, they make good reading. A fifteen-year-old girl, entered and then eviscerated by a crazy scientist, who then writes all over her precious body. There's your novel, or at least the start of it. But that's where the police let it finish." She pulls a final file. Not police-issue, but pink, precisely bound… personal. "What was written on Jezebeth Hooger's body—the crazed scribbled text—to the investigating officers, well that was… irrelevant."

Torgus lays her hand across the file and spreads her fingers wide. "But not to me."

Hatchling smiles and moves his hand toward the file, but Torgus is quicker and tugs it tight toward her body.

His fingers tap against the bar. "Let's not play games."

Torgus shakes her head. "I need to know you're interested. That there's a deal to be done here."

Now Hatchling drops his smile. "Dr. Torgus, I have to say that, of everything I've heard tonight, the only thing that interests me is what you now *won't* say." He points to the file. "If what you have uncovered is suitably… sensational, then perhaps we have a deal. Without it, you have just another crazy-coot killing that I could catch on cable. So let's not waste any more time."

Dr. Torgus swirls her wine about the glass. "Oh, it's sensational, Christopher. It is end-of-the-world, death-of-humanity sensational. And I believe that I have told you quite enough for you to make an offer." She fluffs her hair, laughter bubbling in her throat. "I mean, it's not as though your readership cares what particular flavor the apocalypse comes in."

Her laughter twists to silence as she catches sight of Hatchling's reaction.

"Christopher, I'm so sorry. I didn't mean to imply for one moment that your readership is... that Phobos caters only to the—"

His face is set hard, killing her tumbling apology on impact.

"Listen, *Doctor*, the psychiatric community sniffed you out once before. If you think that by descending from those lofty heights you'll find a second chance, think again. If there's one thing that the pig-ignorant know, it's the smell of shit."

His hand rises to both silence her and to demand the check from the barman.

"I'm sure Phobos wasn't your first choice. This meeting was, no doubt, a fishing trip." His eyes are already pursuing the redhead as she leaves.

Torgus grabs his sleeve. "Please Christopher! Believe me, I—"

But Hatchling is departing fast.

"I suggest you try elsewhere."

 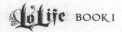

4

OFFICER WALLACE MOLLOY stares into the mirror that hangs inside his locker door. He takes a comb and with slow, careful motions shifts a ginger strand half an inch to the right. His hair is so sparse, its entire arrangement takes only a few strokes. But this evening, Molloy seems impossible to satisfy. He combs it again and again. And now his eyes leave the mirror, rolling left and right, searching out those who still remain in the locker room. A handful of guards linger, shrugging on civilian shirts, ready to sink some beers. Their voices echo off the tiled walls: a barrage of bar suggestions—*I say the Kicking Mule, bound to have the game on*—amid shouts to *have a good night* and warnings to watch out for the rain, *'coz she's a slippery bitch.*

The last reverberation is directed at the locker in the far corner.

You comin', Molloy? You can't get no prettier.

"I'll catch up." Molloy still claws at his scalp with the comb. "You go ahead." And now his purpose is clear. He is waiting for the room to empty. To be the last man standing...

Pondering... panicking.

The click of the old door latch declares that he is finally alone. He slides his fingers into his breast pocket and pulls out the sodden fragment of paper forced upon him by Agnus Day. The confusion of the storm meant that none of the others saw him receive it. Molloy wants to keep it that way.

Not that the guards would comment, even if they knew. They never talk about Agnus Day. Not even to each other. It's a rule to which they all adhere. An unspoken rule. An unbroken rule.

Since Agnus arrived at Morphic Fields, almost every one of them has received a similar piece of paper. At first, the scribbled messages were met with derision. This soon shifted to fear.

The notes revealed secrets, personal to each man. Exposing a truth about their lives. Something that had happened... something that was about to happen.

Some guards bluffed bravado, mocking those who feared the sudden thrust of Agnus's hand.

Some guards became withdrawn, anxious.

But all of them agreed on one thing—since Agnus's arrival, the inmates were... different.

Molloy's wife, kept awake one particular night by his nocturnal churning, had demanded that he tell her what he meant. *Different how, darlin'?*

Molloy had risen to his elbow, struck a match, and lit a cigarette, slowly sucking it into life. "It's like this, Trudy. The prisoners have a law all their own. A jungle justice. And a child killer... well, the law demands *that* demon must receive a particular punishing. Take Ring-Pull, for example—"

Molloy pauses and taps his ash into the neck of a beer bottle. *What in God's name did that kiddie molester do to get such a nickname?* He exhales a ring of smoke and continues.

"They beat Ring-Pull up so goddamn bad, doctor couldn't

put his face back together. But Agnus Day..." The cigarette lolls between Molloy's lips. "He filleted a fifteen-year-old girl, ripped her up like rare steak. But the cons, they don't lay a hand upon him. Not a single finger. It's kinda like they..."

He waves the glowing tip, searching the dark for the right word.

"*Protect* him?" offers Trudy.

Molloy shakes his head. "No... no. They *revere* him."

"And you have no idea why?"

Molloy hesitates. He could tell Trudy about the secrets... the revelations. But instead he pulls her close to him and tenderly kisses the crown of her hair. There's nothing she can do. Best keep this from her.

Along with all the other secrets.

In the locker room, Molloy slams the metal door hard, shutting out all thoughts of his wife.

Screwed to the door's metal plate is a clip, holding his work roster. The date of Agnus Day's execution is looming.

The guards have never once said it out loud, but they all sense it, like the coming of a Louisiana storm: The day the life of Agnus Day is taken, the inmates will respond.

There will be trouble.

Warden Duggin has refused to make the execution date public. It will be announced just hours before, to minimize the inmates' opportunity to prepare any protest.

Molloy can only ripple his lips with the same prayer every night: *Please, not on my shift.*

He folds up the paper fragment in his hand and shoves it through the locker grill. Then closes his eyes and inhales deeply, smoothing his expression into a mask that his wife might recognize as her easygoing husband.

✦

A crash of rain draws his eyes up to the window. The glass shivers. *What's with this weather?* Molloy can't remember a cloudburst going on this long.

He pauses, then snatches his locker open, reaching quickly inside to pull out a thin jacket. He prepares to slam the metal door shut one last time.

But then—the paper fragment falls to the floor, refusing to be ignored.

Molloy grits his jaw. Finally stoops to snare the paper and opens it, eyes locked on the single word upon it.

What the fuck does it mean?

His fist rolls shut and he thrusts the fragment deep into his pocket.

Grotteschi needs to see this.

5

In the metal workshop of Morphic Fields, machines lurk in lines like a hostile robot army, waiting for some spark to revive them. Even in this dead-metal state, they fight against the prisoners. Fingers, feet, scalps, and—on one memorable occasion—an entire face, have been ripped and chewed by these unmuzzled machines. It is not so much that they are dangerous, more that there is a general absence of interest in the prisoners' well-being. Morphic Fields gets paid by the volume of metal goods it produces and so, for the sake of speed, all safety gates have been removed. Many an inmate has gone to the chair with limbs already removed, as if his execution were but part of a layaway program.

One machine churns away in the far corner, throwing sparks. An inmate is hunched over it. When he shifts position, it becomes clear the hunch is not a stance of concentration but the result of a deformity of the spine. The prisoner's hands, however, are nimble and elegantly manicured. This is Charles Grotteschi.

The metal tube Grotteschi welds together is part of a plumbing device, but it reminds him of the sculptural pieces in which he used to deal, before his arrest.

Never seen without his trademark onyx monocle, he was known in every coffeehouse on Manhattan's East Side as the curator of the Hunkypunk Gallery. He dealt in what is known as "wet art"—work from up-and-coming artists. Some of it so radical, like a smear of human sputum on canvas, that critics would often fail to agree on whether it was art or idiocy. All of which made for an excellent environment if—like Grotteschi—you were a confidence trickster with a gift for gathering gullible clients.

It was never Grotteschi's intention to become a criminal. The real crime was how he had been ruthlessly excluded from the legitimate New York art crowd. The cause was his hump, the result of childhood spina bifida. If he was to be cut off by the connoisseur clique, he would deal with those stupid enough to spend ten thousand bucks on a lacquered twist of dog shit. They deserved to be duped.

In Morphic Fields, Grotteschi's academic learning was well known. It was the trick upon which he traded to keep himself removed from the usual prison routine of rape and rough-housing. And since Agnus Day had arrived within these awful walls, Grotteschi's services had been much in demand. Every prisoner who had received one of the obscure revelations had come to Grotteschi in the hope that his vast knowledge would shine some light upon its meaning. And just as many guards had sought the same service, sweeping Grotteschi aside, somewhere unseen, swearing him to silence as they unfolded their own particular paper scrap.

Grotteschi is always happy to offer up his cryptology skills, in return for cigarettes, soap, or soft towels.

He lifts his head from the welding machine, sniffing the air. Sure now that a guard has appeared behind him. Feels a boon of some sort slid into his pocket. Whatever it is, it smells of lily of the valley, a particular favorite of his.

This guard must want some very immediate attention. Grotteschi turns, his hump sweeping just inches from Molloy's chin.

"Good evening, Officer."

Without a word, the guard presents him with the paper. Grotteschi neither needs nor expects any accompanying conversation. All he requires is his onyx monocle, which his privileged position has allowed him to preserve. He withdraws it from the top of his sock, huffs a cleansing breath, then screws it deep into the wrinkled knot of his eye.

It almost falls free as Grotteschi's eyes pop, locked onto the single word riven across the paper: *Scox*.

Molloy lunges forward. "What does it mean?"

Grotteschi pauses and brings a delicate hand to his temple as if awarding Molloy's revelation the greatest care. In truth, Grotteschi is indulging in a little drama. If his interpretation comes too easily, seems too lacking in luster, then its apparent value will diminish. He wants Molloy to feel that there is weight enough in his revelation to merit eight ounces of soap.

Finally, Grotteschi speaks. "This is what I can tell you of Scox. The name refers to an ancient god. He appears in many cultures—Egyptian, Mayan, Nazca—but most prominently in voodoo, where he takes the form of a stork." Grotteschi inhales, ready to embroider this further, but Molloy is already pacing backward, his mouth pumping air, inflating an agonized wail.

"LaTisha's pregnant. That little bit o' trash is goddamn pregnant and she's going to tell my wife. That's what she always threatened to do, but I didn't believe her. But this… this…" His finger wildly agitates toward the paper. "This is a warning! A stork means a baby. And you said Scox is a stork. Oh, this is bad… This is very bad…"

Grotteschi shrinks back as Molloy paces wildly, finally storming away across the workshop floor, loudly lamenting the unbidden secret that his mistress now seems destined to expose.

If Grotteschi's shoulders were not fused to his neck, he would shrug. *Such is human nature.* Give people the thinnest thread of an idea and they will weave their own meaning. What he told Molloy about Scox was true—but as to whether that paltry, adulterous incident was what Agnus referred to—who knows? *Who cares?* Grotteschi withdraws his hand from his pocket and sniffs his pristine bar of soap.

✦

A pleasant hour later, freshly showered and smelling like his mother, Grotteschi lies on his lower bunk bed. He has the cell to himself, a luxury arranged by the accommodations officer. A few weeks previously, the officer had received a prophecy from Agnus, and Grotteschi had maintained that to crack the obscure reference, he would need an extraordinary degree of silent concentration. That same day, a transfer was ordered to a private corner cell, *with a window, no less!* Defying his deformity, Grotteschi danced a little jig that day and cracked the lunatic scrawl of Agnus within the hour. Not that he

delivered the deciphered text to the officer until three days later, declaring loudly that it had drained him dreadfully.

The privacy he now enjoys is precious, but more wonderful still is the window. By day, the hues of sunlight, and by night, sometimes, the sound of rain. A gentle patter to transport him back to autumn in New England. But tonight... tonight is quite different. The rain clatters like nails against the glass, and the howling gale reminds Grotteschi that this portal derives its name from "wind's eye."

He wriggles deeper beneath his blanket... uneasy.

There is a while to go before lights-out. He pulls from under his mattress a selection of books. Dusty and devoid of pornographic content, these academic tomes are rarely borrowed from the library cart.

With a puff of dust, Grotteschi opens up the appendix to *Rabey's Compendium of Myth and Lore*. He finds the precise reference to Scox and with a moistened finger peels open the book at the appropriate page. As his one good eye scans the chapter, he slowly nods, commending his own memory. Scox was indeed a stork god. But Rabey elucidates further. While some cultures attach him to the idea of new life, hence the myth of delivering babies, Scox is far more prevalent in cultures as an omen of evil. Grotteschi wriggles up onto his elbow, curiosity mounting as he reads that in voodoo culture, the stork appears as a "loa," or harbinger of the most feared evil of all, an apocalyptically destructive spirit force that goes by the name of...

Grotteschi eagerly turns the page to find the name. Only to find the top corner gone. Torn off. Taking the vital text with it. These thick waxy pages make excellent roaches, so no doubt some prisoner carelessly puffed away this information. Grotteschi grunts with frustration. His interest had been genuinely piqued.

He thuds the book shut, the resultant gust blowing up from his blanket the fragment of Molloy's revelation. Grotteschi had quite forgotten to file it with the rest.

He reaches below his bed once more, this time withdrawing a shoebox. Beneath the lid lies an avalanche of paper shreds, each one covered in Agnus's manic scrawl. This is Grotteschi's stash, collected from worried recipients, eager for interpretation.

Few of his clients ever asked for their revelation to be returned. Grotteschi could understand that. *Here's your awful truth. Would you like a receipt with that?*

But Grotteschi is a natural hoarder, a lover of *things*. His tiny apartment in Manhattan had an entire wall stacked with leather-bound boxes, filled with knick-knacks and geegaws, pictures and letters. His filing system was deliberately perverse; he labeled each box with the name of a Greek god. The irony delighted him still that the one box he could muster behind bars was labeled *Nike*.

He presses Molloy's revelation deep amid the rest. But as he moves to close the box, something is exposed; an envelope crudely taped to the underside of the lid. Just as a dealer may separate the darkest herb for his own smoking, Grotteschi keeps within this envelope the more obscure revelations. The ones that he has yet to decipher to his own satisfaction.

He rummages around the envelope with a careful finger. Amongst the scraps are some of the earliest given to him. Way back then, Grotteschi found each one fascinating. The whole

 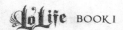

mad distraction of Agnus Day was, after all, still a novelty. And Grotteschi had his own opinion. He readily assumed that this highly intelligent inmate was conjuring a confidence trick. Behaving in a mad and mystical fashion, in the hope that Dr. Torgus would declare him insane, commute his death sentence to life.

So if it is *a hoax*, thought Grotteschi, *who better to uncover it than a kindred gifted trickster*?

But as time passed, and further revelations spewed from Agnus, Grotteschi was forced to admit that something other than deceit was at play.

The more he studied these fragments of text, the more he had come to believe that something fascinating lurked within.

The first bell of lights-out sounds. Ten more minutes of contemplation. Grotteschi pulls out a few of his favorites, running his eyes over the texts, committing every detail to memory so that—as darkness is thrust upon him—he can roll his mind like a marble between the mysterious words until sleep finds him.

The first is a fragment where the handwriting of Agnus is so agitated that only a single repeated word is partially legible. To Grotteschi's eye, it says **chiaroscuro**. This, Grotteschi knows, is a school of art in which light and shadow interplay in the extreme. A style much favored in the seventeenth century by the Italian and Dutch masters. *But what does it mean... ?*

On its own, perhaps nothing. But Grotteschi has another fragment. It bears the name **Emanuel de Witte**, once again written repeatedly and with such fervor, Agnus's pen has ripped through the paper, carving great holes. De Witte was a seventeenth-century Dutch artist famed for his perfect perspective. His works are largely church interiors, all pillars and vast arches. He did not paint in the chiaroscuro style. So what, other than the particular fury with which Agnus wrote both these gobbets, is the connection?

The other fragment that equals these, in terms of manic execution, is Grotteschi's favorite. Its content diverts and distracts him so violently that he momentarily forgets the steel and stone about him. His mind, at least, escapes the jail.

This fragment bears the name **Archilochus**. Grotteschi's passion for the classics means his knowledge here is deep. Archilochus was a Greek poet.

His greatest work was called "The Moirai". This is the Greek term for the three Fates. The word *moira* means "part" or "portion," and it refers to the way the Fates pull the thread until the extent of each portion is reached for each individual human. The thread is then cut and the human's mortality set— their span defined.

What intrigued Grotteschi, when this fragment first came to him, is that the Greek word *moira* is the root of the word *telomoera*, which became *telomere*—the thread that determined the life of a human cell. This had been Agnus's field of research.

The final bell of lights-out sounds. Grotteschi's cell is plunged into darkness. The endless storm rolls on outside and Grotteschi's mind churns: *Are these links of literature and linguistics pure coincidence? Or does something deeper connect Archilochus, the Moira, and Agnus's research into human life span?*

 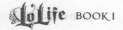

6

SHE BREATHES SLOWLY. A black canvas hood, heavy and smelling of someone else's saliva, has been buckled about her head for the last two hours.

She has been instructed not to remove the hood until ordered to do so.

Her hands, though not cuffed, lay obediently in her lap. She knows that she's been disarmed. Her holster feels lighter. Her .44 Magnum is gone.

She likes her gun. More than the average detective. But that's Alexis Bianco—always more than the average detective. Her file is testament to that fact—a collage of commendations for bravery and reprimands for breach of protocol. A senior officer once said that if a police dog had a record like hers, they'd put it down. She was unsafe off the leash.

They'd even made her do a psych test before her sergeant's exam. The doctor had noted at the start of the session that there was little on file for her before the age of seventeen. He had requested, in gentle, sing-song tones, that she recount the tale of her childhood.

Even as Bianco drew breath, she knew that telling him the truth could flip those sergeant's stripes way out of reach. But here's the thing with Bianco: She has her creed.

Tell the truth and face the consequences.

So she kicks off her shoes and stretches out along the couch, a long story coming. Beginning thirty-five years ago, at the very hour of her birth.

Wrapped in a blood-splattered grocery bag printed with the words WE DELIVER, she was abandoned outside St. Hilda's, a children's home in Bayou Cane. There was no note left by her mother as far as she can remember.

Her memories, etched deeply by events, begin the day she turned five. The same day that St. Hilda's burned to the ground. She knows it was her birthday, because a small, dry cake had been presented to her that morning. She wished it had been a proper birthday cake, with icing and candles, but this dull muffin was all St. Hilda's felt obliged to provide. The fire must have started soon after breakfast, as she has no memory of ever eating the cake. But she does recall that amid the hysterical aftermath, with police and social workers running and remonstrating, she had heard a girl's name talked of in the same breath as the blaze. At first she thought that they had given the fire a name, like they do hurricanes. It was too late by the time she realized that the girl's name was her own and its association with the fire was brought about by a deep suspicion that she, by means of a stolen candle, had wantonly started it.

A week later she was dumped in a foster home. Her new parents, Sterbon and Monica, didn't much like God or his little children, but they worshipped whiskey, a devotion observed from Sunday to payday. They stretched the liquor with a combination of lemonade and federal aid; a weekly sum of ninety dollars came through their door, as long as the kid was under their roof. They never got around to giving her a name. Their dog had always just been Dog, and so Kid would work well enough for her. She could have accepted this lack of a label more easily if Sterbon and Monica hadn't taken the trouble to give the broken-down shack that they called home a name. A plaque on the porch read BONICA—a union of their first names' last syllables. They should have selected the first two, making *Monster*, as this is how they appeared to the Kid. A two-headed beast, locked together, fists flying as they drunkenly raged about the room, hurling accusations, threats, and glassware.

And then, just as fast as any fight would start, it would finish, and Sterbon would stagger to the Kid, half-hidden by the doorjamb and rub her hair with the palm of his hand.

"Y'see, Kid, always best to tell the truth, take the consequences and move on."

Monica would nod woozily, making the wads crammed into her bleeding nostrils quiver like tissue tusks. "He's right, honey. Truth's always gonna come out, so you just make sure it comes outta your mouth first." Monica would finish these good parenting homilies with a smile, absent many a tooth lost to the truth.

As soon as she grew big enough to lift her bedroom window, the Kid was out of there, sliding down the tiles, feeling the first bone-jarring thud of freedom. A life on the streets began—but at least the life was hers.

With her loose mouth and even looser fists, the girl with no name fast got a reputation. She'd tell it as it was, call you out, spit the truth and take the consequences. Her appetite for a fight meant that the first two letters of the alphabet she ever learned were ER. The nurses were kind enough and knew the score, but there were only so many times they could stomach a girl with gunshots to the belly before they called the cops.

So she had to go elsewhere. The streets talked about an old swamp mambo who would patch you up with spit and spells and take payment in liquor.

She took the raft out to the woman's cabin one night, when a wound between her ribs refused to close. The old mambo asked for her name, but she said nothing. The mambo clucked, "Well, I believe I know who yo' are. I hear talk of the filly who weighs no more than a feather but is forever crowing for a fight. And seeing as you won't give me a name, I'll give you one. I'm gonna call you Bien'Cou. It's voodoo for 'Crow' and it means 'a lot of neck.' 'Coz that's what crows are—kinda pushy."

And the name stuck. When she came to New York she changed it to Bianco, Italian-American being an easier blend than Bayou voodoo. But what didn't alter was her pushy nature. She soon attracted the attention of a recruitment cop who worked the ghetto beat. He saw something in her. Took a risk and gave her a book on law enforcement. She ate it up, demanded more. Quick fists soon became quick wits.

The day after her twenty-first birthday, she aced the entrance exam and signed up as a cadet.

At twenty-seven, she made uniform sergeant. At thirty-one, she was moved to plain clothes and joined the toughest ranks of vice. At thirty-three, she made detective with specialist firearm privileges.

 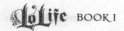

And from the day she strapped on her restricted-issue Magnum, one thing was clear—Bianco would always be more than the average detective.

If she were anything less, she wouldn't be here now. In darkness and alone. Summoned to the most secret of debriefings.

Bianco twists her cheek against the bag. The air inside now tastes of her last meal. Hummus. Had she known what was to happen just moments later—a thump to the skull, a clamp of canvas—she woulda had the salad.

Someone will come. The hood will be removed. The debrief will begin. Or maybe it won't.

The summons, after all, had come from SCURO.

7

DR. TORGUS FLOSSES her teeth, lips snarled back like a dog's. She rinses the clotted thread in a basin. The bathroom is attached to the private quarters of Warden Duggin, who smokes on a pull-out bed in the adjoining room. She runs the faucet to drown out the sound of him.

Dr. Torgus arrived an hour ago, same as each Friday afternoon, to hand-deliver her weekly report. This particular Friday, she had allowed Duggin's hand beneath her blouse. More routinely, she would rebuff any attempt at intimacy. But if the occasion arose that Dr. Torgus should need something—a few days' vacation, an increase in her gas allowance—she would let his fingers twist open her buttons while she wrestled with his fly.

Today had been such a day. Torgus now finds herself in the bathroom, brandishing a flannel, completing the usual kitty-lick that still leaves her feeling dirty.

She pulls on the cord above the mirror. The bare bulb blasts like an X-ray, revealing the skull beneath her face. Torgus averts her eyes.

Sex and death. She shakes her head, a thought coming to her mind that the French call an orgasm *une petite mort*—a little

death. She understands why. She tongues her teeth. They feel loose in her gums. She stretches out another length of floss, and her mind flies in another direction, to the three Fates, pulling their threads. She severs the floss and wonders, *How much longer do I have?* Her life is passing too quickly. There is so much more she wants to achieve.

She's not finished. Not yet.

Torgus bends low, forcing her lips about the faucet, filling her cheeks with water, spitting hard. This does nothing to rid her mouth of the taste of Duggin. The whole building tastes of him, smells of him.

But no matter how distasteful the prospect may be, she must re-enter the room and continue her seduction. She still has to gain the permission she seeks—a very special permission.

She has failed to get any publisher interested in her book on Agnus Day. Her past acts of academic fraud follow her still. So she has devised another plan. A means by which she can get a worldwide platform for Agnus's work. But she needs Duggin to bless this latest and most brilliant enterprise.

If he will just give me a chance to explain my idea. She tousles her hair and tugs off the light, gaining ten years of youth in the gloom.

Her hand snakes around the doorjamb, finds the light switch to the main room and flicks it off. A beam of yellow light persists. Duggin has switched on the television and a corner of the room is bathed in its flickering glow.

Torgus shimmies out of the bathroom and moves toward the window, pulling the curtains shut. Duggin's voice grunts from the sheets.

"You lookin' to go another round, Doctor?"

An apt description for barely two minutes of action. "Suppose I am, Warden. Are you going to refuse me?"

Duggin pats the bed. "Since when did I refuse you anything, *chère*?"

She slides to the next window. Stares out at the lashing storm. Presses her forehead against the cold glass, as if willing an idea to distill.

She must act carefully. One wrong word and he will sniff out her intent too soon.

She listens to the snatches of sound as Duggin flicks past the quiz shows in search of the Friday night games.

"One final chance to get this right, Bobby or it's sudden death…"

"…All eyes are on him as he takes aim… and with the seconds on the clock, this has to be the last shot…"

Duggin flinches as the remote is pulled from his fist. He finds Torgus stroking his arm, demanding his full attention.

"And what have I done to arouse such a healthy interest, Doctor?" Torgus peels back a smile. *One final chance to get this right.*

"I have a proposition to put to you." She aims her words carefully. "Something that could be very good for the reputation of Morphic Fields—"

Before she can shoot, Duggin rolls up from the bed, a rictus grin spread wide. *Sudden death personified.*

"And here it comes…" He swoops, naked flesh flopping. "Let's hear it! C'mon now, let it out!" Spit spills, his mouth now just a bubble from hers. "It's Agnus Day, isn't it? *You want Agnus Day.*"

 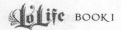

"I don't want *him*, I simply want the opportunity to—"

"—bring down these walls like fucking Jericho! You think you blow my trumpet and get what you want?"

He drags a bathrobe from the back of the door, wraps himself within, and tugs on the toweling cord, as if this binds his resolve tighter still.

"You think I don't know what you've been planning? Those trips to New York, cocktails with this editor and that... You think I only open the *inmates'* mail, Doctor?"

He bares his teeth broader still. "I like to slide my knife where that tongue of yours has licked. Peel open that soft manila."

He wags a finger before tapping it against his eye socket.

"I've seen inside. I know what you've been sending out. What I didn't know is how long you'd burn your knees on my carpet before finally finding the courage to beg for what you really want. My permission to publish."

Torgus rises now, pulls sharply away. Utterly silent as she contorts her face from caustic fury into something quite coy.

"Really, baby. You're acting as if I were deliberately keeping this from you. If I was discreet, it was because I thought you'd be pleased. A wonderful surprise—that I had created something that would attract such worthy public interest in Morphic Fields... in you."

She wants to underscore her words with a tender gesture, but her fingers refuse to unclench from fists. So she sweetens her voice another spoonful.

"Just imagine the magazine headlines: 'The visions of a prisoner, brought to the world by a visionary—'"

He cuts across her like a truck.

"I want Agnus Day dead. No more goddamn portents and prophecies. Just my pretty prison, back to how it used to be. Can't you understand that?"

His breath comes in rasps, slowing slightly as his bare feet pace the cold, tiled floor. He says nothing further. *A good sign perhaps?* His temper may be cooling.

Torgus moves once more to the window. A single pane has blown open a crack and is being sucked against its hinges by the wind. The metal creaks under the mounting strain.

She appears to busy herself with pulling the glass shut. She can hear the repeated snap of Duggin's lighter behind as he attempts to ignite a cigarette.

Her back is still to him. She slowly inhales.

And with seconds on the clock. This has to be the last shot of the match…

"Baby, I just want you to consider the—"

"Answer's no."

His cigarette jabs toward the back of her head.

"Do I make myself clear, Annie? Whatever you're planning—it's finished."

Duggin cannot see her expression. He cannot see the quiver in her fingers as they twist the window latch, tighter and tighter.

She turns to him with a straining smile. Barely moving as behind her the glass shudders under the force of the rain.

 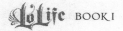

8

A WHITE SHEET unfurls. Twisting through the air. Caught at the corner by a tattooed hand. One of many hands that claw upward, catching at cotton.

The prison laundry is alive with activity.

A long line of inmates heave sheets from shelves as water floods across the concrete floor. The freakish storm has overwhelmed the prison's sanitation system, and water is bubbling up through the drainage grills.

The inmates work with a strange urgency, the sheets billowing like sails of a flotilla. The guards on duty are focused on the rising water and seem unconcerned by the prisoners' silent synchronicity.

At the back of the laundry, an event is occurring that the inmates are concealing. Agnus is on all fours, a lump of charcoal in his hand. Crawling back and forth across the plashy sheets, writing madly as if the cotton were canvas. His entire body quivers. Saliva froths at the corners of his mouth.

And from the shadow of the doorway, Kon'Verse looks on, delivering a signal with a flick of his eyes. A Petra Loa foot soldier nods and disappears, his mission understood.

✦

The first that Grotteschi knows of his summoning is the grip of a hand about his throat, followed by a sharp yank. His socked feet skitter in an attempt to stay upright as he is hauled across the flooding floor, arriving like so much wet laundry at the feet of Kon'Verse.

They are surrounded by a row of prisoners who appear to labor hard. But their tightly packed bodies serve another purpose. They create a barricade, behind which something thrashes in the water. Grotteschi wipes a wet cuff across his eyes, then bolts back at what he sees. Agnus, convulsing and retching as he scrawls across the vast expanse of sheets.

Never before has Grotteschi seen him work on such a scale. And this time, he writes not a word—but a symbol. The same symbol. Again and again. His hand clawing at his own creation.

Grotteschi rubs his eyes, mumbling in excitement. *How long has he… ? How have the guards not… ?*

Kon'Verse towers above him, dark eyes imparting the only question that matters.

What does it mean?

Grotteschi reaches down, fumbling at the top of his sock. Pulls out his monocle and smudges the lens against his cuff. Sinks it into his eye socket and stares again at the symbol.

Jagged lines surround a dark center, in which Agnus writhes, blackening the sphere deeper and deeper with heavy strokes.

The black sun, could it be?

Grotteschi has read of this symbol in many of his books. He knows its origins in Germanic mysticism, and that it always portends evil, but what could it mean here?

He looks on as Agnus scrawls the jagged lines farther across

the sheet, turning the rays into something else, something jointed. Like legs. The black sun now appears... alive. Like an insect.

What manner of creature? And what does it mean?

Grotteschi pokes a thinking finger in his ear, willing an interpretation forth. He opens his mouth, unsure of what will emerge. And then—

A bestial roar erupts.

Not from himself, he realizes, but from Agnus, as his arms and legs violently spasm. He falls to the ground, eyes rolling into the back of his skull.

The cry draws the guards, who now splash the length of the laundry room. Before the first of them breaks through the ring of prisoners, the marked sheets have all been pulled away and bundled into a giant wicker basket. Leaving just the body of Agnus to be discovered, convulsing in the water.

The senior guard bellows, commanding the prisoners to disperse, but they are already marching out in a silent exodus, led by Kon'Verse. He lumbers past Grotteschi. A look is cast. The command is clear.

Figure this out.

The jab of a baton in the small of Grotteschi's back moves him out toward his cell.

Even before he shuffles into the corridor, he is running an imaginary finger along the spines of books massed beneath his bed.

This symbol, this black and mutant sun, does not appear in any of Rabey's illustrations. And in *Le Grand Grimoire*, an ancient tome he knows so well, never has Grotteschi come across a cryptogram like this.

His eye darts up as a phalanx of guards pass by. The inert body of Agnus swings between them.

As they round the corner, the limp head lolls and Agnus's face is revealed.

Grotteschi flinches back against the wall, riven with fear. Until the baton jabs once more into his hump.

He resumes his shuffling stride. Back to his cell… to his books. Which he now suspects will be of scant use.

Grotteschi closes his eyes, seeing again the flash of that face… that mask of inexpressible terror.

Shakes his head, certain now.

The meaning of this last symbol does not lie within his library. Nor within his vast learning.

Indeed… it does not lie within the human realm.

9

"What does it mean?"

Bianco screws up her face, thinking hard. Trying to remember.

Secret Civilian Unidentified...

No, that's not it.

Special Covert Unreported...

Exhales loudly, puffing out the black hood that still wraps her head. Surely someone, at some time, must have told her what the acronym stood for.

Supernatural Classified Unorthodox...

Maybe nobody knows.

She's heard many a cop refer to the SCURO Bureau the "Screw Loose Bureau." Such locker-room ridicule serves to mask a deep unease in the rank and file about this shadow agency and its obscure operation. Rumors occasionally arise of cops who get summoned to a debriefing and never come back.

But Bianco didn't get to where she is today by listening to rumors.

She explores the rough floor with the heel of her shoe. *Not that I know where I am today...*

But there's one thing of which she is sure. She knows why SCURO pulled her in. It was a report she filed on a missing girl called Maddy Pool.

It was a strange case from the start. Maddy was an overweight teen with bad skin and braces. The club where she worked as a coat-check girl was an elite joint, frequented by thin, tattooed creatures with black-painted lips. Any flesh not pierced was scored with self-harm scars. It was an underground club in every sense. Set up in the old city sewers, it had a long track record of members taking their own lives, a fact which found an ironic echo in the joint's name: The Sewercide Club.

Bianco had been called here to bag up wrist-cut sluts too many times before. But this body-collect was different.

There was no body. Just a strange carbon burn mark on the floor of the coat-check kiosk, in the shape of a fat corpse.

Filling out her report, Bianco had used the words *spontaneous human combustion,* even though she knew this phenomenon belonged to the realms of science fiction.

The file must have gone straight to SCURO.

That was months ago... six months at least. Maybe more. A year? No, not a year... Her thoughts are blurring. And with a rush of fingers, she claws at the hood. She is loosing consciousness, her brain operating now on adrenaline alone. With a wrenching tug, the hood comes free. Long, dark hair tumbles out, crackling with static. Heaving back as she gasps for air.

What in God's name... ? Were they just gonna let her suffocate in there?

Or were they testing her? How long before she defied orders not to touch the hood?

Breathing deep, she rakes back her hair, revealing a pale face, sharp with cheekbones. The eyes are dark and deep, close-set like a predator's.

 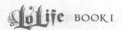

She looks left and right about the room. She's in some kind of derelict loft. The vast space houses vats and pumps, rusted remnants of a soap-making factory. There is still the faint smell of lily of the valley. Strangely at odds with the sinister chill that creeps down Bianco's spine.

The only available light seeps through the barricaded windows. The rays are thick with dust and strain to bounce a few feet from the floor. And so a darkness fills the void above her.

Silent. Still. Rushing as—

—something hurtles down, skimming past her skull and crashing into the floor.

Bianco jolts, looks down. At the foot of her chair is a clipboard. A crude artifact of plywood with paper jammed beneath a rusty clamp.

Bianco glances from the floor up to the darkness, unsure whether she should expect anything more.

Silence. Nothing comes. Then a deafening whine of white noise that finally resolves with a loud sonic pop.

And a cough, as a deep voice crackles from an unseen speaker suspended somewhere in the gloom.

"We ask that you record the events that you witnessed. Be accurate. Be truthful. Good afternoon."

A second *pop* signs off the command.

Bianco pauses, then gathers the clipboard. A pen dangles from knotted string.

You gotta be kidding.

The most feared of all federal agencies and SCURO turns out to be what—a clipboard and a Biro?

Bianco flips the paper. Clicks the pen. Is this another test? If she cracks some combination, will she activate a secret entrance to the real headquarters hidden below?

Her fingers explore the pen shaft and soon she finds a button that, when pressed, releases the barrel. A spring flies from within and a moment later she makes a discovery.

That she can't put the fucking thing back together.

It's just a pen. In fact, without the spring it's less than a pen, as no amount of clicking now can force the nib to come.

Bianco frisks her own pockets, finds a pencil. She stares at the rounded point, almost worn away, and wonders whether enough graphite remains for her to commit her account.

And then she stops, smiles at her own stupidity. Shouldn't she be asking herself a different question?

Am I going to tell them the truth?

The top brass already fear that she is halfway to crazy. What she writes here could confirm it and kill her career.

Bianco licks the pencil's soft tip.

She hasn't lived her life by many rules but one: *Truth… and consequences.*

She grits her jaw, not about to change. And with bold strokes she begins. Three words, writ large:

TORMENTA
The Facts

She moves to underline the title and then halts, remembering she's short on graphite. She needs to keep this brief. Just tell it as it is.

 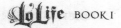

Walking amongst us—looking, sounding, and acting just like us—is a type of demon called the Tormenta. And as demons go, they are particularly...

She pauses. Searches for the right word, settling for:

...fiendish.

Then her pencil halts again. So much to say.

Maybe she should tell it just as Lola told it to her. Because dammit, that girl sure had a way of making it sound simple.

Bianco thinks back to the moment of their first meeting. She had been sucking on a cigarette outside the station morgue, trying to make sense of the autopsy report in her hand. Her latest case was Gina Avner, a hostess at the Sewercide Club. A pretty, pale-skinned creature, no more than twenty-two. But according to the medical examiner, her bones were over four hundred years old.

A mistake, gotta be!

Then it happened: a hand locked hard about her neck and the muzzle of her own Magnum, impossibly pulled from its holster, twitching an inch from her chin.

"Do I have your attention, Detective?"

Bianco found herself staring at a swath of cropped blond hair, the only feature of her assailant visible in the darkness. She mustered a nod.

"Then listen good."

Lola's voice was no more than a whisper but it seemed twisted tight, sinking like a needle into her ear.

"Humans are born with a predetermined life span, an allotted number of years to live. Some consume their spans and pass away. Some have their spans prematurely snatched from them by murder or mishap. But some surrender their lives by choice. Humans call it suicide. Tormenta call it opportunity."

Bianco feels the grip on her shoulder loosen a fraction. When she doesn't move, it loosens further. But the gun goes nowhere. Bianco can still smell its metal breath.

"At the moment of the suicide's death, Tormenta can siphon the surrendered life span. Every unspent year refuels them. Rejuvenated, they will live out these stolen years. And when those years come close to expiration, the cunning Tormenta will begin the search for the next fuel stop. The next fragile human that they can sucker into self-death. Because the life span must be surrendered, not taken. This is the only way it retains its purity and potency."

Slowly, the Magnum lowers.

"From their method comes their name. They torment their human prey into giving up their lives."

Bianco swallows, attempts to speak, but no words come. She licks her lips, easing a path, and tries again.

"You—you say these Tormenta walk amongst us... in plain sight."

"They are everywhere."

"I've never seen one."

"Weren't you listening?"

The Magnum twitches, not committed to retreat.

"They look like humans. In fact, they are the demon species most like mankind." Lola sweeps the finger of her free hand.

 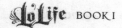

"Take man one evolutionary step back in the natural world and you find the great ape. One step forward in the supernatural world and you find the Tormenta. They share much with us."

"So you're saying that I *have* seen one—I just didn't know."

Lola leans in closer now, almost chummy. "Ever heard one of those stories... about the old guy with a trophy wife who drives him to drink and then to divorce? Stripping the house of everything he's ever worked for. But maybe she deigns to leave him just one thing: his study desk. The one, conveniently, in which he keeps his gun... She's probably gone no more than a day before, broken and bawling, the guy blows his brains out... Or how about the story of the little girl in the church choir, so pretty, so tempting beyond her tender years, she seduces the young pastor. He hangs himself from the church rafters, no doubt compelled by her threats to expose him. Or maybe it's the tyrant boss, who promotes some kid so fast and then—just when the kid has bought the car and the penthouse and run up a ton of debt—he fires him, with the whole floor watching. They pull the poor kid's body out from under the train the very next day..."

Bianco feels her head nod. The department's suicide file is full of scenarios just like this.

"Tormenta come in every human form, each with its own particular grift to get you to surrender your span. Gina Avner kept it old-school. She played the bully bitch."

"And Maddy Pool... was her victim. Gina bullied and abused her until she... But now Gina's dead, one clean shot to the..."

A silence hangs. Bianco glances down at Lola's gun.

"You killed her, right?"

Lola holsters the Magnum. "It's a lot to take in."

"No, I get it."

"Take a minute. Have a smoke. You'll have questions."

"Actually, I got one now." Bianco pulls out her soft pack, taps a stick. "Who the blue fuck are you?"

✦

A bell suddenly shrills from the soap factory wall.

Bianco jolts back to the present. Looks at the paper on her lap.

She has written nothing. And she knows why.

The truth matters. It is her creed. But sometimes, there's a truth that matters more.

Being a cop is about right and wrong. Working with Lola is about this world and the next. And maybe the one after that.

With a loud *shunt*, a narrow hatch slides open in the floor below her chair. She waits for a command, but none comes. And so, with careful fingers, she eases the empty clipboard into the slot, feeling something snare it below, snatch it away.

She's given SCURO nothing.

That may be bad. The slot snaps shut.

Too late now.

IO

THE LONG BLADE of a windshield wiper slashes back and forth. It clears the path of a bus as it hurtles through rain. The side panels of the vehicle are splattered with high-velocity mud, as if the wheels have burst the road's carotid artery.

Beneath the mud, a design on the bodywork can be discerned. Painted in black, it stretches the length of the vehicle. It is the skull of a long-beaked bird.

In giant letters below the skull is one word: STORK.

With a shriek of hydraulics, the tires twist around a tight bend.

Inside the bus, the driver lurches at the wheel and howls with laughter. Or perhaps fear. His full expression is obscured by long, black hair that dangles to his chin.

His hand unclamps from the wheel and fumbles across the dash, searching for a CD. The album cover bears the stork-skull logo. With one skilled hand, he slides the disk into the slit of the player. Stabs at the volume button.

A death-metal track blasts from the speakers. The driver leans back, re-sparks his joint, and mumbles along to the music. The only discernible phrase from the chorus seems to be "...*death is the breath that I wanna inhale...*"

He glances up to his rearview mirror. A collection of heads, hung with unwashed hair, moshes to the droning beat.

A girl removes her leather jacket, studded with the word STORK, revealing beneath a black T-shirt printed with a list of stadium dates, demarcating the path of this fan-club pilgrimage.

She folds the leather with care, as though it were a shroud, then examines her forearm. Old scar tissue hatches the flesh.

Between her fingers she twirls a razor blade. The edge comes to rest on a fresh patch of skin. She intends to score her name— *her new name.* The label given to you by your parents has no meaning—*that's your slave name.* Once you are awakened, as Stork awakened her, you choose a name that has true meaning… true destiny.

The band's lead singer had set an example. When Stork's original front man blew his brains out, he was quickly replaced by a Japanese guy called Hash-Tu. The fans were appalled, until they realized that Hash-Tu was not his birth name. He signed it #2, a name that respectfully signified his position behind Fell Watson as the band's second front man. Immediately, the fans were won over.

She doesn't imagine that she will come up with anything quite so brilliant. But still, she carefully considers all her options. The logical thing would be to select a name made from straight lines. Carving an *o* or an *e* could be messy. She smiles to herself. Even now, so far evolved from the nerdy girl she used to be, she still likes things to be… neat.

She bites down hard on her lower lip and cuts three verticals and two careful obliques—**Livi**—then smiles as the neat incisions barely weep. There is a rationale behind her choice. The child psychiatrist, hired by her parents at the first sign of

their daughter's sudden obsession with Stork, had once let her file slip from his briefcase. She glimpsed her allocated patient number: 57.

Just another can of worms for you to label, eh, Doctor? Fifty-seven varieties of crazy.

And so she chose Livi, a version of the number 57 in numerals. She's kinda rearranged the Roman rules a little bit, but what the hell? No one will ever figure out the meaning of her name. That's the point. Your name is your own private destiny. And her destiny is to follow the band. From coast to coast. Continent to continent, hemisphere to hemisphere.

From this world to the next.

Her iPhone blips and flashes up a road map. Livi checks the mileage, then wrinkles a frown. They're gonna need to stop for gas soon. She flicks her tongue against her teeth, clicking a silver stud like an abacus as she does a quick mental calculation. *We can make another fifty miles.*

Owing to her residual love of order, Livi is in charge of this phalanx of die-hard fans. And she performs her duties with appropriate style. When the fan club was forced to comply with certain federal regulations, Livi grabbed the papers from the city hall clerk and, while the bureaucrat watched, cut her palm and signed the Health & Safety form in blood.

Livi looks about the bus. Blades and needles roll about the seats. Bodies flop against the cool windows. Of all the kids traveling, only half are conscious at any one time. It's no sure bet that the driver will be one of them. More than once the bus has been known to swerve wildly off the highway, the wheel-spin worsened by his attempt to stamp out a burning joint, thudding his foot indiscriminately between the gas and the brake.

As the person in charge of their safety, Livi knows she is doing a pretty poor job. But she mentally blots that drop of guilt. That's the kinda thing that would have bothered her old self. Livi now knows better.

Death is the breath I wanna inhale.

A pale face looms up in front of her. The eyes are deep green and the lips are painted black.

"Hey… hi…"

Livi stares at the eyes. They are so dilated, the pupils look as though they are about to roll down the girl's cheeks like tears. Livi's voice is stern. "How many Vicodin you taken, Ghost?"

Ghost shrugs, the effort dropping her back behind the seat. A sprout of blond hair slowly reappears as she claws her way upward once more.

"So… yeah…" She inhales, determined this time to get a little further into her question. "Don'cha think the skinny kid with the real big…" Her fingers loosely circle her eyes, suggesting glasses. "Don'cha think he's kinda… weird."

Livi looks to the bespectacled boy sat a few seats in front. Accusing any kid on the Stork bus of being weird is pretty meaningless. They all exist way beyond the bounds of normal. But Livi has to agree with Ghost. This kid doesn't fit.

She has her own suspicions as to who he might be.

Ever since the media labeled Stork a "suicide-cult" band, various do-gooders have attempted to infiltrate the fan base. Teen counselors dressed up in leather jackets turn up at gigs, the most dedicated amongst them committing to a little self-harm, blending their scars like tiger stripes amid the true followers.

Livi had watched the skinny kid. The way his eyes swept back and forth behind those big glasses, observing... absorbing.

And yet she hadn't moved to expose him. One thing prevented her from being sure. She's been around enough psychiatrists and counselors to recognize the suffocating air that surrounds them. They might come toward you with open arms, but what Livi saw, held in their outstretched hands, was an invisible feather pillow, ready to smother. This vision was so strong, so real, that the last time her psychiatrist tried to embrace her, Livi swore she could smell feathers.

But this skinny kid... he didn't trigger that nerve. Livi knows this from the time she came close to him. Just a few days ago, when Ghost took too many downers and couldn't be woken.

Livi had found the boy bent deep over her body, his lips almost touching hers. Livi had thrust her hand forward and wrenched him away. And that was when she saw it... in his eyes. A flash of *something*, there and gone—too quick for her brain to give the expression a label. His face clicked to a picture of simple concern. "I was just listening... to see if she's breathing." As Livi protectively gathered Ghost's head into her lap, the pale mouth had twitched and groaned, confirming life. The skinny kid exhaled with apparent relief. "Looks like she's gonna be all right."

As he walked away, sliding back into his seat, Livi's brain had churned over and over, searching for options: *Is he a church worker? A newspaper reporter?* She shook her head, knowing none of these was right. He didn't smell like feathers. *He smelled like...*

Her brain finally nailed it. *A fucking vulture.*

Livi remembers flinching at this strange conclusion. Unsure of what her own instincts were telling her. She decided, there and then, to keep it to herself… until she could make sense of it.

That was two days ago. Livi hasn't spoken to the skinny kid since. But he was never far from her thoughts. And now Ghost shares her ill ease.

Livi pats her hand. "Don't worry. I'll take care of it."

She looks at the green eyes, which flicker shut.

"You look like shit, Ghost. Get your head down."

And with a violent jerk, Ghost's head is thrown down onto the seat. Because the whole bus is lurching.

Livi braces herself against the window, adrenaline forcing her to her feet as she yells at the driver. "What the fuck, Tez!"

He sweeps around his mop of hair, probably facing her, but no features are visible. She can only hear the roar of his voice.

"Suck and chuck, people, we got company!"

And now Livi sees it. A pulsing blue light, closing in behind them. Followed by the whoop of a siren.

And in one swift action, every window in the bus is pulled open and barbs, Baggies, and burning joints burst out of the vehicle as if it were a well-struck piñata.

The driver yells again. "We clear back there?" In his rearview mirror, he sees Livi give a thumbs-up.

With a squeal of rubber, the bus swerves off the road and pulls to a halt. The patrol car slides in smoothly behind.

The driver bundles his long hair back into a ponytail and from under his seat comes a bus company cap. It reads YOUR DRIVER IS TERRY. With a grunt, he pulls it on.

Fuckin' cops.

 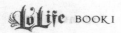

His eyes go now to the side-view mirror. A woman exits the patrol car. Tall and lean, with cropped blond hair.

His eyes crimp with confusion. He leans closer still to the mirror.

She sure don't look like a cop...

II

A WOODEΠ SiGΠ once bore the name of this place, but no living soul can remember what it said. All that remains is the sign's uppermost post—the rest sucked down, year after year, in gentle sips. The same thirsty mud gave this plot the name by which it is known today: Swamp Gravy.

An ugly name but rarely spoken, so the need for something better is unlikely to arise.

The rain is a frequent visitor, dimpling the thick mud. Making ripples that radiate out to a low, lone hut in the middle of the swamp. It perches on wooden stilts, carved with scales like chicken legs. Flecks of paint suggest that long ago a careful hand took time to paint the stilts a rooster red. But the paint has peeled and the cabin is now plucked of any comfort. Roof tiles have sloughed off, exposing rafters, and the wooden steps droop into the water like a broken wing.

The porch boasts just a single shingle. Beneath this shelter squats an old woman, her body arranged in thick, comfortable folds. Dyed yellow hair is piled high on her head like pondweed. Old Fan Fan Bohica twitches a fishing rod and sinks it over the edge of the stoop.

She chews tobacco and a song throbs in the stretching chamber of her neck. The melody—if such it can be called—

 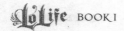

repeats around and around, deeper and deeper. And each time she inhales to begin a phrase anew, she seems to suck the world toward her, drawing the wind around from the east, bending the reeds away from the tide. But throughout her song, Fan Fan's eyes never divert from the tip of her rod.

And so it is with fury that she turns to call behind her. "Ain't I told you once too many times about your shadow?"

A massive black crow lowers itself onto the back of her chair, wings still beating.

Fan Fan jabs a finger at the water. "Stickleback's got eyes on the top of his damn head."

She jabs the rod at the bird. "Maybe I'll just put you in the pot. Problem solved. Problem eaten."

The crow ignores her, shaking the rain from its feathers as if much used to weathering the storm of Fan Fan's irritable welcome.

She slowly sets down the rod and shuffles the folds of her body until her massive form confronts the crow. She looks the bird straight in the eye.

"So—she's back, is she?"

The crow emits a rasping caw. And Fan Fan nods, clapping her huge hands down upon her thighs.

"Guess I shoulda been expectin' her." She heaves to her feet, now talking with the absent care of someone who addresses empty air. "But there's gonna be trouble if she's brought more than one…"

Her tongue is already tutting as she collects a long wooden pole and shuffles to the side of the cabin.

"Last time she came, I told her… told her straight…"

She pokes the tip of the pole into the swamp. "I'm kinda full t'bustin'..."

In the black water below floats a slew of bloated corpses.

✦

The pole sinks again. Each stroke now propels a crude raft. Fan Fan is paddling across the water, through the thick bayou vapors that roll and part to reveal another cabin. Painted black, the windows are barred, and the doors are studded with metal plates. This hut was built to keep something in... or something out.

Candles burn within. It is late, but Lola won't be asleep.

She never sleeps, not the way the living do. She might shut her eyes and her breathing may slow. But her mind remains hitched to the switch of her adrenaline. Ready to respond to the slightest sound, the merest movement.

Which is why it comes as no surprise that the ripple of Fan Fan's raft arouses a shotgun snout. It slides through the bars.

"Jus' me, child. Jus' me."

The rifle retracts. And one thigh at a time, Fan Fan heaves herself onto the tiny porch.

Inside the hut, the walls are hung with weaponry—short knives, long-nosed pistols. A six-foot rocket launcher is braced above the door.

And the tiny tip of a needle glints. It pulls a length of surgical suture through pale skin.

Lola sits cross-legged on the floor, closing a slit in her shoulder with a final stitch.

 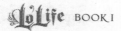

Fan Fan grimaces at the depth of the wound, then inhales, knowing better than to pass any comment. Instead she lifts a green flask of Old Artemis liquor from her apron. "I brought fresh supplies." Her eyes dart to the stack of empty bottles in the corner.

Lola grabs the flask and splashes its contents like hot sauce across the sutured slit. Then she jolts a shot across the back of her head. Her pale blond hair is shaved short, and four fresh rips, raked by fingernails, run down her neck.

The last slug is saved for a split across her eye. The flesh swells blue. But the eye beneath is bluer still. The liquor hits and her lashes thrash against its antiseptic bite.

Then her fist swings again and the flask swoops and smashes on top of the pile.

Fan Fan pulls out another bottle, uncorks it with her teeth. "You know, one day you might try drinking it." She takes a deep chug, smacking her lips and wiping her chin with the back of her hand.

Lola picks up her shotgun, snapping it open, checking the chambers. Picks up a cloth and begins to clean the weapon.

"Now, *chère*, what's troublin' you?"

"She said she'd be here."

Lola's tone is almost petulant. Times like this, Fan Fan is reminded that the ruthless hunter now before her is just a girl. She couldn't have been more than nineteen when destiny dealt her this cold hand.

"Bianco's doing what she has to do. And you should pity her." Fan Fan reaches out, touches the back of Lola's neck. "She doesn't have the freedom you enjoy."

Lola pulls sharply away and Fan Fan inwardly curses her poor choice of words. *Enjoy?* As if one moment of Lola's dark existence could be something to enjoy.

"Child, I simply meant—she's a cop. She got her duties."

"She's off duty. Today and tomorrow. She said she'd be here."

"Give her time."

"One hour."

"I meant, give her *time*"—Fan Fan eases herself into a chair—"to understand your world." Her big feet spread wide. "You got her into this, remember. Your decision." She kicks off her shoes, stretching her toes. "You needed someone to get you information. Trace plates, tap telephones. Without a cop on your side, it would take you twice as long to find your quarry. And you knew she would roll with it. You saw that crow-crazy look in her eye and that lust o' hers for danger—and you worked on that."

A fat finger rises and wags at Lola's head. "But remember this, my lil' muffuletta: The day you chose Bianco, you gave her no choice at all. You just turned up and hit her with the truth. And I don't doubt that everything you revealed is ripping her in two, even now."

Fan Fan exhales; her finger drops to her belly. "An old mambo like me, familiar with the dark side, I can accept you... and all that comes with you. But Bianco's different. Her life is in the real world, at least what she thought was real until you came along. She needs a little time to adjust—to believe all that you're asking her to believe. But no matter how hard it is for her, I can tell you this, Lola." Fan Fan's voice drops to a whisper. "She believes in you."

 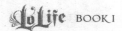

Her old hand reaches out, strokes the back of Lola's head. "She brought you to me, didn't she? To Swamp Gravy, a place where she once felt safe. A place to heal, to hide what you are... and what you do."

Lola slides the polished bullet chamber back into the belly of her Winchester. She rises, pulls on a long black leather coat. Then pauses, looks at Fan Fan.

"The job we do, that's the real fight. The only fight. So how long before she gets that?"

"Soon, child, real soon." Fan Fan taps a finger to her temple. "You already got her here; she understands." Her finger then drifts down toward her chest. "But she's gotta believe. You need to get her here." Her finger taps her heart.

Lola points to the empty space beside her. "I need to get her right here."

She pulls a gun holster from the wall, buckles it about her hips. Tugs on a belt of bullets without looking up.

Fan Fan exhales. "Then I guess you're going."

Lola's lean frame moves toward the door.

"But missy, one more thing."

Lola turns to see Fan Fan's finger jab toward one corner. "When you gonna clean your room?"

A sticky trail of blood arcs across the floor, leading to a bundle of tarpaulin. From one end pokes a pair of bloodied Pumas. From the other, a pulped skull.

Lola exhales. "When I get back."

"No, no, uh-uh. We do this now."

Fan Fan withdraws a large, leather-bound book from deep beneath her apron and spreads it wide across her lap, pawing through pages of handwritten notes until her fingers find a fresh page.

"So let's begin." She nips her tongue between her lips and licks the tip of a pencil. "What was his grift?"

Lola crosses her arms, resigned. "He was passing himself off as a member of a fan club." Lola nudges round the dead head with the tip of her boot. It is the skinny kid from the bus.

"He was following a death-metal band that's famous for its fan base, a bunch of self-harming, soon-to-be suicides. Pretty rich pickings for a Tormenta."

Fan Fan writes in slow, careful strokes. "What was the name of the band?"

"The band—seriously?"

"Every detail, *chère*. Every detail."

Lola exhales, taps her fingers against the holster. "Stork. And the bus was an Isuzu Gala twin-drive diesel. Light blue. Maybe Duck Egg."

Fan Fan puckers her lips. "My love, you may laugh. But I have ambitions." She pats the book. "Come the day the world is ready to know the truth, this little opus is my sure-ass passport to Oprah." She nibs her pencil to the page once more. "How long would you say this boy's been around?"

"Long enough." Lola tenses her shoulders, as if reliving their encounter. "He had a fistful of fight styles."

Her mind flashes back. She's inside the bus, her fist smashing into the skinny kid's skull. He dives down, deflecting the blow, his legs spinning round, cracking her behind the knees, forcing her into the aisle.

"Korean kick-house, for one."

Fan Fan moves her pencil fast across the page, keeping up. "What else?"

"Hapkido. Wrist-lock style." Lola's fingers ripple, remembering.

She is tumbling out of the bus, pulling the kid with her. Their two bodies thrashing through the mud, the rain falling hard. The kid leaps and twists, contorting his hand into an impossible punch that reverses back, connecting with Lola's jaw, jacking her high. She smashes hard into the back of the bus, falls on all fours, gasping for breath. The kid responds with a roar, ripping himself free from the last of his T-shirt. The torso revealed is racked with muscle. He lunges forward, Lola still on the ground. Defeated... or deceptive. As she suddenly launches upward, a length of metal in her hand—the bus fender, ripped away. Too close to halt his attack, the kid swoops down. And with a sucking thud, the metal plunges through his belly. He falls—dead.

Lola rises from the impaled body to see the other kids lined up against the bus, spread-eagled, eyes averted as Lola had commanded. Only one pair of eyes dare to look around—this girl Livi. She stares through the rain in a shivering silence as Lola extracts the fender from the kid's flank. Then Lola halts, sensing eyes upon her, and slowly tips her head to meet Livi's gaze. And with a dark smile, she hoists the bloody fender. "Death metal. My style."

Fan Fan turns the page, her old hand racing to record Lola's account.

"Ah, *chère*, your wits were quicker than his fists. But he was good. Hapkido and kick-house—to learn that many disciplines takes time... and travel."

"To Peru, amongst other places." Lola pulls a knife and slices the twine that binds the tarpaulin. "There was some capoeira, Wari style." She nods toward the unrolling tarpaulin. "Not from the kid. The other guy."

A second head slumps forward, striking the floor.

Fan Fan looks up, eyes wide. "What was this bus—a Tormenta nest?"

Lola shrugs and cranks her jaw, a jab of pain taking her back to the fight.

She's bent over the kid's corpse, momentarily distracted. A fist launches from the shadows, smashing her to the mud. She leaps to her feet, to see a figure hurtling forward. A cap catches in the light, a name upon it, declaring that her attacker is "Terry." But now the driver's eyes are ablaze and his movements fast and powerful, revealing his true nature. He drops his body low, swings his legs high. Boots smashing, catching the side of Lola's face as she swiftly deflects the attack. Blood blasts between her teeth as she crashes down, twisting her torso, her hands thrusting upward. Fingers tensed, hard as blades.

Scything into the driver's neck that cracks hard to the left. He gasps for breath, but too late as Lola grabs his long ponytail and wraps it round his neck, forcing her knee into the base of his skull. As he writhes, his cap rolls into the mud.

Lola mumbles through split lips, "Your driver is sorry." Then yanks back hard on his hair and in one jerk garrotes him.

Fan Fan's pencil pauses. She looks up. "And then?"

"He died. In no particular style."

With a thud, Fan Fan shuts the book and waddles over to the bundled bodies. "Well, if you're done, let's see what they reveal to my old mambo eyes."

She tugs at the tarp and the corpses collapse onto the floor, face down.

Fan Fan begins her examination with the kid, peeling off the last of his clothing. The cotton cracks with hardening blood, revealing a fresh tattoo spread across his shoulder blades. It is the bird-skull logo of Stork. Fan Fan pulls a bottle from her pocket and shoots a stream of liquid across the dead skin. At first, the impact serves to wash away the blood. But as the liquid settles, it begins to sizzle, its acid nature reacting with the air to produce a scalding brew that burns away the surface skin.

Her hand balled into a fist, Fan Fan wipes away the bubbling blisters, revealing beneath an older tattoo that stretches across his shoulder—a spider with eight eyes.

"I seen this one before." Fan Fan flicks through her book, her finger finding a sketch of the same tattoo. "It's the mark of the Ocho Ojos, from Tecate. But that gang hasn't been active since the late nineteen sixties."

She slops another slug of acid across the forearm. A number bubbles in the flesh.

"A prison tag, inked deep. I'd say he did time at the turn of the century."

She rolls the corpse and splashes the last of the acid across his chest. As the flesh boils and Fan Fan scrubs and rubs, another image appears, buried deep in the flesh.

A bird, long-beaked, wings spread.

"What's that, another stork?" Lola leans in close, reaching forward. Until Fan Fan smacks her hand away. "No, no, *chère*. This tattoo is deep. Real old."

She prods at the flesh. "Back when he got this, he wasn't following no stork. Because that right there"—she tentatively circles her finger above the bird—"is Guacariga."

She pauses. Then, with a sudden resolve, the old woman rolls the second body over. An identical tattoo is spread across the driver's chest.

"Well, well… fresh ink, I'd say. Which makes this darling dude a new disciple." Fan Fan slumps back onto her haunches, tapping her chin in contemplation. "It would seem the followers of Guacariga are gathering once more." Then her hand reaches down. She pulls a lump of tobacco from her pouch, agitating it between her palms. "What does this portend—that he comes again?"

Lola knows that phrasing. The way Fan Fan will half-finish a thought, dangle a question. She is playing the wise but haughty mambo who must be cajoled into her tale.

"So, great Bohica—you gonna tell me who this Guacariga is?"

Tracing her teeth with the tip of her tongue, Fan Fan selects the right place to begin her story.

"The Nazca desert, in Peru. You ever seen the creatures drawn in the dust?"

Lola nods. "Yeah, I've seen pictures. A spider, a monkey…" She frowns and then raises a finger. "And a hummingbird"—she points to the tattoo—"that looks just like this."

"And the hummingbird represents a god called Guacariga. And to the Taino people, he is the god of death."

 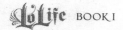

Fan Fan settles into her tale with another plug of tobacco.

"Taino legend tells of two great spirit clans who were at war: the House of the Fly and the House of the Lily. One house had a son, the other a daughter, and they fell in love—ancient precursors of Romeo and Juliet. Their love was forbidden because the Fly was a filthy creature that fed off death and the Lily was a thing of vivid beauty and life. So the young Fly, in a fit of love, did a terrible thing—he stole rays from the sun and turned himself into a glittering creature whose wings were every color of the spectrum. And so was born the Hummingbird. But the Sun God discovered what the Fly had done and he cursed him.

"So when the Hummingbird at last sank his beak into the sweetness of his beloved Lily, he found himself driven to suck... to suck the very life from her. In that moment, wracked with grief and fury, the Hummingbird became Guacariga, the destroyer. His coming signals death, just as it did when he was the Fly. Those who bear the symbol of Guacariga believe he will return. And when he does return, death will come to all mankind."

"How d'you know so much about Taino culture?"

Fan Fan flaps her hand as if it should be obvious. "The Taino people came from the Nazca deserts. They spread to Trinidad and Haiti and then to Louisiana. And that's where Taino culture grew into voodoo." She taps her chest. "Even my own name, Bohica, is evidence of this ancestry. In the ancient Taino language it means 'priestess.' So I take that as a sign that I was always destined to become a mambo... even though some may doubt my powers."

A silence falls. Lola looks up. "I know how powerful you are."

A dark smile passes between them. Lola looks away, unwilling to let Fan Fan see what rises in her eyes.

"What is it, child? Are you having regrets?"

Lola says nothing.

"I sense that something's stirring in you." She pauses, draws a subtle breath. "Do you want to remember…?"

The blond head remains averted in the shadows.

"I don't know… maybe."

Fan Fan reaches out, pats Lola's hand. The gesture is gentle, but the old woman's fingers are stiff with tension.

"No, honey, believe me… you don't."

12

GROTTESCHI WHEELS THE library cart along a narrow corridor. It leads to the isolation wing.

He has secured this duty by calling in a favor from the young guard who accompanies him. Not that Grotteschi ever itches to dirty his hands performing the labors of a prison trustee. But today... he has a particular mission in mind.

There is one prisoner he wants to talk to, and this is the only way that he can secure an audience.

Because this is no ordinary prisoner. This is the one they call Ring-Pull.

The wheels of the cart squeak, a rhythmic pulse that echoes off the walls like an alarm.

They approach the last security gate that quarantines the corridor. The young guard slows his pace. His eyes flick to the unlit length ahead.

"So... you goin' right inside his cell?"

Grotteschi exhales. "No, my plan is to remain outside and slide his book choice, page by page, beneath the door."

The young guard pauses but Grotteschi waits, knowing that sarcasm moves in slow motion around here.

Finally the guard grunts and nods. "Yeah, well, let's see how funny you are when you come out."

His key churns in the lock as Grotteschi ushers the cart through the gate.

"I'll open his cell when you get there." The guard dangles a hand above a panel of buttons. "You got three seconds and then the door shuts, real quick. Could slice that hump o' yours like ham."

Grotteschi trundles his cargo toward the farthest door. Then, quite unexpectedly, a shiver struggles up his spine. Grotteschi halts and tugs at his ear, confused.

How strange!

When he walked down the first length of corridor, the young guard's evident unease had served as a distraction. Now, with him gone, Grotteschi feels exposed to the pounding of his own heart.

Can it be that the prospect of this prisoner actually unnerves me?

Grotteschi had felt nothing, not a flicker of fear as he read the transcripts of Ring-Pull's trial. Even as he scrolled through the tabloids, with their glut of gory details, his hand had never flinched. He appreciated, of course, the ghastly magnitude of Ring-Pull's crimes. To fail to do so—well, that would be inhuman; seven little boys, blond beauties every one, abducted and killed.

All in the same way—starved to death in a shed in Bayou Cane.

But none of this aroused outrage in Grotteschi. What consumed him was curiosity. The opening argument from Ring-Pull's defense was beyond extraordinary. It contended that Ring-Pull was not in his right mind. More than that—not in his right *body*.

 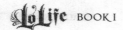

His real name—that is to say, the name on his birth certificate—was Todd Lily. A roadie who lugged gear for every heavy metal band that rocked the East Coast. When his sacrum finally cracked, Lily turned his massive hands to a new trade and opened up Rinky Dink Ink, a tattoo parlor on New York's Lower East Side.

Age fifty-two, he gets blood-poisoning from a dirty needle. Falls into a coma and is pronounced dead.

He's laid out in the morgue. The pathologist makes his first cut and finds running blood. Lily is still alive... or back from the dead. Same thing. *Kinda...*

When Lily comes round, he announces that he is Tenzin Nara, a Buddhist monk. He has no memory of his life as Todd Lily.

Once physically recovered—and with no coverage through his HMO for psychiatric help—he is discharged. And disappears.

Ten months later, he turns up in Louisiana with seven little boys, all dead. When arrested, he said nothing, only that he meant the children no harm. He was simply performing his duty, in search of the Rinpoche.

The county court of New Orleans had not much cared to investigate what lay behind this one repeated word, settling to respond with just one of their own: *execution.*

The inmates of Morphic Fields talked eagerly and endlessly of his arrival and soon bastardized this Rinpoche to Ring-Pull.

Grotteschi's interest had been piqued. Tales of reincarnation had always fascinated him. Lily's belief that he was now a Tibetan monk sounded like a classic case of delusion. He was keen to speak with the man. But Grotteschi was denied any opportunity for such a conversation.

On his first night in Morphic Fields, Ring-Pull's head was so savagely pulped against the lip of a urinal, his jaw could not be reconstructed, and now the lower half of his face is held together by a crude wire brace.

Grotteschi is not even sure whether the man can speak. But he has to find out. Because Ring-Pull is the one who can give him the answers he seeks.

He arrives outside the cell. Wipes his palms down his thighs, conscious of their heavy sweat.

The young guard, far distant on the other side of the gate, presses the button and the door slides open. The space beyond is windowless and dark.

Grotteschi sees nothing, but his other senses quiver to the rasp of wet breath and the sharp tang of urine.

As his pupils dilate, a shadow gains form. A face turns, meshed in metal.

Grotteschi grips his cart as if he might at any moment wield it as a weapon. Then, with a jagged intake of breath, he finds his voice.

"Namaste…" He places his hands together and bows, using the downward motion to conceal the removal of a particular book from the bottom of the trolley. "I am in need of your wisdom."

The silence is filled with the shadow's breath, sieved through saliva. Forcing himself onward, Grotteschi slides the book across the floor. "There is a symbol that defies me. It is not one of our world. I believe it belongs to the realm of the dead. And

so its meaning may lie within this book. I ask for your learning to help me understand."

An arm uncoils from the darkness, draws the book closer. A flashlight snaps on, finds the volume's title.

BARDO THODOL
THE TIBETAN BOOK OF THE DEAD

Grotteschi taps the cover. "It is a nineteen fifties imprint, but wonderfully complete."

The beam of light swings up, catching the edge of Ring-Pull's metal face. Grotteschi spasms, his knees buckling behind the shield of the cart.

He gathers himself, points with a quivering finger. "The relevant page—I have marked it."

Ring-Pull rises from the corner and slides through the darkness toward his bed. The movement releases a fresh stench of human decay and Grotteschi feels a cannonball of bile bowl up his gullet. He swallows it down as Ring-Pull spreads the book across his lap, fingers tracing the selected symbol.

Grotteschi musters a whisper. "You know its meaning?"

A noise shudders from Ring-Pull. A deep, bestial grunt. That comes again, faster now. Harder. Louder.

Grotteschi clenches the metal cart handle.

And as sound explodes about the cell, he realizes that Ring-Pull is laughing.

13

Bıanco can no longer smell the lilies. The old aroma, stuck to the walls of the soap factory has not diminished. But she's been there so long her nose has dulled. She looks at her wrists where her watch should be, remembering now that she was stripped of it.

Then her fingers descend to the floor and riffle through scraps. It's the paper upon which her testimony should have been written, torn to pieces. Real small pieces. Stripping and ripping has been the only way to pass the intervening hours since she made her decision.

The right decision. To say nothing to SCURO. She owes Lola her life.

Because a new life began for her the moment Lola revealed all that exists beyond the human realm.

And the fact that Bianco's alive today, that's down to Lola too.

That one night, when everything changed…

✦

Lola was bleeding so bad the floor of Fan Fan's cabin was as slippery as a slaughterhouse ice rink. It took a yard of catgut and all of the old mambo's sewing skills to patch her up. And

 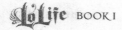

as Lola lay in the corner, forced into slumber by a flask of Old Artemis, Fan Fan turned to Bianco, her voice low.

"Yo' gone tell me what passed tonight?"

Bianco tightened her mouth, twitching her cigarette.

"Ever since I've known you, Crow, you got a sickness. I call it lockjaw." The old woman thrust a bottle of the green liquor beneath Bianco's chin. "Here's the cure. Take as required and talking comes easy."

Bianco grabbed the bottleneck, slooshed the liquor round. And memories licked the back of her mind.

"Do you remember how this all began, Fan Fan? Way back when you and I knew nothing of Tormenta?"

"Child, I always had my demons." She raised her own bottle and, with a smile, took a deep pull from it. Then her smile slackened and she reached out to pat Bianco's hand.

"You got regrets?"

"No, it's just that"—Bianco ground her cigarette slow and hard—"three months ago, before Lola came along, I was just a cop. Plain and simple. Or as simple as homicide gets. Then she drops out of the darkness and into my life. Her DNA says she's one-time dead; her suicide file is on my desk. But here she is, alive and kicking the shit outta anyone who gets in her way. And then she and her Magnum give me a fast education in Tormenta, because she needs my help."

Bianco flipped a smile. "Of course, she doesn't call it help. Lola can take care of herself. She knows how to hunt. She knows every Tormenta game, every grift. She says that all she needs from me is information, the paperwork and passes that'll get her closer to her marks. But the kill—that's down to her. She goes in solo, every time. And I've obeyed. I've stayed away, every time."

Bianco pulled out a fresh smoke. "Except this one."

Her eyes drifted down to the dried blood on her hands, caked across her knuckles. She tapped the soft pack. Pressed on.

"We went to Vegas. Lola said it's a prime hunting ground. A lot of Tormenta operate there. She made it sound like we were going into duck country at the height of the season. But there was one guy she wanted. A casino owner called Jimmy Finny. She knew his grift. He gets a punter deep in debt and then sends his boys round to collect. It doesn't take many visits before the punter opts to blow out his own brains, rather than wait for the boys to achieve a similar result with baseball bats."

Bianco sparked her smoke. "That's top-grade tormenting."

The match dropped to the floor, joining a pile of many. "Finny had built up quite an empire. A ritzy joint on the Strip. A ton of security. Getting close wasn't gonna be easy. Lola needed inside information. So I swing by the Las Vegas Police Department with some cold-case cover story. Ask them about Finny. His movements, his routine. Detective Dirk takes me for a coffee, gives me one of his fancy French cigarettes, and lays out some even sweeter information. He tells me that Finny will always take a face-to-face meeting with the gaming commission. Those guys, he keeps close. So if I'm going undercover, Dirk recommends I get myself a commissioner's ID. That way I can walk right in. I pass this on to Lola. She gets herself suited and booted and, dammit, ya know, she looks badass even with a briefcase."

Fan Fan chuckled, encouraging her.

"I get her a commissioner's ID. And in she goes. Tells me

she'll call when she's done. Like she always does. I'll drive by, pick her up, and then we're smoke."

Bianco stubbed out her cigarette, barely touched.

"I figure I've got fifteen minutes. I walk over to a tobacco booth in the lobby of the Bellagio. I'm looking for that fancy French brand that Detective Dirk gave me. The guy in the booth has a real attitude." Bianco tightened her face, impersonating the clerk.

"Is Madam looking for anything in particular?"

"Thinking about changing my brand. I'll take a packet of the Vichy Grandes."

"That'll be forty dollars."

"Forty dollars?"

"It's a lovely cigarette."

"If I owned the casino, maybe. Wrong brand for a cop."

"Maybe you're the wrong brand of cop."

Fan Fan popped her eyes at this comment. And Bianco nodded.

"Yeah, it hit me too. No way could Dirk afford those smokes. Unless Dirk is dirty. In which case I just walked my partner into a setup."

Her fingers flex into a fist. "I got there in under five. And there she was, under fire. First time I'd seen her fight. And Fan Fan, I gotta tell ya, it's a fine sight. The way she moved about that room, taking all those goons out, one by one. Until Finny stands alone. Then it begins: the main event."

Fan Fan pulled her notebook from her pocket. "Slowly, now; I want to get this down." Her long tongue slicked the tip of a pencil, but Bianco accelerated, lost in her own tale.

"It was spectacular. Fists flying like whirlybirds. And Lola's pulling blades and pumping bullets, any hand, every direction. And Finny—he's just as fast. Faster even. That's what it looked like. Because suddenly, Lola's down. And I'm not thinking. I'm on instinct overdrive. My gun is out and I'm going in. Then I realize, too late—she's not hurt, she's faking. And I've fucked it up.

"Finny turns to me and gets a shot away. And I hear it hit, metal mashing flesh. I know that sound. But I'm still standing. And then I see Lola, right in front of me, twisting through the air, falling and firing her Winchester. She hits Finny. Nukes his neck. And then she's rolling at my feet. A hole this big, right through her chest. She took that bullet.

"I pull her arms around my shoulders and drag her out of there. We're in the car. I'm driving like a maniac. I'm saying, 'I'm sorry, I'm sorry.'"

Bianco closed her eyes, head down.

Fan Fan nudged the bottle in her hand. "She's gonna be all right." Ruffled Bianco's long hair. "You're still her partner."

"We're not partners."

"She's your friend."

Bianco dunked a smile. "We're not friends."

"She'd die for you."

"Yeah. But I'm not sure what that makes us."

＋

A bell suddenly shrills on the factory wall, rousing Bianco.

The last shreds of paper drift through her fingers, falling to nothing. *No truth. Not this time.*

 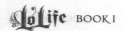

She stands up straight, smoothes her suit. She's disobeyed SCURO, so now there is the issue of consequences.

What fate awaits?

It's easy for SCURO to make a cop disappear. Just deliver some soft-soap story about recruitment to a special operation. All your chief knows back at the precinct is that you'll be on other duties for a while. He won't know where or why or how long until you come back—*if* you come back.

A light blasts on above her head. Bianco blinks, looks about her, seeing for the first time the room that holds her. And instantly she learns a fresh fact about SCURO.

They've got a sense of humor.

The faded sign on the wall reads: THE SOFT SOAP FACTORY.

The slot in the floor slides open for a second time. Something bulges up, soft and rubbery. Flopping out and uncurling onto the floor. Bianco gathers it.

It's a rubber party mask.

The loudspeaker on the wall shivers and crackles. A voice booms.

"Place the mask on your face. Exit the room. Do not speak. Do not remove the mask."

A loud pop punctuates the end of the order as the speaker clunks off.

Bianco slides on the mask. It smells of latex and clings to her nostrils and mouth. She exhales as the door to her room clangs open.

Chin up, she walks out as Einstein.

14

Grotteschi pushes his books down the corridor, fast away from Ring-Pull's cell.

The wheels have lost their squeak, as if the knowledge now borne by Grotteschi is so astounding that it has the power to silence not only him but all he touches.

The body of Todd Lily holds the mind of another.

At first, Grotteschi could not untangle his own thoughts because the fear that shrieked within his skull was so distracting.

Only as he acclimatized to the stench of the cell and the vastness of the shadowed form before him did another feeling start to clamber across his heart: a heavy calm.

The breathing of Ring-Pull, at first so wet with threat, now seemed to impart a soothing rhythm.

And the voice, when it finally came, was deep and round. Grotteschi found himself sitting like a patient child as the mind of Tenzin Nara spoke to him through the mouth of Todd Lily.

"The life that we call ours, we borrow only. Once we die, the life span returns to the eternal cycle and awaits its rebirth. This cycle was my care—my duty to protect."

Ring-Pull pauses, noisily hawking up the drool that escapes from his split lips. Grotteschi shifts, waiting patiently.

"I belong to an elite brotherhood of Buddhist monks. Our

 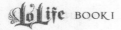

sworn duty it is to seek out the human vessels into which the spans of our beloved masters—our Rinpoche—are reborn. For centuries, this tradition has been upheld.

"Monks such as I travel from village to village, examining every boy, searching for the reborn span of our masters to appear in what we call the Unmistaken Son. But we must move quickly, as once the boy is five years old, it is too late. Human emotions, unwittingly instilled by his parents, will have destroyed his gifts. In short, his mind will now be locked into the human realm—and the spirit of the Rinpoche trapped forever."

Ring-Pull suddenly lunges forward, roaring. Behind his metal mask, his face contorts as if another body is trying to burst out.

Grotteschi shrinks back. *The fight between Tenzin Nara and Todd Lily is not done with!*

Ring-Pull bellows again, then ferociously inhales, swallowing back down the restless fury into the belly of his being. A silence hangs and slowly, he continues with his story.

"When I first died as Tenzin Nara I found myself reborn into the body of Todd Lily. I accepted this as just another stage in my search. The duty to find my Rinpoche remained. I sought the boy in whom he may be concealed. I was not killing these children. I was merely opening their mortal shells."

Grotteschi listens in openmouthed fascination. "Venerable Nara, you indeed have knowledge beyond this world."

He has almost forgotten his original purpose in coming to this stinking cell. Then—he jabs a finger at the symbol on the opening page of *The Book of the Dead*.

"A man… not of his own mind… wrote this symbol."

Ring-Pull nods and rolls up his sleeve to reveal the identical symbol tattooed on his own arm. It is spherical like the sun but the rays are jointed, like insect legs.

"The man Todd Lily was familiar with this symbol, though he had no knowledge of its meaning. The *Bardo Thodol* has long been an inspiration for skin-ink artists. He was simply drawn to this particular totem."

His fingers trace a gnarl of scars that surround the tattoo.

"It was this that he was applying when the infection set in. I sometimes wonder if that is what called me to his body…"

The corners of Ring-Pull's eyes crinkle with a contemplative smile. Grotteschi urges him on.

"So you know the meaning?" Grotteschi wriggles with anticipation.

And with those words, the calm is ripped from Ring-Pull's eyes like a morgue sheet, revealing beneath a face wracked with fear. "Yes, I know its meaning."

His voice strains. "Amid the flow, there are certain spans that come with great power. The power to inflict upon the human realm… infinite alteration." Ring-Pull grimaces. "I never thought to witness it…"

The cell door shudders open. The guard is calling time.

"Witness what, venerable sir?" Grotteschi's body is knotted with anticipation.

Ring-Pull taps a filthy finger on the symbol.

"The accursed Fly, he comes once more. The nemesis of humankind—the Mosca."

 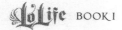

BOOK II

15

A FIGURE SITS in the deepest reach of the Archivum.

A set of shelves, stacked with books, obscures the body, and a table lamp blasts a beam downward, but not up. The figure's face cannot be seen.

But still, there are some clues that prove his identity.

For one: the shirt cuffs.

They tumble from his sleeve, light and lacy. Some might dismiss these details as evidence of dandiness, but he delights in them. As he does in his hair, curled into coils.

Another clue: the cards. A handsome golden deck, laid out in the careful ranks of solitaire. They aid in passing the time, and much time is passed here.

And that's the final clue, the one that categorically confirms who sits within the shadows: the sheer lateness of the hour. Who else would endure the night chill of the Archivum other than Dali?

Dali looks about him. He need not move his head. His eyes are large and swivel in their sockets, soft and silent.

He is alone. His favored state. He gathers up his cards and slides the deck within a velvet pocket.

And then he waits a moment more. Patience, too, is to be prized. He breathes in deep, smelling the leather and the vellum.

And then he slowly extracts a long silver pen, setting it down like a surgeon's scalpel. For in a way, he is about to operate—to make better. The Archivum holds many documents in need of his tender care. Works that contain inaccuracies, half-truths. They need correcting, like a crooked spine.

This addiction of Dali's to add and append, he knows from whence it comes. It is an urge instilled in him during his youthful days, when he worked as a scribe to a scholarly priest. Père Corbeau studied the ancient works of the philosopher Trismegistus. Ten thousand years before the birth of Christ, when the world worshipped a host of deities, Trismegistus wrote of one god who would some day come to Earth in the form of a man. Père Corbeau pored over every word and every time he discerned some deeper meaning, he would charge his young scribe with the task of annotating his copy of the text with a tiny asterisk. Then he would dictate his interpretation and the boy would write, in a fine, light hand, a footnote at the bottom of the page.

This apprenticeship lasted barely two years, but even in that short time, the young scribe became aware that the old priest's mind was growing ever more troubled. With each interpretation, the old man found his faith twisted ever tighter toward the teachings of the Rose-Cross monks, who had long held the works of Trismegistus as the cornerstone of their faith. But the Rose-Cross brothers, or Rosicrucians, as they came to be known, were deemed a radical sect and were exiled by Rome in 1822. So if Père Corbeau's notes were ever discovered, he would be castigated as a heretic. So the old man hatched a plan.

The rules of typography are such that a second set of notes

 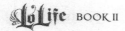

must be signified by a fresh mark—not an asterisk, but a cross-shaped symbol called an obelus. And so it was that the young scribe returned to the works of Trismegistus and, at the old man's command, added an obelus after each asterisk. Père Corbeau then gave him a new, blank book. These new footnotes, in all their rose-colored, heretical glory, must exist in this tome alone. A slim, hide-bound book that the young scribe came to refer to as the *Obelus*. And at the end of each night's annotation, this book would be snatched up by the old priest to be hidden away.

A hide-bound book indeed...

And so this continued—until the night Père Corbeau was discovered on the floor of the church scriptorium with his throat slit, still wearing his habit, dried hard with blood.

Dali never worked as a scribe again. But old habits die hard. And his passion for books continued unabated. He loves not what a book reveals, but what it does not. The insidious intent. The masquerade of meaning. The subtle subtext, sliding another message like a razor blade beneath your eyelid.

Dali leans back in his chair and looks about the Archivum one last time. He is now quite certain of his solitude, and so he reaches up and eases a book from the shelf, gently, as if it were a sleeping baby. Then he sets it down upon the table. This publication will be the first to undergo tonight's process of correction.

The cover is black leather, worn to a shine. Embossed across the front is the title.

THE SINESTRA MANIFESTUM

Dali had first been instructed to read this manual years ago as part of his induction. Standard practice when someone is enlisted in the Sinestra from the outside. And Dali was—in every sense—an outsider.

The information contained within the *Manifestum* is rudimentary, no more than a collection of cold, disjointed phrases. In Dali's opinion, it raises the reader's awareness of the Sinestra much as a tent might be raised, in slow, slotting stages. His instinct was to add a little color and verve and as a result, the manual now sparkles with asterisks.

Indeed, even the very first sentence was one that Dali felt obliged to embellish. The original line read:

The Sinestra is a division of Lo'World security dedicated to safeguarding the dispersal of span. Its sworn purpose it to ensure that mankind is protected from those other entities who endeavor to despoil the span allotted to humanity. *

At the foot of the page is Dali's inky tinkering.

* Let us start at the true beginning. For in the beginning, there was the Source. And the Source created man and bestowed upon him a measure of life. A span of existence. But those dark forces that exist beyond the reach of grace, those foul and fallen miscreants, soon found a way to steal that span. And so the Source sent an army of angels and they were called the Sinestra. And they were charged with the duty of protecting man's span from all those demons that sought to suck it away.

 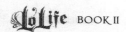

The ink in which this footnote is inscribed is soft and gray, an indication that Dali made this addendum more than a century ago. In those early days, he was still finding his feet within the Sinestra. All he wished to do, by means of this addition, was to record the division's angelic origins.

Then the years passed and his knowledge grew. At first, just facts. But all the same, he felt the need to note his learning and expand again the *Manifestum*'s shallow account. The second chapter is titled "Span," and an asterisk beside leads to a footnote, writ small and at length.

* *To understand span, one should think of it as an echo, reverberating around and around. Span passes from one human to another, as birth follows death. Span has no memory of itself as it cycles. It is just a dose of existence, apportioned measure by measure. But it comes from one shared resource, a whole that connects all mankind. And this universal mass is called the Spanorama. By opening their minds—a process some might call prayer—the Sinestra can tune into the echoes of the Spanorama and detect any untoward fluctuations. If an attempt to siphon span is detected, a Hunter will be dispatched. That Hunter will leave the Hypogeum and walk amongst humans, to seek out and destroy the demon responsible.*

As Dali reads this now, he knows he should refine his own addendum and add a further footnote to explain the term *Hypogeum*. But this can wait. It is a simple matter and can be dealt with quickly. The Hypogeum is the subterranean structure in which the Sinestra dwell. The name itself means no more than "under-earth," and the location of the Hypogeum has changed many times since the Sinestra's inception. The *Manifestum* records the first as lying beneath a field called King's Reach in Staffordshire, England. In 1686, three hundred years after the Sinestra had abandoned this Hypogeum and moved to another, the giant stone slab that marked its entrance was discovered by a the delightfully named Dr. Plot. With the aid of a hefty laborer, he removed the slab and descended the stone staircase that lay beyond, entering the maze of tunnels beneath. Upon his return, he refused to disclose what relics he had found therein, but Dr. Plot later became a master at Magdalen College Oxford, where—by chance or by design?— he dedicated his life to the study of echoes.

The move from King's Reach had been necessitated by the growing workload of the Sinestra. Mankind was expanding across the globe. The task of monitoring the Spanorama threatened to overwhelm them.

A new Hypogeum was established beneath Nottingham Castle. A deep set of tunnels, known as King David's Dungeon, lay beneath the foundations and their vast expanse gave the Sinestra the space they required as their ranks grew. The dungeons were chosen because at their heart was a deep void called Romylowe's Cave. It provided the perfect conical chamber in which the Angelus Superior could pray. This was a new hierarchy within the Sinestra, created in response to their expanding duties. They were commissioned to do nothing but sit within the void, deep in prayer. And with their minds laid open, they would monitor day and night the flux of the Spanorama.

The division of labor within the Sinestra spread far

beyond the creation of the Angelus Superior. Interpreting the fluctuations in the Spanorama and then mapping these disturbances across the globe became a task of its own, and a subdivision arose for this purpose. And as the number of Hunters grew, they required management, and so it was that another tier of administration came into being.

It was at this time that Dali joined the Sinestra, and he was assigned the role of Handler. Into his care was placed a clutch of Hunters. His task was to train them, allocate their targets, and oversee their missions. Within a few years of his arrival the number of Handlers and Hunters had increased tenfold.

But this expansion was not the only change that Dali witnessed. There was another. A monumental alteration to the Sinestra.

And it caused the abandonment of King David's Dungeon.

In the *Manifestum*, this move receives scant mention. A single sentence records the date of resettlement as May 1956 and the location as the Kingsway, beneath the streets of Holborn in London.

The entrance to the Kingsway is a small door at 32 High Holborn. Behind it lies a lift shaft that descends one hundred feet below the streets of London, arriving in an underground city—mile after mile of ironclad corridors and low-ceilinged chambers, all painted a dull beige. This subterranean maze was built as a wartime refuge, capable of sheltering thousands. But from the time of its construction, there was always a sprawling portion kept secret from the public. These covert corridors housed a monumental telephone exchange capable of connecting the entire Western world in the event of an atomic attack. After the war, as the threat subsided, the tunnels of Kingsway were given over to the Public Records Office and four hundred thousand of the Allies' most sensitive documents were hidden here, safe from public scrutiny. When the Public Records Office moved out in 1956, the Sinestra moved in.

The actual means by which they came to take possession is referenced in the *Manifestum* in just one short line.

> *The Sinestra cooperated with terrestrial authorities to effect the occupation of Kingsway.†*

Dali reaches into his coat and pulls out a small, hide-bound book. Its cover is marked with a cross that might, to the untrained eye, suggest that it is a Bible. But any scribe would recognize the mark as an obelus. Just like his old mentor, Dali has created his own book to contain those additions that are too radical to safely sit within the manual's original pages.

He turns to the page that contains this particular footnote.

This entry is absent Dali's florid prose. Instead the tone is stark, suggesting anger. It begins thus:

†By the following means, the Sinestra is forever altered.

(i) It has made certain human agencies aware of its existence and its operations.

(ii) The Angelus Superior, now termed the High Command, no longer monitors the echo of the Spanorama.

(iii) That duty—that precious duty that lies at the very heart of the Sinestra's existence—now rests with a machine, the Helix Vivat. And it was solely in order to install the Helix Vivat into the telecommunication chamber that the Sinestra moved to Kingsway.

 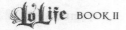

The entry concludes with a final scrawled note, unnumbered and disconnected from the rest.

Trismegistus once wrote, "As it is above, so it is below." The great man was referring to the heavenly kingdom and Earth, but my point is this: The human world occupies the streets above, where mankind runs around, blind and bewildered, governed by ego and self-obsessed order... and so it is below, in our underground world. The Sinestra has become an obsessive bureaucracy with a machine at its heart.

Dali bends the neck of the table lamp, rolling its beam across this old entry. He smiles at the lettering, raw and ragged, reflecting the fury with which it was inflicted on the page. Back then, Dali did indeed deplore the Helix Vivat—a machine swarming with officious operatives who jump at every twitch of the gauge, gripping their clipboards, jotting notes, and filing reports.

But Dali has an eye for beauty, and he could not deny that the Helix Vivat, towering tall with its valves and pipes and glittering lights, was a spectacular creation. Its throbbing and thudding sounds to Dali's ear like music, urging him to bow and bend those long, elastic legs of his. A fey weakness perhaps. But, as Dali likes to say, everybody dances to his own boom-boom.

His obvious delight in the Helix Vivat resulted in the High Command awarding him the honorary title of Master of the Machine. There is little actual duty that comes with the title, but Dali bears the keys to the engine room, and he revels in that.

He has held the post for decades now, and on those evenings when he is not in the Archivum, he can often be found wandering amid the throbbing coils, polishing dials and tapping valves.

The machine does a fine job of monitoring the Spanorama and, in truth, these days there is just one miscreant species remaining that subverts the smooth flow—and that is the Tormenta.

Of all the demon breeds that walk the Earth, Tormenta are the most closely related to humankind. So similar is their physiology that Tormenta can harvest span directly from a human host, as long as the span is surrendered and not stolen.

The *Manifestum*'s entry on these vermin is extensive. But it holds no interest for Dali tonight. He thumbs past those pages, reaching a directory at the back. Drags a finger, finding his own name, listed with his honorary title, *Magister dei Machina*.

He smiles, wondering still whether it was his famous passion for the Helix Vivat that won him the title, or if there was a darker irony to be found.

Did it perhaps amuse the High Command to make him this award, knowing how Tormenta bedevil his beloved machine?

Knowing that he was once a Tormenta himself. Before his defection…

Beside his name in the directory is the date on which he joined the Sinestra: June 6, 1857. And next to the date, a faint cross, confirming that somewhere, Dali has expounded upon his own history.

 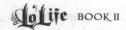

He peels open the pages of his *Obelus*, finds the appropriate place. The entry is extensive—a confession of sorts.

†*This account should begin with a date of birth, but there is none. The boy who was to become Dali was born an orphan. He lived amongst the Taino tribe in Trinidad with nothing but a fierce desire to survive. Which he did by virtue of a silver tongue, his only gift. He was fed by fishermen, whom he persuaded to share their catch, and he was clad by women, beguiled to give him garments.*

When the French arrived and trade began, he saw fresh opportunity. Strong and lithe, he'd stow away unnoticed, pocketing small portions of cargo. Selling it beneath the noses of the French in the Louisiana markets where they docked. He was caught, of course—that was inevitable. But once again, his powers of persuasion saved his skin. He fiddled with their fury until they saw the funny side. The crew took him in and gave him a seafaring name, Tret. It is a term that means the fraction of cargo that is always lost in transportation. The boy was rather taken with his name.

He decided to remain in Louisiana. The prospects would be brighter for a boy such as him, young and hungry for success. The only impediment to his plan was the lack of a patron, someone to provide bare vittles while he made his mark. His prayers were answered by Père Corbeau, a local priest, who took the boy under his wing and trained him in the skills of a scribe. The priest showed the boy nothing but unbridled kindness—a stark contrast to the beatings the man bestowed upon himself. The boy knew that the priest was suffering from a trial of faith, but there was something else eating away at the old man's conscience. Night after night, the boy would hear him thrashing at his flesh with many instruments of penance. Why he should punish himself so was a mystery to the boy, until the night came that the old man crept into the corner of the scriptorium where the scribe slept and tried to lay his gnarled hands upon his naked body. Then he finally understood the urges that had plagued the old man. Tret should have killed him there and then. But something stopped him. An urge of his own that he could neither grasp nor put a name to. But its draw was strong. An instinct… not to snap the old man's neck, but to break his heart.

One dark night not long after, he hears Père Corbeau ripping at his flesh with leather straps. So he enters his room and puts that silver tongue of his to work. Taunting him, teasing him. Whipping him into a frenzy of lust… and self-disgust. Such loathing for his own sick desires that death could be the only salve. And passing him a knife, the boy rouses the old man, there and then, to take the final stroke. And he does. To great effect.

The blood, the boy was prepared for. The horror came from what consumed him next—an overwhelming compulsion to press his lips to the old man's mouth as he lay dying. He fought the urge and, in a frenzy, he washed the room, burned the habit, and tossed Corbeau's body into a bayou.

As he suspected, the old priest was not missed. And without opposition, the scribe claimed his lodgings in the church. And that was where he saw her first. His beloved flower… Rosa Cruz.

She was barely thirteen, but this was a girl for whom spring had slipped soon into summer. Those rounded hips of hers took rest in the pews of the rich, where hers was one black bonnet amongst many. And yet the merest tilt of her brim inflamed him,

 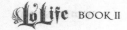

like a rising skirt—a glimpse of thigh could not have roused him more than the flash of her eye. He was bewitched. His heart's sole counterpoise was found. But she was rich and he was poor. These circumstances might have deterred a lesser suitor, but young Tret was persistent. And persuasive.

Every Sunday he would follow her home. Outside her bedroom window was a balcony. Tret would climb the adjacent lamppost and leap across, calling to her. Wooing her with well-chosen words and wild antics. He may have had no coin, but the boy had charm. And he had dreams. He promised Rosa that he would make something of himself and return to marry her, if she would promise to wait.

The night she made that promise was the night that Tret first tasted her upon his lips. But his mouth could barely suck her flavor before his ears were drawn to the click of a lock. Her bedroom door was opening. Her father was entering and the sound in Tret's head became the pulsing thud of his blood as he ran to the window and leaped for the lamppost. His hand missed; his body fell. His chest was impaled upon a set of iron spikes that crowned the post.

In New Orleans, these deterrents are called Romeo spikes. And the longest spike pierced Tret's heart.

The next thing he remembers is awakening. This is most unexpected, compounded further by the fact that the slab on which he lies is in a morgue. The tag upon his toe reads "dead". Before he can begin to fathom what has passed, a hand is clamped upon his mouth and from above a man's voice comes, urging him to silence. He tells the boy that all will be explained. The man is lean and wrapped within a dark cape. Just a wisp of white hair escapes from beneath his three-cornered hat. He inhales a long, rattling breath.

Then, peeling his fingers one by one from the boy's wet mouth, he begins.

"You, my dear boy, are not human. You may look human, you may feel human, but you are not. You are something so much more." The caped figure pauses, allowing each word to settle like a pebble in the boy's mind before continuing.

"If you look back, you'll realize that perhaps you always felt a little different from your peers. That you had an insatiable appetite to taunt and tease—to reduce those close to you to self-disgust. Many children feel this, because many children are not human. Imagine, then, their relief when a kindly, avuncular figure appears one day—perhaps in the park, or as they walk home from church—and gently explains that they are special... very special indeed. Just as I am explaining to you... that you are not a man-child. You are in fact, a Tormenta."

Now the boy's eyes slowly dilate, like blotting paper soaking up the information. And then, cautiously, he speaks. "Père Corbeau—I could have killed him. But I knew... what I wanted more was for him to take his own life... commit the sin of suicide."

The man claps his hands together, as if witnessing a baby's first steps. "Of course, of course! And then you felt an urge to place your mouth on his."

Eagerly now, the boy leans forward. "Yes! Yes! The thought of it revolted me, but still—"

"—you longed to do it even though you were not yet fully formed. Because that is how we feed. We suck up the span the human has surrendered. We can take the allotted years

 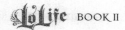

unspent by them. And this is how we live."

He rests a hand upon the boy's shoulders. "This is how we live… forever."

The fingers slide down, arriving at the gaping wound in the boy's chest. "Now this… should not have happened quite as it did, and the fault is mine. I failed in my duties. And so I failed the Legion of Gehenna…"

He tugs the boy's shirt up to cover the ragged chest wound and rolls on with his explanation.

"The Legion of Gehenna are an elite group of Tormenta, chosen for their skills, to seek out and awaken those of our kind. It is a great honor to be called as a G-Man, and each is designated an area to monitor—a beat, if you like. We fit ourselves into society as best we can, as doctors, teachers"—he taps his own chest— "the local undertaker. And when we see a child who harbors a Tormenta spirit, we watch and we wait, choosing our moment to awaken the child to its true self. And this we accomplish by use of our clave." He now lifts a long, iron shank that hangs from his belt. At one end are jagged teeth, like those of a key.

"We thrust our clave into the child's heart. This act, of course, kills him as a human. But his Tormenta self will then take over and consume him fully."

He lets the clave fall back to his side. "My intention was to induct you in the usual way. I was simply waiting for the right moment. But too late. Before I could make my move, you fell and there I found you, impaled upon the Romeo spikes. I pulled you down and told myself that there was nothing I could do. If you die before your Tormenta self is awakened, then it is over. You expire as any human would.

"I thought the very least I could do would be to bury you. And so I brought you back here, cleaned you up, and then—to my astonishment—you revived. Of your own accord. I can only guess that the spike through your heart served the same purpose as my clave. So I suggest we do not dwell on how it came to pass…"

The G-Man grabs the tag that hangs from the boy's toe. Taking a pen, he amends the word DEAD to ALIVE.

"Because there is much for you to learn about our ways. For example: it is customary to take a new name at the beginning of one's Tormenta life. And you must choose carefully—names have enormous potency! Humans vaguely know this—they sense that a given name can sometimes shape their future. But most dismiss this as the stuff of superstition."

He shakes his head at this further evidence of human ignorance. "If they but knew the true power of a name…"

"I have a name. It's Tret."

The G-Man's hands fly upward. "No, no! We must change it and I will tell you why." He jabs a finger high, to indicate his first reason. "You are of Taino descent. Not good." He leans in close. "Many centuries ago, the Legion of Gehenna was betrayed and it was by a Tormenta of Taino descent. This Tormenta was allowed into the inner sanctum of the Legion; then he deserted, taking the Legion's secrets with him. He returned to his tribe, and much of what he disclosed became woven into the Taino mythology. For this reason, Tormenta have viewed the Taino with particular suspicion, as humans who know too much. Thankfully, the passing years have fogged the meaning of these stories, and with each retelling, they have blurred and drifted away from the dangerous Legion secrets that they once contained. But all the

 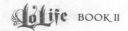

same, we need a name that erases anything of your Taino past. Second"—he jabs another finger toward the boy—"the name you got from the French sailors, it has a different meaning in Creole. Tret means 'traitor,' so if you're set on staying in Louisiana, I'd select a more endearing epithet."

The man smiles. "A name will come to you—trust me."

Tret's eyes go to the wound in his chest, then his fingers follow, exploring this body that he thought he knew. That is no longer human. No longer dead or alive.

What name befits a creature such as he?

His eyes finally arrive at the tag on his toe. In his haste, the G-Man crossed out all but the last D of DEAD, *before adding* ALIVE.

The boy's eyes widen. He sees it now. D-ALI. *Just as he is between two worlds, so his name will be between two words.*

And from that day onward, he lived as Dali... and as a Tormenta. He thrived in this new role, exhibiting a talent for tormenting. Humans fell like apples, and he rose quickly up the ladder of Tormenta society, inevitably catching the attention of the elite Legion of which the man spoke. They recruited him to their ranks, presenting him with his own clave. Each clave is cut uniquely, like a key, so that by its bite, it can be seen who effected any awakening. And over the years, many Tormenta bore the scar of Dali's clave. Because Dali served in spectacular fashion, until the day arrived when he—

Dali closes the *Obelus*. The entry continues, but he has spent too long on this distraction. His original intent was to find another name within the directory. His finger flicks at speed.

And then he finds it, listed numerically amid the index of Hunters: 101A.

She was one of his operatives—a protégé in whom Dali had taken a particular interest. But now she has gone rogue. Exited the Hypogeum on a mission, never to return. Deceiving him. Deceiving them all.

He should perhaps have seen it coming.

In her eyes, there was always a spark—the girl had *something*. She was without doubt the best Hunter he had ever trained. Fast, strong, and without mercy. He had never seen her like before. But more than that, he liked her. For all her brutish prowess, she had an inquiring mind. Forever asking questions.

He remembers the last question she posed, as he was strapping her into her weapons, readying her for the hunt. Her eye had gone to the implement that hung from his own belt.

"Why do you still wear your clave?"

Dali had smiled, choosing his words carefully. "Ah, *chère*, to reflect upon the horrors of one's past is the surest means of keeping one's future pure. I cleave to this tool, lest I forget."

✦

Dali leans back in his chair, the wood creaking like bones. Looks across the table to the seat opposite.

Hunter 101A had accompanied him here many times and Dali witnessed, much to his surprise, that she had an avid appetite for reading. He introduced her to the works of Trismegistus, and she was much intrigued by the fact that the philosopher's name translates as "The greatness of three."

 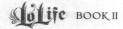

Her natural curiosity led her toward the other works of faith inspired by him.

Dali had cherished her companionship, and such was his ease that one cold night he read aloud to her the contents of his *Obelus*. He expected many questions as he closed its covers, but just one came from 101A.

"What happened to Rosa?"

Dali had flinched, as if this question were a bullet. Then he slowly inhaled, straightening his tie.

"Do you know the story of Romeo and Juliet, *chère*? Their hopes of reunion were held in the hands of a priest." His eyes had suddenly locked onto hers. "Never trust a priest who keeps his hand hidden."

Dali stares at the now empty chair then slowly closes his eyes. Picturing her. Gun in hand.

She is out in the world, killing Tormenta. That much the High Command knows from sporadic reports. She has been sighted in Las Vegas, New York, London. But she is not killing to order. She is killing as she wishes. On her terms. By her choice.

But why?

Why turn her back on the Sinestra? Under their care, she was kept safe in the Hypogeum and regularly supplied with span; she could have lived forever. But out there, in the human world, she will live only as long as her last dose endures. And that could be months, years… or days. That's the thing with span—you just don't know when yours will run out.

But she is gone. And Dali has his suspicions. He believes that what ignited her rebellion was something that she read. Something she discovered hidden in one of these books. A revelation that turned her mind… twisted her heart.

His large eyes roll from left to right, looking at the vast array of shelving that once held four hundred thousand secret documents and now contains the many books of the Sinestra with perhaps as many secrets.

He slides his Obelus into his pocket, rises to leave. The High Command will not care as to the cause of 101A's desertion, only that he allowed it to happen. Or possibly even encouraged it. There is every chance that they may suspect him of provocation. Because Dali, the infamous defector, cannot escape his past.

He strides from the Archivum, entering the low, iron corridor that leads back toward his quarters. He needs to feel the cool touch of a flannel and refresh his collars and cuffs. Because soon he will be summoned to account for her desertion.

And when that moment comes, he must convince the High Command of one thing: that he will retrieve her… dead or alive.

16

A FLAG RIPS and rolls against its pole, caught in a raging wind. It bears the insignia of Cherry Point Military Training Base.

Far below, mud flies. A platoon of marine cadets double-times it through the dark.

Their bodies are humped with munitions. Their boots barely clear the ground. They have been at this since daybreak and now night has fallen and the temperature has dropped below freezing. Exhaustion gusts from their mouth like exorcised ghouls.

Alongside them runs their drill sergeant, seemingly untouched by the grueling exercise. He chews on his cigar and bellows another chorus of call-and-response:

"You can't fail, that's what I said."

The marines respond: *"Sergeant's gonna shoot us dead."*

He pounds up front. *"Only way to save your pride."*

"Do it first with suicide."

With a roar, the drill sergeant finishes the cadence with the cry of "BOHICA!" The marines all know what this means—Bend Over Here It Comes Again—as their taskmaster blows a whistle and breaks out into triple time. The shattered marines dig deep, strive to keep up.

He waves them past, looking for the stragglers. Allows the

cadets to disappear into the night ahead as he watches and waits for the one he knows is missing. He bites down hard on his cigar and smiles. "Looks like we're outta Tampax."

His head swivels at the sound of distant boots. A silhouette appears, stumbling with exhaustion.

The name sewn to the pocket reads PAXOS. Blood falls onto the khaki, dripping from the young cadet's mouth. At first in thin dribbles, then a gusting spume as—WHACK—a fist thuds into his jaw.

"You goddam piece of green Greek shit!" The drill sergeant launches another blow, cracking the cadet across the back of the skull, hurling him down into the mud.

"You know why I call you Tampax?" He yanks the cadet's bloody face up from the mud. "Because every month I see you back in basic, and every goddam month you bleed."

The boy attempts to speak, but his mouth is pulped by another blow.

"When you gonna learn, Tampax? You'll never make it. And each month you try, you achieve just one thing. You bring down every other cadet. Because if one fails, we all fail. That's the marine way. And thanks to you, everyone is gonna have to run the course again tomorrow. Now won't that make you popular? Bet you can't wait to tell the boys. But my advice is this—don't sleep tonight, Tampax. 'Coz in their wild excitement, in their unbridled happiness, your fellow cadets may get rowdy. They may express their joy… physically. You git me, Tampax?"

He bends his big body, whispering, "I'd say you're a dead man, Tampax. An' worse than that—a dead man without dignity. So here's my deal. I'll leave you now to contemplate your fate. And I'll leave you this." His gloved hand produces a single bullet.

"Now, rules forbid me to distribute live munitions. But this is how I see it: I'm not giving you a bullet. I'm giving you a way out."

Private Paxos tries to take the bullet, but his hand jerks so violently with sobs that the sergeant is forced to take the boy's fingers and wrap them tight about the tiny shaft.

"That's one inch of honor you're holding there, son."

The silhouette of the sergeant disappears into the darkness. Private Paxos falls into a ball, howling. As he gasps for breath, he drags a muddy sleeve across his eyes, breathing deep and rolling to his knees. With one hand, he reaches up, pulling his gun from its strapped position across his backpack.

His other palm uncurls, revealing the bullet.

He sniffs hard, gathering concentration as he slides the bullet into the chamber.

It takes both hands to place the gun against his temple. One bears the weight of the weapon. The other tries to quell the violent tremor of his fingers. The snout connects to his head and—

KA-BOOM!—a boot kicks the gun from his fist, thudding him into the mud. He looks up, stunned, to see the long silhouette of a woman beside him.

Walking away—toward the approaching figure of the drill sergeant.

Over the crashing rain, the cadet can barely hear their exchange. The woman seems to say, "Close, but…"

The drill sergeant furiously chews down on his cigar.

His fingers twitch over the gun holster at his waist. The two shadows stand in silence, then—both hands fly, guns draw, shots explode.

The cadet watches the blasted body of the sergeant sprawl into the mud.

The woman slides her gun back into its holster. Strides past Paxos. "Get up, kid. And make yourself worth saving."

And then she's gone.

✦

Slamming down into the seat of a military jeep, Lola yanks the casing from the steering shaft, twists the starter motor, and guns the vehicle, splattering mud across the massive corpse of the drill sergeant.

Size counts for nothing. Lola learned that long ago. It's about how long a Tormenta has been around. If they keep stealing span, they stay alive. And if they're smart, they use their time to hone their fighting skills. Because all Tormenta know that there are Hunters out there, dispatched to bring them down.

But that *guy—he shoulda been sharper.* Sure, he had a good grift going.

A hard-core cadet is fast to fall on a bullet if dishonor looms. But Lola sees it often—if the grift gets too easy, the Tormenta gets lazy.

She mashes the gas and glances in the rearview. The cadet is staggering to his feet. Lola shrugs to herself. She got the job done. That's what matters.

And then she sees it. The cadet pulls on his fallen helmet.

 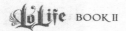

And something bolts into her mind. Sharp as a bomb frag. *A memory.*

Too quick for her to grasp it—more a feeling.

She was once in training.

Even though she had told Fan Fan to take her memories, wipe them clean, right back to that moment when all the hurt began—she can remember some of what happened before.

Someone taught her to fight and kill.

She knows who, she knows where, and she knows why. But what she no longer remembers is... why did she turn against them?

Lola shakes her head, erasing the moment. It doesn't matter. Every morning, she gets up and she knows what she has to do: *kill Tormenta.*

She needs no more than this to function.

But in recent weeks, something has been stirring within her, like a waking beast.

Her hands grip the wheel. She did the right thing. She is safer, stronger... not knowing.

She has a duty. She has a purpose.

But maybe she needs more than this to live?

17

Dali sits alone in the gloom of the High Court. The narrow tunnels of the Kingsway do not allow for grandiose chambers, and so to gift this gray-walled place some measure of pomp the walls are hung with paintings of classical interiors, all marble pillars and lofty cupolas. The largest canvas, by Emanuel de Witte, shows the interior of a Dutch church, a masterpiece of precision and perspective. But Dali suspects that it has pride of place because at its center, painted small, is a group of magistrates sitting about a table. And stretched before Dali is a table. In due course, his accusers will surround it.

Dali knows the drill. They will make him wait. Force him to settle on the chair with the small, spherical seat that buries into his buttocks, as if this pelvic prod is a foretaste of the probing questions yet to come. But Dali feels it not. For him, the agonies of the turncoat reach much deeper. Down into the realm of self-respect.

When he was a member of the Legion, he ranked highly. Seen by many as the brightest star, destined for greatness. And none revered him more than Vassago, a long-serving member of the Legion who had failed, for lack of flair, to further himself. He could only stand by and watch in awe as Dali would detect, distract, and divest Tormenta children of their human selves, releasing them swiftly, painlessly into their new existence. Oftentimes Vassago would break out into applause, gushing praise, scurrying to Dali's side as if by standing in his shadow he might siphon some of this skill. But Dali would sidestep, slip away. He found Vassago's fawning adoration sickening, like a stinking lily, too sweet beneath his nose.

It was Dali's one gnawing regret that when he defected to the Sinestra, Vassago slavishly followed.

But what's done is done.

And those days are done, too. Dali enjoys no glory here. The maverick genius he exercised as a Tormenta finds no favor in the rule-bound regime of the Sinestra.

He casually crosses his legs, neatens the seam of his pants as the iron door to the High Court groans open. The tribunal panel is entering.

The silhouettes settle one by one into their seats, their faces masked by shadows. A figure to the right of the table speaks.

"Since the Sinestra accepted your defection, we have done much to accommodate one of your… type… within our ranks. We supply you with span so that you need not feed your habit by other less acceptable methods. And more than this, we have shown you enormous trust."

"Which I have neva' abused," Dali forcibly reminds them all, his deep twang resounding.

Another figure leans across the table. Even before the face hits the light, Dali knows who it will be. And the glinting eyes confirm it.

Vassago. Of course.

He smoothes a long, black wig, evidence of his senior rank

within the Sinestra. And with the tresses smooth against his scalp, he serves up a smile. The expression seems one of support, but the cold pleasure it radiates suggests that Vassago is enjoying Dali's discomfort.

"I am sure Dali does not question for one moment the sincere regard that the Sinestra have for one such as he. After all, both he and I defected at the same time, under the same circumstances, and witness how high I have risen. There is no prejudice at play here."

Just a preference for dull obedience.

Dali returns the smile like a twisting blade.

Leaning back in his chair, Vassago tips his palms upward as if his next comment is of no consequence. "My only question is why you devote so much time to the care of the Helix Vivat. Your honorary title does not require that you spend hour after hour—for want of a better word—tinkering."

The Lord Chancellor leans forward, eyes tight. "Don't you think you should explain yourself, Dali?"

"Fo' want of a better word, no."

A silence hangs, ruffled only by the swish of lace as Dali tweaks his cuffs.

Vassago grits his teeth, then slowly retreats. "Very well, then. To the business in hand."

He thuds a thick file onto the table. "The unfortunate matter of Hunter 101A."

Dali has his face under absolute control. No twitch. No tremor.

Vassago takes his time, peeling open the file, smoothing his palm across each page.

 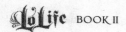

"She has been rogue for quite some time, it seems. But she continues to target Tormenta. So"—his large eyes roll up to meet Dali's—"should this fact make the High Command think her desertion acceptable?"

"I say it would be uppity to presume what the High Command thinks, or even that it thinks at all."

Wigged heads turn and glances are exchanged as if the council members are searching for a handle on this insult.

Vassago presses on. "We do not find it acceptable. Not at all. Rogue is rogue, regardless. And still you have done nothing to retrieve her."

"I had hoped to resolve the situation before it required intervention."

"What you hoped, Dali, is of no consequence. What you did was subvert protocol. You do not have the authority to make such a decision. Need I remind you of your rank?"

"The frequency with which you do suggests a great need, indeed, on your part."

Vassago shivers, his tongue thrashing to find a riposte. But a silencing hand rises from the figure at the head of the table. A face tilts partially into the light. No element of the wig can be seen, but the eyes are enough to let it be known that this man will have the final word.

"With regret, Dali, I order you to retrieve Hunter 101A and oversee her termination."

Dali bows his head, respect to this man readily given. "Ver'well, Commander General. There is a Hunter available who I believe—"

"I will determine the choice of Hunter." The Commander

General snaps his fingers toward Vassago. "Lord Chancellor, your recommendation."

A flash of enamel confirms that Vassago is smiling as he passes a single sheet into the Commander's waiting grasp.

Dali stiffens, knowing already what comes.

"You will send Hunter 666A."

18

In the index of the Manifestum, 666A is not listed amongst the other Hunters. His entry is included in a final appendix, titled simply "*Post Scriptum.*"

And there is no asterisk beside his name, though there is an obelus, suggesting that whatever annotation Dali chose to add, it was for his eyes only.

Dali sits now in the gloom of his quarters, the *Obelus* open on the table before him. His fingers find that particular addendum. It says only this:

> †*Remorse, you are made flesh in him! More than the act that first begat you.*

It is dated October 1858. But the encounter that forced Dali's hand to this cryptic quip is still fresh in his mind.

He closes his eyes, summoning the memory. And sees himself as he was—dressed in the crimson hues he favored in those days. He is walking to the farthest reach of King David's Dungeon, bound for a low, domed structure hewn from the rock. It is known as the Megiddo, and it welcomes few.

Nothing of its obscure entrance and narrow walls invites investigation.

As he enters, what strikes him first is the stinking air. And the guttering light from a rack of candles. They are suspended high above a naked body, prostrate on the floor.

The skin is alive with wounds, bubbling upward as wax falls from above, striking hard, sizzling hot.

The naked figure lies unflinching, arms spread wide, devouring the agony.

Rising smoke summons the stench of burning skin, and Dali plugs a kerchief to his mouth, the white lace flashing as he sinks further still against the wall. Hunter 666A is drawing breath, rousing himself, rising slowly. His body uncoils muscle by muscle.

Eyes open, black as exit wounds. Narrowing as they detect a figure in the shadows.

Dali dabs his lips and devotes undue attention to his kerchief as he plants it in his pocket.

"Please forgive if I transgress yo' time of contemplation…"

Stepping into the candlelight, Dali sees strange artifacts hung upon the walls of the Megiddo. "Your time of worship, perhaps. My ignorance is shameful. I apologize."

A final flourish to his kerchief. "Yo' see, I myself follow no faith. Live and let live and let die and let live—that's what I say."

Nothing issues from the mouth of Hunter 666A, but the eyes make a clear demand.

"Of course, to the cuttin' of the crap." Dali draws a file from within his coat.

"A mission most urgent."

Dali extends the bundle of papers, awaiting the Hunter's gathering hand. But nothing disturbs the air. The only movement

 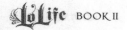

from Hunter 666A is to pull a black cloth tight about his loins.

Ah, silence—the half brother of insolence.

If Dali is going to assert his authority, this is the moment. He may not have trained Hunter 666A—that duty fell to a member more than a thousand years ago—but Dali still outranks him. He need not endure this... this...

This what, exactly?

Dali runs his tongue across his teeth, sharpening his smile sufficiently to skin this rabbit.

"I hear nothing but praise for your dedication. Your impeccable preparation. And I sense now that you'd appreciate some detail." He flicks open the papers. "If you don't mind, I'll read straight from the file."

Dali emits a dry cough. "The mission is to retrieve Brother Spino of the Chiro Scuro." His eye drifts down. "I spy a tiny footnote here, to which I shall refer."

Another cough, drier still.

"The Chiro Scuro is a human vigilante force, founded four centuries ago by a Rosicrucian monk called Brother Magen. Its sworn duty is to combat demon infiltration on Earth. Brother Magen, an exceptional scholar by all accounts, was translating the works of Trismegistus when he fell foul to violent visions. Endless, raging brainstorms that revealed to him the many realms of the Lo'Worlds and all the demon creatures that dwelled therein."

Dali taps the page. "For a footnote, I find this rather fetchingly described, don't you?"

Hunter 666A responds in the same way that granite doesn't. Dali goes on.

"Brother Magen committed his visions to a great series of books, and around these revelations the Brotherhood grew. It took the name of Chiro Scuro—the Hidden Hand. The name reflected the need for the Brotherhood to maintain its secrecy. The Holy Roman Church was quick to denounce them as dangerous fanatics."

A fingertip is licked, a page turned slowly.

"And so the Brotherhood sought the protection of Ignatius Loyola, the Black Pope. Such is the name given to the leader of the Jesuit Church. Ignatius shielded the Chiro Scuro and allowed them to pursue their hunt for demons. He created a library called the Collegio Romano, and upon its endless bookshelves, the revelations of the Chiro Scuro were successfully concealed. Every book was written in a coded language devised by Brother Magen. And without doubt, the most precious, the most momentous of these books is…"

The final page is turned. "The *Kata Strepho*."

A short pause, as Dali leans forward. "The title is Greek for 'I Overturn,' and I do believe the word *catastrophe* derives from it." The briefest of smiles. "I knew a priest long ago, and I gathered a little talent for translation…"

In the ensuing silence, Dali's eyes sink back to the page.

"The *Kata* tells of Brother Magen's most fearful vision—a mighty conflict. But more than that… we don't know. It is written in his most baffling code. That is quite the pity of it all."

Dali closes the file, smoothing the cover with the flat of his hand.

"That a human, a lowly monk, should have been gifted these visions… Let us just say, it is most frustrating. It is hard

 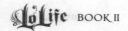

enough for the Sinestra to police mankind and safeguard their existence without humans themselves getting involved. We constantly feel like a peacekeeping force plagued by local, amateur guerilla activity. But the Chiro Scuro cannot be ignored, and so we have learned to tolerate them. However, relations have suffered a severe set-back because the Sinestra have accepted into their ranks a certain defector."

Dali arches a gentle hand upon his own chest. "It seems the Chiro Scuro will never trust a Tormenta, no matter what badge he wears."

With a smile, bitter as a lemon slice, Dali turns on his heel, pacing the floor.

"Relations have recently worsened further still. King Victor Emmanuel of Italy has embarked upon an onslaught against the Holy Roman Church. The Vatican is to be plundered. The books of the Collegio Romano are undoubtedly in danger. So I myself—as an avowed lover of books—have made an offer to the Black Pope. I've suggested that the tomes of the Chiro Scuro be sent to the Sinestra, where I will oversee their care and personally ensure that they are cherished. The Black Pope has reluctantly agreed, and all the books have been delivered into my care—all, that is, but the *Kata*.

"This book has been borne away by one rebellious monk, Brother Spino. He seems determined that it shall not be surrendered to me. But now we have got word he is in Prague. One assumes the book is still with him. So, he must now be found. And when he's found, he will tell us where the book is hidden."

Dali pauses, suddenly aware that his hand has clamped into a fist. He casually concerns himself with uncurling each finger.

"I hope that I have made it quite clear that if the *Kata* were ever to get into human hands, if they were to decipher its contents… Well, let me jus' say this. Once you find Brother Spino, yo' must question him without mercy."

Dali rolls the file into a baton and presents it again. His voice follows, tightened to a whisper. "I understand that it violates protocol to retrieve a human. Indeed, some in the Sinestra have voiced doubts that any Hunter will accept this mission. But my retort is this: 666A is not *any* Hunter."

Dali thrusts the baton closer. "So—what say you?"

To the best of Dali's recollection, the shadow before him said nothing. Not one word. But Hunter 666A took the mission file and returned three days later from Prague, bearing in a sack the severed head of Brother Spino. The face, crushed beyond recognition, confirmed that no amount of questioning had elicited the location of the *Kata*.

✦

And it is with the memory of this pulped skull clear in his mind that Dali rises from his chair and exits his quarters in long, furious strides. Down an echoing hallway that narrows to a stairwell, twisting to a spiral, sharpening his fast descent until the last raked incline delivers him to the door that yawns open, drawing breath. It reveals a bunker, lined with lead so thick it can withstand an atomic blast. It may not be the Megiddo, but its purpose is the same. It is where Hunter 666A comes to suffer his remorse.

Dali enters the blackness and traverses the cold floor. The

 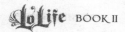

chill is the same as in the old Megiddo. And it is filled with the same aroma of burning flesh. Hunter 666A rises from the floor before him. Just as before. But this time from Dali, there come fewer words.

Just two…

"Go fetch."

…as he passes over the file on Hunter 101A.

19

THE WALLS OF this bunker may be lead, but one is secretly hinged, opening inward.

The space behind would feel like a tomb were it not for the ceiling. It is hung with knives, strung from chains.

A hand, scarred and hardened, reaches up. The blades twist and dance like wives in a harem, flirting for selection.

One by one, the knives are picked and plunged point down into a table. A figure, clad in black leather battered to a shine, steps from the shadows. His gaze falls upon the weapons.

"Have I not chosen you twelve and one of you is a devil?"

Hunter 666A reaches forward, collecting a knife that quivers in the center of the table. It is made from a single seamless shaft of silver.

He slides this blade into the sheath against his heart. Then, one by one, he conceals the remaining weapons about his body. The last item gathered is the dossier passed to him by Dali. Hunter 666A smoothes his hand across the file cover, then bows his head, the movement coming with the beat of a ritual.

"What will ye give me, and I will deliver her to you?"

With a slow tenderness, he kisses the target's number: 101A.

Eyes open, his head lifts, the ritual of departure complete— almost.

His torso heaves against the leather as he bends to attend to his final task. Picking up a delicate china jug, he pours water into a flowerpot. It holds a bloom.

By candlelight, the flower has the silhouette of a rose, but the color is hard to determine. Darker than red, deeper than blue. The flame finally reveals it to be that rarest of things—a black rose.

On the pot is pasted a label, hand-inscribed: The Judas Rose. The paper is cracked and yellowed. Adhered to the terracotta, almost two centuries ago, by the hand of Brother Spino.

✦

The young monk could never have imagined that a day begun by labeling roses would end with a Hunter's knife pressed to his throat.

But his life since joining the Chiro Scuro had been wonderfully eventful.

Brother Spino was recruited to their ranks in 1855, selected for his great skills as a cryptographer. The hidden language of Brother Magen was fast slipping from the Brotherhood's grip, and with each passing generation, his original learning was becoming ever more obscure. To forestall this encroaching ignorance, the young Spino had been assigned the most urgent of tasks—to complete the translation of the *Kata Strepho* before the onslaught of Victor Emmanuel reached the doors of the Collegio Romano.

But with the sound of hooves pounding, Brother Spino found himself running from Victor Emmanuel's mounted soldiers, clasping the *Kata* to his chest like a breastplate.

He knew his orders. In the event of an attack, he must deliver the *Kata* into the charge of the Black Pope. A deal had been struck, and in these desperate times, the protection of the Sinestra was presented to the Brotherhood as the only way to keep their sacred scripts secure.

But Brother Spino ran and ran, as he had never run before.

Dear Lord, if they but knew the prophecy that I have here deciphered, they would never surrender the Kata! *Not into the hands of a Tormenta defector!*

For six days Brother Spino ran, neither eating nor sleeping, determined to make it over the Alps. His final destination was decided by his feet. Worn down to the bone, they called a halt in Prague.

The same feet also found him a friend. The eyes of an elderly apothecary were drawn to the monk's sandals that seeped blood. He introduced himself as Jorgi Baresch, extending a hand so knotted with ague, it seemed a poor advertisement for his craft. But his insistence that he would help the monk with no want of payment proved irresistible.

Clutching the *Kata* below his robes, Brother Spino submitted to Baresch's ministrations: His feet were soaked in pungent unctions and wrapped in cotton. The tender treatment took hours, but Brother Spino said nothing. Exhaustion played its part, but more so the fear of discovery kept him silent. None could know who he was, or his purpose.

The silence is filled by old Baresch, who juggles a jolly conversation as he works upon the wounds, boasting of his ability to diagnose an ill through observation alone. He tells of a liver rot he diagnosed by the way his patient allowed his

 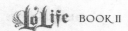

tongue to loll from his lips. And of a lover's complaint identified by the way the lady used her fan.

"And you, Brother, I know that these are not pilgrim wounds. You are in flight, for your very life."

The comment is tossed, but the upward roll of Baresch's eye reveals his intent to surprise. And he finds the young monk's mouth ajar.

"Do not fear, Brother. I will say nothing." He seals the last of the healing cotton strips across Spino's feet. "You cannot know how glad I am of your coming. Dear Brother, I am much in need of a holy man." His old head drops and his hands fall into his lap, a figure of crude prayer.

"This is why I ask for no payment—so that you might serve me in return and hear my confession."

Brother Spino reaches out, fingers clasping the old man's shoulders. He feels the old muscles twitch with tension as Baresch tells his tale.

"The priest of our church, I cannot go to him. He castigates my trade in potions and calls me sinful. But believe me, I practice no magic. The ways of darkness I abhor. And that is why I know, in my heart, that what I sense, what I see... these terrible visions... they come from God."

"What do you see, old man?"

"I beg you, do not think me insane!"

Already on his knees, Baresch slumps further still, grasping the hem of the monk's cassock. "I must confess that when I look into the eyes of a certain woman... I see a *demon* staring back at me."

His words tumble out, old hands wringing as the story of his suspicions gain form. Emily Duvall arrived in Prague a year before. Unknown to any in the city, she soon gained a foothold, taking over the old flower shop that stands just two doors down from this very apothecary. Her golden hair and clear blue eyes attracted customers, but most were quick to comment that it was her delightful conversation that drew them more.

Baresch himself was struck by Emily's clever quips and one insightful comment in particular stuck in his mind. She one day tossed up the observation that those who come to a flower shop are always at the extremes of ecstasy or agony—buying a bouquet for a new lover, or a wreath for a loved one lost. She told Baresch that she liked this best about her profession, that she met mankind in such exquisite throes.

As he bid her farewell, Baresch felt his shoulders shaking at her witty wiles. With laughter, so he thought. But when the shaking refused to abate, he realized to his horror that what shook him was a creeping chill, an abstract of unease. As the lovely Emily had talked of her clientele, he had seen something in her eyes—something hungry, something waiting...

"...like a vulture, Brother Spino. Like a vulture, certain that a corpse is bound to drop. Now you may say, 'What would this pretty creature want with death?' But here's the thing..."

He beckons the young monk closer, as if lowering his voice diminishes the madness of his words. "That flower shop has stood for forty years, but only since Emily Duvall took charge have so many grieving widows and broken-hearted Romeos ended their woes in death."

Baresch brings his hands together in prayer. "Forgive me, Brother Spino, but I believe there is an evil in her. She takes

hearts already broken, and with cunning words, she grinds them to dust."

His hands now spread across his face, as if he fears his eyes should meet those of the young monk. But then he feels the gentle touch of Spino's fingers.

"You are not mad, old man. Far from it. You see clearer than most." Brother Spino smiles. "You have done right to confess your fears. I know what manner of demon she is. And she will be destroyed."

That night, Brother Spino sent word by way of messenger to the Black Pope, telling him that the Sinestra must be alerted to the presence of a Tormenta. He gave the location but asked that no one be told the information came from him, for fear of his own whereabouts being discovered.

While he waited for a Hunter to be sent, Brother Spino determined to use the intervening days to do as he had been taught by the Chiro Scuro; to interfere in Tormenta activity.

The first step was to get close, and this proved no problem. His monk's robes were quick to attract the eyes of Emily Duvall as he sampled, sniff by sniff, the flowers in her shop. The touch of her fingers, lingering too long as she helped him wrap lilies, revealed her ruse. She would see if this celibate monk could be seduced into despair.

He plays along, requesting to spend more time at the shop as he does so love to be amongst the blooms. He tells her of his skills in calligraphy and offers his services. He could label the pots, if that would please her. She agrees with eyes wide.

And now, praise God, Spino will play his part in a grand perversion of Emily's intent. He will eavesdrop on her conversations with each fragile customer, until such time as the Hunter comes.

Which turns out to be a Friday. One that begins for Emily Duvall much as any other. She waters the blooms and brushes bugs from the leaves, careful not to disturb any spiders. Arachnids she admires for their webs, such works of patience and precision. She places the prepared pots in the window and opens the shop door with a smile. And with a slash too fast to flee, a second smile is opened up across her neck. Blood gushes upward. Through its heavy descent, a figure looms, knife in hand. Raised to strike a second time.

Emily clamps a fist to her own throat, stemming the flow, and pulls a blade. Thrusting at the black mass that descends upon her, meteorlike.

Yet, the advantage of that first strike is too much. Overwhelmed, out-bled, Emily falls.

She knows this Hunter who slays her. He walks tall in Tormenta legend. And so she knows his signature of death. With her own hand, she sweeps her hair clear of her neck. When the blow comes, her tresses hang uncut, in all their glory, from her severed head.

The silence that ensues is broken only by the lightest of footsteps. In the doorway has appeared Brother Spino. He looks about the debris of combat, flowers fallen, pots cracked.

"I will see to this, Hunter. Your work here is done."

The monk averts his eyes as the head of Emily Duvall is thrust into a coarse sack. But the Hunter's voice draws his attention back.

"My work here has not yet begun."

 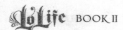

Brother Spino has barely the time to crease a frown of confusion before a knife creases a contusion of blood from his neck.

"You are Brother Spino?"

The monk twitches a nod. He cannot see the Hunter's face above him, hidden in the shadows. But he feels the voice, hot and wet with sweat.

"Upon your pride I relied. You unmasked her. She was yours. So you came to see her die. And now you are mine."

Brother Spino tries to speak, each word forcing the blade deeper into his flesh. "You seek me? But why? I am no one!"

"You are Brother Spino."

The Hunter's face sweeps down, bursting into the light.

The monk's eyes bulge, his voice gulps. "I know who you are… who you were."

His pale finger rises, no longer shaking. Now stiff with excitement as it jabs toward the Hunter. "I see you… *Judas Iscariot.*"

At the sound of his name—unspoken for centuries—the Hunter recoils. The blade twists in his hand. Brother Spino feels the edge sink deeper, then—a slight release.

"How do you know me?"

The monk inches along the tightrope of his explanation.

"Some within the Sinestra are sympathetic to our brotherhood. We hear word of what occurs within the Lo'Worlds. And we heard of you. Your arrival was indeed of extraordinary interest to a Christian brotherhood such as ours."

"Call me traitor, I care not!" The knife resumes its original bite.

Pushing on against the pain, the monk inhales. "We do not call you traitor. Because we know of Boaz."

Slowly, the knife peels from his throat. But the tip still tilts toward the monk's heart. The merest twitch commands Brother Spino to continue.

"Before Jesus called you, you were a fighter. A rebel against Roman enslavement. Young and headstrong, you believed that when Jesus said he would free his people, it would come by a great uprising. Imagine your confusion, then, when Jesus said that there would be no war. That the battle must be fought in the hearts of men…"

The Hunter grimaces, grinding down whatever emotion threatens.

"Boaz had been a rebel with you. Fought at your side against the Romans. He whispered in your ear. 'Judas,' he said, 'we are men of action! We need to raise an army. And every man who follows this prophet is one less for our ranks. He is not come to free us, but to make us happy in our slavery.'"

The Hunter's head sinks, the first impulse of a nod.

"The truth is, Boaz roused you to betray Christ. But the moment your lips touched your master's cheek… you knew what you had done."

His chin upon his chest, the Hunter's voice is crushed to a whisper.

"He turned to me and said, 'What thou doest, do quickly'— and I knew I had betrayed the Son of God. But too late…"

His voice plummets to a grunt, dull with hurt. Then just breath, drawn hard.

"Go on, my son."

 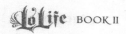

"In fury… in despair… I drew my sword in search of Boaz, bent on his death. But he was not to be found. And as I stood alone, I knew his slaughter would mean nothing. The only death that would bring relief was my own. I looked up to find myself beneath a tree, boughed like gallows—a confirmation from God. I pulled a belt about my neck. I remember the bite of the leather, the swell of my tongue, rupturing against the roof of my mouth.

"And then—nothing. Darkness. Until I awoke, chained hand and foot. A face above me telling me, with deep assurance, that all will be explained."

Judas shrugs, gathering himself, hardening his tone. "The rest you can guess. You know well enough the methods of the Sinestra."

Brother Spino shakes his head. "In fact, no. I'm aware only of the tales passed down from generation to generation within the Brotherhood. Many aspects of the Sinestra's operation are unknown to me. So please, continue."

The knife is suddenly back, thrust up hard into a nostril, drawing blood.

"Is this your game? To trick me into betraying my new masters, some fresh treachery for Judas?"

Brother Spino tries to shake his head but the action screws the knife deeper. "No, no, my son. I have no such intent!"

"How can I trust you?"

"For this reason alone: No matter how we finish this exchange—as allies or as enemies—my death will ensue, at my request. And so nothing you tell me will ever be heard by another."

The knife slowly exits. "You are a curious man."

The monk delicately dabs at his nostril, sniffing up the blood that threatens.

"Curious indeed. To know more."

Judas lowers himself to the floor, sliding the knife into the sheath beside his heart.

"The Sinestra always appoint a Handler to induct each new arrival. I received mine. His first task was to explain what had come to pass, what I had become, the domain that I was now in and—most importantly—the choice that lay before me."

"So what had come to pass?"

"Boaz was a Tormenta. He had identified me as a furious young man, volatile and therefore vulnerable. He played upon my passions and drove me to an act that was certain to destroy my mind. When I came to surrender my life, he was waiting. But he must have been much in need of my span, because he struck too soon. Death was not fully upon me when he pressed his mouth against mine. To attempt to siphon span before it is released—this is the greatest sin a Tormenta can commit. Because in this way, there is a mixing of essence, and a human gains Tormenta traits."

Brother Spino leans forward. "And that same human—now neither dead nor alive, human nor Tormenta, arrives in the Lo'World, dark realm of the Sinestra."

Judas nods. "Tormenta make this mistake rarely, and so the delivery of such a human is a precious gift."

He exhales, half a smile roused by the memory.

"The Sinestra are good at what they do. Most persuasive. They soon convinced me that I now had a purpose. The Tormenta

 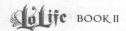

trait I now harbored would act as a disguise, allowing me to move amongst Tormenta society, get close enough to kill them."

"And the Sinestra would train you to fight, until your skills matched theirs."

"My own death has been denied me. I saw no other road to repentance." Brother Spino flinches at this. Then finds his voice, eyes wide.

"You still seek forgiveness?"

"Yes."

"From whom?"

"God."

The young monk tries to sound indifferent, but he delivers the next words with the tension of tossed china. "You still believe?"

"I still believe."

Now Brother Spino cannot contain himself.

"Then you are truly of our calling. It was not by chance that you were sent. The Sinestra selected you because they thought you heartless enough to kill a holy man. But they could not know what higher force was at work. The one force beyond all others. The One True God."

Now he meets the eyes of Judas with cool assurance. "This simple world of man, the obscure realms of the Lo'World… and the many, many domains beyond… they are all just folds in God's robe. This is what we believe."

He leans in close. "This is what you believe."

Now daring to place a hand on the shoulder of Judas, his last words come with a smile. "And this is why you will heed my calling to serve."

Brother Spino's hand now slides within his cassock, withdrawing a thick tome. The gold script on the leather reads *Kata Strepho.*

Judas's eyes fall heavily upon it.

"Then you know of this book." Brother Spino allows himself a wry smile. "But you will not know of the prophecy it holds."

As he opens the book, the ancient pages crackle. "I myself have deciphered only the first few chapters." His fingers explore the waxy text with a lover's tenderness.

"The Bible tells us that the End of Days will come, when the Enemy will rise and Christ will return to defeat him. But though that may be the last battle... it will not be the first. Before that final onslaught, the Enemy will send forth his creatures of destruction. To wreck mankind, bring him to his knees. And the worst of his envoys is the Mosca. The Mosca is a Tormenta of extraordinary power. He is identified in the *Kata* by the letters INRI... Inexorible Nihilator, Rex Immortal—a master of destruction, an unkillable king who will draw all other Tormenta to him, uniting them and in a mighty wave they will drive humankind into mass despair and suicide. And so Tormenta will, at last, claim dominion. His coming is talked of in Tormenta legend. And did they but know this, the beast has come before... risen into a human form, but upon each occasion, the Sinestra have succeeded in bringing about his death before the Legion of Gehenna could find and awaken him. The Legion have little to go on—just what legend tells them. That to find the Mosca they must look for Scox, his harbinger, who will blaze like a star and reveal the dark messiah."

Brother Spino inhales, suppressing a fresh quiver in his voice. "Each time the Mosca has come into a mortal shell, the Legion have gotten closer to finding him. We fear—I fear—that the next time, they will succeed. The G-Man they dispatch will awaken him. And if he does, only one thing can save mankind. It says within the *Kata* that if the Mosca rises, God will bring forth its counterpoise, the Moera, and a battle to end all battles will ensue."

Brother Spino raises a hand. "I know what question comes." He slowly closes the *Kata* with a soft exhalation. "What is the Moera?"

Brother Spino slides the book back inside his cassock. "To that I have no answer." He rises now, tightening the rope of his belt. "I had not time to decipher that far. So I cannot say from where or when the Moera will arise. But I can tell you this: Someone within the Sinestra is intent on its discovery and its destruction. And that is Dali."

Judas rises slowly. "I have been loyal to the Sinestra for more than two thousand years. You ask that I act against one of their number, upon this, the word of a stranger."

"We are brothers in God. Strange only is the bond that binds us."

As if in prayer, Brother Spino places his hands together, gathering patience.

"I am sure of it—Dali plans some treachery."

This word sweeps past Judas's ear like a spear. "What manner of treachery?"

"He watches for the Mosca, to usher his arrival into the human realm."

Brother Spino shakes his head, mouth tight. "His behavior has always been suspicious, strangely self-serving. The Chiro Scuro has never given credence to his defection. And with the Brotherhood disbanded, some other force must keep the *Kata* from Dali. I believe it should be placed in the hands of Man. God will find a way to bring the book before the eyes of those who can decipher it."

"So what do you ask of me?"

"The Moera will be sent to save us, and this time, Judas, you must become this savior's best defender."

"You would entrust me with this task... knowing who I am... what I have done."

"God knows what you have done, Judas. And he chose to bring you here, to me... today." He bends down, collecting a potted flower that stands alone on a shelf. It is a black rose. He thumbs the label that he himself inscribed.

"To keep remembrance of what we once were is the surest way to keep our future pure." He lifts the rose and presents it to Judas. "You were once Judas the traitor. Now you will be the thorn that protects the precious rose." Judas accepts the plant in cupped hands.

Brother Spino exhales with a smile. "And now you must kill me."

Judas grits his jaw, stifling confusion. But Brother Spino just smiles. "If you don't, they will suspect you. Hunter 666A never returns empty-handed. You must defile my corpse, a sign of your frustration that I would tell you nothing. Then return to them unchanged, the same brute they dispatched. In this way, you will keep Dali's trust. Until such time as you can unmask him."

 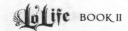

Judas draws himself up, inhaling slowly, sliding the silver knife from the sheath at his heart.

Brother Spino kneels and tilts his head forward. "What thou doest, do quickly."

The hand of Judas flies.

✦

Two hundred years later, the Judas Rose quivers in his tender touch as he pours the last of the water from the jug. Then Hunter 666A rises, pulls a long coat about him, and strides toward the doorway.

This fresh command to retrieve a rogue Hunter—he welcomes it. It provides him with the chance to venture abroad.

Because the time has come. He is sure of it. For Judas has read every page of the *Kata* deciphered by Brother Spino. And when he deposited the book in the care of Baresch, as Spino's written instructions demanded, he was led to a secret panel in the apothecary behind which all of the monk's books and journals were hidden. From these works he gathered deeper knowledge, and over the years, he added to it, drawing information and intelligence from every quarter, studying every sign and portent.

And now he knows it. He *feels* it.

The Moera is about to rise.

As the doorway slides shut behind him, the chamber trembles and above the rose, the whole wall shimmers. It is alive with black petals. The bush is huge across the wall. And Judas's commitment to his secret cause is now as vast across his heart.

20

A LIBRARY ARCHES, bold with grace, born from the fact that it belongs to Yale University. The silence within is thick and only one sound chips at the air, a rhythmic tick of wood. The sound of a walking stick perhaps, though the impact seems more weighty.

The sound increases as a figure nears. Swaddled in chaplain's robes, the old man bears no stick. But the inch between his cassock and the floor reveals the source of the sound. A wooden leg, heaving onward as the old man makes his way between the library tables. A gentle nod and smile to each student blurs the purpose of his journey. There is only one table that genuinely holds his interest. It stands at the farthest end of the library and despite its giant length, it seats just one student.

The boy's face is shrouded by a tangle of long, unruly dreads. It is only when he jerks back his head, to jolt the dregs from a Fanta can, that his face can be seen. Dark skin. Green eyes. His earbuds throb to a hip-hop sub-bass.

A South Central baby born to a junkie mother, some kind of freak gene made him a genius and now he's riding a scholarship outta the ghetto. That's what he told everyone, and it made for a good story.

The truth was somewhat different.

 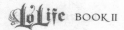

He was born to Mr. and Mrs. Massenberg, a wealthy professional couple who lived amid the trimmed garden borders of Hancock Park, Los Angeles. His mother, victim years ago of a traffic accident, did have an addiction to painkillers. In her late forties, she was reconciled to a childless future and so was shocked to find that pregnancy, not menopause, was the cause of her recent malaise. Her first horrified thoughts were of the fetal effects of the painkillers she had been taking. She was indeed warned that the baby's development might be affected.

But Mary Massenberg was a woman of faith and, praise God, the boy child is born healthy. The first year of life for Norris Massenberg Jr. passes without incident, but come his second birthday it is clear that something is amiss with the boy's mental development.

It is too fast.

In kindergarten, rumors of his prowess are leaked to the press. In a review by a local black magazine of a piano recital given by young Norris, the journalist coins for him the mo' better name of Mo'Zart.

His talent for music was just one facet; mathematics came just as easily. A memory for numbers meant that at just seven years old, he could replicate equations more than a thousand characters long.

Colleges and consortiums clamored to co-opt him but Mrs. Massenberg refused, holding fast to her odd and only child until Yale finally pried him free at eighteen.

No big deal to Mo'Zart. He thinks this brain-funk thing is overrated. He knows the Mayan alphabet by heart, but so what?

He's one month off nineteen and he's never seen a woman naked. Try milking your man-ham to a headful of hieroglyphs.

He'd taken his arrival at Yale as a chance to reinvent himself. The smart church suits, so beloved by his mother, have been replaced with baggy jeans and New Religion boxers.

But the threads and dreads change nothing of his brain. It is a beast inside his head that demands feeding. And night after night, Mo'Zart finds himself back here. Drawn to the library.

Compelled by one book.

The same book that is spread before him now. A thick, ancient tome. Mo'Zart's fingers slowly trace across each page. The dark, waxy text within is a mass of symbols, arranged in complex patterns across the parchment.

Beside the book is a pad, crammed with notes. Mo'Zart's pencil dashes again as he sees a symbol reoccurring, recording its position.

He jolts as a hand falls on his shoulder. Then exhales as he sees the familiar old face above him.

"How ya doin', Father Wexler?"

"Good, good, my son. And you?"

"Kinda slow today. The code has changed again. Every chapter. I feel like I'm always going back to first base."

The hand pats a gentle reassurance. "You have made great strides, Mo'Zart. But tell me this: What you've found today, in this chapter, does it alter anything of… anything of your last translation?"

Mo'Zart flips back a page in his notebook, "Nope, I'm still pretty solid on that." His finger finds the line as he reads it aloud. "…the three will become one and then it shall rise." He shrugs and taps his pencil like a drumstick on the table's edge. "Question is, *what* will rise?"

He flips his pad to another page. Revealing a sheet filled with one word—*Moera*—densely doodled.

"I mean, what d'you think, Father? What *is* the Moera?"

Mo'Zart feels the old hand rise from his shoulder, but he does not see the uncontrollable tremor that now possesses it.

Father Wexler turns away, his voice strangely hoarse as he tosses encouragement.

"Keep at it, my son. With persistence, I'm sure… all will become clear." And he is gone.

Mo'Zart returns to the manuscript, then suddenly bolts back in his chair.

A man in a sharp black suit now sits opposite him. Mo'Zart blinks.

Where the hell…?

He looks back at the departing figure of Father Wexler. Did the old chaplain bring him here?

The man in the suit flashes a smile at Mo'Zart, then looks down at the reading matter in his own hands. His brow furrows, suggesting that whatever he studies, it is something as testing as the manuscript before Mo'Zart.

Mo'Zart jabs his pencil between his dreads and scratches his head, resisting the temptation to ogle what lies in the stranger's hands.

His eyes fix once more on the maze of glyphs before him and, with a crack, he turns the ancient parchment to a fresh page.

The man responds with a deep inhalation. Then loudly, "I don't understand this."

Mo'Zart glances up. The man, roused to irritation, taps his reading matter with one hand.

"Most baffling." He thrusts up the paper. It is a takeout menu.

"The way it's written—very confusing." He jabs a finger at the laminated words. "The pizzeria's called Treble Belly. Very clear. That's written right here. You get three slices of pizza for the price of one. Then down here on the right, it says, 'Thursday night is three-for-one.' But no explanation. What does that mean? Three people can get triple portions for the price of one treble meal? Or that one person gets three trebles, which would make nine portions of pizza? Really very unclear. The way it's worded."

Mo'Zart says nothing. Looks left and right. *Someone punkin' me?*

Looks back to the guy. Flashes a smile.

"You know, dude, if you venture to the diner, you will find there many wise women who will reveal all to you. Called a waitress."

The man says nothing. Then with a sudden thrust, he thuds his hand down on Mo'Zart's giant manuscript.

"That's some big book all right."

Mo'Zart flinches, then snaps his shoulders forward, mouth tight. "You don't touch that."

The man relaxes back into his chair, long legs extending, ignoring Mo'Zart's tension.

"I read it. Some of it. Years back."

Mo'Zart chills his tone, keeping it cool with the weird dude. "You didn't read this book. This is the Voynich Manuscript."

"No, it isn't."

Mo'Zart taps two fingertips onto the parchment. "Yeah, it is. This *is* the book."

"It's the *book,* of course it's the *book.* But Voynich—?" The man shakes his head. "It only got that name by chance."

"Right. And you, the dude with the mind-fuck menu, you know all about it?"

"When it was discovered by old Jorgi Baresch, the cover had been removed. So no name. No title. That's where the mystery began."

Mo'Zart lays down the pencil and pushes back his chair. He stares at the man, taking in the cropped red hair and long copper sideburns that frame his face like a centurion helmet.

"You want to talk to me. You seem pretty set on that."

The suit says nothing.

"I don't know you, man. You're too old to be a student and dressed like that, you ain't on a professor's paycheck. I mean damn." He takes in the cut of the black suit in long, admiring sweeps. "Those are some sick threads."

With one hand, the man smoothes the jacket. "Hand-reeled Thai silk." His fingers flip the lapels, revealing the merest flash of a gun.

Mo'Zart tenses, hands flat on the table. Exhales slowly. "What do you want?"

"Pizza."

✦

The back booth in the Treble Belly pizzeria is in almost total darkness. A yellow bulb splutters above.

The face of the man, once again seated opposite, flickers as if lit by flames. This hellish effect is unnecessary as Mo'Zart's wacko meter is already jacked to the max.

He jerks back against the booth as a fist lunges forward. Then uncurls and hangs midway across the table.

"My name is Agent Petrus Bex."

The hand is tentatively taken. "Mo'Zart."

"Except… you got that name by chance. Your birth name is Norris Massenberg Jr."

"You the law?"

"Yes."

"What kind? I mean state, federal—how high we talking?"

"The highest."

Petrus Bex rolls his hands upward to reveal a tattoo in the center of each palm. It is three crosses, combined to make one crucifix.

"I… I don't understand…"

"Good, that means we're getting somewhere."

Bex signals for a waitress. A steaming coffee pot appears and two mugs are filled to the brim. "You guys ready to choose?"

"Give us a coupla minutes." Agent Bex flashes a smile that makes him appear, for less than a second, like quite a nice guy.

The waitress slides over a bowl of sugar and sashays away. Bex pulls three sachets of sweetener and opens them one by one as he talks.

"Jorgi Baresch was an apothecary with a small practice in Prague. In 1860, he finds a book abandoned in his shop. The cover is ripped away. And the pages within are filled with an ancient coded text. Baresch was already thought by many to

 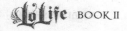

be a practitioner of black arts. His local church had excluded him because the priest claimed Jorgi to be possessed with demonic visions. So when he was found with this book in his possession, rumors raged that it was the work of the devil. These accusations worsened when Baresch stubbornly refused to say how the book had come into his hands. One story said that he was given it by a murderous monk, who slaughtered a local florist called Emily Duvall and then disappeared into the night.

"Baresch labored hard to clear his name, insisting that the book held a message from God. The rest of his life was devoted to deciphering the code. But time was short. He died a broken man just two years later, with not a single page of the mysterious book deciphered.

"He had no close family, and those relatives who descended to pick at his carcass were quick to sell off the manuscript, which had, by this time, gained some notoriety amongst cryptologists and collectors. It was bought at auction by the wealthy philanthropist Wilfred Voynich. Voynich treated it as a fanciful oddity and delighted in showing it to his high-society friends. It becomes known as the Voynich Manuscript and is celebrated as a marvelous conundrum. On the death of Voynich, his widow bequeathed it to Yale University, where it has remained ever since."

He takes a jolt of coffee, wincing at the bitterness.

"I was a student at Yale. Years ago. Mathematics was my forte. But something drew me to the manuscript. As if it were an equation that, with one revelation—that value of x—I might resolve."

He stirs in another storm of sweetener. "It took time before I realized that the manuscript is more than just a code to be cracked. It is a lure, a magnet—to draw out those minds destined to join us. Minds like yours."

He samples another slow sip. Mo'Zart taps the table, urging more.

"To join what?"

"SCURO."

"What—who now?"

Bex smiles through the steam of his coffee. "You cannot imagine what you have achieved. More than I ever did. That manuscript is the *Kata*. It tells us of the Mosca and the Moera. You translated the one line that proves everything. That to rise… the three must become one." The eyes of Agent Bex for a moment seem lost in some strange ecstasy. "That is our creed."

"Whose creed?"

"SCURO's."

"Yeah, you keep makin' that noise."

Agent Bex sets down his coffee, eyes sharp. A perfunctory smile. "Once you join us, all will become clear."

"But not before? Like some crazy game-show shit, huh?" Mo'Zart affects a quizmaster's voice. "So, kid, you wanna take the car or open the mystery box?"

"You want the car—it's yours."

A set of keys tumbles across the table toward Mo'Zart. After only the slightest hesitation, Mo'Zart gathers them up, wide eyes on the fob. An Aston Martin icon dangles from it.

"It's parked outside. Every agent gets one. And a suit. And as for the mystery box? Well, you've already opened that, kiddo.

 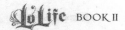

You cracked a crucial clause of the *Kata*. So that tells us you got the right stuff."

Mo'Zart's eyes are still fixated on the glittering fob, but he hears the voice of Agent Bex rolling on.

"We're looking for the Moera... the three becoming one. You wanna jump on that train? Or d'you want to go back to your old life and forget this ever happened?"

Mo'Zart jerks as another voice cuts in. The waitress has returned. "What's ya choice, kid?"

Agent Bex answers for him, jabbing a finger at the Thursday night special.

"He's gonna take the three-for-one."

21

An OLD HAND smoothes the parchment of the Voynich Manuscript. The pages have lain silent since Mo'Zart's recruitment. But the old chaplain knows it is for the best. It had been he, after all, who informed the Primus Pater of the Chiro Scuro, Nero Loyola IV, that another mind had been called to the *Kata*. And it had been such an unexpected pleasure to see dear Bex again. Wexler had made the call that resulted in the agent's recruitment almost thirty years before.

But Mo'Zart he missed more than he expected.

Even the pages of the manuscript seemed to mourn his loss. Father Wexler strokes the parchment as if giving the ancient tome some comfort. As he moves to turn the page, the edge catches his finger, slicing it thinly, drawing blood. Before he can lick the tip, the slit has opened further still, ripping like a fault line down his finger, along his arm. Splitting faster, reaching his chest and racing up his neck to deliver a deep and gaping wound, as if drawn by a knife, severing his neck to the spine.

And then—

—his old eyes flash open. He is standing upright, untouched. His finger barely snagged.

His mind, playing tricks... no more.

 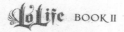

He exhales. He has not been plagued by such a vivid event since the days of his youth, when he first joined the Brotherhood. And even then he was ordered by the abbots to suppress these "attacks of the mind."

He remembers protesting, loud and long. Was it not through violent visions that their founding father, Brother Magen, had first seen the truth?

But he was silenced. The Brotherhood, he was told, is not the same as it had been in those early days. It was forever altered by the attacks of Victor Emmanuel. Driven to disperse, hounded into hiding, the members had lost much of their learning during these dark years of suppression. It was to be more than four decades before the Brotherhood would gather again, at the turn of the twentieth century.

They amassed in Spinkhill, England, under the protection of Joseph Pole, patriarch of a powerful Jesuit family. To reflect the changing times and to aid in the concealment of their true agenda, the Brotherhood assumed the name of the Society of Curators for the Understanding of Religious Orders. Amid a fashionable Edwardian interest in spiritualism, the society attracts little attention and continues its work as the century rolls on.

Then comes war. And once again the world changes. Responding to information that Hitler is collecting relics and recruiting occultists, a secret contra-unit is established by the Allies under a covert title: The Ministry of the Unnoticed. Its task: Halt the Nazis' mastery of magic. And it is under this initiative that the Brotherhood finds an opportunity to truly reunite and return to being an active force.

Brother Wexler was one of the many young monks transferred from the Chiro Scuro's quiet cloisters to join the Brotherhood's field operation. Still technically operating under the guise of the Society of Curators for the Understanding of Religious Orders, this new proactive division took the acronym SCURO.

Agent Wexler relished his duties in SCURO. He proved to be effective in the identification of Tormenta, who were enjoying a juicy existence within the ranks of Nazi High Command. But his active career was brought to an abrupt halt. Word reached SCURO that a Tormenta had infiltrated a branch of Le Maquis, the French Resistance, and was persuading many young underground fighters that the only honor left to them, in the face of Nazi rule, was suicide. Trekking across a field in northern France in search of the Tormenta, Agent Wexler found a landmine first; his leg was blown away at the knee. And just like that, for him, the war was over.

He was relegated back into the cloisters of the Chiro Scuro, where the monks quietly supported the field operatives of SCURO with a combination of prayer and paper pushing. Brother Wexler soon learned, to his dismay, that the fight against evil demanded an absurd amount of administration.

It therefore came as something of a relief when he was offered the post of chaplain at Yale. The Chiro Scuro had used their contacts within the university to subtly control this position for many years, ever since they had reason to believe that the Voynich Manuscript was, in fact, the *Kata*. While the Chiro Scuro, with its extraordinary powers, could have easily had the book removed into its care, Primus Pater Nero Loyola IV had seen an alternate opportunity. Some of the greatest young minds in the Western world would pass through the doors of Yale. If the mysterious tome was ever to be decoded, where better to seek the right minds to help accomplish this feat?

Father Wexler, as he would now be known, accepted the chaplain's role willingly. And over the coming decades, from the hallowed halls of Yale, he observed the ever more extraordinary evolution of SCURO.

By the end of the twentieth century, SCURO operated as a shadow agency aligned with the many other obscure offices of U.S. Intelligence and Homeland Security. Funding from the deep coffers of the Jesuit Church ensures that SCURO is well resourced. The Church's connections reach high into the realms of politics, military, and law-enforcement. Their powers are as wide as they are dark.

Which is why the extraction of a student from Yale is such an easy task. All the papers required to explain the temporary research post offered to the student are furnished to the university administration, friends and family.

But still, Father Wexler had been sad to see Mo'Zart go. Perhaps because he knows how special the lad is. He succeeded, after all, in deciphering that most precious gobbet of the code. But in his heart, Wexler knows it is more than that. He had a real affection for the boy.

Is that why he haunts my visions now?

Because the horror the old man has just experienced was not a warning to him, but a clear knell of danger to the boy. The manuscript was charged with his energy. It was to him that the pages spoke. And they were speaking to Wexler just now, urging him to pass their warning on.

They pursue the boy. They will find him.

The manuscript thuds shut.

And the robes of Father Wexler fly as he slips through a doorway at the back of the library, hurries down a darkened hallway that runs beneath the library. His destination is a chamber, deep within the underground archives. A telephone is installed there, a secure line where Father Wexler can call the Chiro Scuro directly. He uses it rarely. Sometimes to deliver good news that a fresh student has shown interest in the Manuscript.

Sometimes to declare danger.

He increases his pace, the clatter of his leg echoing from the walls as they narrow toward the doorway.

Then he halts—and the echo falls silent a moment later. But a moment too long. He heard the fragment of another footfall. Wexler turns, peers into the gloom. Sees nothing. And pulling his robe tighter about him, he presses on, opening the door to the chamber. Reaching out, raising the phone. His hand extending toward the old dial.

✦

A hand grasps a shoulder and gently shakes. "Primus Pater, I am sorry to wake you. But there is a call. Father Wexler."

Silk sheets roil in the half-light. A voice rumbles. "Wanting what?"

"He won't say. Just that this is a matter for the Primus Pater and no other."

A fist uncurls from the sheets. A golden ring, carved with

 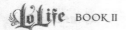

the symbol of the three crosses, is wrapped about a finger, which snaps against a thumb, demanding the phone.

A large black receiver is delivered. Dry lips approach, slicked by a tongue.

"Father Wexler. You have my attention. Use it well."

Nothing comes from receiver. Just a muffled gasp that rises into a desperate shriek that twists into...

...a dull buzzing tone.

The line is dead.

22

Bianco breathes slowly, this time inhaling the sweet latex stench of the mask she wears. Einstein's nose inflates and flops with every exhalation.

She looks through the eyeholes, surveying this new space. It is a vast, dark warehouse, stacked with crates. The only light comes from the open door to the chamber that held her.

And from two other doors, to two other chambers. And now she realizes that two other figures stand alongside her in the darkness.

One wears a Tweetie-Pie mask. A small man in a crumpled suit and slip-on shoes. Bianco knows he's a detective even before she sees the badge on his belt.

His fingers fidget. Bianco recognizes his type; this place will be freaking him out. He's just a simple cop who does things by the book. No arguments. No questions. He'll have written everything down, just to get outta here.

Bianco smiles beneath her mask. *Bet you sang like a canary.*

Then she hears it, a muffled voice. The detective is mumbling something… one word.

"Sulphur. Damned sulphur…"

Bianco leans in. "I'm pretty sure that smell—it's lilies."

The masked figure to her left snaps its fingers, reminding

 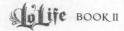

them to stay silent. She turns to see a tall, barrel-chested Marilyn Monroe. Bianco sweeps her eyes past the detective's badge, down a long pair of legs to his feet. Size thirteen at least.

And something sparks in Bianco. *Dammit, I know those feet!*

A sound smashes the memory before she can grasp it. A rhythmic beat. Loud and echoing.

All three masks turn toward the footsteps. A silhouette strides through the darkness, haloed by a blinding beam of light suddenly released by an unseen door.

Before the figure comes to a halt, a voice fires off an introduction.

"My name is Agent Petrus Bex. Detectives, welcome."

His lean form thrusts from the light and he falls into an easy pace, circling his guests. Bianco's eyes go to two deep, ragged scars that slit the agent's skull where his ears should be. The wounds look fresh, no more than forty-eight hours old. From behind her mask, she tries to take a closer look, but he is behind her, striding on.

"Thank you for your attendance here today. Your reports will be reviewed and researched and in the event we find cause for further investigation, we will do so with a wonderful rigor. So rest assured, you have done your duty, and whatever you saw— whatever you *think* you saw—it is now in the hands of SCURO."

His lips stretch wide into a smile, as if wedged around a stick of dynamite. The threat is clear.

"From two of you, we require nothing further—"

His fingers snap and a second figure appears from the shadows. A young agent in a sleek black suit. Unruly dreads dangle down his back. A second impatient snap prompts this cadet to produce all three clipboards and pass them to his boss.

Bianco exhales behind her mask, low and slow.

She can see that two of the boards contain a mass of handwritten notes. Hers is the only one empty.

"There is, however, one of you"—Bex glances up, his face clenched like a fist—"with whom I must speak at greater length."

His eyes swivel. "Detective, this way please."

Bianco jolts as a heavy hand drops onto Tweetie-Pie's shoulder, leading the little man away toward the door. The young agent follows behind.

Agent Bex's voice bounces from the darkness.

"Do not remove your masks until instructed. Do not attempt to leave before the timed lock disengages. Do not hesitate to ask if you have any questions." A pause—less than an atomic second. "No questions. Very well. And so we thank you both. Good afternoon."

The door slams shut.

A bolt shoots.

Then silence.

Marilyn Monroe shifts from one huge foot to another. "So, what d'you figure?"

Sweat runs down the side of Einstein's face. "Fifty-fifty that we're fucked."

The rubber muffles her voice and she's glad of it. She wants to maintain her anonymity until she is sure who Marilyn is. She has a pretty good idea. Even though the probability of this being correct is so whacked-out, it would blow even the real Einstein's mind. But life's like that. One big curved universe, throwing balls.

 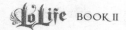

She looks again at those feet. *It has to be Bambi Siggurson.*

It's been ten years at least, but her mind replays the sound of those size thirteens, pounding the gravel of the training circuit at cadet school.

This was where they met—sort of. It was more like they met, then pulled away, then met again on the bend, then pulled away on the last five hundred yards of track that lead back to base.

Bambi Siggurson was her biggest competition for the Silver Wings, the badge awarded to the cadet who graduates with the highest marks.

And back in those days, Bianco had been all about the competition. Maybe because she knew who she was, a one-time perp trying to step over that thin blue line. But something in her told her she would need to be twice as fast as the next kid to stand a chance of outrunning her past. She'd sized up the other cadets on her first day and seen no physique to touch hers. But the Siggurson guy, she had to admit, looked good. Long-legged, lean… and a loner. That's what made him dangerous. She knew his type. *He ain't here to make friends.*

She'd need to keep an eye on him.

And right there was her first problem. Siggurson was so goddam fast, she'd lose sight of him before he hit the first bend. He would easily outpace Bianco over the first two miles. But she would smile as Siggurson, along with most of the other male cadets, pounded past her.

Yeah, bye-bye, guys. I'll be seein' ya.

Those teen years spent fleeing from the cops, when she just kept running—mile after mile until she made it all the way back to Swamp Gravy—her legs are now limbs that don't know how to quit. Bianco may be slow on the sprint, but over distance, she's a goddamn machine. By the third mile, she's thudding past red faces. By the fourth mile, her feet are flying past boots that can barely clear the dirt. And by the sixth mile, there is only Siggurson left ahead of her. The last five hundred yards to the finish would see them shoulder to shoulder. Sometimes she'd take it. Sometimes Siggurson. Always in silence.

They never spoke. That's how they both liked it. And how it stayed, until that one particular day.

It had stormed since morning. Only Bianco and Siggurson were dumb enough to still attempt the circuit.

Bianco felt the rain lash hard against her face. And behind, gaining ever closer, was the thump of Siggurson's Reeboks. Her muscles burned with lactic acid, starved of oxygen in the soaking air. But she *can't stop. Won't stop.*

Must stop!—as a lightning bolt shears a branch. A ton of wood drops hard into the mud, missing her skull by inches. Bianco swerves, grasped by a hand that pulls her below the shelter of a massive oak.

The hand relaxes, releases. Sinks down to hers, palm extended. "Bambi Siggurson."

Bianco takes the hand, shakes it, aware of the weirdness. They've seen each other every day for five weeks and with just eight days to go, they're getting around to this.

"Alexis Bianco."

The hands drop apart. There is no more to say. But the silence held between them grows too heavy and it slips first from her grip.

"Bambi... That's... kinda unusual."

 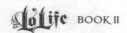

"Yeah, well… my mother was killed in an accident. A hunter in the woods shot her dead. The local kids saw the funny side. Called me Bambi. So I took the name on myself. Then it stopped being funny."

Bianco grimaces and shifts uncomfortably. "That's some story, but hell, you could tell it better."

She glances up. And sees the expression on Siggurson's face. Their long resistance to conversation means that Bianco can read him from his eyes alone. And now she knows with absolute certainty that he has never shared this story with anyone before.

Siggurson's hands agitate the hood of his tracksuit, pulling it over his head. "Rain's easing. We can make it back."

Bianco watches as he tugs the cords tight, concealing his face. Then she jerks a thumb at the track. It's awash with mud.

"Okay, but we walk. Game over. No points to anyone, agreed?" She extends her hand to shake on the deal and Siggurson takes it.

At an easy pace, they start back toward base. Random topics of conversation drop into Bianco's head like bowling balls, all of them dull, detached, designed to pass the time. So she jolts with surprise when her own brain makes a weird selection and rolls out of her mouth…

"Ya know, Bianco isn't my real name."

Siggurson says nothing but he turns to look at her from inside his hood. Bianco shrugs and continues.

"There's no record of my birth name, so… I chose one. Or more like, it chose me. *Bianco* means 'crow.' And I guess I got the label because I'm always crowing. Like I just can't keep quiet about how many times I've beaten you at weapons assembly. And how I always ace you on the shooting range. And how many times I beat you on the seven-mile."

She grins at Siggurson and through the rain she sees his eyes narrow as he suppresses a smile.

"Yeah. Suits you. Got those scrawny crow legs, too."

"All the better for beating you, Bambi."

He yanks down his hood and jabs a finger toward a dirt track that cuts through the woods.

"The ten-mile. Right now."

She holds her palms up to the torrential downpour.

"In this?"

"You chicken, Crow?"

She grins and with a surge of mud, she's gone. Accelerating down the track. Siggurson pounds after, heels flying.

He beat her. That time.

And every time after. If Bianco thought that anything had passed between them that day in the rain, she was wrong. Siggurson never spoke to her again and for the remainder of the training, she savored second place so many times it tasted like vanilla.

✦

Bianco licks her lips, releasing the mask that clings to her mouth each time she inhales. She looks at the familiar line of Siggurson's body. The years have been good to him. Doesn't look like he's gained a pound.

Bianco rolls her shoulders, feeling the weight of everything

 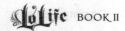

she knows bear heavily upon her. She may look the same, but she has changed beyond recognition.

She exhales. Reaches up, ready now to remove her mask.

23

A DRUNK SLUMPS across a bar, tink-tinking his empty shot glass, looking for the barman. "Hey, man! Where you hiding?"

He lifts his glass and peers through it, as if the thick base might bring his world into some sort of focus.

He cranks his head left and right and something catches in the prism. A wisp of gold. He lowers the glass to see that on the bar is a deck of cards, spread in columns. The backs of the cards glitter with an intricate gold design.

A figure sits by the cards, close to the window.

The drunk lugs his head round. "Pretty dandy cards, man." His eyes pucker, searching for the figure's face. But nothing can be seen. The gloom of the bar conceals his hair and neck, and what escapes of his face is hidden behind an enormous pair of binoculars, pressed to the eyes.

The lenses are turned toward the window. They survey the only building opposite—a derelict soap factory.

The barrels of the binoculars twist, fixed on the factory door. The figure slowly exhales.

Patience… With patience this plan might just work.

The cards at his elbow suddenly flutter upward.

"Solitaire, eh?" The drunk clumsily pokes at the half-completed columns. "How 'bout you ditch that game and deal a duet."

 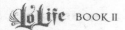

The barman appears, wiping the bar and nudging the drunk's sprawling arms back into a manageable mound. "Eyes front and center, Donny. The dude don't want to play."

The shoulders of the figure tense, then roll—a shrug, perhaps.

"No inconvenience, my friend." His pale hand descends, collects the cards. Slowly shuffles. "I have time to kill."

"There ya go, man!" The drunk snorts, slaps his hand down on the bar. "Name the game."

"I propose a battle of my own design." A smile flashes, like the silver plate on a coffin lid.

"Sweet, man. What's the rules?"

"The aim is to find the Mosca." The hands cease to shuffle. "The rules are constant, unchanging. The rules of eternal balance. And they state that if the Mosca rises, so will the Moera."

The cards are placed one by one face down on the bar. "But where to look?"

The hand hovers over a card. "The Legion have played this game many, many times… and lost."

He turns over the ace of hearts.

"This being so, my plan is to change the game-play. And if we cannot find the Mosca, then we will seek out the Moera."

The ace of hearts is set down on top of another card.

"And *that* will lead us to what we truly seek."

He turns over the card underneath. It is the ace of spades.

"The Mosca and the Moera. Their fates are locked together for eternity. Like star-crossed lovers…"

The drunk rumples his face, trying to keep up. "So how d'you win?" The figure sweeps up the aces, then adds a king and a jack to his hand. "You get your enemy to play into your hand." A long finger taps the king. "To the death."

The drunk grunts. "I don't get it, man."

"But you will, *man*." The hand gestures to the mash of humanity in the bar. "You all will."

The figure is already turning away, binoculars rising, racking focus. Fixed upon three silhouettes that exit the factory opposite. It is Agent Bex, that new dreadlocked recruit, and, shuffling in tow, a small detective.

The Chiro Scuro seek the Moera. So follow the agents and when they find theirs, we shall find ours.

Fingers snap as the figure orders another pomegranate martini, dry, with a twist kicked to the side. Knowing that elsewhere, his precise orders are already in action. His plan has begun.

The martini glass is jerked forward, purple juice spilling onto the card caught beneath. The hand slides the card out, glancing down.

It is the joker. *Of course! How perfect!*

A bitter smile as the card is crumpled deep into his palm. Too long has he been regarded by the Legion as a trickster. Worse, a traitor.

But when he succeeds in finally awakening the Mosca, the Legion will embrace him again and forgive his past betrayal.

He would have succeeded long ago, were it not for Agent Bex. He has indeed proved to be an admirable adversary. He covers his tracks to perfection, guards the information he garners with a fist of steel. No word on the Moera has ever slipped his grip.

There have been times when the entire enterprise seemed

 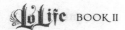

doomed to failure. Then—this new recruit was taken on. A kid who has not yet acquired Bex's invulnerable exterior.

A chink in SCURO's armor.

The challenge, then, is to find the right geegaw to distract the recruit. Something that can get close to him. Something… or someone.

The hand slowly slides a queen between the king and the jack.

24

THE TREBLE BELLY pizzeria is alive on a Saturday night. In a back booth, a pair of hands toy with a menu. Opposite, another pair of hands fold and unfold a piece of paper, their owner glancing at the text within.

"Says here you like music." A boy swallows hard, the collar of his shirt bulging. "I like the classics."

The girl opposite has her hair pulled tight into a ponytail. It tugs her face taut. "What, like Springsteen and shit?"

"Debussy… and shit." He exhales hard. Unfolds the paper again. "So, what else do you like?"

He halts as a voice comes from above. "I like this booth."

Someone stands by their table, clad in a long, hooded coat. The boy attempts a smile, tips up his palms. "Hey, guy, we're on a date."

The hood swivels from the girl to the boy. "I don't like your chances."

The figure thuds into the booth, the ripple of the impact launching the couple onto their feet. They hurry into the aisle.

Booted legs uncurl below the table. Long and muscular. Hands rise to the hood. They are pale and delicate.

From beneath the fabric, blond dreadlocks tumble, concealing a face that is etched by a strong jawline. Only when the face turns, pierced and tattooed, does it appear to be that of a woman. An Amazon creature.

Her features are African but her skin is white. Eyes are ice blue. The woman is a black albino.

Everything about her—color, race, gender—is made of contradictory mixes.

She snaps her long fingers, demanding coffee.

A waitress stomps up. "Black or white?" Maybe she intends the jibe... maybe not. One cold glance from the woman and the waitress quickly offers cream, resolving any doubt.

These fucking humans...

As the waitress scurries away, long black fingernails tap the table. Then idly gather the sheet of paper abandoned by the boy. It's a dating agency profile sheet. The top box is filled with a name and the box below is labeled TELL US A LITTLE ABOUT YOURSELF.

The woman grins. *Yeah, just imagine that...*

The name box she could fill in: BEE-BEE. But only a human could fit his or her life into a single text box.

Bee-Bee's life stretches over nearly three centuries.

She was born in 1744 in Trinidad. At the age of fourteen she was captured as a slave and shipped to New Orleans, where her strange albino looks attracted much attention. As a thing of interest, she was sent across the Atlantic to the French court. Painted in her tribal colors, with a black stripe across her eyes, she was presented to the young dauphin and given the name Melissa, from the Greek for bumblebee, prompted by her black and yellow coloring.

Melissa soon became a favorite and her quick wits brought

her to the attention of the court's high chancellor. He controlled the espionage that ceaselessly flowed between the French and Spanish courts as the New World brought them closer and closer to war. Melissa's strange appearance meant that she could pass as any nationality, because no one had ever seen her like before. More important still, it had become clear, in the midst of the lascivious antics of the French, that Melissa's sexual preference was wonderfully fluid. Men and women found her irresistible, and she happily obliged both.

A marvelous quality in a spy.

And so it was that Melissa moved between the two courts, playing both sides, politically and sexually. Her prime loyalty, always, was to herself.

Until the day she met Perfidia.

Perfidia was a handmaid, newly recruited to the Spanish queen. There was something about her that was both cruel and magnetic. A perfect contradiction. No wonder Melissa fell fast in love.

Perfidia encouraged these passions, telling Melissa that their destiny was to be together. When Melissa was ordered to return to the French court, she refused. The savage punishment she received at the hands of the chancellor all but left her dead.

Yet to Melissa, death would be preferable to separation from Perfidia.

As Perfidia washed the deep lashes across Melissa's back, she whispered a proposal. They would commit joint suicide and be united forever in death.

Melissa willingly agreed and swallowed a spoonful of poison.

As the last gasp left her body, her consciousness flickered.

 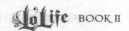

She saw Perfidia not lying beside her, but bearing down, thrusting her mouth upon hers, violently sucking…

And then… nothing.

All that was found by the chambermaid the next morning was a smoking carbon ring upon the floor.

And Melissa awakens in Lo'World, delivered into the Sinestra's care. When her new masters explain that Perfidia was a Tormenta and that she duped her, Melissa's fury knows no bounds. Her first instinct is to break free of this place, return to Earth, and seek Perfidia's death. Then her handler in the Sinestra explains that Perfidia is already dead; her failed attempt to take Melissa's span will have condemned her. Melissa rages that she must have vengeance, and so what sweet relief she feels when she is told that there is a means by which she can get even. She can be trained to become a Hunter, and while Perfidia may be gone, she can vent her fury against every other Tormenta that crosses her path. Without hesitation, Melissa agrees and becomes Hunter 696B.

She soon gains a reputation as one of the most ruthless to ever serve the Sinestra, taking mission after mission, slaughtering Tormenta. Until one day, when she learns a certain truth about Perfidia. About her motives all those years ago…

And as a consequence, Melissa's loyalty to the Sinestra is instantly and forever destroyed.

Her old duplicitous ways return. She drops her Hunter number, releases her yellow dreads, reinstates the black stripe across her eyes from her tribal days, and takes the name Bee-Bee.

A killer for hire.

Part human. Part Tormenta. Entirely mercenary.

Another snap of her fingers brings the waitress back to her table.

"What's hot?"

The waitress jerks a pencil toward a picture on the menu. "Hottest we got. Topped with three types o' chili pepper."

Bee-Bee smiles. "The Treble Rebel. I like that."

Bee-Bee peels a ten-dollar bill from a roll. "You make it quick, and you make this." The bill goes down on the table.

The waitress bobs and scoots away, all smiles now.

Must be my Tormenta side that makes me expensive, 'coz humans are so damned cheap.

The money roll slides back into her pocket. The generous girth suggests it must be ten thousand thick.

Last week she accepted a new mission. She has a new target. And she expects him at any moment.

✦

A giant key swings and Mo'Zart slides it into the lock of the factory door. One grinding clunk and the latch slides shut. Mo'Zart attempts to slip the key into his suit pocket, but its long shaft resists, as if the key is determined to poke from his pocket and observe the journey the boy makes to the back of the building.

Agent Bex waits in the darkness, a cigarette in one hand, the other resting in a relaxed—and yet restraining fashion—upon the shoulder of the short detective.

His voice carries cleanly on the night air.

 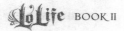

"Detective Gobis was just telling me he hails from Sulphur City. Born and bred."

"And soon to be dead?" Detective Gobis titters at his own grim jest. "Hey, just joking, guys. I know that SCURO aren't… that you would never…"

He looks from one agent to the other, searching for some chink of camaraderie.

Agent Bex opens a smile, like the priming of a bear trap. "I suggest you forget any preconceptions you may have about SCURO. We are not what you think we are."

Gobis shifts from one foot to another. "You don't know what I think you are."

"Believe me, Detective, you do not have that caliber of imagination."

Agent Bex waggles a hand, instructing Mo'Zart to come closer. "The cellar door, please."

Mo'Zart fumbles inside his jacket, pulling another giant key and slotting it into a padlock that seals a set of storm doors in the ground. The thought strikes him that the last time he manipulated keys so large in proportion to his hands, he was a baby and the Playskool keys were strung across his crib.

And working with Agent Bex, he sure feels like the baby. He has yet to see any real action. And tonight looks set to be no different, as his boss ushers Detective Gobis down the cellar steps before raising a flat hand that halts Mo'Zart in his tracks.

"You may not attend this interview."

Mo'Zart grimaces, head down. "So this is how I learn? The three-monkey method? See nothing. Hear nothing—"

"Say no more. And avoid insolence."

Bex pulls a cigarette, sparks a match, draws deep and slow. Taking his time. Either the cigarette is sweet enough to savor or Bex is considering, with unusual care, what he utters next.

"This detective worked on a homicide." Smoke seeps from the side of his mouth. "A fifteen-year-old girl was found in a motel room, ripped from neck to hip one hundred and forty-four times."

Mo'Zart jigs in the cold. "Did they get the guy?"

"*She* was the guilty one."

Mo'Zart balks, eyebrows up. "What did she do?"

Bex taps his ash like a ticking bomb. "Maybe nothing." He takes a long last drag. "Maybe everything."

The same jerking gesture that casts down the cigarette instructs Mo'Zart to leave.

"Go get some fresh air."

Ten minutes later, Mo'Zart finds himself stomping through the dark streets. He's been in the agency training program for nearly a month.

When will he start to get a taste of the good stuff? When's 007 gonna get the girl?

Speaking of which…

Mo'Zart glances at his watch. Maybe he can make good use of his time. A few nights back, he met this cool chick, or more like, she met him. The girl had some stones, just sliding into his booth, smooth as…

Mo'Zart smiles. She was kinda tall and the thought did cross his mind that she might be more man than him. But all suspicions were allayed when she allowed Mo'Zart's drunken hands to roam free. Suddenly, boy got game. And he got her number.

 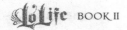

Mo'Zart pulls out the napkin with her digits and flips open his cell phone. She picks up on the second ring.

What d'ya know—she's in the Treble Belly, just down the street. Says she's gonna order for him, so be sure to get there quick.

"How do ya like your coffee?"

"Like my women." Mo'Zart cringes at his own bad line.

In the diner, Bee-Bee leans back and snaps her cell shut with a smile. She's not sure that they serve trisexual coffee.

25

Thᴇ ʙᴀsᴇᴍᴇɴт ᴏғ the soap factory smells quite different. It has a sweet, searing tang that forces Detective Gobis to jam his sleeve to his nose. He knows the stench well.

"You got a body down here?"

Agent Bex strides ahead between a maze of vats that fill the basement. "What you smell is old rendered fat."

Gobis relaxes his sleeve half an inch. "Smells human."

"I believe they used pigs. Now please, if you will…" Bex gestures to a metal chair that stands alone amid the vats. "Make yourself comfortable."

Detective Gobis fails in this first task as his buttocks overspill the small, cold seat. A tight-fitting jacket rides up about his waist and a toupee struggles with equal difficulty to cover his scalp.

"Do you smoke, Detective?"

"Why, you gonna set fire to me?"

"You are quite the joker, Detective Gobis."

"Guess it's a defense mechanism."

"Not much protection against a bullet."

Gobis shrinks back as Bex's face sweeps down. The scars of his severed ears ripple as he hikes a smile.

"I jest, Detective."

Something cold and hard suddenly presses into Gobis's

 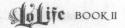

chin. His eyes roll slowly down, pooling with relief as he sees it's just the metal edge of a clipboard.

"Your testimony." Agent Bex urges the metal edge a little deeper into the folds of the detective's chin. "It contained certain facts relating to the case of Jezebeth Hooger. Facts for which you could find no adequate explanation."

"Sir, I just saw what I saw and reported it. I'm only a cop. I don't need to know everything."

His words twist to a gasp as the corner of the clipboard kinks his wind pipe.

"But *I* need to know everything."

Bex withdraws the board. "In your own time."

Which feels to be fast running out, so Gobis draws breath and begins. "It started the day that Jezebeth Hooger was murdered—"

A thin finger rises, wags disagreement. "It started long before that, Detective. The true beginning, please."

"All right, we can do it that way." Gobis shifts on his seat as if his ass is searching for the start of the story.

"So this is going back some, but, yeah, I was the detective on duty the night of Agnus Day's suicide. Or supposed suicide, because there was no body. Just a goodbye note and a big ol' carbon burn ring on the floor. And no corpse. Now, if it had been anybody else, the file would have been consigned to the Cold Case cabinet. But this guy had a fancy academic reputation, and the chief wanted us to show some huff 'n' puff, a little effort. So we dusted for prints, took a bunch of pictures. Then I filed it as a missing persons. And forgot it."

He halts, jerking a finger up toward his mouth. "I do smoke, if you got one."

Agent Bex produces a soft pack, taps a cigarette. Gobis takes it, glancing at the logo.

Never heard of this brand. But I guess that figures.

Agent Bex clicks his lighter, the sound like the snap of fingers, commanding him on.

"So the Agnus Day case goes cold. And seventeen years later, I get called to a homicide scene. A motel in Sulphur City. Sounds routine, until I get there."

He glances up at Agent Bex. "You musta seen the pictures? They were everywhere. Every newspaper. Every news channel. Little Jezebeth Hooger, fifteen years old and all raped, ripped up, and written on. And lying on the bed right alongside her, catatonic and covered in her blood, is her killer, Agnus Day. Not that I knew it was him. No way. The pictures I'd seen when he went missing, he was this skinny, bearded scientist. This guy was all muscled up, a machine. But the DNA pegged him. And that was surprising. But then the lab boys take Jezebeth's prints, and what d'you know…"

The cigarette sizzles half an inch. "Coincidence is a funny thing."

"God's favorite joke, I hear. Continue, please."

"They match her prints to a set of unknowns taken from the scene of Agnus Day's disappearance. But Jezebeth Hooger is only fifteen years old. She wasn't even born then."

Gobis takes a last, long drag. "So I file a report. And this one I ain't forgetting anytime soon. Until the chief takes me aside and says that I'm to wipe my memory clean of those prints. The prosecution has an airtight case. The killer was found with the victim. What nobody needs is a piece of the puzzle that doesn't

 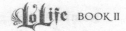

fit. It has to be an error. And he promises me personally that he will send the prints away for review. And meanwhile, I should keep my mouth shut until Agnus Day is safely put down.

"I thought I could live with it. It's not like I'm so squeaky clean. I got dirt under my fingernails—what cop hasn't? But when Agnus went on death row, that dirt on my hands... felt sticky like blood. So I told the chief, I want to know what happened to the evidence review. I wanted proof that the fingerprints were some kinda freak mistake. Guess you could say I made some noise. So when I get brought in by SCURO, I'm thinking two things: Either I'm gonna get some facts... or the facts are gonna get me."

He looks up to see that Agent Bex is writing something on a piece of paper. The shred is ripped from the clipboard and passed to Gobis.

"Please look at that number. Have you ever seen a man with this number tattooed on his arm?"

Gobis takes the paper, glances at the number. Shakes his head. "He may have gone by this name."

Bex gestures with his finger that Gobis should look at the reverse of the paper. "Is it familiar?"

Gobis flips the paper fragment and now his eyes bulge wide. "Well... well of course I know this name, but how could I ever... How could he be..."

With a waft of his hand, Bex draws him to silence. "Thank you. I just had to be sure." His lips tighten. "So, we are grateful, Detective Gobis, for what you have provided. Thanks to your concern for the truth, we know where we should direct our search."

"For what?"

"That is not your concern."

"So what now?"

Agent Bex slides back his jacket, pulls out his gun.

26

"So, Bianco, 'd you make sergeant?"

"I scraped some stripes."

"Thought you'd be way up there. You were always so hungry."

"Maybe I lost my appetite."

"You—never!"

Siggurson's words follow her as she drops her mask and walks away across the warehouse, her attention caught by something. A glint of metal. She arrives at a crate and reaches in between the slats. Smiles as her fingers feel the familiar shape of her gun. Retrieves it and slides it into her holster. Siggurson is immediately by her side, fishing his own weapon from the box.

"All right, so I say we blast the lock and get outta here." He buckles the gun tight beneath his arm, looking about the warehouse for the door. "I don't know who or what SCURO is, but soap never smelled so much like bullshit."

He glances up at Bianco. She is slowly buttoning her jacket over her holster, taking her time. "Hey, what's with you? Don't you want to get out of here?"

"The door's at twelve o'clock." She jerks a finger toward the back of the warehouse, then sets off, following her own command. Siggurson moves up alongside.

"You've changed, Bianco."

She strides half a pace in front of him, voice low. "I saw some things. Now the world don't look the same."

"C'mon, we both work homicide. I've seen every way a man can die. You deal with it. Move on."

"Yeah, you're right. That's all there is to it."

Siggurson shakes his head, unrolling a smile. "Don't tell me there's a little bit of real woman buried deep down in there? That whole job-is-not-enough thing. There-must-be-more-to-life shit…"

"Actually, there's more to death, Siggurson."

A gunshot explodes, from somewhere deep below.

Before the echo dies, Bianco and Siggurson are pounding toward the door. Siggurson pulls his gun and shoots the lock. In a shower of sparks, the metal bursts open. The stairs beyond shudder under their descending feet.

Gunfire erupts again, directing their pursuit down toward the factory cellar. They survey the floor, looking for an entrance. Race outside. Find the storm doors wide apart.

Siggurson is first down the steps, gun high. Bianco sweeps behind, weapon high, ready to cover. Back-to-back, in tight formation, they enter the basement.

And then they see him: Agent Bex, aiming his weapon at the figure of Detective Gobis, who stands quivering with his back to one of the vats.

Siggurson shouts an order to Bex to drop the gun.

As Bex turns, Siggurson sees only the approaching mouth of the agent's Luger.

But Bianco sees something else—a strange expression on

Bex's face. Which twists to agony as Siggurson's bullet shears through his hand.

And as he falls, his skull explodes upward. Struck by another bullet. Another shooter.

And then Bianco understands.

The barrel of a sawn-off shotgun emerges from behind the vat. Followed by a shadow with its arm tight around the detective's neck. The attacker had been holding Gobis as a human shield, until Bex was fatally distracted, allowing the attacker to let off a kill shot.

Realization passes like lightening from Bianco to Siggurson, a moment before a bullet slices past their heads. Siggurson's neck is hooked down by Bianco as she reacts first, releasing a shot as the attacker pounds up the steps of the cellar, the limp body of Gobis slung under one arm. Bianco's bullet rips through a storm of blond dreadlocks that swirl as the attacker turns, firing with one hand. Effortlessly. Accurately.

Bianco's shoulder explodes, the force of the impact cracking her backward and hurling her to the floor.

Siggurson reaches out, grabs her jaw, and twists her face to look into her eyes. She's alive. Then sweeps his gun through the darkness, finding just silence.

Leaping to his feet, he strides to the body of Agent Bex, rolls him over. His halved skull rocks like a bowl of bad fruit.

Strides back toward Bianco. Hauls her to her feet and, bearing her weight, makes for the stairs to the storm door.

In thudding steps, he rises and hits the air, stumbling as something tangles in his feet. Spread on the concrete is the motionless body of the other young agent. Blood seeps from the back of his skull.

Siggurson moves to walk on, Bianco now his priority. But halts. He cannot escape his training. He sets Bianco down and goes back to the kid. Listens for breath. Nothing.

Feels for a pulse. Nothing… then, something. Faint but real.

He is alive.

Siggurson's eyes shoot up. Sees an old Ford Tahoe in the abandoned yard of the factory.

The hood pops. Wires fizz. The engine revs.

The unconscious cadet rolls across the backseat and Bianco slumps forward on the passenger side as a size-thirteen boot crushes the gas pedal and the car roars off into the night.

27

LOLA'S CHEEK LOLLS against a leather headrest. She is slumped in the bucket seat of her '71 Dodge Challenger.

This is one hot day for a stakeout.

Her eyes flicker open, looking across to the passenger side. The seat is empty.

Bianco should be here.

Then Lola shakes her head, mouth tight. *My weakness. That I want her with me.*

She tenses her spine, stretches her neck. She doesn't need her for anything.

Apart from maybe keeping her awake. On these long observations, Bianco's conversation was as relentless as the radio.

When was their last hunt together—a month ago? They'd been in the car for three hours and Bianco was still talking.

"Hey, Lola, you ever shot with a .44 Magnum? Massive kickback. It pulped my palm black and blue the first few months. But I've never seen you carry one. And ya know, I got an interest in what weapon you use. I'm your partner. You should try it. You'd like it. You like Clint. And Clint likes Magnums."

"Clint hates having a partner."

Bianco laughed. Lola liked the sound of it. Hard and loud, like a dog's bark.

She can't remember the sound of her own laughter.

A lot of things I don't remember.

Lola's eyes close. She breathes deep, feeling fatigue fold about her. Opens them again, fixed on the empty seat. The only thing that rolls on the leather now is a tiny container of half-and-half.

Without Bianco, Lola needs coffee.

A hot cup sweats on the dash, capped tight with plastic. Lola picks up the half-and-half, places it between her teeth, and pierces the foil lid with her incisor—a standard cop maneuver for avoiding spill.

She'd learned that from Bianco.

She'd learned a lot from Bianco. About how to tap phones, bug buildings, trace registrations. She can even log on to the police database for fingerprints, bullet matches, and ViCAP.

And Bianco had gained some skills in return. She was getting pretty quick at spotting Tormenta grifts.

Lola plugs in an earpiece and looks up at the building where she's parked. The Hoyle School of the Dramatic Arts.

This stakeout had been Bianco's idea.

She was buzzed to tell me. Her first find.

Bianco had taken her to a sports bar on the outskirts of town.

She leans across her frothy beer. "I was watching this show about acting classes, how they break the students down, really mess with their minds, telling them that they have to destroy their own persona to get into the mind of another character."

Bianco talks at speed, excited by her own discovery. "So I'm thinking, drama students are pretty tender meat. So what

 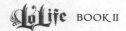

happens if you add some devastating criticism, tell them they will never be good enough—"

"Is this going anywhere *specific?*" Lola hates this bar. She wants out.

"It's going right there."

Bianco points out of the bar window to the Hoyle Academy opposite. "Hilda Hoyle, prime English bitch and the toughest acting coach outside of New York." A photo slides over. A small woman in winged spectacles. "Students pay a fortune to get enrolled. They say that Hilda will either make you or break you. So I pulled up the student records. Seven suicides in nine years."

Lola lifts her chin, eyes front. Bianco has her attention.

"Even to an amateur like me, that school looks like an Oscar-winning grift."

✦

The listening device crackles in Lola's ear. A class is getting under way. A woman's voice shrills.

"*You were deadly dull last week. All of you. I hope today that someone might light the darkness with a glimmer of talent.*"

Lola slugs down the last of the coffee. Its bitterness stings her tongue. But still her eyelids fall.

The leather seats are hot. Almost midday.

The half-and-half container drops from her fingers. Lola's breathing slows. Then—

Her body spasms, like a falling dreamer. Words crackle in her earpiece: "*I want you to take a good long look at your face.*

You see the problem? No one else wants to look at it."

Lola's eyes roll beneath the lids. The words trigger something. A memory...

A fat, pallid face stares into a mirror. Removes thick glasses. Tries to apply red lipstick, but the downturned mouth is sobbing, lips quivering, sending the lipstick in chaotic scrawls down the chubby chin. The image shifts... The lipstick becomes a trickle of blood, running down a slashed wrist.

You will never succeed. Your life, my dear, is worthless.

Lola bolts forward in the car seat, breathing hard. How long was she asleep?

Slams from the vehicle.

Boots pound up the stairwell. Burst into the studio to find the room in darkness.

But Lola's eyes soon adjust to see a familiar congress taking place in the far corner: A young girl's body is sprawled across the floor, pale and lifeless. A telltale froth bubbles at the corner of her mouth. In her hand is a bottle of pills, spilling outward.

Lowering down, jaws agape, is Hilda Hoyle. She presses her lips hard onto the girl's mouth and begins to suck.

A glistening, twisted, blue coil of span rises, snaking down Hilda's throat. She gulps hard, drawing it further. The last coil rises. Hilda inhales, ready to ingest, when...

...she hears the thud of approaching boots.

She rises. Her outward appearance is a bundle of knitwear and pearl-rimmed glasses. But as she opens her mouth and roars, her Tormenta nature rises to the fore.

And Hilda strikes the first blow, showing that she has put all her years to good use. She hustles left and right, back and forth

 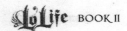

with dancing speed, her fists, clad in heavy rings, lashing and smashing into Lola's defenses. The backs of Lola's hands pour blood but she matches the old woman, blow for blow. Until Hilda bobs low, landing a punch deep into Lola's belly. The breath blown from her, Lola staggers backward. A dangerous dip in her guard, forced down by Hilda's lunging fist cracking across Lola's temple.

Lola swirls back, aware that her opponent is drawing up her fist for a final blow to her skull. And as the old woman's small feet dance in for the kill…

…her shoes slip, rolling chaotically, the soles sliding across the pool of pills spilled from the bottle of barbiturates. As Hilda flails and skitters, Lola bundles her fist and launches hard, cracking back Hilda's head until the neck snaps.

The old woman falls dead.

In the corner of the room, the girl does not move. A length of span, half extracted, trails from her mouth. It glistens wet and blue, like a long-exposed vein. But its tubular structure is not tissue. It is a tight, pulsing vortex of energy.

As the girl suddenly gasps for breath, the span is sucked back down. The last few inches, pulled from Hilda's mouth, are tainted black.

The girl bolts upright. Looks around her. "What happened? She said I should… and I wanted to die… but… ?"

Her eyes go to the body of Hilda and then to her own hands, which wiggle with life. With a smile, she looks up at the tall, blond stranger who stands before her.

"You saved me?"

"Kinda."

"I'm alive!"

"Half-and-half."

The girls frowns, confused.

Lola pulls out her aviator shades. "Everything will be explained."

Slides them over her eyes.

She knows what's coming next.

In a blinding blast of light, the body combusts. Leaving just a charred void in the floor.

Lola turns and exits.

28

A BLISTER SIZZLES, brown and sticky. The glowing tip of a cigarette rises from flesh. The filter slides between the lips of Bee-Bee, who sucks hard, refreshing the heat before she lowers the tip back onto her forearm, searing another circle.

Then twists her wrist, admiring her handiwork.

The length of Bee-Bee's arm is covered in a delicate trellis of scars and blooming blisters. Her neck is ringed with kiss-cuts, and carved onto her chest, above her heart, is an inverted *K*.

She sucks on the last inch of her cigarette, creating just enough heat to score another swirl. The hot tobacco bites and a cry explodes.

Not from Bee-Bee. From a man, in agony.

Why won't this dumb fuck just give up what he knows?

Bee-Bee is bored and wants this over with. She pulls out a small mirror. Checks her reflection. Sweeps back her dreads. The edge of the mirror, prettied with pearls, captures a gruesome sight behind her. Gobis is stripped naked and bound to a chair, a mass of needles implanted into his flesh.

His interrogator sits in silhouette beside a table. On the table is a box, coiled with wires. Beside the box, gold cards turn. His captor is playing solitaire. Passing time, as he waits for Gobis to recover from the last pulse of pain. And as the detective's bloody head lolls up, another blast is discharged.

His body spasms.

Bee-Bee exhales, twisting her dreads.

Talk or die. Or better still, both.

She snaps her mirror shut. Inquisition is definitely not a spectator sport. "Why don't you let *me* try?"

The Interrogator declines her offer with another voltage blast.

Fuck you, I could make this sweat-ball talk.

Bee-Bee has recently discovered a talent for interrogation. She always knew she was a skilled assassin. Her training in the Sinestra taught her how to kill with repetitive efficiency. Same moves, like a dance routine.

But since she became freelance, she's added her own little half-step.

Before she finishes off her target, she takes a moment to ask a few questions. More precisely, one question.

Do they know where she will find Perfidia?

Because Perfidia is not dead. She lives!

The Sinestra lied to her. Just as they lie to all the half-dead humans whom they wish to turn into Hunters.

Bee-Bee knows this because she asked the right question, of the right Tormenta.

The finest Tormenta she had ever had the pleasure to make bleed. Her fingers trace the *K* carved onto her heart. It stands for *Kave*. And Kave stands for no one.

This was all she knew of him the night the Sinestra sent her on a mission to kill Kave. She was still an obedient operative back then. Her hard-core commitment was the reason she was

 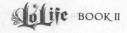

selected for this particular task. Because to bring down Kave meant almost certain death. No Hunter had ever succeeded. But now, she was told, it must be done. There had been "an incident." Most unexpected. But it elevated the destruction of Kave from something that the Sinestra might simply relish into an event upon which they now relied.

She found Kave easily—too easily. That was the first thing that made her suspicious. He was alone in an old salsa dance club. The gray-green walls were soon splattered with blood as she and Kave fought furiously. Hand to hand, blow for blow, she felt the casual sweep of his attack as if he were merely deflecting her fists until something more fun suggested itself.

And then, as she gasps for air, mustering a last assault—he smiles. "Such spirit. I see now why Perfidia fell for you."

At these words, confusion combusts with rage and she launches forward, sending him crashing to the ground. He falls with effortless grace. And does not resist as she strips his torso bare and chains him to a chair, a knife drawn and pressed against his throat.

"What do you know of Perfidia?"

Kave rolls his head, dark hair falling from his face. "It hurts to even say her name, does it not?"

The blade whips, delivering a careful, shallow nick at the base of his neck. Bee-Bee's voice is hoarse with fury. "I ask you again. What do you know of Perfidia?"

Blood slicks Kave's sternum. He lifts his chin, eyes unblinking. "Cut me as you wish, Hunter, I will not be persuaded. But cut yourself and I will talk."

She jolts, confused.

But Kave smiles. Something in his eyes, his voice... something she cannot explain. Only feel. And she feels her knife rise.

"Above your heart, make a cut. Downward and oblique."

Her hand shaking with a strange tension, she finds herself obeying. The edge sinks into her skin, slowly slicing. The searing pain is strangely cooled by the steel of the blade. As her flesh peels, her lips part, releasing a soft gasp.

"Exquisite agony that lessens the pain of a broken heart."

The tip of the knife shivers from her flesh, attempting to return to his throat. "Tell me of Perfidia!"

"I will not be persuaded by my own pain. Yours, however, I find irresistible."

The knife slowly curves back toward her own body, as if borne on the wave of his words.

"I can tell you three things, Hunter. But I want a cut for each. A triangle, of sorts, is what we shall carve. Because what we have with you and Perfidia is a love triangle. You have made the first cut." He looks at the delicate oblique incision. "And so, the first thing you should know is this: The Sinestra lied to you."

He relaxes back into the chair, as if the chains that hold him could be shrugged from his shoulders at any time.

"Perfidia is not dead."

She feels her muscles twitch. Kave has instilled just the sound of Perfidia's name with an agonizing power.

"So now to your second question, which I guess to be this: Why do they perpetuate this lie?" His eyes move like magnets to the knife. "A second cut, please. One end touching the other, to form a point."

Bee-Bee stares at her own fist as it raises the blade, cutting deep. The blood comes fast.

Kave nods, satisfied.

"They know that when they tell a half-dead human what has befallen them—and more importantly, who did it—the victim's first instinct will be to wreak bloody vengeance against that particular Tormenta, the one who drove them to take their own life. But the Sinestra cannot let that happen. They need a Hunter to kill according to command. They must serve just one cause: theirs. So they tell the Hunter the Tormenta who turned them is dead and, in so doing, hope to divert all that hatred toward the world of Tormenta in general. Not that you should hate Perfidia. She did nothing but love you."

The knife wavers in Bee-Bee's fingers like a metal tongue.

"Which of course begs the question: Why did she persuade you to your death?" Kave smiles. "The third incision, when you're ready."

The blade arrives on her skin as if to finish the triangle along the base. It halts at the sound of Kave's voice. "No. Not there. Place it across the top, balanced on the point." He flashes a smile. "You must not complete the triangle until you find her."

With a steady hand, Bee-Bee obediently makes the last cut.

"This mark will remind you always that the one you search for will complete you." He tips his head to one side. "And by chance, it looks like a *K*, so you will not forget who taught you this lesson."

She mutely looks down at the raw edges of the scars.

"Now this I tell you as a kindness. So be grateful and come to your knees."

Bee-Bee mutely drops down before him. He parts his legs, the action commanding her to bring her torso between his thighs. Her head hangs in submission.

"Closer. Chin up."

Her ear arrives at his lips. His tongue brushes the soft, pink ridges as he whispers.

"Perfidia loved you. But you were a human and she a Tormenta. She could never change. But you... some part of you could become Tormenta. She could bring that immortal transformation upon you. By committing the greatest sin known to our kind—take a human span, your span, while you still lived, and so ensure your arrival in the Lo'World. She knew then that you would be returned to Earth and although the Sinestra would have caged and controlled your Tormenta traits, by making you hate that part of yourself, Perfidia had to believe that fate would cause your paths to cross again. And when you meet... when your hands are once again upon each other's bodies, the love you once shared would return and prove stronger than the hatred honed in you."

Bee-Bee's head dumbly rolls back, mouth open.

"What she did, she did only so that you and she could one day reunite and be together forever. Perfidia loved you. She still loves you." Kave lowers his mouth. "Release me."

And as the chains fall to the ground, so does Bee-Bee, hard onto her back...

...with him fast upon her.

Pushing her down. His breath thundering into the curve of her neck as he forces the last of her humanity from her, filling her with a hot rush of Tormenta ferocity.

 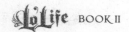

And so it is that Hunter 696B walks away as Bee-Bee.

And each time she looks upon the *K* cut into her chest, she sees a triangle that awaits completion. Its final side to be moved into place. So that each of the three lines conjoin.

Three becoming one.

✦

She jolts as Gobis screams—this time releasing a cry that gurgles to a deathly silence.

The Interrogator rises up in the darkness. Lays down his cards. "Well, there we have it."

Gobis's limp form slumps, lifeless.

"Or, more accurately, there we don't."

Bee-Bee saunters toward the corpse. "You want me to clear this up?"

The Interrogator hisses furiously, like escaping steam. "What I want is information!"

He inhales, calming himself. A gloved hand taps the curve of his chin. "What was it that he told Agent Bex?"

His head turns at the slightest of sounds. Something has fallen from beneath the toupee of Gobis. A shred of paper, hastily hidden. The yellow color reveals it to be the scrap given to him by Agent Bex when he asked him if he recognized a particular name. The Interrogator's gloved hand sweeps the fragment up. It is so soaked with sweat, the ink has seeped from the paper. It is illegible. The fingers crush it, thwarted.

Bee-Bee kneels down, peeling back the hairpiece. The ink has left a reversed imprint on his scalp.

She pulls her mirror, holds it against the mark. The reflected words read:

Judas Iscariot 666A.

The gloved hands slowly come together, fingertips tapping in contemplation. "Judas, well, well! We must find out what he knows."

Bee-Bee pulls on her long coat, preparing to leave.

"If you want me to bring *him* in, the price is double." Knives slide, one by one, into her belt.

Her employer emits a pellet of laughter. "I would never use you for such a task. This one requires sharp wits."

Bee-Bee spins the last knife in her hand, tempted to show him just how quick her thinking can be.

29

A HAND THRUSTS a knife upward.

"Could we get another? This one's dirty."

The old waitress at Fat Tuesday's whips the steel away and lashes out another with a grin that makes you wonder what she's thinking.

"And more coffee, please."

A steaming pot appears, carried by a busboy. And as he tops off the two cups, what he's thinking is clear: *Why the hell is she with him?*

The woman has creamy skin and auburn hair that curls like maple syrup. The older guy beside her, balding and hunched in a waffle-knit cardigan, looks like a dessert delivered to the wrong table.

But their intertwining hands declare them lovers, to the untrained eye.

However, a figure sits behind their booth, listening in with a highly trained ear. It is Lola, slowly stirring her coffee.

The couple are discussing their hurried wedding plans. Lola smiles as she hears the man excitedly anticipate the reaction of his friends and family.

"They're gonna adore you, Love Muffin. Just *adore* you." He nervously kneads her hands like dough. "They'd never think I'd catch a peach like you."

"Ah, Bubsy, you silly man." She giggles, eyes down.

He sweeps a fat hand across his head, drawing up a skein of hair from the top of his neck, spreading the ends across his scalp. The woman tweaks his cheek.

"Bubsy, don't fret. You look just fine."

"And I feel even finer." He sniffs and smiles. "I was only half alive until I met you."

Lola sweetens her coffee, shakes her head. How many times has she seen this particular grift—the old Heartbreaker.

Most Tormentas have plied it at least once in their careers. Perhaps they may invest it with a little variation, but in essence it remains the same: raise the target's hopes beyond reason, then dash them at a time designed to deliver maximum shame and pain.

And for this guy, tonight is the big night.

✦

There is no moon, which serves her well. Lola takes up position in the shadows of the parking lot. She watches as Bubsy's battered Saturn pulls up.

She knows the plan.

Bubsy will go into the café first, where his family has gathered. He will then deliver the wondrous words of introduction to his bride-to-be. Their devotion may seem sudden and, to some eyes, unlikely. But they are in love. And with every reassurance to his incredulous family that this woman is sincere, he will sow the seeds of his own imminent humiliation.

Love Muffin will be alone in the parking lot, waiting for her cue.

Lola checks her weapons belt, pulls it tight, ready to take out her target before those cute kitten heels hit the tarmac.

The engine is killed and the headlights dim. Bubsy squeezes from the driver's door. As he waddles round the car, he sweeps his hair forward, tugs down his shirt. Then turns back into the open passenger door.

"You sure you want to do it like this, honey? We could just walk in together. They're gonna love you, I promise."

Love Muffin smiles coyly from beneath her curls. "You've never brought a girl to your family before. I want this to be special. I want you to tell them how much in love we are."

He strokes her cheek and his voice catches and cracks. "Didn't think a day worth living till I met you."

She tenderly collects his hand and returns it to his side. "Go along now."

"I hate to leave you."

"Honey, we got the rest of our lives together."

Bubsy wipes a cuff across his nose, sniffs happily. "Yeah, you're right. Till death do us part, eh?"

Then his face twitches as a thought stings. "Speaking of which, you got the gun in the glove box, right?" His eyes scoot about the desolate parking lot. "I don't like to think of you out here alone."

"I'll be fine. Nothing's gonna happen to me in five minutes. But yes." She flips open the compartment. "It's right here. Loaded and ready. You happy now?"

He looks about the darkness one more time. "Never can tell what's out there. Always plan ahead, I say."

In the shadows, Lola exhales hard.

Plan ahead. Right.

It's only because Lola kinda likes this fat-boy fool that she's put so much thought into this hit.

If Lola makes the kill here, the cops may find evidence of murder and Bubsy may just cap himself from grief. So instead, she's gonna render Love Muffin inactive, take her and the car away to another secure location, and finish it there. That way, for at least the first few days, Bubsy can think that his lovebird has merely flown the coop. Nerves. Cold feet. But she'll be back.

Sure he'll hurt, but he'll have friends and family around. With luck, he'll get over it.

And if he doesn't?

That's life. She can do no more.

Lola pulls on her gloves, flexes her fingers, the leather creaking. She slides her eyes from the shadows, watching him waddle toward the café. He turns back for one last wave.

And Lola finds her eyes drawn to his face.

Not his face… his eyes. The look in his eyes. That heaving emotion.

And something ignites, exploding across Lola's brain.

A spasm grips her. Forcing her to the ground. Her arms lash about her head as blinding pain erupts. But in her mind, a memory blazes.

A man. Long dark hair. Eyes so blue. Gazing at her with that same yearning. That desire.

That love.

His mouth, so close. Whispering words amid kisses.

"I am not who I was, Lola."

 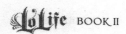

His hands on her breasts, his arms tight about her. Her body surrendering. Rising up, as—

A voice shouts loud, "Miss, you all right miss?"

Her eyes bolt wide.

She doesn't know how long she's been out. It is a sheriff's boot that rouses her from the tarmac. The parking lot is strobing with blue lights.

"A nasty sight, fo'sure. Guess you just fainted plain away. How's them legs now? Can you get up for me?"

Lola slowly rises, breathes deep. Looks around. Yellow crime-scene tape flutters about Bubsy's car. His body lolls from the passenger side, his bald-spot problem permanently cured, as the back of his skull lies somewhere across the pavement.

The sheriff raises his palm, shielding her view. "Best not to look. All very sad. Some kinda Romeo and Juliet heartbreak, far as we can figure. But he did it himself, we know that. His gun, his hand. So don't you worry now."

The deputy glances about the parking lot. "There ain't no gun-crazy on the loose. You're safe to go on your way. Quite safe."

But Lola is already gone, striding into the darkness. Thudding her fist against her treacherous brain.

The memories are coming back, like a cancer.

And now they are affecting her ability to do her duty.

She has never before lost a human. But now, in the space of a few days, she barely saved the drama student and now this— the mark is dead and the Tormenta has fed.

Lola flips up the collar of her coat. She's gonna get this head of hers taken care of. Fan Fan Bohica can do whatever it takes, pull her frontal lobe outta her nose with a coat hanger if she has to.

She is better, stronger… not knowing.

Lola thrusts her hands in her pockets, turns a corner at speed. And flies hard against the wall as a metal pipe smashes into the back of her skull.

30

A HAND MOVES up Lola's thigh, forcing her hips to the ground. She feels her spine arch sharply, but not in resistance—in blind compliance. Her head rolls, her neck extending as a heavy breath rushes against her skin. Her mouth releases a groan that rises from the pit of her stomach. Her face twists again. Finding the chill of a stone floor, she...

...snaps hard into consciousness, bolting upright. She is alone. It was a memory.

Her eyes rapidly adjust to the gloom. She appears to be in the crypt of a church. She attempts to look about her but her head throbs at the first twist. She lifts her hand to explore the back of her skull, to find her wrist jerked to a halt just a foot from the floor. It is bound by a rope that's attached to... something. She can't see what. The light source illuminating the wall suddenly moves, swinging from side to side. It comes from a lantern, and the movement suggests that whoever holds it is approaching.

A figure arrives above her, thrown into silhouette by the low-held lamp. Lola shields her eyes with her free hand.

"Who are you?"

The voice is cracked and low. "Are you prepared to listen?"

"That wasn't my question."

The lantern lowers further still, the glass now hot against her face. "Are you prepared to listen?"

Lola sinks back against the wall, her body relaxing. Then, with a roar, she lurches forward, loading her full weight behind a raging punch that wrenches at whatever bolts the rope. Feels metal give with a groan. Punches outward again, the rope cutting deep into her skin. But this time, the tension holds.

She shrieks and thrashes a third time. Blood flies. She remains tethered.

Sinks back down, jaw tight. "I'm listening."

The lantern retracts, shrouding Lola once more in darkness. But she feels the figure come closer.

"The Sinestra released me on a mission, but I walk the world on a cause of my own."

Lola's eyes narrow. "Okay, now I'm really listening."

The lantern rises, illuminating a face scored heavily with scars.

"My name is Judas Iscariot. But you knew me—knew *of* me—as Hunter 666A."

Lola nods, smiles darkly. "Yeah, that's right. You refused to quarter with the rest of the Hunters. I kinda respected that." She grins now. "The weirdo in the Megiddo."

Her smile drops at the rush of a blade. Judas lunges, metal flashing, slicing deep…

…across the ropes that bind her wrists. The coil falls to the floor and Lola slumps back against the wall, exhaling hard. She rolls her wrists, feeling the blood seep back into her fingers.

"Thank you."

Her hands jolt as a book is dropped into them. The purpose of her release is now clear. She gathers up the small red volume,

twisting it back and forth, looking for a title. And as the lantern is swung close to give her light, the spine glitters. Embossed in gold leaf are three words: *Fuga di Spino.*

She moves to open the cover, but a growl from Judas halts her. "You do not know how to read."

Lola cocks her head. "Yeah, I kinda *do.*"

"With your eyes, perhaps. But not with your heart. And your heart must be open, or a book will deliver just words yet no meaning."

"Meaning what?"

"That first, you must listen." The light bathes the book in her lap.

"A *Fuga* is a diary kept by those who are in flight from persecution. It often represents a last chance to record the creed that condemned them. When all is lost and capture is nigh, the *Fuga* will be left in trusted hands. This is the *Fuga* of Brother Spino. He left it in my care. Because it holds his lasts words on the Moera and the Mosca."

"The what... and the *what*?"

The lantern rises and slides onto a nail in the wall. As Judas lowers himself onto a stool beside her, Lola sees him entirely. She recognizes the bite of many blades and the puckered kiss of bullets. But across his torso, like the surface of the moon, are strange, cratered wounds. Some ancient, some fresh. But all of them, she is certain, self-inflicted.

Judas drags the stool closer.

"I will tell it to you, just as it was told to me. In simple terms. But then you must read." His finger thuds against the book. "So you can fully understand."

He closes his eyes, as if taking himself back to the moment when he first heard these words.

"The Mosca is the dark messiah of legend, whose coming will unite all Tormenta. The Moera is the defender of humanity. If the Mosca rises, so must the Moera. But the Moera can only rise when three become one."

Lola sits in a moment of silence. "And that's your idea of keeping it simple?"

"You have questions?"

"Always."

Judas rolls a hand, encouraging the first.

"Tormenta screw the system all the time. And they don't have any kinda messiah making them do it. So I don't see what difference it will make if this Mosca rises. What's one more dick at an orgy?"

"Such disrespect!"

"Just my kinda simple."

Judas clenches one hand into a fist. Wraps it in the other and grinds it slowly, milling particles of patience. Then, with immense control, he speaks.

"Tormenta are lone creatures, highly competitive. Fighting for each other's hunting ground. This internal competition keeps them fragmented as a force. If a leader were to rise, with a promise of domination, Tormenta might unite. And with this army at his command, the Mosca could deliver on that promise."

Lola nods slowly, jaw tight. "Mankind wouldn't stand a chance."

"Not without the protection of the Moera." He raises the *Fuga*. "Brother Spino's recorded the portents of its coming. And how

 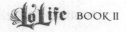

we can protect it, become its guardian and hold it safe until"—he leans in close, his voice low—"the three become one."

"Meaning what?"

Now Judas leans back, a dark smile spreading. "Ah, the *meaning*." His eyes gaze into the darkness. "If words are flesh and bone, then meaning is spirit."

Lola snaps her fingers. "Hey, Jude-dude, feels like we're at the city limits of simple again. Turn around and run it past me one more time."

Judas grunts, stiffening his spine. Then nods. "You are right. It is important you understand this, though Brother Spino barely grasped it himself. He had just begun deciphering this phrase when he was forced to flee. But in his *Fuga*, I read his attempt at interpretation."

Judas gathers up a length of rope from the floor. "When we are born into our human selves, we have one life. When our span is taken, we enter a second state, part human, part Tormenta." He folds the rope in two and twists the lengths together. "What, then, if we were to find the Tormenta who holds our original span and—somehow—claim it back. Would we not then enter a third state?"

Judas bends the rope a third time, twisting the three lengths into a single thick pillar. "Stronger and stronger. Three, becoming one."

Lola's eyes lock upon the rope and she feels her mouth form words. "The greatness of three…"

Judas looks up, eyes narrowing. "What did you say?"

Lola shakes her head as if freeing her mind from its own grip. "It's… I think it's something that I read. Something I remember."

"It is the meaning of Trismegistus." A voice comes from the darkness. "You have read his works. Well, well! I am impressed."

A hooded shadow shuffles forward, arriving before Lola and uncurling a hand from within a long sleeve. The flesh is withered from the bone. The hand hangs unshaken.

The old monk acknowledges Lola's refusal with a nod. "Of course, my bad manners. You wish to know who offers you welcome."

He lowers his hood. "My name is Brother Jolusa. I belong to the Chiro Scuro."

The shaven head beneath is pulpy with black and purple rot. He smoothes a last shred of hair across his scalp and settles into a thronelike chair that Judas sweeps beneath him.

"I apologize for my appearance." He wipes a hand across his muddy habit as if that were the thing that offends. "As a brother-hood, we rarely venture forth. But these are serious times."

His eyes then rise like embers and land upon Lola's face. Burning deep.

"We appreciate that we are asking you to absorb a vast amount of information. But time is short. And our enemy is strong." A gray fluid, like ashes in milk, bubbles at the corner of his mouth. "I should perhaps say 'enemies,' as the Legion of Gehenna number many. And their sworn duty is to awaken Tormenta, not only in the hope that they will find the Mosca, but to ensure than when he rises, his army is vast."

He lifts his left hand. This one is sheathed in a glove. The fingers wrap about a rose-colored cross that hangs at his neck.

"The calling of the Chiro Scuro is to counteract the Legion.

 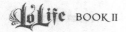

We must therefore guard the Moera. But before we can guard it, we must find in which body it will rise. No easy task, but one in which Judas has miraculously succeeded."

Brother Jolusa reaches out like a proud father, stroking the bowed head before him. "He followed the instructions in the *Fuga*, looking for the signs and portents, gathering information from all quarters, heavenly and human. And by these means, after many longs years of searching, he discovered Agnus Day."

Judas suddenly jerks up his head, eyes alive. "It is he! I am certain of it!"

Brother Jolusa twitches his gloved hand, silencing this interruption. The glove then continues upward, dabbing the drool that drips from his chin.

"And thanks to his relentless searching, not only do we know *what* Agnus is, we know *where* he is. Locked inside a penitentiary called Morphic Fields, where he awaits execution. Now, this should present no real obstacle to our accessing him because the Brotherhood has under its command a powerful agency—SCURO."

His mouth twitches, not in a smile. Something other. "Ah, SCURO! Our public face. Our eyes and ears and, inevitably, our fists, when action is required. But over the centuries, SCURO has lost remembrance of its sacred origins. Increasingly it behaves as a secular agency. One that still professes to serve our holy order but that all too often questions its orders."

He sinks back into his throne. "Judas went to the head of SCURO. The illustrious Agent Bex. And he told Agent Bex that he had found the body in which the Moera was about to rise.

He asked for SCURO's intervention to get Agnus Day released. One call from Agent Bex could have effected that. SCURO is empowered by the Brotherhood's lofty connections within the ranks of human governance. But Agent Bex failed to hear his higher calling... and did not make that call. He agreed only to conduct his own investigation into Agnus Day. If he should find sufficient proof, he would act."

Brother Jolusa jerks forward, his mouth tight as an anus. "I ask you, where was this agent's faith? Was he so far fallen that he should demand proof! Faith is belief in the absence of proof!" He sinks back. A smile rises. "But Bex was not prepared to listen. So what use were those ears of his?"

His smile lets laughter escape, like smoke beneath a door. "So you know what Judas did? He pulled his knife and in two strokes he sliced those ears clean off Agent Bex's head."

The laughter erupts into a roar. "One, two, one, two, and through and through!"

The old monk claps a hand upon his thigh, throwing back his rotten head and bellowing with delight. Until his eyes catch Judas. His head is held by hands that quiver and clench.

Brother Jolusa swallows his last guffaw. "A vile act, of course, for which Judas immediately repented."

Judas grunts, his voice low. "I found a church and I fell to my knees."

"And there I found him. In the White Lily of the Trinity, that little church beside the old soap factory." Jolusa turns to Lola. "Perhaps you know it?"

She shakes her head and Brother Jolusa smiles. "Of course you don't. One such as you, so young, so lithe and healthy." His

 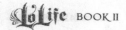

baggy eyes linger on her body. "The Lily of the Trinity is famed as a place of holy cure. I went there seeking a miracle—and found Judas. A miracle indeed."

His gloved hands dabs his chin, careful not to dislodge the rotten flesh that still clings. "Judas told me of his discovery and of what had come to pass with Agent Bex. I assured him that I would help. I would insist that SCURO offer more than just a promise to investigate Agnus Day. I would make Agent Bex take action."

Jolusa taps his gloved fingers against the arm of his throne. "But that course of action is no longer open to us. Because Agent Bex is dead."

Lola snaps her head up, eyes locked on the monk now as he struggles to his feet.

"And as a consequence, action falls to us." Yellow eyes sink down to Lola. "And to you."

"Me?"

"Judas and I must go to Morphic Fields and effect the release of Agnus Day. You must halt the Legion of Gehenna."

"At the risk of repeating myself… *me*?"

Brother Jolusa signals to Judas. "Restore her weapons to her." Then he turns with a flash of black teeth. "You will not face the Legion in its entirety—although from what I hear, a Hunter such as you would relish those odds. By tradition, the Legion selects one from their number to seek and awaken the Mosca. It is deemed quite the honor. So you find that glorious G-Man and finish him before he completes his task."

"You know who the G-Man is?"

"We are certain of it." Jolusa shuffles close. Lola shrinks

from the warm, wet stench. "It is the deceiver, the duplicitous defector. It is Dali."

Lola feels her fists instinctively clench. "You're wrong."

"We expected some resistance. You and Dali were close. Like father and daughter."

"Like Hunter and Handler."

"He favored you. And yet you weren't the best."

"He must have thought I was good enough."

"I don't think it was your goodness that appealed to him. Quite the opposite."

Now Judas appears at her side, whispering hard against her ear. "For centuries, a Hunter has not broken ranks. And then you go rogue. Strange, indeed. Then, stranger still, Hunter 696B departs. But this is what intrigues us the most: Hunter 696B is a far more fearsome predator than you, and yet the High Command of the Sinestra devote all their attention to *your* loss. Because even the High Command suspect that Dali played a part in it."

"He played no part."

Judas smiles. "Still so loyal!"

Lola thins her lips, each word cracking with the precision of a whip. "He. Played. No. Part."

"And yet he is deeply involved with your retrieval."

He thuds a mission file against her chest. "My orders to kill you. Signed by Dali."

Lola grabs the file, throws it to the floor. Judas tenses, eyes wild as he lurches forward. But Brother Jolusa raises his gloved hand, halting him.

"From the moment Dali offered to shield our holy books,

 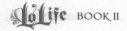

there were those within the Chiro Scuro who suspected him. We believed he had a secret motive. He was looking for information. Some gobbet, deciphered from our texts, that would allow him to predict the Mosca's rise."

Brother Jolusa rolls up his hood, turns to Judas. "Did you not hear me? I said *return her weapons*."

His gloved hand jerks and Judas reaches into the shadows. He pulls out a belted cache of guns and knives. Slings it to the floor. The old monk turns, and although the hood masks his eyes, Lola can feel them upon her. Like thumbs, pushing down.

"Who knows how long you have, child? By leaving the Sinestra, you condemned yourself to live off just your last dose of span. Unless you had the forethought to bring a supply with you?"

The head within the hood cocks, awaiting an answer. Then slowly shakes when none comes.

"So, then, the clock is ticking. Put whatever time you have remaining to good use. Serve the cause of righteousness and deliver us from Dali."

Judas offers his arm for support as the old monk shuffles toward the door, one final question slipping free.

"Ask yourself this, child. What do you really know of him?"

And then the door creaks. And they are gone.

Lola stands alone, her weapons about her. The *Fuga* splayed on the floor. And the door open.

She could just take her guns and leave. Or take her guns, shoot the old man and maybe even the Judas dude—and leave. That sounded all right.

Or she could take a moment. And think things through. It has always been her weakness that she acts first, thinks later.

Ah, chère, *those trigger wits of yours…*

Lola grunts, something close to a laugh. Maybe the old man is right. What the fuck does she know of Dali?

What can she remember?

She closes her eyes, summoning an image of Dali's long face. But the image is hazy. Her memories of the Sinestra had not been touched by Fan Fan. But, just as the removal of a tumor can damage the surrounding tissue, Fan Fan's treatment had caused her to lose many memories of Dali and her time in the Hypogeum.

And what she does remember is random, snatched… dreamlike. She's like Alice in *Through the Looking-Glass.*

Off with his head! says the Queen of Hearts.

Dali always carried a pack of playing cards with the gold insignia of the Sinestra upon the reverse: two long keys, stood back to back with their teeth turned out, the two loops together like eyes. A skull is what Lola always saw. And she saw this design every day. It was painted on every door along the corridor where the Hunters had their quarters. Identical doors, stretching down the Kingsway, like a pack of cards laid out in a game of solitaire.

She had counted the occupied quarters once in a moment of idleness, and, by coincidence, there were fifty-two Hunters then in service. Their rooms are simple, almost monastic. But the food is good and the Sinestra provide meticulous medical care. And the confines of the rooms matter little. Most Hunters spend their days in the training arena, constantly sharpening their fight skills. Knowing that their Tormenta foe will be doing the same.

But as Lola walks that corridor, with the occasional Hunter lifting his head to glance at who passes, she knows what

controls their loyalty. Their hatred of Tormenta makes them fight, but what keeps them obediently returning to the Sinestra for the rest of their lives—is life itself.

As long as they serve, they will be served span. And their lives will be infinite.

And while the life of a Hunter may be hard, the Sinestra presents a better proposition than many of the other Lo'World divisions where misfits such as they—neither dead nor alive—endure for eternity.

Lola continues along the corridor toward a staircase that spirals down to the training arena. The metal shudders under the heavy boots of Hunters that descend in silence.

Lola looks down at her own feet. They are bare. She wiggles her filthy toes.

Maybe train later.

That's the thing about forever. There's always later.

She swerves left past the staircase and toward a giant set of doors at the end of the corridor. The gold-scripted sign above the arch reads ARCHIVUM.

✦

A pair of snakeskin boots stride down the dull vinyl floors of the Hypogeum. The heels are spurred with rowels made from spinning hearts. Although as they spin and invert, they look more like spades.

The boots enter the Archivum and halt by the head archivist's front desk. The hairless little man raises his head and stokes his welcome with as much fury as the rule of silence will allow.

Dali smiles and nods, aware of what provokes his irritation. Follows the archivist's laser gaze to a table in the center.

It holds a pile of books, stacked high on all three sides like a barricade. The ancient gold text on each spine reads *Collegio Romano*.

From behind the books comes the rhythmic buzz of earbuds and the occasional involuntary half-sung phrase. Dali reaches across and withdraws a stack, revealing a pair of bare feet, perched on the table.

Lola sits behind, a book open on her lap, tapping a pencil to the bass line. She smiles as she sees Dali and pops out her buds.

"Hey, Père D."

Dali glances back toward the archivist, who ogles them above his spectacles.

"He doesn't like you playing music."

Lola exhales and punches off her player.

"He doesn't like you marking the books."

Lola lays down her pencil.

"He doesn't like... you."

Lola gasps, faking horror.

Dali patiently clasps his hands behind his back. "Yo' could make yourself more popular by adherin' to the simplest rules. For example, keeping to your appointed collection time."

He produces a glass vial that shimmers with a blue liquid. "Word reached me yo' forgot your dose."

Lola takes the vial, uncorks it, and downs the span in one gulp. Dali nods, satisfied. "I'd be most grateful if yo' could remember to attend. My duties don't include room service."

Lola returns the vial to him. "You know Père D, the fact

 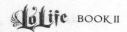

that I forget should make you happy."

"And yet I feel no such elation."

Lola leans forward, pressing home her point. "First thing most Hunters do on their return is claim their span, because that's what keeps them coming back. The fact that I forget must mean that I'm just happy to be here."

Dali runs a hand down the pillar of books. "And always right here." His fingertip taps the top book. "What are yo' looking for, *chère*?"

Lola shrugs, leans back. "Maybe nothing... maybe everything." She thuds the huge book in her lap shut. The cover's title reads *Codex Gigas*. "Don't you think a Hunter should exercise her mind?"

"She should tend her wounds." Dali points to a recent scar at the cusp of her left breast. It has an unhealthy yellowish tinge. "That looks odd."

"Next mission I'll take a bullet to the other one and make them even." Lola tugs down her vest, making her point but revealing more skin than Dali finds comfortable. He twists his head away, masking the movement with an averted cough.

Then snatches up another topic. "I also hear that yo' have been absent from training."

Lola rises now. Leans deep across the table. "With the greatest respect, so what?" Leans deeper still, their faces almost touching.

"I've never failed on a hit. I'm as fast as I need to be."

Dali holds her gaze. They are chin to chin. "Confidence close to arrogance."

"Which one are you?"

Her eyes bolt open, the dream vanishing. She has been asleep. The deadweight of her arm upon which her head is slumped suggests that she's been out for hours. But something roused her. A sound that comes again and louder now. A noise she knows too well—the rasp of metal on bone.

Her hands whip about her body and, clad with weapons, she exits the crypt into the catacombs beyond. The low tunnel, as if blown like an instrument, delivers a dreadful sound. Heavy sobbing.

Gun drawn, Lola pursues the sound, to discover in an alcove the heaving form of Brother Jolusa, hunched over the body of Judas. His breath comes in sharp jags as if he is performing some muscular task. At the sound of her approach, his hood swivels round and he gathers Judas to him. The naked torso is wrought with wounds. Brother Jolusa inhales and sobs again.

Lola sinks to Judas's side. His skin is still warm, but he is dead. The weapon still impales his heart. With a quivering hand, Brother Jolusa pulls it clear.

It is Dali's clave.

Teeth gritted with grief, he thrusts it before Lola. "You know this device! *Is it not proof enough?*"

But Lola's focus is not on the clave. It is on the hand that clenches it. The old monk's glove has been removed, revealing a contorted claw, twisted not from disease but an ancient burn. Jolusa hurriedly drops the clave and sinks his limb once more into the leather. Then gathers Judas into his lap, stroking his hair.

"Dali's name was once Tret. And our name defines our destiny. Dali was ever the traitor!"

His eyes flash beneath his hood, finding Lola. Burning deep.

Lola nods. Slings her rifle across her back and exits into the dark night.

31

THE BACKSEAT OF the Ford Tahoe smells of cinnamon and vanilla. Mo'Zart has had time enough to enjoy this sweetness. His face, slicked with sweat, has been stuck to the leather for over six hours.

Donuts. Someone sat here and ate donuts.

And there's a whiff of coffee. *Damn, I'd love a hot, black—*

He winces hard and fingers subtly rise to explore the back of his skull. It oozes blood like jam. An hour before, a similar blast of pain had brought him back to consciousness. But he's keeping his wakeful state to himself. Until he can remember what happened at the Treble Belly diner and how he ended up in this car. And whether the two cops up front intend to help him—or harm him. So for now, he's going to keep his busted head down.

A man's voice comes from the driver's seat. "How much farther?"

Bianco lolls on the passenger side, her seat reclined. "Not far."

"I haven't seen one sign for Swamp Gravy."

"It's a hideaway. Thus, it's hard to find."

The Tahoe rolls to a halt at a fork in the road. Two dirt trails wiggle away through the heavy undergrowth.

"Which way?"

 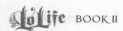

"That way." Bianco jerks a hand to the left. Siggurson wrenches the wheel, churning mud as Bianco suddenly throws her hand to the right. "No, other way."

Siggurson stabs the brake, kinks an eyebrow.

Bianco shrugs. "Didn't I just say—it's hard to find? And most times I'm driving. Kinda automatic pilot. And o' course most times I'm not distracted by a bomb site where my biceps used to be." She points to a wound on her arm, crudely choked by a necktie.

The Tahoe swings to the right and Mo'Zart lurches across the backseat. He knows who these cops are; it was his job to set up the briefing session. They are hard-core homicide detectives, both with reputations for getting results. He's read their history. So he knows that he had better fill in the gaps of his own recent past—and fast.

He remembers arriving at the Treble Belly diner... spying those blonde dreads in the back booth. He sits with her, takes a gulp of the coffee that she has waiting for him. It tastes weird, kinda like cherries. Then he remembers talking and talking— and then a blast of pain.

He grits his jaw, bracing himself against the back of the seat as the road turns rocky and the chassis bucks and bounces.

Siggurson grips the wheel like a bronco rider. Glances at Bianco, who clamps a hand to her wound.

"Still raw?"

"Like sushi."

Siggurson turns his eyes back to the road. It's fast churning into mud. In the distance, across the bayou, is a lone hut on chicken-leg stilts.

"This is where we're going, Baba Yaga's shack?" He shakes his head. "I'm trusting you on this."

"You made the decision not to call for backup at the factory. The right decision. But from that moment, we pulled ourselves off the radar and now we have to stay that way. At least until we know who ordered that strike and who the intended target was."

"But that gives us a few days at most. Then your chief and mine are going to start asking questions about where we are."

Bianco shakes her head and smiles. "Ah, young Skywalker, you have so much to learn."

She reclines back in the seat. "SCURO will have tied that off before you even got the summons. As far as your chief knows, you've been on a special operation. Too high up for him to have clearance. No information on when you'll be back... *if* you'll be back."

Siggurson turns in his seat now to face her. "All right, Einstein, so you gonna tell me how you know so much about SCURO?"

Bianco rests her head against the cool of the window, feeling that familiar bayou heat rise on her neck, sink down her thighs. She shifts on the leather.

"I could tell you a whole lotta things, Bambi. But better that you ask Lola."

"Who's Lola?"

She jerks her head toward the cabin. "When we get there, you can make that your first question."

"And what about him?" Siggurson glances at the body of the cadet in the backseat. "He may wear a SCURO badge, but his

 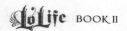

key let the killer in. You think he knows anything?"

"He doesn't know how to keep his mouth shut, that's for sure. But I'd say she loosened him up."

"He was drugged?"

Bianco sniffs the air hard. "You're not getting that? Pentothal oxide. Smells like cherry pie. One dose and this little virgin woulda told her anything."

"I don't think so." Siggurson shakes his head. "Pentothal oxide leaves crystal deposits at the corner of the mouth."

Bianco hikes herself around to get a better look at the inert face on the leather. "I see crystals."

"That's cane sugar."

"It's Pentothal crystals. I smoked you in chemistry class, remember that?"

"I remember what sugar looks like."

"All right, so you want me to taste his face, 'coz I will. I will taste that kid's face."

The cadet launches upward, suddenly wide-awake. "She's right—she's right. Detective Bianco is right. There was something in my coffee. Tasted like cherries."

Bianco blips a "told you" at Siggurson, then turns her eyes to the backseat. "Kid, you got instant likability. What's your name?"

✦

Fan Fan crinkles her eyes, filtering the sun. Stares down the narrow slip of road as a car slowly approaches, sliding to a halt beside her.

Yellow hair swoops low. Fan Fan leans deep into the

passenger window, her gaze going straight past Bianco to lock on Siggurson.

"He's pretty."

"He's a cop."

"He's a pretty cop. And you're a pretty cop. Now ain't that somethin'?"

Bianco grimaces and moves to exit. The old woman still hovers at the door.

"Fan Fan, may I?"

"*Chère,* if you don't, I sure will." The old woman cackles, her smile just for Siggurson. Until she sees Mo'Zart shuffle out of the back door.

Her eyes sweep up and down his scrawny frame, then she throws a question over her shoulder to Bianco. "Your lunch got a name?"

"That's SCURO Agent Mo'Zart. We're keeping him on ice. In case we need him." Bianco unhooks the rope of the raft, ready to make the drift across the bayou. Glances up toward Lola's cabin.

"She around?"

Fan Fan appears behind her. "No, child. She's been gone fo' a while."

Bianco tightens her grip about the rope in her hands. "She'll be all right. She always is." Looks up to see Siggurson arrive beside her. She tosses him the punt pole. "I'm guessing you'll be great at this."

Minutes later, Fan Fan is leading the way in her own boat, rippling across the soft waters as dusk descends. In the raft behind, Bianco and Mo'Zart sit on either side of Siggurson, who slowly punts.

 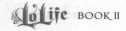

Bianco loosens the necktie about her arm, probing the wound. "So, skipper, with Lola gone, I'm gonna have to do my best to make you understand this weird new world you just walked into. And you, kid..." She jerks her head at Mo'Zart. "You gotta back me up, because it takes some very powerful persuasion to grip a human mind and make it open... make it listen to truths beyond imagining."

Siggurson lets the pole trail in the water. Looks at Bianco. "So what made you listen?"

"Big fat gun."

Siggurson smiles. "Well, I've got nowhere else to go. And not much else to believe in. So let's start."

Mo'Zart cautiously raises a hand.

Bianco shrugs. "What's that, a bathroom request?"

"I was just... just going to suggest that maybe we start with the incident that brought Detective Siggurson to SCURO's attention."

"You read my report, kid. You already know why I was there."

Bianco leans forward. "Maybe he does. But I don't. And I just might find it interesting."

Siggurson nods and looks out at the bayou as if searching for the right place to begin.

"There was a psychiatrist, a woman, Dr. Jellowitz. She was hired by the commissioner to counsel officers who suffer trauma on duty. Who maybe feel guilty that they failed to save a victim, or maybe they shot and killed the wrong person. The stats on uniform suicides are rising."

Bianco leans forward, instantly hooked.

"But there was something not right about Dr. Jellowitz. I

couldn't put my finger on it. Nothing specific. Just that—the questions she asked, the way she probed… as if her intention was to drive the hurt deeper."

He pauses—then punts the pole harder.

"So I decide to do some digging on her. Find out her background. And I come up with nothing. The only information I can get is that since she started acting as the precinct psychiatrist, the suicide rate has gone up. Two officers in ten months. So I tell this to the chief. But he blows it off. And nothing changes. She's still practicing. Then one night, by chance, I see her out in the parking lot of a bar. And I confront her. 'Who are you, lady? Because my gut says you're no healer.' And she answers my gut pretty directly, with this hammer blow. Next thing I know, I am fighting a woman. Which goes against everything I am, but on this occasion she's turning what I am into pulp, and unless I fight back, she's going to kill me. She had such a fist on her… and speed. Unbelievable. Then she whacked me hard in the back of the skull and I fell."

Siggurson pulls the raft to a halt alongside the cabin. "I made a report. And a few months later, I get the call from SCURO."

Mo'Zart claps his hands on his thighs, his confidence thawing. "SCURO had their suspicions about Jellowitz. And you confirmed it."

Siggurson bends to tether the raft. "So—who was she?"

As he rises, Mo'Zart tentatively swings an arm about Siggurson's shoulder "Dude, let me tell you a lil' somethin' about women like her."

✦

 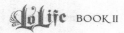

Five long hours later, Siggurson lies awake on the porch swing. A small, floral quilt suggests that this has been turned into his bed for the night. From one end of the frame, a lamp dangles. But Siggurson's eyes, deep in thought, are set on the glitter of stars above. Inside his skull, his brain sparks with an explosion of new information. A fresh vision of the world, broken and reset. He shifts a hand behind his head like a pillow, staring out into space.

That one question we've all asked—are there other beings out there? Suddenly it is answered. *Yes, there are other life forms. But they're not out there. They are right here. Walking amongst us. Looking like us, acting like us, silently planning.*

Patiently waiting.

Bianco and Mo'Zart had given him a moment to absorb the existence of Tormenta. Sitting around the fire, empty bottles of Old Artemis glowing with reflected flames, he knew they were being patient. Probably remembering how they had reacted when they first heard.

Siggurson's response was to shoot off a magazine of questions.

"So Tormenta live for centuries and they don't decay. But their bones must show age under the microscope. That means if a Tormenta's body were ever found and a pathologist got hold of it, the bones would show the body to be unnaturally old. They'd be exposed."

Mo'Zart had fielded this one, leaning back. "Sometimes Tormenta do make mistakes; they fail to feed and they die. And sometimes Hunters neglect to properly dispose of a body after a kill. But for all the times that this has occurred, it has never exposed the existence of Tormenta. Because neither the Sinestra nor SCURO wants that. Mankind is to be protected. Tell humans the truth and they may try to fight back themselves, which would mean inevitable defeat. So if a Tormenta body falls into human hands, that event will be concealed."

Bianco, stripped down to her vest, is dousing her wounded arm with the liquor. "That was how I first got hooked into this. I was investigating the homicide of a club owner called Gina Avner. She was a Tormenta—not that I knew—plying this goth girl death-is-beautiful grift. Teenagers fall like plums if you squeeze them right. And Gina was good. Then she turns up dead in my precinct morgue and the pathologist laughs as he shows me the bone report. The lovely Gina is one hundred and ninety years old. Now back then, that result struck me as pretty funny too. And I'm thinking, 'Damn this case is getting weirder and weirder,' because just a few months before we'd had a report of a suicide in Gina's club. A girl called Maddy Pool. But when we got there, no Maddy. No body at all—just a carbon burn ring on the floor. So I make my report and next thing I know my chief tells me SCURO's taking over the investigation and I'm to keep this"—she twitches her nose—"clean and clear out of it. Then I get the summons to the debrief and I'm smelling the lilies."

"So you're telling me no one has ever retained evidence of them?"

Bianco shrugged. "Tormenta know what they're doing. They're good. They never stay long in any one place because a grift can only play for a while before it starts to draw attention, like you sniffing out Dr. Jello-tits."

"They have to keep moving, like sharks." Mo'Zart uncorked a fresh bottle, offered it to Siggurson. "If they hang around, not only would their grift grow old, but people would start to notice that they don't age."

He twirled a finger through his dreads as if unwinding this information directly from his brain.

"They are born into human bodies and, just like the rest of us, that body can dictate what you do in life. Let's say you're a Tormenta and you find yourself in the body of a pretty little girl. The smart thing may be to hit fifteen and stick. Because there's a bunch of grifts that are gonna work for you—the Little Lolita, the Heartbreaker, the Jump-a-Juvie—"

"The what—?"

"It's a popular one. You seduce a nice family man, then drop the bomb that you're underage. That turns a momentary lapse into statutory rape. Just add whiskey and a gun and most times—you got span. Or let me give you another example. You're a Tormenta, prone to fat, not so fine looking. You might decide that a little gray at the temples and some senior swagger will generate the best grifts for you. So you let your body age until you reach just the right amount of reassuring seniority. Then you can ply something like the Gimme-All-You-Got grift. You hide yourself in society as an investment broker and wait until a nice rich client entrusts you with his fortune. You keep him happy with some fake paper profits for a while and then, when you need your next hit of span, you pull the plug and he loses everything. Most rich folks would rather eat a bullet than starve in the gutter. So, boom—span. I could go on, but you get the picture."

"So if they keep taking span—let's say more than they need just to live—can they get younger again?"

Mo'Zart shook his head. "No. But they'd sure like that capability. There's much about their bodies they don't understand—just like we don't understand how cancer happens or why belly fat sticks. And, like us, Tormenta are always trying to figure out ways to evolve and become even better. But so far, they don't know how to use span to reverse the aging process."

"But they do know about spandex." Bianco chucked her empty bottle on the pile.

"What?"

Mo'Zart turned to Siggurson. "She means spanDX. This is, I guess you could say, a form of synthetic span."

"Which would be needed to feed the Hunters. Because they are part Tormenta."

"Bang on, Bambi, my man. You're gettin' this fast!" Mo'Zart rolled a gappy smile. "All right, so listen to this. The Sinestra labored long and hard to develop an extract of span that could be used, kinda like fuel, to top up a Hunter's tank. They tried many formulas, working under the project code name Dextra—kind of an opposite play on Sinestra, I guess. And finally, the tenth formulation worked. And span Dextra Ten became spanDX."

Bianco raised her bottle with a smile. "Spandex: It stretches your life."

Mo'Zart looked at Siggurson. "You've known her a while. Was she always this funny?"

"No, it's a new symptom."

Bianco ignored them, pressing on. "You know what my first

 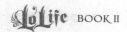

question was? How come Tormenta don't just get together, overwhelm humanity, and set us up like farm animals. Then they can just milk us for span. Forget all about their grifts and take the easy route. It's like us having to persuade a cow to die so we can get the meat, instead of just smashing its skull."

Siggurson nodded. "Smart question. And the answer is—?"

"Kinda scary." Mo'Zart grinned and then fell strangely silent. His eyes lowered to the last of his liquor as he swirled it round the bottle, in no hurry to deliver this final revelation. Then he stiffened his spine, sank his drink, and continued.

"Like I told you, Tormenta are sharks. They hunt alone. And they defend their territory against other Tormenta who may try to come in and feed in their waters. This competition and distrust amongst them has hindered them from ever operating in unison. But if a Tormenta were to rise with the power to unite them, to show them how different the world would be if they worked as one force… then everything would change. And mankind would be finished."

Mo'Zart looked up now, mouth tight. "The book I was translating—the *Kata*. It predicts that this Tormenta will rise and lead his kind to domination. A messiah called the Mosca."

✦

"Hey, those flies are gonna bite ya."

Siggurson jerks awake, almost falling off the swing. Bianco stands above him, pointing to the lantern. It swarms with insects.

She reaches out and kills the flame, plunging the porch into darkness. Just the moon illuminates them now.

Siggurson hoists himself up onto his elbow. "You can't sleep?"

"This kinda stings." She tweaks her arm, now bound in clean cotton.

"Let me see it." He beckons her closer.

"Big feet. Big hands. You don't look so gentle." Siggurson smiles.

"Trust me."

Bianco lowers herself onto the quilt, unwraps her wound. With careful fingers, Siggurson probes the tender split. "The tissue has a lot of previous scar damage. You been caught here before?"

Bianco winces. "Maybe. I don't remember." She feels him probe deeper. Grits her teeth to talk. "So anyway, Doctor, I got a question. How come you knew about that other doctor, the psychiatrist?"

"I was referred to her for therapy."

Bianco jolts. Not from pain this time, but surprise. Her voice stays cool. "You were seeing a shrink?"

"Chief made it mandatory. To check my 'emotional stasis.'"

Bianco silently suffers the discomfort of him rebinding the wound. Feels she can't make a sound, in case a question escapes. But as Siggurson ties the last knot, he takes her shoulders and turns her toward him, knowing what she is burning to ask.

"When my mother was shot, I was with her. The bullet passed through her body, impacted my head and lodged inside my skull. The doctors told my father that the best option—the only option—was to leave the bullet in there. It may not move. It may stay in one place forever. In which case—I will live."

"And if it does move?"

"Then I'm dead."

Bianco looks away, his calm unsettling her.

"But then why become a cop? Why do a job that gets your head cracked every goddamn day? Why not do something quiet, work in a library, in a bookstore..."

"And what—die a little every day?" Siggurson shakes his head, smiles. "I'd rather live myself to death."

His finger traces a scar down her neck. And then slides to her shoulder where another old wound still leaves its bite.

"You're not so very different. Throwing yourself into the front line, every time. You've fought every sort of psycho."

"But you've fought a Tormenta, with no preparation at all. That's pretty impressive." She feels the heat of his eyes upon her. "I haven't—not yet." Swallows hard, forcing a laugh. "So I guess once again, you've gotten there first, Agent Siggurson."

His hand is still on her shoulder. The touch is light, but to Bianco it feels as if gravity is sucking his skin into hers. She makes her mouth speak. "So, tell me about it. What was it like?"

"I don't remember much. It was so fast. Unreal. I'd never seen anyone move like that. Like her limbs were on fire. And when she hit me, the force of it... But then I landed a blow. Just here." His hand touches Bianco's sternum. "And I felt her skin. Just for a split second. But it was warm, soft. Then she threw me back. I hit a wall. She thought I was knocked out. She let her guard down, just for a moment. But I took it. Pulled my piece and got a shot off. I saw it draw blood from her, just here..."

His hand now on the curve of Bianco's neck.

She shivers at his touch. Breathes deep. "Then what happened?"

"She spun me round"—his fingers trail down to Bianco's breast, circles its soft cusp—"and she hit me."

Bianco's voice is just a whisper. "Where?"

"Just here." Siggurson takes her hand and places it on his cheek.

"And then?" Bianco leans in deep, mouth open.

Siggurson descends. "I fell."

32

LORD CHANCELLOR VASSAGO lurks in the shadows. His back is against a set of iron doors that shudder and boom.

Although he has never passed into the room behind, he knows what lies there. Huge cylinders that drive the Helix Vivat.

The carved sign above the doors declares the room the Ingenium. Vassago has previously pondered this rich and ancient term. The word *engine* shares the same stem as the word *ingenious*, and appropriately so. Just as an engine pumps away, so a mind will churn ideas.

Vassago's fingers idle by the lock. The only key to the Ingenium is under Dali's charge.

Ah, Dali, what pistons of ingenuity pump and plot within your mind? Why do you spend so long in the Helix Vivat chamber?

Though this question may tantalize, it does not trouble Vassago. A mere trifle compared to the greater question he has concerning Dali: What madness caused Dali to first betray the Legion of Gehenna?

Vassago would never forget that fateful day, one summer in 1857.

He and Dali had been bestowed the greatest honor by the Legion—the task to seek out and awaken the Mosca. For the first time in centuries, the Legion had succeeded in finding a human vessel ahead of the Sinestra. The sign had been clear. An explosion had occurred at a munitions plant called Harris Cox. The factory sign blazed bright in the flames, burned down to the last length, which now just read s cox. And among the staggering, blackened victims caught in the blast, walked a small boy. He dragged a burning toy in his hand, a wooden puppet of a bird—a stork. At the sight of it, Vassago had gasped in excitement—without doubt, the harbinger Scox.

Dali gathers the child and, with Vassago at his side, bears him away to a quiet spot and raises his clave above the boy's chest.

Then he pauses—hearing the distant, distraught shrieks of the child's mother, searching for her boy. Before Vassago can stop him, Dali ushers the child up, slapping his legs hard to propel him out of the darkness and toward his mother, who gathers him up with wrenching sobs.

Vassago stares at Dali, aghast. "You have condemned us both!"

Their defection to the Sinestra was the only path now open to them. Despite an instinctive reluctance to absorb these one-time enemies, the High Command of the Sinestra knew that their inside knowledge of the Legion of Gehenna would prove invaluable.

Vassago shivers as if waking from a dream. His eyes flash wide. Then narrow to slits as they glimpse a shadow, moving between the pipes of the Helix Vivat.

Vassago slides into the light. Coughs discreetly, then—"Dali?"

The familiar lean silhouette emerges, buttoning his jacket. "Vassago."

"During office hours, I'd prefer you to use my title."

 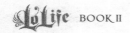

"O' course, Lord Chancellor."

Vassago never tires of the strum of those words across his heart. The many painful years spent in Dali's shadow now just a distant memory.

He would like to think that his promotion is testament to his greater qualities. But deep down Vassago knows the truth; Dali's brilliance always will outshine his own. It is only the quirks and foibles exhibited since he joined the Sinestra that have made Dali unsuitable for promotion. It was struggle enough for the rank and file of the Sinestra to accept the admission of two Tormenta. But they had no alternative. They needed these defectors if they were ever to get an answer to the question that plagues them: Who are the Legion of Gehenna and what is their true purpose?

The actions of the Legion run counter to Tormenta behavior. As a species, the demons are loners and ferociously territorial. They do not welcome the arrival of other Tormenta on their patch. And yet the Legion quests tirelessly to awaken more and more of them.

Vassago's instinct was to immediately divulge everything to the Sinestra, so great was his desperation to find sanctuary. The Legion were no doubt already in their pursuit. But Dali, of course, kept his heels cool. He assured full disclosure, in time. And promised that when they understood what credo drove the Legion, they would find both him and Vassago endlessly valuable—and eternally grateful.

And so the years had passed with Dali keeping himself to himself and Vassago slowly, surely rising up the ladder, surpassing his former master.

Oh, unsurpassable joy!

He casually strolls forward, allowing his hand to trail along the giant banks of oscilloscopes that map every pulse of the Spanorama. He watches for Dali's quake of displeasure. Vassago knows how Dali hates anyone to touch his beloved machine.

"Why do I find you here, Dali?"

"Perhaps because yo' are looking."

Vassago taps one of the green, flashing scopes. "And what are *you* looking for?"

Dali's eyes go to the glass gauges that dance green, like emeralds alive. "I find it beautiful."

"To the untrained eye, I do agree it is a mesmerizing miasma. Each pulse and wave crashing to the next. But what might the trained eye see?"

Vassago leans in deep toward one scope. The green light bathes his face, giving him a deathly pallor. "Do you recall, in our former lives, when we were so misguided and misruled... our doctrine was quite contrary, even in the smallest detail, to that of the Sinestra. For example, in the Legion we were told that span does hold a memory of its former self. And this being so, it would theoretically be possible to track one particular skein of span and follow its arrival into human form. You recall that lesson, do you not, Dali?"

Vassago waits for a response. Dali smoothes his lapels, turning smartly.

"I recall my lessons in grammar, and rhetorical questions do not require an answer."

Dali moves to walk on but Vassago sidesteps before him, blocking his path.

 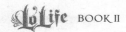

"But my real question is this: What do you believe, Dali? Given time, could this machine track one skein of span all the way through to the human realm?"

"With patience, all is possible. And now, Lord Chancellor, I have a question of my own. What is your intent in coming here?"

Vassago rolls his neck like a goose. "Intent? That strikes too harshly. I come in hope." He jerks a smile. "You and I, we are the same, Dali. We should be allies, not enemies."

"You are my enemy? I am most grateful fo' that clarification."

Vassago stiffens. Forcing his smile wider. "Ah, how we joust, we two!" Leans forward, pulling Dali close to him in a cold embrace. "You can trust me." Grasps him tighter still. "For we two are one."

Something in Dali's body pulses. Like an unsheathing knife, he pulls himself from Vassago's embrace.

In insolent silence he exits.

Vassago feels spittle gathering in the corners of his mouth. Swallows it down, squeezing a calm expression across his face. Turns to the shadow who appears behind him.

"I think my point is made, sir. He defies the *Manifestum*, which clearly states that span has no memory of itself. He is, for want of a better word, a heretic. And a dangerous heretic. For he can be searching for only one measure of span—and you and I both know what that is."

A head of white hair appears. The height and extravagance of the wig reveal that this is the Commander General of the Sinestra. He walks forward, hands clasped tight behind his back. "Increase the surveillance. If he makes a move…" The

Commander General hesitates, as if the evidence before him somehow jars with his gut instincts.

"I am authorized to act?" Vassago keenly completes the order.

Silently, the Commander General nods.

33

A MATCH SPARKS, then drops into a glass ashtray. A sheet of paper catches alight, curling tight in the flame.

Words written in thick ink cover the paper, but the fire gnaws at every edge. The opening line is already gone. The following sentence is consumed up to:

...the police case notes, discovered three years ago by Judas. These documents suggest that the root of Agnus Day's madness lay in the fact that he never grieved for his daughter. Instead, he threw himself into his study of telomeres. When he could not break the link between immortality and cancer, he grew steadily mad. It was at this time that he began to believe that he was seeing the ghost of his daughter. The image of a young girl would appear at his window, sometimes leaving messages written in the condensation of the glass.

Every message says the same: that he must take his own life and join her.

All evidence in his laboratory suggested that he obeyed this ghostly command. But no corpse was found, just a carbon ring. This is because the "ghost" at his window was an artful Tormenta called Jezebeth Hooger. She saw the opportunity to exploit the loss of his daughter and taunt this wretched man to suicide. One fateful night, she waited in the shadows for him to place the noose around his neck.

But Jezebeth was inexperienced. She knew the dangers of snatching a span too soon, but all the same, she lost patience as his body twitched and spasmed. Her haste meant that he was delivered to the Sinestra and was returned to Earth as a Hunter.

For years he performed his duties well. No longer the frail man he had been, he stood strong and fearsome. His only weakness was the memory of his daughter. No amount of mental training at the hands of the Sinestra could erase her memory. But the Hunter did a good job of keeping his pain hidden—leading his Handlers to believe he was done with his human past.

Then one day, in a filthy skin joint, he sees a girl, dancing in a cage. She looks so much like his daughter—his heart pounds. He drinks heavily, eyes locked upon her swaying body. He doesn't know what animal urge is driving him—grief, lust, anger—but he slides money across the bar, enough to buy her for the night. The girl is Jezebeth.

She's plying her new grift, seducing men and then exposing her tender age. She's had success with quite a few family guys, God-fearing salesmen and the like, who'll eat a bullet in a parking lot sooner than face a charge of statutory rape.

Jezebeth doesn't recognize the man who buys her that particular night. But it is done—a Hunter and its original Tormenta are reunited.

The result was the madness of Agnus and the murder of Jezebeth. Bloody and brutal and most bizarre. For when they found her carved-up corpse, it bore a prophecy, written in blood and ink. An account of the end of mankind.

And so it is with much excitement and deep trepidation that I conclude the greatest mystery perhaps is solved. This forbidden union is the first incredible step toward—

Flames gust upward, snatching the last words away, crackling them to ash. A silhouette relaxes back behind a desk. Reaches for a deck of cards. Shuffles slowly.

Fascinating. Perfectly fascinating...

A card is selected from the center of the pack. Laid face up on the desk. The ace of hearts.

What are the chances!

A long finger strokes the gold edge of the card. This chance is real. And so close. The chance to infinitely change this world and the next, forever.

And so...

It is time to leave the Hypogeum.

In truth, he quite enjoyed his last perambulation. The pomegranate martini was surprisingly good. So he will walk abroad again.

Not walk, actually. He will ride. And in some style.

Humans may be pitiful, but for their invention of the automobile, they deserve praise.

Particularly for the grace and might of the Mercedes Maybach.

A marvelous machine.

34

A HAND NUDGES it back up. The cap is too big. Maybe because she's a woman. And maybe because the cap was made for her father. Mercedes Toolan comes from a long line of drivers. Her father named her after his favorite manufacturer and probably set her destiny there and then to be a driver. But she loves her job. Even on nights like this.

She tips the cap back once again, hauling the car off road.

This wasteland is known as the Wrips. An abandoned dockside where whores heave up and down like whalers. As Mercedes steers half a million dollars' worth of car between the derelict warehouses, all the security advice from her Toolan forebears comes to the fore of her minds. She knows the drill. Headlights off. Vehicle tracking on. Isolate just the near-side back window as operational. The rest of the vehicle goes on lockdown.

A knuckle raps on the glass partition behind her. Mercedes jerks, thrown from her thoughts.

For chrissakes, who knocks on the glass anymore?

This is a fully tricked-out Mercedes Maybach with a voice-activated intercom system. Where has this dude been for the last twenty years? She had thought there was something odd about the way he dressed. Kinda... *English*. No, weirder than English. More like—

 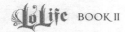

A second rap, harder this time. Mercedes squashes the brake, bringing the car to a smooth halt. Her gloved hand depresses the intercom.

"Anything you require, sir?"

She knows he can hear her. The sound of his breathing issues from the speakers. But nothing more.

Mercedes mutters, releasing the button. "Suit yourself, Mr. Strange Suit."

She looks at the shuffling buffet of whores on offer. Grandpops always said you could tell more about a man from his choice of whore than his choice of suit. Mercedes cracks a smile.

Then this guy must be something south of evil.

Her cap slips down but this time as she tilts it up, her eyes bolt wide. Someone—*something*—is hobbling from the darkness, heading toward the car. And the opening back door signals that the person approaches at her client's request. It looks like a woman, long skirt flapping. A tattered goatskin bag slung across hunched shoulders. But as the figure nears, Mercedes can see no face, just yellow eyes. But she is sure now it's a man. No, weirder than that.

It's a monk!

She feels the door thud shut behind and waits for the rap on the glass, signaling her to drive on. None comes. But a chill strikes. Creeping up the back of her neck. *Something don't smell right about this. And Pops always said, "Listen to your nose.*

"And look with your ears."

Mercedes presses the intercom button. The client switch has been disabled. First thing any chauffeur tweaks. The client thinks he has set it to privacy, but the driver can override.

Mercedes has done this many times before, she likes to think always with good reason. But never has she heard a conversation such as this.

It begins with a long rattle of breath. Then a voice comes, cracked with age. Must be the monk.

"Good... good evening, sir. We meet again."

There is no response. Another haul of breath. "Have you perhaps had time to digest the report I sent on Agnus Day? I wrote every word, exactly as Judas told it to me."

Silence, just the creak of leather. The old man presses on.

"And this evening I can report more progress, sir. The rogue Hunter, 101A—she has been turned to good effect. She now believes that Dali is the traitor and is bent on his destruction. And Judas is dead." A grunted laugh. "The famous fearsome Hunter, slain by an old man such as I! Proof indeed that misplaced trust cuts closer than a razor."

A rasping silence.

"Is there anything more you require, sir?"

A response comes, in the form of clicking fingers. Some kind of command.

"Ah yes, I did not forget. You were very clear that I must return it." The whisper of metal, withdrawn from fabric.

"Might I ask how you acquired it without being detected?"

Again, no response. Just the chink of glass as the drinks cabinet is opened and a bottle is removed.

"You are most generous, sir. Most generous."

The door clunks and then comes the sound of feet, departing.

Mercedes looks in her side mirror to see the hunched old monk shuffling fast across the Wrips.

What in God's name was all that about?

And what object had the old man returned to her client? She had heard the sound of something long and metallic, withdrawn from inside his robes.

A gun. He's given him a goddamn gun!

Mercedes sits rigid, picturing the back of her head like a pumpkin conveniently placed at arm's length for smashing.

The silence in the car never sounded so loud. Then—

TAK! TAK!

Her head flies forward, jolted by the sound of the knuckles on glass. Mercedes obeys the order, eases the gas and pulls away.

✦

In the back of the Maybach, the client sits in virtual darkness. A row of white teeth places the face in the center of the long leather seat. The amount of exposed enamel reveals the client to be smiling.

And the laugh that ensues has a signature hiss.

For this is Vassago.

And this is his plan, coming together tremendously well. A campaign of keen complexity. Hardly the work of an "imbecile"!

His smile snaps down to a grimace. That was the word that Dali had chosen to describe him, when reporting to the Legion on Vassago's first disastrous attempt at an awakening.

He had been working as Dali's apprentice for some time and seen him perform the ritual frequently. The day came when Dali deemed him able to perform his own. A girl-child had been found, ripe and ready. Dali had stood back as Vassago pulled his clave and sank it into the girl's chest. He waited for the awakening to begin, but instead the girl began to writhe and squirm. A madness came upon her and she rose up flailing wildly. Screaming and pounding her head against the wall as if bent of self-destruction. It was too late when Dali yanked the clave from her chest. She fell dead. And Vassago's clave hung from Dali's fingers. Only then did Vassago see the truth.

The clave was not his.

He had fallen prey to an ancient trick, wrought upon him by the Chiro Scuro. These wretched monks would forge false claves, bless them with holy water, and then plant them in place of the real thing. The Brotherhood's name, meaning "hidden hand," came in part from their need to remain in the shadows of the Church. But there was another, darker practice behind the name. As men of God, they could not kill with their own hands. But neither could they passively stand by when their powers of detection alerted them to the imminent awakening of another Tormenta. So the monks trained themselves, with a fanatical zeal, to be wondrous fingersmiths. The Legion member would feel no more than the brush of a shoulder in a crowd and the deed would be done—a false clave supplanted. As this device would ultimately be wielded by some other hand, the monks would have committed no sin.

A victim of this tactic, Vassago was accused of negligence, and in disciplining him, Dali spared him not at all.

Now Vassago would show a similar rigor. Dali would be ridiculed, routed, and ripped apart. And what pleased Vassago most: This would be ensured by the same trickery that had trapped him. At their last encounter, when Vassago had spontaneously embraced Dali, he had switched the clave. Vassago's nimble fingers had been well prepared. Hour upon hour of practice had culminated some weeks before in a successful rehearsal, in which Vassago had supplanted Dali's favorite deck of cards with an identical pack. Dali neither felt the subtle switch nor, as the days went by, seemed to notice that the cards were not his own.

And every game of solitaire that Vassago played thereafter, twisting Dali's cards between his fingers, fed his confidence that Dali's clave would easily follow.

Vassago strokes the clave that rests on the leather. His plan is now to return to the Sinestra with this bloody instrument and news of Judas's death. What further evidence of Dali's treachery could they need?

And with all suspicion focused on Dali, Vassago can quietly set about the next stage of his plan. To subtly place himself close to the Moera—and wait. For the Mosca will come, drawn irresistibly to its counterpoise. Then Vassago will watch keenly for the sign of Scox to finally determine in which human vessel the Mosca resides.

Vassago will then awaken him and return to the ranks of the Legion—a hero!

The city lights glitter through the tinted glass. His gloved hand presses a button on the control panel and the glass partition slides down.

Mercedes flashes her eyes up to the rearview mirror.

"Anything I can get you, sir?" In the reflection, she sees his finger gesture for her to pull over. The Maybach rolls to a halt. The partition remains lowered. Mercedes understands that she should, as a courtesy, face her client. And she is indeed curious to see his face. And yet…

Her spine seems to fight against her, resisting the twist. So she must force herself around. And in the darkness cast by the tinted windows, she can see no face. But her eyes go to a long, metal shaft on the seat. She tenses, then exhales, seeing now that it is not a gun. Just a large, keylike device.

She pumps a smile.

"You know, sir, you've still got another hour."

He says nothing. And she feels that same chill seep down her neck.

"Perhaps there's somewhere you'd like to go?"

Her cap slides down. She nudges it up, forcing a laugh. "I gotta small head."

She doesn't even see the gun. And the silencer means that nobody hears it. Just a sharp *TAK! TAK!*

Vassago slides it back inside his jacket. Looks at what's left of Mercedes's head.

Real small now.

35

BROTHER JOLUSA FEELS a splash of rain. A storm is coming. He hikes his robes to speed away across the Wrips, weaving between the whores, his hood pulled low. The girls grab at this monk, just as they would any john.

Thunder booms. His speed increases.

But still one whore follows him, proving particularly persistent. Perhaps she has noticed that he clutches something tight within his hand and assumes it to be valuable.

To her it would be worthless. But to him, it is everything.

Life itself!

He slides a blue glass vial into his goatskin bag, buckling it tight. How many lives has he betrayed in its pursuit?

He feels the girl closing in. Quickens his pace.

His breathing rasps. He cannot delay. He needs the span! He glances down at his hand. The flesh is now so rotted that the rising wind can shear it from his bone. He must find some dark corner, escape this girl's attentions and immediately imbibe.

He swerves into a warehouse. An old earth-moving machine is rusted with its claw outstretched, as if offering concealment. The old man shuffles within its giant embrace. Throws back his hood and hurriedly uncorks the glass vial. Raises his fleshless fist, ready to chug it. Then… The vial is snatched away. Jolusa shrieks, twisting his head to see who assails him. From the darkness steps the girl. She lashes a hand about the old man's plashy neck, pinning him to the wall as his gloved hand desperately flails, trying to reach the vial that she holds a taunting distance from him.

Her face lunges forward. It is Lola.

She sweeps her lips close to his ear. "One word exposed you, old man. *Traitor.*" Her grip tightens. "How could you know that Dali's name was once Tret?"

Sputum oozes from Jolusa's mouth like juice from a squeezed orange as Lola presses on. "Y'see, Brother Juicy, ol' Père D didn't share much. And he certainly did not share with many. So there is no good way that you could come by that information. But he told me things. And here's one pearl from the wise man: Never trust a priest who keeps his hand hidden. I think some holy man taught him that lesson the hard way. And I think that was you."

Rain plummets through the roof, striking Jolusa's hairless head, mulching the flesh into a putrid gravy that trickles down his crown. "Now, I'm guessing that you trade secrets for span. The good news is, I'm in the market to buy. Bad news is, life just got cheap. So I'm gonna need all the secrets you got."

Jolusa gurgles his agreement. Lola loosens her grip just enough.

He draws breath. "I am in the service of the Legion of Gehenna. Six months ago, one of their members commissioned me—"

"No, no old man. We're going way back, right to the day

when you first met Dali. I want to know everything." Lola thrusts his head hard against the wall. "And you better hope I believe you." She slides the vial inside her belt.

"Hunter, I can give you proof." His eyes urgently dart to his goatskin bag. "If you permit me…"

Lola nods but keeps a careful hold as his hand sinks inside the bag and emerges with a letter. The paper is so old, it frays at the creases. She recognizes the meticulous script as Dali's. But the words? Could the same cold hand she knew so well, the one that withdraws at the most accidental of touches, be the same that penned this passionate appeal?

Rosa, my beloved!

I have been gone from you so long, you must think me dead. And in truth, I am. My heart died the moment I left you, and though I might still breathe and my body perform this physical charade, I exist not. Life without you is worse than any death.

I must tell you now what came to pass the night when you were last mine.

Our kiss sealed a promise. That I would leave and make my fortune, so that your family might accept me. All I asked in return was that you meet me again. The day you turned twenty-one, you would go to the Church of Our Lady's Tears on the corner of Parliament Square. I promised to be there, to claim you as my bride.

But how could I know that just moments after we exchanged this vow, I would fall and my heart impale upon the Romeo spikes below your window?

My life ended, Rosa.

But a new life began. One in which I was forced to immerse myself, driven by one sole desire—to forget you, my love.

The pain of separation was unbearable and never lessened. For so many years, I hid my sorrow until an inevitable catastrophe occurred, one that overturned my world.

You will understand better when you have read what became of me, but here I will say just this: I was ordered to commit an act that would unleash a lasting war against mankind.

But I refused.

Not from pity—I cared little for mankind. What stayed my hand was my love for you, Rosa. All humanity would suffer from my action, so I saved the world—solely to spare you.

I wanted you to live to see your twenty-first birthday. For in my heart, an idea had taken root. If you had ever truly loved me, you would keep to our avowed reunion.

With no word from me for so many years, you would have every reason to believe that I had forsaken you. But if you loved me as I loved you, then your heart would compel you to come to the church.

And so, I came and hid myself amongst the shadows. I could not let you see me. How could I ever account for the monster I had become?

I waited all day, in such exquisite agony. Feeling dusk fall behind the church windows. And then, as the last of the day disappeared, I saw you. Your face was veiled but I did not need my eyes. My half-corrupted heart sang out to you as you looked about the church, searching for me. I heard you whisper my name. And I felt your sorrow as you stood there, utterly alone—as you so believed.

 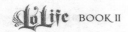

My heart raged. Every muscle in my body yearned to reach out, to touch you and say—I am alive! I am here! I kept my promise!

But then you were gone, stopping only to kiss the gloved hand of the old priest who stood by the door.

I decided in that moment to write you this letter and entrust it to that priest, so that he might pass it on to you when you next come to church.

Read on. For in the pages that follow, I have described all that I was and all that I have become. And I implore you, once you have this understanding, to ask yourself one question—can you still love me?

If the answer is yes, my dearest, then send me word by this priest. And we shall be together once more, and this time, for eternity.

For eternity is what my new life offers. I will begin my account with this wondrous element, so you might see how

Lola turns the page over. Nothing. There is no more.

Her grip tightens, posing her question so clearly, she need say nothing. The old monk squirms, the rain making him slippery in her fist. "I no longer have the rest of the letter. I burned it. It was just an explanation of his Tormenta awakening, his days in the Legion, his defection—all events of which you know, nothing more."

"No doubt he paid you handsomely to deliver this letter. And you betrayed him."

"I wanted no part of this lovers' subterfuge. But then he produced a purse and yes, I did begin to warm to the role, a lovers' go-between. And perhaps I would have even performed my duty. But the girl killed herself just hours after coming to the church, owing to a broken heart, or so I heard. So I kept the letter, useless now, and opened it. This was no sin, as I was no priest. I had been defrocked long ago. Had Dali seen my hand, he would perhaps have guessed."

Jolusa raises his scorched claw. "The Jesuits are brutal." His eyes fix upon it. "But I deserved this discipline. My life was one of sin."

The old man's eyes suddenly narrow with half-remembered glee. "Can you imagine, then, my elation when I read Dali's explanation of span? The ultimate elixir! With span, I could live my life over and forestall my assured destiny in hell. And so, using the information supplied within the letter, I sought out the Legion of Gehenna and struck a deal. I gave them proof of the traitor Dali's whereabouts and in return, they supplied me with span."

The happy recollection of this smart barter rouses a chuckle, cut short by Lola's fist, which indicates she finds nothing funny. Jolusa resumes his story with a straining inhalation.

"The Legion demanded that whilst I persist in living, I serve their cause. I was directed to infiltrate the Brotherhood of Chiro Scuro and report back on their activities. And so, under the name Brother Jolusa, I began my life of espionage. With much success. Even Judas was an easy dupe."

He crinkles a smile. "Turns out I lie real good."

Another boom of thunder delivers a torrent of rain, roaring through the roof. Lola shouts to be heard above the gale that rises. "Who were you meeting tonight?"

"I don't know." Jolusa's eyeballs bulge, her fist closing. "That is the truth! I have never seen his face."

A slice of his own rotted face falls away, pounded from his skull by the torrential rain. Jolusa shrieks.

"I die!" His clawed hand grasps at Lola's coat, imploring. "My span!" He can see the blue glass vial, tucked into her belt. "I must have it! Give me my span!"

Lola does not release her grip. She watches with cool fascination as the rain strips the remaining skin from his face, a long-delayed death at last devouring him.

The last of his lips wash away with the words "I trusted you!"

"Guess I lie better."

36

DALI'S BOOTS APPROACH the doors of the Ingenium. The iron booms and shudders, like bone plates that cage a raging heart. His hand withdraws a long key, cranks the lock, and eases one weighty door aside. He enters a chamber that heaves and pumps with four cylinders, conjoined by a vascular mass of wires. The noise is deafening but Dali seems oblivious. A pressing purpose urges him on and he turns sideways to slip between a slew of pistons, arriving at another door, this one is so low it could be easily missed, the opening key so minute that one might think it merely winds a clock.

Dali has no time to waste and enters quickly. The tunnel that lies beyond the door is tight and dark and he has to bend and shuffle to enter it. The walls are laden with dials and gauges that extend into the darkness. These machines do not form part of the Helix Vivat. They are the fossilized remains of the old telecommunication system that once occupied the Kingsway. In its day, it represented the cutting edge of human technology. When Dali first discovered it, he was full of admiration for the system's ambition. And he found himself musing upon how far human telecommunications have come since those early days. He'd heard that modern governments could listen into every mobile telephone conversation taking place across the entire globe. And by taking just a snippet of a conversation and feeding it into a computer, they can track down one voice from the cellular roar of billions.

Perhaps this had been his inspiration. For the thought would not leave him.

Somewhere in that vast expanse of span was the measure that once belonged to his beloved Rosa. What would he give to find that span! To watch it arrive once again in human form... to feel that she was alive.

Not that he would make an approach. That was never his purpose. He just wants to feel that somewhere, in the temple of another body, Rosa still waits for him.

This thought—idle at first, then compelling—proved potent. And he found himself pondering on how small a fragment of voice was needed by the human computer to tune into one person. Could he not then find a fragment of Rosa, isolate its frequency, and then tune the oscilloscopes of the Helix Vivat to search for her span?

But here his hatchling plan halted. For what did he have of Rosa? What fragment of her could he conjure that might provide her frequency?

All he had of Rosa were his memories.

And then one night—a breakthrough. He was in the Archivum making a small amendment to one of the books of the Collegio Romano. It was a biography of Brother Magen and it mentioned that he often drank an alcoholic distillation called artemisia. The biographer called it a poisonous brew and even suggested that it might be the cause of their master's hallucinations. Dali felt compelled to add a footnote. He wanted to point out that

Artemisia is the scientific name of the wormwood herb and therefore the drink referred to was probably no more than absinthe. A heady liquor but unlikely to engender the vast and violent visions that plagued Brother Magen.

As he made this footnote, a memory sparked in Dali's mind. He was transported back to his early days in Louisiana, when he was just a boy, sailing on the trader ships. As part of his initiation into the crew, he was taken to a filthy strip of New Orleans known as the Artemisian Quarter. On every corner stood an absinthe house. The plan was to find him a whore. But young Tret's curious eye was drawn to the other dark doorways of the quarter—the mambo parlors. Inside a sailor could find a cure for every pox or ill. But Tret heard tell of one cure offered by these women that struck him as exceedingly strange. And yet, many a sailor requested it. It was the removal of their memory. Leaving in their wake their loves as their duty pulled them from port to port—what a sailor wanted was to forget. To have every memory of the face they loved cut from their minds. And the old mambos, skilled in this craft, would—for a bottle of artemisia—happily oblige, sometimes carving entire decades from a man's mind. On the walls of the parlors hung hundreds of poppets, little dolls sewn up from skin. Tret heard tell that each poppet held a man's memories, keeping them safe lest he should one day want them returned. The curious boy had asked if a man had ever come back to reclaim his past. But his sailor comrades gave him no answer, instead shouting down this sour talk, keen as they were to return to their task of Tret's initiation.

Dali never forgot this mambo magic, and it instilled in him

 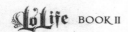

a firm belief that memories are made of matter. They are as much a part of our bodies as blood and bone.

And as he mused upon this, the idea struck him. Hard and wonderfully sharp.

If Rosa existed in his memory, then a sample of her as real as blood could be summoned forth from his own mind.

Which is why tonight, as every other night, Dali comes to this secret tunnel and places, with painful precision, a series of deep needles into his skull.

The needles are soldered in bulbous lumps to wires that have clearly been stripped from elsewhere. These connect, via heavy brass jack plugs, to the back of an oscilloscope extracted from the Helix Vivat.

The pulsing green signal jumps as the last plug clunks into place. And Dali grimaces, feeling the first jolt of the needles. A thread of blood runs down his scalp. The ready kerchief that Dali wields suggests that this is suffered often.

And then he exhales and closes his eyes. Silently mouthing her name as he searches for her in his memory. And, upon finding her, he smiles. And opens his eyes, locking them like missiles on the scope. Watching as the green light sweeps round and round. Waiting for that particular fluctuation.

One day, Rosa, my love… One day…

37

"It's dead."

"It's not dead. It's asleep."

"Spiders don't sleep, stupid."

A stick pokes at a tangled black mass. It is stuck at the center of a web, strung between the iron legs of a park bench.

Lola shifts along the seat, giving the two little girls some space to conduct further experimentation. The girl who wields the stick is a snub-nosed golden cutie. Her playmate has raisin eyes, stuck in a little muffin face. She tries to take the stick from her blond friend, who prods at the web.

"Don't tease it. You'll kill it."

Cutie-Pie twists to Mini-Muffin. Lola sees the furious look delivered.

Kid, just leave it. Better she torments the spider than you, because she is bent on hurtin' something.

Too late. The stick lashes out.

"Spiders should die because they are ugly. Just like you." The stick misses, but the words hit their mark and Mini-Muffin struggles to her feet, her voice rising to a sob as she lumbers away.

Damn, I sure hope I was one of the cute crowd.

Lola has no recollection of growing up. Fan Fan took those childhood memories along with any clue as to why she left the

Sinestra. Lola doesn't know why it all had to go, but Fan Fan musta had her reasons. As far as Lola knows, her life began when she woke up in the Lo'World with Père D's old face smiling down at her like a gator.

Lola swings out her long legs. Runs a hand through her cropped blond hair.

Cutie camp. For sure.

She folds her arms, scans the park. Taps her boot. *They'll be here soon.*

Children tumble before her, a tornado of teasing, taunting, tears, and tantrums. Lola smiles and shakes her head. It's the one thing that always gives her pause for thought: She may hunt Tormenta to save mankind, but the truth is, your average vanilla human is still a pretty vicious creature.

Look at what they routinely inflict upon each other—they bully as children, persecute as adults, break hearts, wreck lives. Every damn thing that Tormenta do, except Tormenta have an excuse: They do it to survive. Humans do it… because they *can*.

So why? Why save mankind?

Père D always said it was a curse of her nature, to be constantly asking questions.

Chère, your chromosomes may be XX but you got a helluva big Y in there.

She pulls her coat about her, closing out the chill. She misses him. And she knows that if he did authorize her execution, he had his reasons. There is something more at play and she is going to find out what.

She looks at her watch. Scans the park one more time. *Where are these guys?*

She gave them very clear coordinates and she knows that they use state-of-the-art navigation systems. That's the kind of hardware you need if you're a reclusive brotherhood with ambitions to fight evil on a global scale. Rumor has it that the Chiro Scuro have disciples buried deep in every software giant from Seattle to Singapore.

Linked to the world by their own personal iGod.

Lola jolts as the bench bows beside her. Two men have sat down. They wear long gray coats, but their robes, a dull brown, are still visible below the hem. Their feet are sandaled and fallen leaves have gathered from their trudge across the park, wet and muddy, crammed beneath their toes.

The man closest to her reaches down to flick away the offending foliage. His fingers are brown and crinkled with age but the heavy gold rings wrapped about them suggest that great authority has accrued there with the years.

His voice rumbles. "Why here?"

Lola glances at the second figure, a younger monk who pulls his coat about him, eyes anxiously scanning the park.

"I know you guys don't like to… venture forth. Security risk and all that. But this kids' park—safest place I know. A mass of moms on the lookout for any kinda threat. I promise you, nothing weird gets in the playground. In fact, honestly, you guys are the weirdest thing here."

"Still your mouth!" The younger monk gawps with fury. "You must address Primus Pater Umberto with respect!"

The Primus Pater pauses from his delicate task of leaf removal to raise a silencing finger, then turns to Lola. "Our first duty is to God. So our place is within our monastery. It is

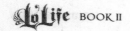

278 **LoLife** BOOK II

for this reason that SCURO was established, to operate in the outside world. To act 'in loco' on our behalf."

"Yeah, well, you wish."

Umberto thins his lips, tasting insolence, but Lola presses on. "You have one agent dead and a spy in your ranks. Or you did, until I got loco on his ass. So I think your boys at SCREW-U just found themselves way outta their league."

"You may be rogue, but I see you have lost none of that Sinestra charm."

"Yep, that shit sticks like tar."

Umberto gathers his hands in his lap. "The loss of Agent Bex is unfortunate. And that miscreant Jolusa is—"

"*Was*, thanks to me."

Umberto exhales, withdrawing his feet from an onslaught of muddy toddlers. "Can we please get to the point of this pleasure trip?"

Lola leans forward, voice low. "Judas tracked down a Hunter who he believed had reclaimed their span. If he's right, this could be the first sign of the Moera rising. And if the Moera is being summoned into existence... well, we know what that means."

"*We* know what that portends. But that you should have this knowledge is most—"

"Irrelevant right now." Lola sweeps her hand, moving on. "Judas was murdered, and in a Chiro Scuro safe-church. That tells me he was on to something. So I want to finish what he started. Find the Moera and keep it safe until the Mosca rises. Which means we act now."

"As you so propose in your report." He unfolds a tattered

napkin from a diner. It is inked with hurried notes. "An intriguing choice of paper."

"I was kinda short on time."

"But what intrigued me more was the detail of your information. For example, how was it that you found us with such speed?"

"I studied the books of the Collegio Romano. There's nothing about you guys that I don't know."

The younger monk leers, eyebrows arched. "You don't strike me as a scholar."

Lola lurches, eyes hard. "Would you prefer I strike you as a Hunter?"

Umberto thrusts a finger, commanding silence. Then his long yellow nail descends, poking the serviette. "This information. You say Judas was the source. And he was certain that this"—Umberto peers down at the scrawled notes—"this Agnus Day has passed into the third state."

Lola nods. "That's what he believes."

"Then if you are to act upon it, we will need to know your plan… your strategy. We must understand it, as that will determine what documents we provide you with—the right one, to meet your chosen cover story. So please, what is to be your approach?"

"Get into Morphic Fields. Get Agnus Day out."

"That's not a plan. That's a to-do list."

"All right, so how about you tell me what clearances you can get me and I'll just work with that."

Umberto smiles, his teeth tea-brown. "My dear, I don't think you quite understand." He pulls up the collar of his coat,

successfully shrouding all but the bulb of his old, shaven head. "There is no quarter of the globe that lies beyond our reach. We have access that exceeds that of every temporal investigative agency on Earth. Over the centuries, the wealth of our church has succeeded in ensuring that our followers reach the highest office in every field of politics, military, law enforcement."

"Kinda like the Masons?"

Umberto smiles, muttering within his collar, "Yes, that diversion has been most successful." His fingers click. "Brother Scarbo, the corroboration documents please."

The young monk pulls a large envelope from beneath his coat. Passes it to Umberto.

"These documents will get you access to the prison."

Umberto passes her the set of papers.

"Thereafter, as you seem keen to improvise, I refer you to the appendix page. If anyone questions your activities, ask them to call one of the names on this list and your authority to act will be corroborated."

Lola's eyes widen as she reads the names. "Man, when you say you have guys at the top..."

"At last, we impress you. You've no idea how much that means."

Now it is Lola's turn to flash her eyes at the old man's sarcasm. He smiles and sinks his hand into his sleeve, removing a final piece of paper. A ragged remnant, containing a dense extract of text.

"This I suggest you digest."

Lola takes the piece, examining its fragile state.

"We collected it from a source within the prison. It confirms that Agnus Day is plagued by visions and that these prophecies have a considerable hold over the inmates at Morphic Fields."

"So you believe that Judas is right?"

"Ah, my child, what I believe... Let us not venture there." His old hand rises, wafts. Dismissing her.

Lola stuffs the papers inside her coat and with a scout's salute she rises from the bench and departs across the park.

✦

Brother Scarbo watches her go, then leans in, his head respectfully bowed.

"Primus Pater, can she be trusted with such a mission? If what she says is true, that the Moera is rising, then that must mean—?"

"That the Mosca rises also." Umberto sinks deeper into his hood, muffling his voice. "Yes, my son. He comes to bring his dark dominion. But God will not forsake us."

Umberto conceals the last of his face. "The Moera will rise... must rise."

Brother Scarbo places his hands together, the prayerlike pose serving to quell a rising tremor. "But Primus Pater, is it not the sworn duty of the Chiro Scuro to always seek the Moera—to act as its guardian? How can we send a Hunter on such a quest, untested and alone?"

Umberto's eyes roll within the gloom of the hood, coming to rest like hot coals upon Brother Scarbo's pale face.

"She will not be alone, my son."

 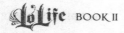

38

"YOU SURE it's dead?"

"Of course it's dead."

Mo'Zart nudges the charred creature about his plate. "So what you callin' this food?"

Bianco wipes her plate with a slice of bread. "With Fan Fan, you never know. She just pulls something outta the bayou and fries it to death. Mystery meals. Kinda Agatha Crispy."

Mo'Zart leans into a laptop that stands open by his plate. He vigorously stabs at the keys and his long dreads jiggle about the collar of a pink and yellow bowling shirt.

Bianco jabs her fork toward the shirt. "So what you calling that look?"

Mo'Zart doesn't take his eyes from the screen. "I guess when Siggurson threw me in the back of the car, he forgot my weekend bag."

He returns for a moment to his breakfast, chasing the meat with his fork. "Turns out I'm a bleeder. The suit was real messed up. So the old lady gave me this."

"Real tasteful."

Mo'Zart pauses, the fork hovering in front of his mouth. Then his nose twitches. "And what's that smell?" He twitches his nose closer to his plate.

"That's not breakfast, that breakdown. Decomp." Bianco leans back toward an open window. Peers out at the shallow waters below. "We need some pike to come by. Those things can rip through a corpse like a wood-chipper."

Mo'Zart balks. "You have a body out there?"

"Nope." Bianco swats her hand as a blowfly buzzes. "Whole bunch o' bodies. Bundled up like dust bunnies."

Mo'Zart shakes his head. "This place is 'ucked up to the *F.*" Chews on his last bite and tries to cut another.

Bianco watches him struggle. "Kinda bony, ain't it?" She leans back, nodding. "Yeah, pretty sure it's pike."

Mo'Zart blurts the mouthful back onto the plate, shoving it away. Wipes a sleeve across his mouth, then pulls the laptop toward him. "How old is this thing, like what—an Atari?" He lowers his ear toward a whirring sound. "Processor is full of bugs."

Bianco is stalking the room with a rolled-up newspaper, following the drone of the blowfly. "It's all we got here. But you're a bona fide brainiac, so you should be able to log on with a waffle iron, right? Keep trying."

The blowfly lands on the window frame. Bianco raises her arm. Then lowers her eyes to the porch outside. Siggurson sits on the steps. Beside him, carefully laid out, is a row of weapons. He examines each one. She watches his fingers deftly snap and slide one clip after another. And her body tenses, a visceral memory of his hands sliding down her belly.

Did last night mean anything to him?

Bianco mentally swats herself. *Think straight!* Siggurson has a bullet in his head. He's trained himself to live in this moment

and not think about the next. One night with her isn't going to smash down that wall.

KER-RESH! She wallops the paper against the wall, shattering a china plaque. The pieces fly high, then clatter to the floor.

The fly casually drones on.

Mo'Zart chirps from behind the screen. "You get it?"

Bianco bends to pick up one of the pieces, a multicolored fragment. She's seen this plaque a thousand times. The piece she holds is the beak of a hummingbird. The picture shows the bird with its wings spread wide, glittering like the rising sun. There is a Taino proverb underneath. Fan Fan has told her what it means. Bianco can't remember exactly how the old woman translated it, but she knows that it is an ancient warning of sorts, something about mortal dangers at sunrise.

And right now, it feels like it's giving her a warning: *What happens at night might not feel so smart in the morning.*

She jolts up as Siggurson strides in. "You got it?"

"I'm working on it." Mo'Zart hunches lower over the machine.

"How much longer?" Siggurson slides the magazine from a Luger.

Mo'Zart raises his hands above the screen. "Look at my fingers. They're cramping. You're asking me to go through every case that Gobis handled. That dude was old. He could have been a cop for thirty years."

"I'm guessing, thanks to you, he's retired with a bullet now." Siggurson clicks the magazine lock.

A chair scrapes back. Mo'Zart rises. Leans on the table, head low. "Is this how it's going to be?" His face rises from the mass of dreads. "I made a mistake. I let my dick do the thinking and that bitch outsmarted me with a cup of kooky coffee. But I am going to make that right. And you need me. Because you're looking for one homicide report, with no name and no date, and so only a brain like mine could find that with a deadbeat laptop and a connection so weak you might as well use voodoo for Wi-Fi. Maybe you should think on *that*."

A silence quivers, his declaration made.

Siggurson slides the Luger into his belt. "To get back to your original question, yes. This is how it's gonna be."

A sound comes, the slap of water, sending Siggurson's head jerking toward the window.

Bianco waves a dismissive hand. "That's just gators."

She drops down into a chair beside Mo'Zart. Lays a hand on his shoulders. She feels the muscles tense, ready to rebuff her.

"I know you wanna make things right, kid. So you got no choice—you crack this. Because the report that Gobis wrote— that's what got him and Agent Bex killed. Not you. So keep fishing. And get yourself off the hook."

Mo'Zart lowers his shoulders, drags a sleeve across his eyes. "I guess if I could come up with the right keywords, I could launch a spider. That could get through ten thousand files a second, the whole police database. But I'd need the right word. One that would be relevant to that particular report. But I never saw what he wrote. Never even spoke to the guy."

Bianco slumps back in her chair, her mouth dropping open as an idea drops, big as a bowling ball.

"Sulphur."

"What?"

"Try sulphur. 'Damned sulphur.' That's what Gobis said, right before Bex came in. I thought it was weird at the time but standing in that old factory, with the masks on and the stink of lilies, everything felt weird.

Mo'Zart shrugs. "I can try it."

Fingers fly across the keyboard, then he jerks a thumb toward Siggurson. "What about him? Maybe he has more."

Bianco turns to Siggurson, who stands by the window, scanning the water. He pulls the Luger from his belt and thrusts out of the door.

"No, I'm pretty sure we've had all there is to be had from him."

At the bang of the porch door, Mo'Zart looks up. "Where's he going?"

"Takes a while to get used to the sounds of the bayou. He thinks he hears something, but it's just a sly old gator."

"They dangerous?"

"They sure are. Man-eaters. Nothing more dangerous in the bayou." She sits back in the chair. Then...

...bolts up. *There* is *one thing...*

And then she hears it. The crunch of bone. And racing through the door—she sees it.

Siggurson slamming hard against the wall, his nose already bloody and his arm jerked high, an inch away from cracking from the joint. The final thrust averted by—

"Fucking stop, goddammit!" Bianco thunders down the porch.

Siggurson expels a gasp, shot with blood. Peels his eyes

from the wooden wall to see Bianco approaching. She comes to a halt. One hand now upon her hip, the other gesturing to whoever holds him.

"Siggurson, Lola." Her hand swings back. "Lola—Siggurson."

The fist about his neck releases. He pulls his face from the wood. Turns to see the figure behind him. Body like a gun barrel. Blond hair cut like a bullet.

He cranks his neck, flexes his fingers.

Bianco shrugs. "Lucky for you she wasn't hungry."

She turns to Lola and the two women fist-bump. The gesture is easy but the connection lingers a beat. "You've been gone a while."

Lola drops her fist and looks to the door as something unfamiliar in a pink and yellow shirt bursts out.

"Seems so."

Lola's eyes assess the kid as he approaches. The bowling shirt, the screw-top dreads, the voice unbuttoned to an awestruck mumble.

"You must be… I mean, are you an actual real-life one-time-dead supercharged—"

BING! The computer chimes as if the cookies are baked. Mo'Zart's body jolts, then jigs with mounting excitement.

"And you know what that means. That sound. That means, my dear amigos, that I have a hit. I have found it. I have found the file!"

He bounds off, his dreads alive and shirt flapping.

"Who's that?"

"His name's Mo'Zart. And he's not as stupid as he looks."

"Hell, he couldn't be."

 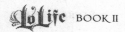

39

It is DEAD, even though the eyes seem strangely alive. It is a trick of the candlelight, the flicker caught in two shards of mirror that sit where the eyes should be. The skin is human, but hardened and yellow, stitched together with black sutures. This voodoo poppet is one of many that hang from the wall.

A black hand reaches up, perusing the poppets, touching one and then another before finally selecting the one that hangs at the very last of the line.

"Come, come my little one. You are where it ends."

Fan Fan's fingers close about the doll, lifting it down. Wrapping a shawl about the little head as she lowers herself into a rocking chair.

Her face flashes back and forth in the candlelight. Her lips are painted black and her jaw is cracked with a beard of white paint. Her fingers, stained red, nudge back the folds of the shawl, revealing the neck of the poppet. A jagged line of red encircles it.

Fan Fan's eyes roll upward. Hung from the ceiling is what's left of a crow. The head has been ripped clean from its neck. The last of its blood drips onto a silver plate below. The plate holds long black thorns, soaked and sticky.

Fan Fan's fingers tweak a thorn from the pile. Her throat

produces a throbbing chant as the spike hovers. With a howling incantation, she thrusts the thorn down hard into the head.

✦

He's dead! His neck is severed, splitting apart as if it's blowing a kiss. His long, dark hair is thick with blood, as he falls…

Lola bolts awake, clutching her head, the memory searing through her brain. Lurches to the bars of her cabin window, clinging tight to the metal, head down.

Her shoulders heave as the pain passes. She lifts her eyes, bloodshot and wet.

Flips open her phone. Stabs a number, her body rippling, awake.

She hears a phone chirp in the cabin across the water.

The line connects.

"Dammit, Lola…" The voice is clotted, but clearly Bianco's. "What the hell time is this?"

"Time to go."

✦

The clock on the car dash flashes 4:15 A.M. Lola's fingertips are cold from the kinked blood supply so she uncurls her grip from the steering wheel. Rolls her neck.

Mo'Zart and Bianco are in the back, silent. Maybe asleep. They are obscured by four large black suit bags that hang from a hook. Beside her is Siggurson.

 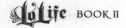

She's been driving for five hours down the straight and narrow road that leads to Morphic Fields. All roads lead here, it seems. The Gobis file that Mo'Zart found was that of Jezebeth Hooger. That takes them to Agnus Day. So, too, does Lola's mission. No coincidence. Something is massing, drawing from all quarters. And accelerating. Lola feels it.

She grits her teeth as she feels something more. A stab of pain behind her eyes. Another memory, poised to attack, she is sure of it. She swallows hard, smothering its sting for the moment.

Pushes the gas. Tilts back her head and breathes deep. Feels the ba-boom-ba-boom of the road studs under the tires. The car is drifting. She pulls it back into the center of the narrow lane.

Siggurson rolls in his seat. He, too, is drifting. Asleep now, but any moment he'll speak, certain that he's been awake all this time. Lola glances at his face, loose and soft, cheeks softly billowing with each breath. Would he care that she had seen him in this gentle state? She can't remember what guys care about. Maybe she's never known that kind of thing.

Maybe no guy has ever cared for me.

Her head suddenly jerks. That same cold, sharp pain—as something pierces her memory.

Black hair. Blue eyes… his face bloody.

She exhales with the ache.

"Maybe I should drive." Siggurson hauls himself up, drags a hand across his mouth, reaches for the soda can that slides across the dash.

Lola grips the wheel tighter. "I'm fine." Accelerates, arms straight.

"You like to drive?"

"Crazy about it."

Siggurson sets down the can, nodding. "You don't trust anyone else." He arches his back against the seat. "So, after all the talk last night... one thing's troubling me."

"Just one?"

"I like the details to fit."

"I bet your house is pretty."

Siggurson exhales, patient. "If a Tormenta is born into a human body, do they know what they are, right from birth?"

The hanging bags peel apart like a stage curtain and Mo'Zart's head pops through. "Can I field this one, boss chick?"

Lola says nothing, so he grasps this silence as grace to proceed.

"I struggled on this particular question, but Agent Bex had a great way of explaining it."

Mo'Zart sweeps the bags to one side, clearing his stage, and then reaches forward to lay a hand on Siggurson's shoulder. "You ever been to Vegas, lookin' for a little action?"

Siggurson swings his eyes to Mo'Zart, like a pair of wrecking balls. The small hand shrinks back and the kid quickly changes tack.

"I mean, a lotta people do. Particularly folks who have a taste for the unusual. They all meet up in those wild hotels; some even hold conventions. So one day, Agent Bex is sitting at the bar of the Bellagio and he's watching all these people arrive. They're dressed up like plushy animals. They actually call themselves plushophiles. And the only way they can have sex is if they're zipped up in a creature suit. And the other person, well they have to be dressed up all funny-bunny too."

Mo'Zart leans forward, finger raised. "Just for your education, they call the act of sex 'yiffing.' But I digress. So anyway, Agent Bex is looking at all these foxes and ferrets, mice and monkeys, and he asks himself, 'How did these people all find each other?' I mean, the urge to yiff is a pretty weird thing to admit to. Not something you can just drop into conversation. But look at them, hundreds of them, all gathered together in a Vegas hotel, exchanging information and experiences, the knowledge of their rare urges ever growing. So, thinks Agent Bex, if plushophiles can find each other, congregate and thrive, then of course, so can neophyte Tormenta. Their urges, to hurt those around them, to thrill at the suffering of others—this is no more shocking than slipping on a fur suit. So, putative Tormenta may not understand their impulses but once they reach out and find others like themselves, the Legion will soon follow, and their awakening will ensue."

Siggurson nods. "I get the picture."

"But y'know, some never discover the truth at all. If a G-Man don't find them, a Tormenta might go through life driving people to despair, maybe hating themselves for it— never even knowing why. They just live and die a plain ol' mean bastard, not knowing how to draw span and extend their own evil lives."

Siggurson scratches at his stubble. "So some are awake, some are dormant." Siggurson turns to Lola. "And you, what are you—you're like one part human, one part Tormenta?"

"She ain't no cheap cocktail, man!" Mo'Zart slams his hand down on the seat. "Don't you get it?" His hand rises behind her and hovers as if wanting to touch a live power line. "Lola is as good as it gets."

Lola flashes her eyes at Mo'Zart in the rearview mirror *Down, boy.*

Siggurson shrugs. "So you tell me, Lola, how do you see yourself?"

"In the mirror. Just as often as I can."

A silhouette of Bianco's head rises up from the back. "Are we there yet?"

Mo'Zart slumps back next to her. "We're eighty miles from the prison but a long way from him really gettin' it."

Bianco runs her tongue across her teeth, fluffs her hair. "Kid, we've had time. We've had proof. He's had six hours and home-brewed liquor."

She leans forward to Siggurson. "It's fucked up. But as cops, what do we do?"

"We fuck it down a notch."

Bianco nods, leans back. And her eyes return to the window. "We're heading into a storm."

Mo'Zart dips his head. "An unholy storm."

"No, Captain Dramatic. *That* storm." Bianco's finger pokes at the window. Up ahead a lightning bolt shears down to the swamp. She puts her hand up to the window, shielding her eyes to get a better view.

Then her neck flies back in a violent jerk as the car slams to the left, sliding across the road.

Lola's hands are off the wheel, clawing at her head. She roars in pain and twists wildly as the car spins out of control.

Siggurson lunges, grabs the wheel hard, tightening the spin

 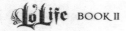

until the axles spiral to a halt in a stink of burning brake pads.

Silence—as one by one, they lift their heads. Look about them.

Lola is the last. A thread of blood unravels from her nostril. She drags her sleeve across her nose and turns to Siggurson.

"You drive."

BOOK III

40

THE MEMO ON the envelope is handwritten and says only:
Read this, then *call me.*

He pulls a single sheet from within. The print is faint, a poor
photocopy. He holds it closer to the light.

*Ray D'Sola was born Osca Bosque twenty-seven years ago. His
parents were well established in the Rio de Janeiro jet set. His
father, a plastic surgeon, married only once but changed his
bride's face with a tireless dedication. Osca grew up believing
that Egyptian "mummies" got their name from being covered in
bandages, as this was his perception of his own mommy.*

*On evenings when his parents entertained, Osca's hair would
be slicked and his shoes polished. A maid would then usher him
through to the lounge, where his father would instruct him to
play Chopin's Etude no. 4. On the polite applause that greeted
the end of his choppy performance, he would be removed back
to his rooms.*

*The only occasion when any attention was paid to young
Osca was at the age of twelve, when a doctor diagnosed him as
suffering from meningitis. Osca had fallen into a coma and the
news was broken to the parents that the child was not expected to
survive. His mother wept, dabbing her eyes to stop her mascara*

running. In fact, she lingered by his bedside so long she almost missed the party she was due to attend.

His father prepared for the worst, tracking down a colleague from medical school who was now known for his beautiful mortuary work. He could guarantee a beautiful corpse, which in Rio meant a great deal.

His parents were adamant—no expense was to be spared. However, the costs were ultimately limited to a number of irritating cancellation charges. Osca lived.

Perhaps it was born out of a desire not to disappoint his parents, but when the child emerged from his coma, he insisted that he was—in fact—quite dead. He maintained that he could feel a constant swarm of flies about him, attracted by the stench of his rotting guts. He referred to a residual red blotch on the back of his hand (a disfigurement typical of meningitis) as his "death spot."

Osca was swiftly diagnosed with Cotard's syndrome—an unshakable belief that one is a walking corpse.

Physical illness was regrettable, but for his parents, madness was one affliction too many. The Bosques took the opportunity that a move to New York provided to redefine their relationship with their son. At the age of thirteen, with every comfort he could wish for, the boy is locked up in the penthouse suite of their skyscraper apartment.

For hours at a time, all alone, he would stare at the windows of the surrounding buildings. They looked like picture frames, enclosing vignettes of life. He requested a telescope and soon found that time passed quickly when peeping on one's neighbors.

He began to draw on postcards—reproducing the shape of the

 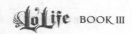

New York windows, and capturing what he witnessed through the glass. Sometimes moments of happiness, acts of kindness. But more often than not, what the boy saw and recorded in obsessive detail were extracts of despair. These were his favorite. They excited him. He knew that this was not right—not natural. But it was the reality of what he felt—and evidence of his own contention that he was indeed dead. Only a corpse could have a heart so hard that the sight of a man blowing his brains out (as the boy had once actually witnessed) would raise a smile and generate an appetite. That was the way he described the pang he felt.

His life (or death state, as he preferred to term it) changed entirely when he was fifteen years old. One of Osca's many nursemaids had taken a particular interest in the boy. It broke her heart to see him locked up and alone, with just his endless postcard sketches. She discreetly arranged for a psychiatrist to visit, a soft-spoken woman with the fortuitous name of Dr. Mother.

She began by talking with Osca about his "death spot." What if she could make it go away—would he then be alive? Osca confidently assured her that he had tried everything to remove it (the burn from an attempt with bleach had made it only bigger)—but he encouraged her to try if she wished.

The following day, Dr. Mother returned with a tattoo artist whom she introduced as Mr. Todd Lily. He looked at the ragged-edged blotch on the boy's hand. After a little consideration, he got out his needles and began to work. An hour later, he blotted the skin and told Osca to take a look. He had transformed the blotch into a blazing sunburst. The shape was perhaps a little uneven, but the effect could not be denied. The death spot was gone.

This was the beginning of Osca's new life. Dr. Mother had birthed him anew.

At seventeen, he changed his name to Ray D'Sola, emancipated himself from his parents (taking with him a hefty payment to keep his "imprisonment" secret), and set about creating a new persona.

Ray D'Sola became an artist and a business whiz. At nineteen, he had turned his postcards into an installation at New York's prestigious Hunkypunk Gallery. From there, the Revelation Project had sprung.

It began as an underground movement, with people writing anonymous revelations about themselves on postcards and leaving them hidden about the city—inside library books, beneath coffee cups in Starbucks. The human urge to declare one's darkest thoughts and exploits found voice and the project was soon transferred to the Internet, spawning a global audience and—of course—merchandise, books, events, and flash-mob parties.

The media—jerking its knee in response to another Internet trend—rushes to link the Revelation Project to an increase in youth suicides. The dailies work hard to find individuals who submitted anonymous postcards and then went on to take their own lives.

With a wonderful aptness, Ray D'Sola immediately sets up a suicide counseling agency called Rays of the Sun. Manned entirely at his own expense, the groundbreaking outreach program rapidly puts all other such agencies to shame. This masterstroke rips the moral high ground from beneath the media's feet and the Revelation Project continues its unbridled ascent.

He turns the paper over. The reverse is blank. Clearly just this one page has been prized away from its rightful owner.

He pulls the phone close. Dials a number. It connects on the first ring and a woman's voice immediately asks, "You've read it?"

"Yes, Marta, I've read it."

"And?"

"It is pleasingly accurate."

"They want to run it in the weekend edition. Center spread."

"Marta, I have made my fortune from the secrets of others. I was bound to become a target. We both knew this day would come."

"It calls your mental acuity into question."

"You mean it portrays me as a loon."

"Yes."

"Do you think I'm a loon, Marta?"

"I think you're a *fool* if you ignore this."

"So, as my attorney, what do you propose, Marta?"

"We offer them an exclusive, an on-the-record interview. Your whole life story. They'll want some gristle, but at least we control what bones we throw them."

"If that's what you suggest, then I agree. Make the call. Put it to bed. And then... off to bed with you." His voice softens. "I can tell from the echo that you're in that marble tomb you call your office."

"It's still light outside."

"My dear, that's the moon." He sighs. "You really do live up to your name, don't you Marta? You are the constant martyr to my cause."

"If that means you work me to death, then yes." She strains a laugh.

"Ah, Marta, you once again turn it into a joke. But I know what you have sacrificed for me, for all your clients. These last ten years, when you should have been falling in love, building a family, having a life—you have spent chained to your desk. And now... you have left it all too late."

The familiar silence comes. That glorious absence of sound that is, in itself, the sound of the target being hit. She doesn't know how to respond to a compliment that cuts so deeply.

"I'll speak to you tomorrow, Ray."

"Yes, Marta, sleep well."

He hangs up the receiver and jots a quick memo. He'll get another bottle of her favorite bourbon sent over. As a thank-you... and a failsafe, to be sure that she always has sufficient alcohol at hand, for when the tragedy of her pointless life finally punctures her heart.

D'Sola settles back into his chair. The black leather blends into the shades of granite and slate that prevail in his vast Manhattan penthouse. He plugs a set of headphones into a laptop. Clicks his in-box and retrieves his daily e-mail from the duty therapist at Rays of the Sun.

It opens with a host of audio files attached, each labeled with a name. He transfers one after another to his desktop.

This ritual began as a piece of PR. He'd made a public promise some months ago to visit the agency on a regular basis. The purpose was to evidence his involvement in its operation. On one visit, a worker keen for him to understand their methods played a tape of a call received that day—a heartbreaking account from a man who was sitting with the phone in one hand and a gun in the other. Ray had listened in rapt silence. All those present had been struck by his determination to listen to the very end. Such consideration, from the entrepreneur whom so many called a conman.

Since that day, Ray has insisted on getting the tapes sent to him regularly, such is his active and ongoing involvement.

D'Sola looks at the file names. Sees one labeled DOLORES.

He smiles. *That bodes well.* The name Dolores means sorrow. He selects the file, relaxes back, stretches his legs, and unbuttons his fly. As a despairing voice plays through the headphones, his hand trails down to his groin. And once again he finds that familiar sensation rising—that appetite he felt as a child. But now, as a grown man, the feeling has gained a hardened, more urgent edge. His blood pumps as he listens to Dolores, slurring her words as she pops pills and swills whiskey. She drones into the phone, increasingly oblivious to the male counselor on the end of the line. And then her final death sob comes and D'Sola groans with pleasure. His head lolls; his hand falls away.

He knows this is wrong, so very, very wrong... but every man has his particular lusts. Just so happens that D'Sola's fetish is... *What would you call this?*

What is the word for someone who gets sexed up on suicide? That perplexes him still. D'Sola has surfed for solutions. He's invested in some very expensive therapy. He's even read books. And come up with nothing. It's not necrophilia. It's not sadism.

It's something... *other.* There are days when he feels he might be the only one in the world who feels this.

But never a day that he cares.

He slips off the headphones, buttons up his fly.

He can keep this secret—we all have secrets. He looks about his apartment, filled with artwork from the Revelation Project... and smiles. Turns at the rasp of a subtle cough. In the doorway stands a squat man in the gray of a chauffeur's uniform.

"Will you be needing the car again tonight, sir?"

"No, no, Wilson. You may leave."

"I appreciate that, sir. My wedding anniversary, so she'll like to see me home on time."

"Of course. But I'll need an early pickup tomorrow. Regretfully I must meet with... people." His hand flicks across his diary. A name is scrawled. "Wilson, do I know a Marty Starr?"

The old man shakes his head. "I don't recall that name, sir."

D'Sola flips the diary shut. "I'm sure all will become clear. So off you go. And have an enjoyable evening."

"Oh, I will, sir. Much to celebrate. God is good and my world is a happy place."

D'Sola clips a smile and makes a mental note to replace Wilson with someone a little less blessed.

41

MARTY STARR sits uncomfortably hunched with a cell phone at his ear. A voice barks from the speaker. "Call yourself a producer? You can't produce shit, Marty. So either you get this mess sorted or you're finished. You get me?" The line goes dead.

Marty lets the mobile slide from his hand. It falls into a hammock of trousers that's gathered at his ankles, sat as he is in a toilet stall. He sighs. He kinda misses the days when phones had a cradle and calls would end with a resounding clunk. At least you knew they were over.

You're finished, Marty Starr. You can't produce shit.

He rises from the toilet and stares into the unsullied bowl. How true. Even his bowels have turned against him.

Squeezing from the stall and pulling tight his belt, he shuffles to the basin. Stares into the mirror. Lolls his tongue. He needs a shave. Dammit, his tongue needs a shave.

He exhales, barely fogging the glass.

You're dying, Marty. And you know who's killing you.

It's the band. Marty Starr has managed Stork from the very start, when Fell Watson was the lead singer. Death metal was just beginning, but Fell immediately understood how to harness despair to the same three chords and make platinum sales. Self-scarring, suicidal teens swelled the band's fan base, even before Fell blew his vocal cords out the back of his neck with a revolver.

Marty was under pressure from the label to get a replacement—and fast. He wondered where he would find a kid with the same authentic aura of death. But life is strange—and on the day that Fell's funeral was uploaded to YouTube, a guy walks into Marty's office—Japanese, maybe… hard to tell behind the curtain of black hair—and declares that he's the one. Says his name is Hash-Tu.

Marty listens to his demo and it blows his mind. He can't get the contract printed fast enough. But six months on, he is feeling the pain of this hasty decision. Hash-Tu has raised the affinity with suicide from something obscure to the central core of the band's existence—or impending non-existence, depending how seriously one takes the lyrics of their songs.

Hash-Tu's deadly antics onstage are now drawing criticism from the mainstream media, as suicidal postings on Facebook constantly reference Stork lyrics.

The head of the Scorpious Records laid it out to Marty in their last bitter exchange: Stork is one high school shooting away from being dropped by the label.

The launch of the new album *Rocker Lips* is fast approaching. Hash-Tu wants to stage a performance outside a prison as an execution is taking place within. He plans to call the event the Rocker Lips Apocalypse. The rest of the band, who look to Hash-Tu like a lethal Jesus, insists that this is a brilliant idea.

All Marty knows is that they can kiss Walmart stocking the album goodbye. Marty has put his own money behind this

 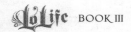

release. If the album fails, he's finished. He begs the band to see commercial sense. As they slam the door behind them, Hash-Tu challenges him to come up with something better.

Two bottles of Grey Goose later, Marty has nothing. Just a liver so swollen you could mash it to pâté.

A Bible is splayed on the floor. In his drunken desperation last night, he must have leafed through the final chapters, searching for any compromise on the theme of Apocalypse. It lies open at the Book of Revelations.

And then inspiration strikes—the Revelation Project. This is the answer!

He will persuade the band that the album launch should be done in association with the Revelation Project, with CDs hidden alongside postcards about the city. Hash-Tu is sure to love the tacit heritage of self-slaughter that comes with the project. Meanwhile, Marty can claim to the label that Stork is aligning itself with a reputable counseling agency that has done so much good work in the field of teen suicide.

It is a slam-dunk win-win... if only...

...if only he can first persuade Ray D'Sola.

Marty blinks again into the washroom mirror. On the other side of the door is the vast marble lobby of the Revelation Project's headquarters. His appointment with D'Sola is only minutes away.

He rolls his tongue about his mouth. It looks and tastes like feathers. Marty is rarely given to nerves, but everything is riding on this.

And he is not the only one vying for D'Sola's attention. It took two weeks just to get this meeting, and sitting in the lobby is another contender, with another pitch to hitch her wagon to the Revelation star.

Marty inhales and exits, eyes flicking to his competitor, who fidgets in the lobby.

✦

Dr. Torgus is careful not to look up. She refuses to be deterred or distracted. She has her pitch memorized. She keeps her eyes fixed on her hands, casually folded in her lap.

She's recently taken to wearing gloves. Sleek, black leather affairs. The purpose is to conceal the liver spots that leopard her hands, but the effect is to suggest a constant readiness on her part to commit murder. And right now, motive mooches dead ahead in the shape of a man, shuffling from the bathroom in a cheap chino suit.

Torgus clenches her jaw. It had taken a week of studied silence to convince Duggin that she had abandoned any ambitions concerning Agnus. Then, with the warden's focus eventually averted, she approached the Revelation Project. Call by clandestine call, she clawed her way through the entourage of Ray D'Sola, at last eliciting his private office number. With an audience achieved and the day finally upon her, she is crushed to find herself in competition with others, clamoring for his commercial attention. It seems that D'Sola likes to keep the pressure up. Likes to see people sweat.

As her competitor settles into a seat on the opposite side of the table, Torgus feels perspiration prick her armpits. She lifts her elbows to allow air to flow, skillfully disguising the move

as a reach across the table to gather one of the glossy books. She feigns interest in the title and then—her hands twitch in an unexpected flash of genuine curiosity. The book she holds is titled *The Poems of Archilochus*. Torgus flicks through the thick, silky pages. Archilochus's work is very obscure. D'Sola must be quite the aficionado of Greek poetry to know of him. A smile cracks her thick lipstick. *Torgus* is an ancient Greek name. Her roots are in this culture. Has she perhaps stumbled upon the most perfect icebreaker? The door to D'Sola's office swings open.

Dr. Torgus and Marty Starr look up together.

42

It is one of those Louisiana days when you just can't beat the heat. No point fighting it. Might as well just pop that top button and stretch out those legs just as far as you can.

Police Chief Willy Lyon has been heeding this advice the entire day. He thuds a pair of buckskin boots upon his desk.

His officers have their own lil' wisecrack: "You know what the chief's name is short for? Willy Lyon-His-Ass-All-Day."

But he doesn't care. It don't bother the chief at all. He runs the station his way and it works. All about good delegation. Which is why he likes to have a lotta female officers. Back at county hall, the sheriff thinks that Chief Lyon is some kinda poster boy for progress, recruiting all these women. But here's the truth: They work harder. Simple fact, they just do. Quicker with their caseload. Quicker with the coffee.

Chief Lyon smoothes a hand across his head, taming a mass of sandy hair that circles, via sideburns and a beard, his entire face. Pulls a file from his desk. Then he opens his mouth to shout a name, demanding attendance. A yawn bubbles up at the same time, turning the summons into a gurgling, Tarzanlike bellow. In the operations room beyond, where the chief's many and varied noises are well-known, Detective Blaise Dunkel rises to answer the call.

He appears at the door, swilling his coffee. "You want me, Chief?"

"As a matter of fact, I don't. I want Detective Bianco, but she's been assigned to some secret-über-hush-hush somewhere, so I'm settlin' for you. It's a suicide."

"That sure is her specialty."

"Plus she shakes up a fine iced latte."

"Yeah, they *are* good."

"But you're the best I got right now. So this one's yours." Chief Lyon skims a finger across the file. "It's a suicide, no doubt about that. Forensics show residue on the victim's hands, and he's a drinker. Got a hospital record that says he's tried this stunt before. Just about sober enough this time to get the gun in his mouth, I guess."

Dunkel slurps the foam from his coffee. "So what's to do? Sounds like we can wrap it and stack it."

"Wrap it and stack it?"

"That's what my old chief—"

Lyon's boots thud to the floor. "This ain't Walmart, son." He hauls his huge chest up to his desk. "You're new and maybe my candy-sweet karma has confused you. But I have earned a little kickback. Thirty years of service, four bullets, thank God none in the ass. So I do things right. You best learn that. And what we got here"—he wafts the file—"is a little cleanup in aisle four."

He flicks to the last page. "There was another person present… a kid called… I dunno, there's no name, just a number. Says here he's some kinda rock star."

Dunkel grimaces, as if another shot of shit has just been added to his coffee. "That so, sir."

"Yeah, fronts a band called Stork. Some kinda"—peers closer, frowning—"'death metal grindcore.' You ever heard o' that?"

"I'm a little bit country, sir."

Dunkel catches the file as it frisbees toward him. "Dig some. Usual questions."

"Sure boss. And… what are the usual questions? I mean, if we know it's a suicide."

"Reckless endangerment, son. Gotta be sure Mr. Rockstar didn't push him to it."

"Oh sure, that, yeah… I got it, sir. I'm on it."

Lyon tilts back his chair, shaking his shaggy head as the detective disappears down the hallway.

For a guy called Blaise, he sure don't burn too bright.

✦

On the wall of the interview room an old-fashioned digital clock flips numbers, marking the seconds and generating a relentless *SHIK-SHIK-SHIK*.

Seated on one side of the table is a uniformed male officer. Opposite is Hash-Tu. His long black hair hangs like a curtain across his face. In his hand is the pen he was given to sign his statement. He tap-taps it on the table, finding the off beat with the *SHIK-SHIK-SHIK* of the clock, creating a nerve-jangling non-rhythm.

The officer grips the edge of his chair, veins pulsing with tension. Wanting to reach across the table and skullfuck the kid with the pen. But he can't. The freak isn't even under arrest.

 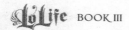

He's helping with their inquiries.

As the door swings open the officer bounces to his feet. "All yours, Dunkel."

His exit has sufficient speed to generate a waft of air that peels apart Hash-Tu's hair. Just long enough for him to glimpse the sweating detective who now settles into the seat opposite.

"Sure is a hot one today." Dunkel runs a finger round his collar, then opens the file, papers clinging to his palm. "We'll try not to keep you long. A few questions is all."

Hash-Tu stares at the shiny face before him. Breathes deep. Smells the detective's discomfort.

"If you could just explain to me what happened."

Hash-Tu says nothing out loud. But his mind unfolds the question with great care.

The beginning part, he can explain. He was in his dressing room. It was the last night of the official tour. Marty was there. He was drunk, of course. Raging and weeping, begging Hash-Tu to reconsider his decision to stage a concert outside Morphic Fields. It was bad enough that Stork would choose to perform as an execution was taking place, but to select the death of Agnus Day—a perverted child-murderer, for chrissakes—that will kill the album.

"It's fucking goddamn professional suicide! I'm begging you—"

Marty had fallen sobbing to his knees, and once again, Hash-Tu felt it rise within him: that very particular thrill that came when he witnessed a person in the throes of despair. It's been this way his whole life. The misery of others feels like silk upon his skin.

Guess that's just the way I'm wired...

He tells Marty that he has brought this upon himself. He had promised the band a collaboration with the Revelation Project, and, in truth, Hash-Tu had liked this idea. The project's creator, Ray D'Sola, was someone he wanted to meet, because the guy was an artist in death. His personal contribution to America's suicide culture deserved recognition. But Marty had clearly failed to impress, as D'Sola had selected another project with which to partner. When Marty delivered this news, Hash-Tu experienced an emotion that he later identified, with a little research, as disappointment.

So the sight of Marty prostrate before him, pleading and pawing, provided him with some small pleasure. One that would be improved if Marty would just kill himself. That's what Hash-Tu wanted.

That's what he always wanted.

And this is the first element that he cannot explain. Not to himself. Certainly not to this decaf detective.

So he opens his mouth a fraction and provides just this: "He was sad. He pulled a gun. He shot himself."

Detective Dunkel writes rapidly. The gathering momentum suggests he's expecting more. So the pen hovers mid-air as Hash-Tu concludes not so much a statement as a haiku.

"That's all you know?"

"Yes."

Hash-Tu doesn't lie. It may not be all that occurred. But it is all that he knows. The rest of what ensued is beyond his understanding.

As Marty lay dead, gun in hand, brains in bits, Hash-Tu felt the most tremendous urge to kneel and press his lips upon the man's cold mouth. He sucked hard, aware at first of the dead tongue drawing up into his mouth, then—fighting a gag reflex—he sucked some more and then he felt it... something rising out of Marty, pulsing, alive, released from this dead shell. Entering him as he inhaled again, sucking harder, swallowing it down and feeling...

What?

An incandescent euphoria. A deep need, spectacularly satisfied. But as the giddy high passes, Hash-Tu wrenches his mouth from Marty's corpse. Rises to his feet.

No way of knowing what had just occurred. What he now felt.

This may take a little more research...

✦

He sits back in the interview chair as Detective Dunkel passes him a card with the station number on it.

"If you gain any further insight... understanding... into what happened, please let me know."

The card sits unclaimed, despite the fact that Hash-Tu is quite certain he will be seeking further insight and understanding. But not into Marty's death.

Into why he has never felt so alive.

43

WARDEN DUGGIN is a short man. Very short for his weight. And always short for his age, right back to his childhood days. At five years old, even on tippy-toe, he had not been able to see inside the long wooden box that lay in the front room of his house. But he knew that his mother was inside it. She had been there for a few days, surrounded by white lilies. Kept close until her burial, as was traditional. But with the '50s boom, his parents were the first generation to get central heating, and no one in the family had stopped to think of the ripening effect this might have upon a corpse. And so, although young Duggin was unable to see his mother's body, he sure could smell it. And judging by the way the brown and withered lilies stank, his mother, he imagined, looked the same or worse.

Then came the day that four men, in identical sharp black suits appeared at the door. They had come to take her away. At the time, young Duggin was unaware that the removal of his mother roused any horror in him. But then, two years later, his father took him as a treat to a music show. The first act on was a doo-wop quartet, the Fly Boys. They walked onto the stage in their identical sharp black suits and young Duggin felt hot, clotted bile rise up in his throat, erupting from his mouth and splattering across his lap. He recalls hearing a voice scream out that he wanted the men to go away—but it didn't feel as if the voice were his. The most intimate memory, the only thing that he recalls as feeling real, was that his vomit smelled sweet as lilies.

Amid his screams and violent squirming, his father held him down, trapping his wrist against the seat, embarrassed, insistent.

The men won't hurt you, boy. Just stay for the first song.

✦

Duggin suddenly bolts from the memory, roused by a sharp, female voice.

"Let's begin by getting something clear."

He looks up. Four sharp black suits stand before him. Two women. Two men. It's the brunette who speaks. "This prison is ours, Warden. For as long as we want it."

Duggin smears his palms along his thigh. These agents had walked in unannounced and spread themselves in a line across his office, hands clasped up front, the pose identical... disturbing. It has taken Duggin until now to master his childhood chill. He looks to the window. The rain beats, relentless, but he takes calm from the rhythm. Breathing deeper, slower.

Until the brunette breaks out from the line and begins to pace the office.

"We are here because word has reached the Federal Bureau of Prisons that, under your command, a disruptive force has been allowed to spread unchecked within Morphic Fields." She curves around a bucket that collects rain from a split in the ceiling. "You've permitted one prisoner, Agnus Day, to gain a psychological hold over the inmates, and that's one sure way to make the Bureau snippy. So we have been dispatched with full authority to end this nonsense now."

Duggin blinks as if Bianco's words are individual jabs in the eye. "Now, I don't know what your personal record is on the control of narcotics and firearms, but let me tell you this: There is nothing more dangerous in a prison than the spread of an idea. And you have allowed, without intervention, the entire inmate community to develop an addiction to the prophecies of one man."

She straightens her lapels, rolls her hands, knuckles down upon the desk.

"Our charge is to clean this mess up and, with your cooperation, we'll pass through like a dose of chlamydia. You won't feel us. But if you stand in our way, start swinging that dick—you'll be pissing blood. Do I make myself clear?"

She reaches inside her jacket and produces a thick sheaf of permits and subpoenas.

They slap against the desk. With a hesitant hand, Duggin slides on his spectacles. Scans the contents. Then, in disbelief, draws the papers closer still. These clearances are mighty high. Sky-high. A man might get a nosebleed just from reading the signatures.

And then the papers are gone, swept up in Bianco's hand as she rolls them tight, replacing them within her jacket.

"I will be heading up this operation, so I'll need an office and a dedicated phone line." She clasps her hands behind her back. Walks down the line of her fellow operatives, passing

 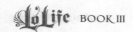

Siggurson. "We will need a barber and a set of prison blues. The library must be cordoned off"—she slaps a hand on Mo'Zart's shoulder—"and get him every gigabyte you got."

She walks on past Lola with just a razor's edge of a glance and… says nothing.

Then turns her back on Duggin. "Our first objective is to debunk Agnus Day in the eyes of the prisoners. Make them see that his voodoopalooza prophecies are bogus. Once he's robbed of their respect, his hold will be gone—and we can haul his ass from Morphic Fields without fear of reprisal."

Duggin appears to be listening, but his eyes are on Lola. He stiffens as she breaks from the line, moves toward him.

Bianco shoots her cuffs. "And let's be honest, Governor, you don't want Agnus here. He's been nothing but trouble. So I'm pretty sure a lot of what I've said sounds good to you."

Duggin puffs his cheeks and puckers his lips into a balloon knot of contemplation. Feels Lola close on his right side. But still he risks popping one last question.

"So I assume that the Federal Bureau has cleared all this with the Ministry of Justice and Washington?"

Lola leans in. "I want to kiss your mouth to stop you saying such ridiculous things."

44

HER UNDERWEAR IS somewhere. She wore black, of course. Her best Victoria's Secret, because this was to be her big seduction. The vinyl floor in Duggin's private chamber is dark gray, turned black by dirt, and Dr. Torgus had removed the thong with such alacrity the elastic launched across the room. Now the only secret of this underwear is where the fuck it landed.

She had been hiding on the other side of the door, waiting for her weekly meeting with Duggin, and today she was keen to get to the meat of it. Then those four agents had walked in.

On the other side of the wood, hands gripping her short skirt, pantyless and gasping, she had listened in horror to their mission brief. They were going to take Agnus from her.

Not possible! Not now! Not so close to the arrival of Ray D'Sola...

With her old face and broken credentials, still she had succeeded in persuading him to come. Just to witness, with his own eyes, the sheer mountain of material generated by Agnus Day. More than a book—an *installation*. A phenomenon. Nostradamus for a new generation. Secrets of the past. Revelations regarding the future. Dr. Torgus remembers telling herself to *shut up!* as she pitched the idea in D'Sola's office, hurling reason after reason at the coconut of his head. And then—joy of joys—the word *yes* had been handed to her. The smallest word that felt huge in her arms as she walked from the office, giddy and giggling.

Now she has nothing. No hope. No plan. No panties. And their chilly lack is forcing her to tweak her stride, when every muscle in her body urges speed.

Her hands contain the swirl of her skirt and, flanked by two guards, she minces in tight-hipped, tight-lipped silence down the central prison corridor, arriving at the final corner cell. The one with the window.

✦

A slender finger drifts back and forth. Grotteschi lies on his bunk, white iPod buds plunged deep into his ears. Inside his head, Mozart's *Requiem* unfurls. The slim device is a treasured perk from a guard who was particularly troubled by a note from Agnus. The actual wording of the revelation now escapes Grotteschi, but he had found a mild interpretation that gave the guard relief.

Grotteschi inhales as the key descends to a mournful B-flat—then yelps as he is sharply yanked upright. Eyes bolt open to find Dr. Torgus bursting into his cell, guards in tow, jangling keys.

"What is the meaning of this… !"

He is silenced by a hand that thrusts his hump against the wall, holding him fast. The face of Dr. Torgus flies forward, an inch from his. He can taste her breath. Coffee and stomach acid. She raises her thumb and forefinger, the merest pinch apart. "I am *this* close…"

Grotteschi shrinks back. "*Less than*, I'd say—"

Her spit hits his lips—"*this* close to getting everything back." She stares, eyes wide, fogged by her fury. "My reputation. My life. And then this happens."

"Must *this* happen?" Grotteschi waggles a finger at the guards who rip up his room, yanking blankets.

Torgus's upper lip curls like a safety gate rising on a band saw. "They show up with their papers, as if my plans count for nothing. Giving me no chance to change his mind, to put my case, to put my ass on his face until he says yes! That's all I wanted!"

"So reasonable, thus phrased."

The guards tip out his drawers as Torgus grinds on. "So now—a change of plan. I am forced to go beyond those means."

"Beyond the ass?"

A guard reaches under the bed. Pulls out a pair of shoes and a small wash bag.

"You understand, I must have total control."

"That may require medication."

The shoes are searched with probing fingers and the wash bag is unzipped, soaps spilling. Torgus swings her eyes to the bed as the guards comb through the contents.

"Everything must be in my possession. All that you have is now mine."

His pockets are turned out like dog ears. Gum sticks fall. Grotteschi gestures down. "Can I minimize the mess by confessing now that I keep two balls inside my scrotum?"

His insolence gains him a sharp punch to the sternum. He falls heavily to the bed, his sudden weight forcing something to dislodge from the springs below.

The thud of a box hitting the concrete floor.

A guard falls to his knees, retrieving the Nike shoebox. He peels off the lid and presents the contents to Dr. Torgus. A mass of paper shreds, covered in text.

She takes the box, cradling it in her arms, looking at the many prophecies within. "This holds the future that Agnus saw. And now, it is my future." She strokes the box, a smile rising. "What *is* the meaning of this?"

She lays her hand upon the lid, exhales, and, with a spin of her heel… is gone.

The cell door slams and clunks. Grotteschi lowers himself to the bed and sweeps aside his precious soaps from the pillow. Pokes his pockets back within his pants. And then he lifts an arm upward, snaking it beneath his shirt to where his twisted spine lurks. And out from his collar, Grotteschi pulls a handful of paper, the loss of the bundle reducing the size of his hump. He then carefully slides them into the pocket next to his heart. He had sensed that such a raid might occur and had prudently secreted the most precious of the papers beside the most untouchable part of his person. He smiles and, with a soft grunt, settles back down onto the bed.

He listens to the rain, battering against his window. How unnatural that this storm should be so unrelenting.

The skies know it. Heaven itself is horribly aware. *Something comes…*

From the moment of his encounter with Ring-Pull,

Grotteschi knew that momentous events were now unfolding. He could not know what form they might take, nor when the catastrophe might come. But he knew that fate had dealt him a card to play in this game.

He slides his earbuds in and sighs as the glorious *Requiem* floods his ears.

If this duty brings death, then I am ready.

And the scattered soaps fill his nose with the scent of lilies, the traditional flower of the funeral.

45

LOLA'S BOOTS STEP out onto the prison roof. The flat surface swims with rainwater. She pulls her long coat about her and strides to the edge, forcing ripples hard to the gutter. She hears the boots of a guard follow, two paces behind. Clad in hooded black rain gear, he looks like a slippery tadpole, slung with a gun. Young Officer Trill has been assigned to accompany this agent, but halfway across the roof she holds up a hand, commanding him to stop.

She sweeps her eyes across the roof and spies the twelve-foot tower of a ventilation shaft. Rusted rungs creak beneath her weight as she mounts it. Rising up, high enough now to survey Morphic Fields in all its sodden shame.

The surrounding swamp has drunk its fill of water, but the storm tortures it with more, forcing it to swallow rain that bubbles back up, rising around the prison perimeter like a burgeoning sea.

Flanked on all sides by fifteen-foot fences, Morphic Fields seems to float like a frigate, torn from the world by the black water. The watchtowers at each corner groan in the wind like masts.

Lola closes her eyes. She did not come here to look. She came here to feel. To release, for a moment, that Tormenta streak within her—that shard in her soul. If another like her walks within these walls, sharklike, she will feel it.

Lola breathes deep, opening the mental cage in which she imprisons her darker self, and instantly, the power she has disciplined herself to use solely for combat purposes bursts free, roaring through her mind and body. Lola tenses every muscle, riding this beast, feeling it rage, following where it leads. Opens her eyes, her every sense heightened now. Ready to search.

Is he here? Is the Mosca already amongst us?

And then she feels it. Like the death throes of a dark star, a wave of energy rises from the entire prison and breaks across her body.

She staggers back. Stumbles to find her footing, her body quaking. Officer Trill splashes up to the base of the tower.

"Ma'am you all right?"

Lola says nothing, hauling heavy breaths. Trill tips up his hood, his young face twitching, a mess of emotions. "Thought you were gonna jump for a moment there."

Lola thrusts out a hand, commanding him to stay back from the tower as she fights with herself, forcing her Tormenta side back into its cage. It resists, screaming inside her head, trying to wrest control of Lola's mouth. Her smile flashes at the guard below and, like a distant echo, she hears her own voice say, *"You've thought about jumping, haven't you, kid? Because you feel the evil that approaches. You sense it coming. So maybe you should jump, before it pushes you."*

Lola grasps her head between her fists, forcing this thing down, expelling a jagged grunt as she slams her mental cage shut and condemns that sliver of her soul to darkness once more.

Slowly rises. Eyes wet with strain, she stands above Trill, a pulse jumping wildly in her neck.

He flips a faint smile. "It'll pass, ma'am. We've all had it— kinda feelin' outta sorts. I blame the rain." He tugs his dripping hood. "No good for the brain."

He suddenly lurches back as Lola thuds down from the ventilation tower, landing before him. And with a snap of her fingers, they are on the move again.

✦

It's gonna take one hundred and twenty-seven steps to get back down from the roof. Trill had counted them on the way up.

He has taken to counting and collating his surroundings— lightbulbs in the corridors, floor tiles in the washroom. He likes to keep his mind occupied. To stop it from wandering. Because Officer Trill's brain has recently been prone to restless roving.

And now he's finding it harder and harder to deny the knocking dread inside his head.

He accelerates to keep up with the agent. She now strides toward a set of steps that lead underground to the medical isolation cell.

And as they descend, he finds himself counting a fresh set of steps. Mouth shut, but shouting the numbers loud in his mind.

Sixty-four, sixty-five, sixty-six... The emergency ward of Morphic Fields lies deep beneath the prison, hewn from the bedrock. The steep stairwell and many doors lend the ward its security. They also spare it from the rain, and this tunnel is one of the few places in the prison that remains unflooded.

Sixty-seven, sixty-eight, sixty-nine... They reach another door. A guard shuffles to his feet, tips back his cap, exposing a face that's pale and wrinkled, as if his years of subterranean duty has rendered him unable to withstand sunlight. He cranks his key in the lock and swings his door to reveal another stretch of steps. Then turns, his eyes fixing upon the blond figure that accompanies Trill. As she moves to pass, a book is thrust hard against her.

"So must ye descend before ye can rise." The guard's voice rattles with unreachable phlegm.

Lola stares at the old guard as Trill swiftly dips between them, snaring the book, then waves it harmlessly. The cover is emblazoned with a mass of golden crosses. "It's just an ol' Bible. He's taken to passing it to anyone who... descends." With a thin grin, Trill turns. "Now, Bob, I don't think this agent needs your protection. She looks pretty handy to me."

Trill strains a laugh as he eases past the old guard and pushes the door wide for Lola.

She thuds down into the darkness and Trill follows. They silently sink deeper and Trill feels the beat of his mind against his skull. He breathes hard and looks down. In his hand is the Bible. He knows for sure that there are forty gold crosses on the front, but he will count them again and again.

✦

On those occasions when Officer Molloy found himself on isolation duty, he would always volunteer to take the final

 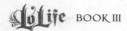

stretch of corridor, guarding the last door before the cell itself. His reasoning was that if he were to be forced deep into the bedrock, he might as well take the spot with the sweetest acoustics. Because Officer Molloy loves to sing, and on this last stretch, the granite walls afford a wonderful echo.

But the stone no longer resonates to his tenor. He hasn't sung for a while. Not since his beloved Trudy left him. Ripped from his arms by the revelation that his mistress is pregnant.

Just as Agnus had predicted. On the paper he gave Molloy was written one word: *Scox.* Grotteschi translated that as a stork, foreboding evil. News of this baby would wreak destruction— and, as ever, Agnus had been right.

I shoulda listened to him!

"You hear me, Molloy?"

Molloy spins round to see Trill before him. "I said, open up."

His finger gestures to the door behind Molloy. The sign reads MEDICAL ISOLATION CELL, but the heavy rack of locks confirms that the purpose of this room is less about care and more about concealment.

Trill's thumb now jerks over his shoulder. "The agent here wants to talk to Agnus."

Molloy jolts as a blond figure steps from the darkness. She looks like a woman but scares him like a man.

He gathers himself, rubs his narrow chin. "Is that so? The agent wants to speak with Agnus." Molloy pulls up his keys, cranks the lock, and gives what could be a grit of strain... or perhaps, an amused smirk.

"Well, let's see what we can do, shall we?"

The door swings wide. Inside a figure sits, withered and wild with hair. On the wall behind, lit by tiny, flickering lights, is a metal frame.

Lola enters. Takes up a position in front of Agnus. He doesn't move.

She lowers to her knee to find his face. And then she sees that the metal frame is a surgical device. Tubes coil from his chest and wires connect his head to a monitor, the flickering lights of which create the strange illumination.

His eyes are wide, unblinking.

And his mouth sags open, dragging air, but locked into a silent, catatonic gape.

Lola rises to her feet, pulling out her phone. Flips it open. It connects in one ring. "Can you talk?"

✦

Bianco snaps her phone shut. Increases her pace. She thinks better when she walks. And just as well. She's got a lot to think about and a long way to walk. The rain means that she and her escort of guards can't cut across the yard to reach the library, so they are making their way through the long circumference of corridors. The two guards each push a plastic-wrapped cart stacked with prison files. The wheels squeak, and to Bianco's ear they seem to throw a constant question. "*So… ? So… ? So… ?*"

So what are we going to do now?

She looks to see the guards are pointing left. That hallway twists away into the distance.

"Why not down here?" She points to the broad gray corridor before her.

 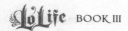

"Ma'am, that way is through the gym. The prisoners are taking their exercise in there, on account of the rain."

"So?"

Bianco flicks her fingers, a gesture to open the gym. A guard thumps a button and an electronic motor heaves the doors apart. High up on the observation platform, armed guards prime their weapons, put on edge by this entry. The command is yelled for all movement to cease and the gym falls suddenly silent. Each prisoner compensates for this enforced immobility by charging his eyes with a body's worth of muscle, punching his weight at Bianco. Following her every step across the vast room. Their faces are tattooed with a gang mark that Bianco knows very well. She has seen these horizontal stripes crosshatched by the bars of a holding cell many times. These prisoners belong to the Petra Loa. Her hand instinctively moves beneath her jacket to her holster. Finds it empty. Remembering now that she'd agreed to the warden's demand to surrender her weapon. Her eyes rise up as a giant of a man emerges from the center of the gang, lumbering toward her. The distant rifles prime and point, but Kon'Verse is allowed to approach. Bianco feels as if her limbs are made of metal and this giant man is a coil of magnet. His eyes draw her to a halt.

"You will fail if you fail to see him."

Bianco's eyes flick up to the gantry. The guns are trained upon them but something tells her the weapons are poised more to ensure her attention than to contain this convict.

She looks back to Kon'Verse. "See who?"

He lets the basketball in his hand drop, like a god releasing a planet to its fate. And the sound of it striking the floor seems to act as a signal. The guns withdraw and the exit door slowly grinds open.

Bianco strides out, breathing hard, furious at herself. Throws back one glance, finding all eyes upon her. Stiffens her spine, shaking the feeling that she is trapped—*and yet somehow, these prisoners seem free. Unbridled by these walls.*

She pounds down the last few yards of the corridor and thrusts open the doors to the library. Mo'Zart is already inside with a fleet of guards who unload boxes of inmate records.

Bianco fires two words, like warning shots. "Plan B."

She signals for the guards to leave them. As the doors swing shut, she turns to Mo'Zart.

"Agnus is alive but a dead end. Lola's seen him. The warden's got him plugged up, just enough to keep him breathin' until he's off his property. But that's it. There's nothing we can get from him."

She paces around a tower of boxes. Drops to a desk. Pulls a clean pad of paper toward her. "I need to write while I think." Frisks her pocket. "You got a pen?"

"Just this one. But it's red." Mo'Zart pulls it from his shirt.

She snaps her fingers for him to throw it. Snatching it from the air, she scribbles with the nib until the red ink flows. "I don't like to write in red. Reminds me of school. Like teacher has corrected me. Like I've gotten something wrong."

Mo'Zart drops into the chair beside her. "But we've got it right, right?"

On the pad she draws two pin men. "We know what we've got to do. Find the Mosca. And find the G-Man who has been sent to awaken him. That ain't changed. Just how we do it."

"And how fast we do it. Because I looked up the medical notes, and what Judas told Lola—it all bears out. Agnus went into a vegetative coma three weeks ago. Now, if this is some kinda chrysalis stage for him becoming the Moera, then the Mosca has had time enough to close in. Both he and the G-Man could already be here."

"But we'd know if the Mosca had been awakened. There'd be seven shades of shit already falling, right?" Mo'Zart nods. "I'd say we're in time... but by how much?"

Bianco taps the pen like a metronome, quickening the tempo of her thinking. "If Agnus can't speak, then we get a hold of everything he wrote and we talk to every prisoner who spoke with him. Whatever information we get, we have to piece together ourselves until it shows us who the Mosca is. And as for the G-Man"—she thrusts the pen at the files on the trolleys—"those are the employee files. We look at everyone who's arrived in Morphic Fields since Agnus began to have his visions."

"I've already made a start on the prisoner records." Mo'Zart jerks a thumb at a two-foot stack.

"You read all those? I was gone thirty minutes, tops."

Mo'Zart taps his skull. "Kinda my thing. And I found this." He unrolls the file in his hand and spreads it on the table. "It gives me an idea about what we should do first—"

A finger sharply taps the table, halting him. "You know why it's called Plan B? It's short for Plan Bianco. *I'm* running the show. *I* say what we do first."

"So you got me boiling these exceptional brains, and you don't want to taste the gravy?"

Bianco says nothing. Mo'Zart looks at her. The silence strains. Broken only by Bianco's tapping pen. Then, "So what you waiting for, kid, an eight-bar intro?"

Mo'Zart smiles, peels apart the pages. "It's a classic bait—and-wait." He taps the name on the file—*Charles Grotteschi*. "This one prisoner was closely associated with Agnus. Very closely. He acted like a kinda interpreter, decoding every revelation. So all we gotta do is get Grotteschi to open up to Siggurson once he's inside."

"And how do we do that?"

Mo'Zart pulls out a page from Grotteschi's file. "I know every book this dude ever checked out of the library, and one in particular… gives us an opportunity."

Bianco takes the prison file, flicks through it. "Grotteschi's done time. An old con like him will smell a cop through kryptonite. The minute Siggurson makes an approach, starts asking questions…"

"He won't. Grotteschi will come to him."

"Why?"

"Because he'll find Siggurson irresistible."

46

GROTTESCHI'S FINGERS CRAWL over the muffin. He is pulling it apart but not eating it.

He finally prods a lump between his lips, but it lodges in his mouth, parched dry by excitement. His eyes are locked on the prisoner seated opposite him in the mess hall.

The morsel squats in his throat until his brain finally engages and pumps words from his mouth, forcing the muffin to expel in an explosion of crumbs.

"That's some big ol' bullet hole you got there."

The freshly shaved head of the man opposite bears a cratered scar above the ear. His eyes rise, stare at the hunchback, then sink back to the meal. Grotteschi knows that it's hard to get a new con to talk. The smart ones stay silent until their position in the hierarchy is first confirmed by their fists.

But Grotteschi cannot wait. He'll risk retribution.

This is just too extraordinary to ignore!

The strange events leading to this moment began earlier that morning. Grotteschi turned up for his trustee duties to find his book trolley parked outside the library doors. The duty guard informed him that the library was—for the moment—out of bounds. This being so, the books ordered by the inmates had been loaded onto the cart, ready to go. At the time, Grotteschi barely cared about this wrinkle in the system. In fact, it spared him the task of trawling the shelves to collect the same old sticky paperback porn.

Quite happily he took the trolley from the guard, along with the delivery list. With his good eye already monocled, he wandered off, pushing with one hand and holding the list with the other, scanning the titles and cell numbers. Then, with a muted squeal, the monocle pops from his eye. He comes to a halt. Pulls the list closer.

There it is. In black and white. His name—and beside it, a book to be delivered. But he has not ordered it. Not this time. In truth, he hoped never to see it again.

It is the *Bardo Thodol: The Tibetan Book of the Dead*.

Who would have sent it to him? Who knew of his encounter with Ring-Pull? Not the guard who escorted him; he'd never set eyes upon the book. Only Ring-Pull… and so now, only Ring-Pull could be sending it back to him.

But why? As a threat, a taunt? No, no, this made no sense!

Grotteschi is certain that, in that one fateful encounter, he saw the true spirit that now occupies Ring-Pull's mortal shell. It is the spirit of Tenzin Nara, a gentle, seeking mind who sought to help him in his search for the truth to Agnus's visions.

He would not tease.

But might he share? Yes, yes! This is the answer!

Tenzin Nara wants to send Grotteschi a message, a clue. And so, with a trembling hand, he pulls the book from the trolley, rattles the pages back and forth—and then he finds it… a fly, squashed between the covers. Its sticky body has been used as a crude glue to affix a scrap of paper.

 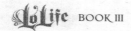

Just like he said... the accursed Fly... the bringer of death.

Most certainly this message is for him.

Grotteschi peels the note free. It is short and elegantly written in red ink.

A bullet in the head.
He should be dead. But he did not die.
And this one man
Can tell you more than I.

Now, a few short hours later, Grotteschi finds himself before this man.

It must be he! That bullet wound to the head, so deep, and yet he lives. This is the man that Tenzin Nara foresaw.

And now Grotteschi must engage with him, find out what he knows. Share with him his own meager findings.

But where to begin? He may be quite unaware of his destiny, oblivious to the answers that lie within his bullet-riddled brain. The wrong approach may break no silence, only bones.

Think, Grotteschi! Think!

But all that comes is the most common of con greetings.

"So... how long you got?"

The shaved head rises again. This time the inmate speaks. "Life."

Grotteschi scours the face before him, searching for a clue that this man knows of their shared destiny... some awareness of the realms beyond.

And then it comes. The man leans closer. "But not necessarily this life."

47

"WILL YOU QUIT scratching?"

Mo'Zart's voice crackles from a tiny device lodged inside an ear. Above the ear is the scar of a bullet wound. Siggurson's finger scratches at it again.

"C'mon, sounds like we've wired up a canine."

Siggurson grimaces. Drops his finger.

He stands in his cell, tin bucket in hand. It is slop-out time. He waits for a bell that finally shrills. His cell door slides open and he steps out onto the iron gantry. Below and above him, the cell doors clunk and slide and a hundred slop-out buckets clang down on the walkway. Siggurson grits his jaw. Undercover in a jail always stinks. The buckets are emptied and he eases back against the wall. From the gantry above, droplets shower down.

I am outta here before shower time comes around.

He turns his eyes straight ahead. Sees Grotteschi outside his cell, talking to one of the guards. The merest flick of his old finger gestures toward Siggurson.

✦

 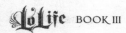

In the library, Mo'Zart is surrounded by open files and laptop keyboards. A speaker crackles as Siggurson's mic picks up another voice. The tone is gruff, with the edge of a whisper.

"*The old hunchback tells me you got a talent, a talent for... metal-work. He wants to show you around the shop before the shift begins. I've given that my blessing. And if I ever need a blessing in return... I may call upon your talents. Do you understand?*"

Mo'Zart's dreads dance as he swivels in his chair from one terminal to the other. Fingers punch up information.

"This is good, Siggurson. I got the workshop log here. Grotteschi's in there every day. That says to me that he thinks it's a place of safety. He's taking you to his sanctuary. Looks like he's buying it."

Bianco leans forward, her pen tapping like a conductor's baton, slowing the beat. "But don't underestimate the old guy. He's smart." The pen taps on, counting down to her conclusion.

"We're gonna need another beat. Some kind of detail that'll convince him Siggurson's got the gift."

◆

In his concealed earpiece, Siggurson can hear Mo'Zart's fingers hammering at the keyboard. And in his cell, summoned by a sharp hiss, he looks up to see the finger of the guard reach in and beckon him out. The finger then wordlessly directs him toward Grotteschi, who is already on the level below. The hunchback urgently jigs back and forth, beckoning Siggurson to come down and join him. As he descends the metal steps, Mo'Zart's voice buzzes in his ear.

"This guy Grotteschi has got some kinda good game going. All sorts of favors. A CD collection, art books, cigars... but most of all, soap."

✦

In the library, the speaker now transmits the echo of footsteps. A change of surface. Concrete. Siggurson must be entering the workshop.

Mo'Zart rattles at the keyboard. "And when it comes to his soap, Grotteschi will accept only one fragrance: lily of the valley."

A heavy clang of metal pops the speaker. Mo'Zart cranks the volume as another voice comes, muffled by fabric and movement. But it is clearly Grotteschi.

"*We have these pieces. Different shapes, different fixings. Our job is to put them together. We rarely know what the end item is destined to be—a plumbing fixture, a valve, perhaps. And never do we have instructions. Perhaps they existed once, a mystery all of its own. So the trick is to examine each piece until the piece speaks to us and tells us where it goes.*"

Mo'Zart dinks a frown. "Why is he telling Siggurson this?"

Bianco recognizes the careful tone. "The guard is too close. Grotteschi can't speak freely."

"*I was just saying to Office Bilfinger here, I saw those dexterous hands of yours and I knew that your talents should be applied to the metal shop.*"

Mo'Zart nods to Bianco, her instincts right.

"*So he's allowed me the chance to show you the ropes before the shift begins. Officer Bilfinger knows what a puzzle this work*" *can be… and he has had some personal experience of my own ability to solve puzzles, isn't that right, Officer? So let's begin. And the first task is to wash from our hands all trace of grease. So, Officer, I'll just show the new boy where the basins are."*

A rush of water drowns the sound of the mic. Mo'Zart fiddles with the pitch, thinning the bass to bring out the thread of conversation.

"Please, my boy, don't use that fecal treacle they call liquid soap." The disdain in Grotteschi's voice sets the signal crackling. *"I have something of my own."* The rustle of a pocket, the crinkle of wrapping paper. *"Lily of the valley."*

Mo'Zart taps furiously, then pulls the mic close. "Mary's tears, Sig. That's another name for the flower. Tell him that, then wait for my cue."

✦

Siggurson twists off the tap. Turns his head to Grotteschi and delivers in an empty monotone. "Mary's tears."

Grotteschi slowly pulls his hands from beneath the faucet. Water drips from his fingers. And in his eyes, something bubbles.

"You know about Mary's tears? That is such a rare extract of knowledge." Grotteschi watches as his new apprentice closes his eyes.

"Your mother's name was Mary… and you lost her when you were still a child."

"Did this come to you in a vision, my boy? Tell me! Do you… do you then know about my mother?" Grotteschi staggers back, grasping the edge of the sink, gasping for air. Forcing his mouth to form words. "Yes… yes… you see everything."

He hauls a deep breath, gathering calm. Then casts his one good eye upward. "When my mother bathed me as a child, she would cry. She always assured me it was nothing—just the soap. That the fragrance was Mary's tears and, with her name being Mary, it was bound to make her eyes water. A kind story, to keep me from knowing that what truly made her weep was the sight of my crippled spine." Grotteschi hauls a deep sigh. "She took her own life, and many cruel tongues wagged that no mother who loved her child could do such a thing. But I know my mother loved me—why else would she spare my hurt and blame her tears on the fragrance of lilies?"

A hand launches out and grasps Siggurson's sleeve, quivering with an ecstatic energy. "Your gift is strong, my boy." He stares deep into Siggurson's eyes. "And in you… I sense that your mother… your mother somehow has made you what you are. Gave you life, but also death…"

Another commanding bell rings.

✦

Mo'Zart dials the volume down as the bell's blast threatens to blow the speaker.

Then he turns to Bianco and sucks a low whistle. "That's some gameplay from Siggurson. He's got Grotteschi believing they share some mommy mojo. How'd he do that?" Mo'Zart returns to his keyboard, shaking his head in admiration.

The roar of a machine rises. The bell marked the start of

the metalshop shift. Mo'Zart tries to adjust the pitch again but nothing comes.

"I can't get anything. Sig's on his own."

"So we wait."

Bianco says nothing more. But her mind twists a smile. *Ah, Grotteschi, you've got the gift and you don't even know it.*

The jig-cutter is a two-man machine, and at the sound of the bell, Grotteschi is quick to claim it. It will keep Siggurson at his side and their conversation can continue. And it suits Siggurson's purpose, also. The blade descends every ten seconds and its piercing squeal means that Siggurson's answers to Grotteschi's questions must be cut short.

"My boy, what do you know of Agnus Day?"

"I am here because it was destined."

The blade screams, churning sparks. Grotteschi waits for it to rise, impatience riddling his feet. At last, it lifts…

"You have seen him in your visions?"

"I hold a book. And in the book, I see the meaning…"

Grotteschi squirms away from a spray of sparks. "Agnus brings us a warning but I cannot decipher it. Which is why I prayed for one such as you to be sent."

Mo'Zart tries the volume again and winces as the jigsaw grinds from the speaker.

"Still nothing."

Bianco looks up from a stack of files. "We wait. And while we wait, we read."

She slams a file shut. Quickly pulls another. "So far I've counted a hundred and seventy new intakes to Morphic Fields since Agnus got here. Anyone of them could be the Mosca or the G-Man. Without something from Grotteschi, I'm gonna die of paper cuts."

Suddenly, the flush of a toilet. Siggurson has made it to the confines of a cubicle. His voice hisses from the speaker.

"Listen up! This is what I've got so far. Agnus wrote hundreds of prophecies, thousands maybe. All of them cryptic, most of them crazy. But according to Grotteschi, some do hold a deeper meaning. Two in particular. Grotteschi calls them the Poet and the Painter. Don't ask me why. Thing is, we gotta get these pieces and… piece them together. To see the bigger picture. So the one he calls the Poet, that prophecy was given to a heavyweight called Kon'Verse. Grotteschi has arranged for me to have an audience. Kinda loose arrangements though. Basically, he's just given me a code word that should stop Kon'Verse from pushing my teeth so far down my throat I gotta clean them with a toilet scrub. If I can get close, get him to talk, maybe he'll give up the prophecy and we can get to work."

✦

Siggurson's eyes are set on a hulking kiln across the concrete floor. The Petra Loa gang move amid the hot pipes. They are not working, but the guards make no attempt to coerce them.

As Siggurson nears, he feels the heat of their eyes upon him. He takes a final pace. Looks up, a long way up, to find Kon'Verse's eyes.

He's surprised by the crack in his own voice. Coughs to claim control of it.

"So, you interested in Greek?"

Kon'Verse stares at him in silence.

Siggurson feels like he's cut the red wire and the bomb's still ticking. One of Kon'Verse's crew takes a step forward, head cocked like a rooster's.

"You wanna say that one more time?"

Unsure that he does, Siggurson inhales. "Greek… poetry."

Sounds worse. The gang moves a step closer, but a low exhalation from Kon'Verse halts them and the twitch of his giant hand signals that this stranger may approach.

"Grotteschi sent me."

Kon'Verse inhales and slowly lowers himself to sit on the base of the kiln, as though it were an iron throne.

"Then we will talk of one thing." He spreads a hand on each thigh. "The meaning of my revelation." His fingers are thickly tattooed with roses. They clench, rippling thorns.

"Time was, Little Bit rapped and his words were cheap. And he soon found himself a foe. Got into a dissing war. Things got outta hand. His foe's daughter ends up dead. Little Bit didn't pull the trigger. Maybe one of his crew did it, but he ends up here all the same."

From his pocket, he pulls a folded piece of card, passes it to Siggurson. It bears the words, in a savage scrawl:

Came he once as Archilochus with words that killed. He will come again by that same name.

"At first, I could find no meaning in it. The hunchback told me Archilochus was a Greek poet. What was I supposed to understand from that? And yet—I knew Agnus intended this for me. So I meditated upon it. And I found my meaning."

A tattoo of thorns climbs up his neck, as if they bear his head like a windblown bloom. "I cursed my imprisonment as unjust. But then this revelation showed me the truth. What killed little LouAnne Titley may have finished with a bullet, but it started with my words. I was guilty. And suddenly, with that realization, the anger that raged inside me subsided. And there came great peace. And I knew that I must make amends. That Little Bit must die to pay for her death. And so I killed off that identity. And Kon'Verse came to be."

He gently smoothes the crumpled card across his palm. "This is the meaning that I took from Agnus's words. A meaning that spoke to me and helped me make sense of my fate. But I know that this holds another meaning. One that relates to all mankind."

Siggurson stares back at the black eyes upon him. Feeling their gaze enter deeper through his skin as Kon'Verse leans in close.

"The hunchback may be fooled by your games. But I know the truth, lawman. And I know this too, that you were sent here for a purpose. So take this…"

He slides the scrap of card toward Siggurson.

"…and set its meaning free."

48

THE MOUTH OF Agnus Day sags uselessly. He can't talk.

So Lola has gone to Plan B. She's ordered up every recording of his police interviews and psyche assessments.

She stands beside his bed, the tapes spread out on the blanket. Picks up the first. In the underground gloom of the ward, she can barely read the label. She twists it to catch a glimmer from the flashing lights of the medical machinery.

PROPERTY OF SULPHUR CITY POLICE DEPT.
INTERVIEW: AGNUS DAY

She slots it into the player. Plugs in her earbuds and sits back, eyes closed as the old tape hisses and pops into action. A long burst of tone. Then a gruff voice announces:

DIX: The time is twenty-two hundred, June sixth. This is the interview of Dr. Agnus Day in connection with the homicide of Jezebeth Hooger. Attending officers are Sergeant Don Dix and Detective Judah Gobis. Dr. Day has been offered an attorney and declined. Please confirm this for the tape.

AGNUS: I decline an attorney.

[*Sound of a chair scraping back*]

GOBIS: So, Agnus, can I call you Agnus? Y'see, I feel I know you. I've worked a case on you before. [*A cigarette lighter snap; deep inhalation*] As fate would have it, I was the investigating officer on your suicide. Or what we thought was your suicide. Guess I can wrap a ribbon around that one now. But I remember it well. It was all about your daughter. That's what we thought. Her death. That's why you took your life. But here you are, very much alive. But Jezebeth Hooger is dead. So you need to tell us about that, Agnus. Tell us everything that happened tonight.

AGNUS: My duty was to protect her. To save her.

DIX: To protect who, Jezebeth?

AGNUS: To save her.

GOBIS: Hey, where're our manners, Agnus. You smoke, don't you? Here's a fresh pack. Crack it open.

[*Cellophane crackling, chairs creaking*]

GOBIS [*whispering*]: I think he means his daughter. She died of cancer and he was supposed to be a cancer specialist. That was the guilt that pushed him over the edge.

DIX: So he's confusing Jezebeth with his daughter.

 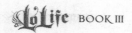

GOBIS: He's got seven pints of someone else's blood down his shirt, Dix. I think he's confused about a lotta things.

[*A throat-clearing cough*]

GOBIS: So, Agnus, can you tell us about your daughter?

AGNUS: I will tell you about Maddy.

DIX: Your daughter's name was Lily. [*A fist thuds onto a table.*]

AGNUS: Are you listening? You must listen. It is important that you remember this.

[*The voice of Agnus becomes strangely clear, not thick and stilted as before. Sharp as a pin.*]

AGNUS: The first thing you need to understand is that Maddy Pool was an ugly child. Blubber-skinned. Thin hair, like an insect nest wrapped around that large cranium. Her teenage years brought no improvement. All those vile hormones just swelled her body bigger and bigger. So she took a job that kept her in the shadows, as a coat-check girl in the kiosk of the Sewercide Club.

This underground music den ran in the old pipes beneath the city. It was the creation of Gina Avner. Now Gina was a cream-skinned delight, with a lithe body, pierced and tattooed into a temple of pain. The girls who frequented the club were equally spectacular creatures, wrapped in black and obsessed with death. Nothing made them so happy as despair. Particularly the despair of others. Maddy was taunted by Gina without mercy. The naughty girl once slid a razor blade beneath the kiosk window and told Maddy to cut that ugly face right off her skull. And every night, as the thin, gorgeous girls danced into oblivion, Maddy would wonder if death, so celebrated in this club, might be just the thing to set her free. And so one night, she walks to the river and lets her huge body roll in. She tries to breathe the stinking water in; she wants to welcome death. But something in her fights back. Refusing to die. Rejecting death. And her legs beat and her arms crawl and her fingers find mud and, heaving hard, she drags herself from the water. Lies on the edge of an old abandoned reservoir, into which the river empties. Glad that she is alone to wallow in this shame. Not shame that she attempted suicide. Shame that she lacked the courage to see it through. Regretting already that she permitted her primal instincts to overwhelm her desire to die.

And then she sees him. A boy—a man. A little older than herself. Black hair. Blue eyes. Walking through the reeds. He says he's an entomologist... a fly hunter. He didn't mean to disturb her. But seeing her distress, he stays. He reaches out a hand and gives his name: Kave. An unexpected friendship sparks. For Maddy, it quickly grows to love. And so, just days after that first bizarre meeting, she cannot contain her joy when he says he wants to take her on a date. And he insists that they go to the Sewercide Club, so all the girls who taunt her can see her in the arms of an adoring man.

When the night comes, oh, Maddy's excitement is quite marvelous! She can barely slick her lipstick straight. She has squeezed herself into a red dress that so constricts her blood supply, her face is soon a matching crimson. But she will endure it—just for tonight. Because this is her night. And when Kave takes her hand and sweeps her into the throbbing club, she is delirious. They dance and swirl until she is giddy. So giddy, in fact, that she can't be sure of the exact moment when Kave's hand slipped from hers. And without her glasses she can't be certain that what she's seeing is real. So she waddles closer. And there it is. Gina Avner—her long cream arms wrapped around Kave, kissing him deeply.

The last thing Maddy remembers is crashing into her kiosk, ripping off her dress, pulling out the razor blade from the back of her diary, and slashing it across her wrists.

And as she falls to the floor and her head rolls, she sees a shadow in the doorway. And she knows it is Kave. He rushes to her side, gathers her in his arms and brings his lips down to hers. She feels his kiss… but not a kiss. Something other. He is sucking hard, an unnatural force dragging something from within her.

But she will not give in to death. And just as she did beneath the water, she fights back. Rising up, swallowing back down what Kave had tried to siphon from her and then…

Nothing. Blackness. Until Maddy's eyes bolt open and—

✦

Lola's head jerks. Eyes blink hard in the half-light.

Have I been asleep?

She looks down. The tape deck lies on the floor, cracked, as if it has fallen from her grip. Picks it up, frowning. The cassette inside is knotted into the mechanism. Which makes no sense.

It was playing. She heard it. All that stuff about…

She snatches up a folder and tugs out the printed interview transcripts. Flicks through. And finds… nothing. No mention of Maddy Pool. No record of that part of the interview. Lola chucks down the papers and hitches herself onto the bed to sit cross-legged before Agnus.

If it wasn't coming from the tape, then it was coming from him, somehow…

This is some kinda weirdo voodoo.

Lola stares at him. With his skin all stinky and yellow and his head spiked with monitor needles, Agnus looks like one of Fan Fan's thorn-headed poppets.

She always said they spoke to her.

So speak to me, Agnus. Tell me who Maddy is.

Silence. Nothing moves and then…

…a hand rises.

Not his… but hers. Lola watches, wide-eyed and mystified, as her arm extends, fingers pulling a wire from the machine. Its sharp tip draws blood from her finger as she yanks it free. Then, inhaling hard, she forces the thornlike tip deep into her own scalp.

A trickle of blood runs down her forehead as her fingers pull another wire, thrusting it deep into her skull. Her obedient hand returns to the machine, stripping the wires one by one, stabbing each sharp thread into her head until her cranium is linked to Agnus's by a shivering, silver web.

Blood streaks her face. She stares up.

 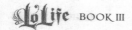

This is what you wanted.

His mouth still sags, but she clearly hears his voice.

It is necessary.

What do you want me to do?

To remember.

His voice suddenly explodes like a bullet within her skull.

Know thyself.

Lola's body arches in the grip of a violent spasm. She reaches up, one hand clawing at her head to rip the wires free, but her other hand wrestles with it, fighting against herself—as memories flood her mind.

She sees the heavyset face of a girl, eyes swollen and red. And she knows: *This is Maddy*.

And she knows: *This is me*.

She feels herself entering a lumbering body. And she hears the shrieking taunts, feels the sharp jab of fingers. And the hot burn of shame. She tries to run, but as if in a dream, her legs are leaden, refusing to escape.

Then blackness and…

…another torrent of memories, faces, voices, tears, and screams, crashing down upon her, drowning her. She gasps for breath as if the past is bursting her lungs and then…

…blue eyes. Black hair.

Kave! My savior!

Her breathless mouth. A kiss. Her hand in his.

And love. Such love. Like sunlight. Warming her body and then…

…it burns. It scalds her heart. It boils her blood, so she must cut her skin to cool it down, to let it chill against the ground.

And then he bends to take the last of her.

Kave! My traitor!

Her lifeless mouth. A kiss. Her span in him.

Lola leaps from the floor, roaring, ripping free. Spinning to her feet at the sound of the cell door bursting open and the thud of boots.

✦

Officer Molloy enters first. He waves a hand, halting the guards behind him.

Every eye is on the strange agent who ranges back and forth, breathing deep. Her blond hair is clotted with blood, running in thick streaks down her face.

Taking neither his eyes nor his rifle from her, Molloy chucks a command over his shoulder to Trill.

"Go tell the warden."

Trill's voice trickles from behind. "Tell him what?"

"That Agnus is awake."

Lola turns, eyes fast on Agnus.

The old man's sagging mouth slowly tightens to a smile.

49

BiΛΠCO GLAΠCES ΛϮ the sign on the library wall that reads 'quiet please', then inhales and bellows at the top of her voice. "Two-nine-three-six-four."

"Okay, I'm getting closer."

Mo'Zart is deep in the library and high on a ladder, running his finger along the reference numbers on the uppermost shelf. "Scroll down and see if he took out any others on Archilochus."

Bianco taps the computer. The page lists all the books checked out from the library by Grotteschi. She shouts over her shoulder, "No, just that one."

"I got it!"

Mo'Zart pulls a book, jams it between his teeth, and scoots down the ladder like a firefighter, landing with a thud. As he bounds across the library, Bianco snaps her fingers, encouraging speed. Mo'Zart wipes the cover on his thigh and drops into a chair, flips the book open.

Bianco hovers behind, leaning deep. "So, what have we got?"

"Apparently, no sense of personal space." Mo'Zart tucks his shoulders tight. "It don't help with you bent on my shoulder like a crow."

She leans in deeper still, black hair swishing. "In Taino, *bianco* means 'crow'. Perching's my natural state."

She jabs her finger down hard on the book and Mo'Zart grunts, pressing on. Flicks the pages, each one bearing a poem. The paper is yellow and stiff, crackling in his fingers.

Bianco's nose is almost in the crook of his neck. "What are we looking for?"

"I don't think the answer is in the actual poetry. Agnus talked about Archilochus himself, the man. And when he says, 'He came once before,' that has to be a reference to the Mosca. We know the Mosca has come many times before, and the Sinestra have always successfully struck before the G-Men could arrive to awaken it. So maybe there is something, some shared similarity that links each incarnation of the Mosca. We find that, then we know what to look for in this new coming."

Bianco glances again at the tattered card Siggurson gathered from Kon'Verse.

"This says that he'll come by the same name."

"We can't take that literally. The Greeks love to play with their names." He raises a finger, skewering an example. "Plato's name was actually Aristocles, but he got the name Plato from being fat—*platon* means 'broad.' So first we find out what we can on our guy."

Mo'Zart spreads wide a page titled "Archilochus—Extracts of His Life," and Bianco snaps her fingers. "Read it."

Mo'Zart dips his head, eyes scanning back and forth.

Bianco snaps again. "Out loud."

Mo'Zart sits up, book in hand. Clears his throat.

"'The poet Archilochus was born in 680 B.C. on the Greek island of Paros. He was famed for the savagery of his verse, which would often take prominent dignitaries as its theme

and subject them to vicious ridicule. In Greek society, one's reputation was valued above all else, and to be reduced to a laughing stock for many, meant ruin. Numerous accounts of performances given by Archilochus would make particular mention of the strange pleasure that he appeared to derive from seeing men and women crushed by his poetic scorn.

"'However, despair struck Archilochus himself when he fell in love with a beauty called Neobule. Archilochus courted her earnestly, but her father, Lycambes, grew ever more reluctant to the union as Archilochus's reputation for cruelty grew. When he ultimately withdrew Neobule from the engagement, Archilochus set his mind on vengeance.

"'At the feast of Demeter, where all of noble society was drawn, Archilochus rose and delivered the most scathing attack of his career. The poem's subjects were Lycambes and his once-beloved Neobule. They were mercilessly parodied until both ran weeping from the feast.

"'Soon after, their bodies were found hung in the temple gardens. Father and daughter had committed suicide, crushed by Archilochus's words. The poet was inconsolable. He cried out that he did not know what so possessed him to drive others to their destruction. One account records him tearing the robes from his body and crying to the sky, "What beast lives within me, that I must be a stranger to myself?"

"'Archilochus wandered into the desert, imploring none to follow him. But intrigue followed him to the end. According to an account rendered by a scribe in Lycambes's household, an unknown man attempted to pursue the poet as he fled. His name is not recorded, and the scribe notes that he was unfamiliar with the strange legion the man attested to serve. When he questioned him as to his intent, he replied, "To kill Archilochus, if you so call it death." However, in a final twist, before the legionnaire could reach him, Archilochus was slain in a duel by a man known only as Corvus.'"

Bianco is pacing, thinking aloud. "I see a connection. Archilochus killed through his words. And Kon'Verse, his lyrics... his rhymes... They got a young girl killed. Just like Neobule."

She flexes her fingers as if the idea is growing in her grasp. "I looked into his eyes and I saw something there... something beyond the natural."

Mo'Zart shakes his head. "If Kon'Verse were the Mosca, his every instinct would be to kill the Moera. And I've read the records. Kon'Verse has been close to Agnus all along... and the old man ain't dead yet."

"I say we play safe. Get him locked in isolation."

"I say we need him."

Mo'Zart sees the steel grit in Bianco's eyes. He holds up a hand. "Will you hear me out?"

He flaps the hand, beckoning her over. With his other, he punches up an image on the screen. "You know how I got recruited, right?"

Bianco walks around the desk toward the screen.

"The Voynich Manuscript at Yale. That's what SCURO uses. Like a brain magnet." Mo'Zart scrolls through online images of the book's strange pages. "This chapter is right where I'd got to in my translation when Agent Bex found me." He jabs at one page, singling out a symbol in one corner. "This is the sign for Scox. And Scox, the flaming stork, is a herald, so it always appears close to the symbol of the fly—the Mosca." His finger sweeps to a winged rune.

"Like Lord of the Flies?"

"That's the devil himself. Let's say that the Mosca is one of his fierce lieutenants. But this is what I want to show you." He points to a thin, triangular rune. "This symbol is known as *Thurisaz*, or, in Anglo-Saxon, *Thurs*. It appears frequently alongside the symbol of the Moera." He points to a sign that resembles three threads intertwining as one.

"So what are you saying?"

"Thurs is the rune for protection and defense. It means 'thorn.' Now look at this." He leans across to another computer that displays the prison records. Taps in a reference number. The file picture that comes up is of Kon'Verse. Tattooed rose thorns climb up his neck and reach across his jaw.

"He was drawn to those tattoos because his name—his birth name—was Ursus Blackthorn." Swivels to Bianco. "And that shows us his destiny. Like Judas with his black rose. And Brother Spino—in Latin, that means 'thorn.' Kon'Verse is just one in a long line of guardians."

"So he's not our guy..." Bianco exhales, fists clenching against the edge of the desk. "Where does that leave us?"

Mo'Zart spreads his hand over the poems of Archilochus, then folds the wings of the book shut. His eyes flicker as if a thought is passing through his head like a butterfly.

Bianco sees his expression. "What is it?"

Mo'Zart grimaces, failing to capture the idea before it disappears. "Your name means... 'crow'?"

Bianco exhales. "Yeah—so?"

Mo'Zart twists his pencil in his dreads as if trying to unscrew an idea that is buried too deep. "Could it be that there's…" He snaps back into focus. "It's nothing. Maybe nothing. We need more to go on."

"But tell me we've got something here. That Archilochus holds some clue to the identity of the Mosca?"

Mo'Zart nods, chin in hand. "It's one piece of the puzzle. We just don't know where it fits."

50

"YOU CRAZY WHACK-SNATCH! What the fuck have you done?"

"If you'll just let me speak—"

"I'm sick of that mouth of yours! It sucks like mud and spits up trouble."

The raised voices are muffled by the door, but Officer Trill knows how to skulk. His parents' refusal to get a divorce and readiness to get drunk meant that Trill perfected early the art of lying low and listening up. He moves his ear close to the hinges.

The warden and Dr. Torgus are really going at it.

"Woman, you're destroying me!"

"I would never hurt you—"

"You'd pull my colon out through my cock if you thought it would drag you outta this shit."

"Ray D'Sola is a celebrated philanthropist. I've persuaded him to come here... to meet you. To memorialize a prisoner—your prisoner—in your prison."

"You're an idiot."

At a bellowed command Trill is quick to appear, flapping through the door in his rain poncho. He sees Warden Duggin behind his desk, kneading the back of his chair, killing the leather.

"Get over here. I'm kinda sick o' shouting."

The officer moves closer, finds himself beneath a split in the ceiling. The rain splatters down the back of his hat.

"Trill, I'm finding it tough to talk to Dr. Torgus without getting testy, so I'd like you to tell her just what you told me."

Trill turns to Torgus. Her hair is wet and stuck against her scalp, gray roots showing. She looks like a raccoon spooked from a trash can.

Leaning back against the desk, she muzzles a grimace. "Tell me what, exactly?"

"Ma'am, it's like this. We heard this scream. More like a roar. And we rushed into the cell and there he was. Agnus Day. With this strange ol' smile across his face, looking right at us, eyes wide, and that agent lady, well now she was all blooded up and breathin' hard, and Agnus Day—"

"Is *awake*. That's the point." Duggin strides toward the window, snatching up a pack of cigarettes. "I had a chance, one chump chance to get Agnus swept outta my chimney, nice and quiet… an unconscious con. But now all my bunting goes right back in the fucking box. One whisper that he's awake and the Petra Loa will be baying to get him back in the general population."

Torgus drums her nails upon the desk. "So—I have a proposition."

A dart of her eyes suggests that Duggin should dismiss the guard. As the door closes behind Trill, Torgus eases herself forward.

"Consider this. You do not return Agnus to the cell block. Instead, you declare an ongoing concern for his health. He would, in your opinion, fare best in the care of the infirmary.

 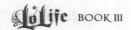

That means he rides the prison train across the desert. To ease his journey, I will administer one of the many anti-anxiety drugs that I am licensed to dispense. The dose will be necessarily high, such is Agnus's state of distress. Sadly, he will experience a very rare, *very* adverse response to the sedation and never again regain consciousness. As the federal agents will no doubt insist on traveling with him to the infirmary, they will be aboard the train to witness his death, in full knowledge that you, Governor, are miles away in Morphic Fields. You clearly had no hand in his unfortunate passing. I doubt they will demand much investigation, as his death puts a very final end to their concerns about Agnus's undue influence."

Duggin chews the filter of his cigarette. "And what do you want in return?"

"Next to nothing. I simply want the chance to sell Ray D'Sola the publishing rights to the prophecies. To do that, I first need Agnus to assign those rights to me." Torgus reaches inside her jacket and produces a document. "Once I have his signature, I will… sedate him."

"And Ray D'Sola?"

"His interest is in Agnus, so he'll bypass the prison and accompany me on the train." She moves in closer still. "You won't feel a thing."

Duggin's face relaxes a twitch. Torgus seizes the moment. "Trust me, honey—it'll work."

She slides her fingers down, finding his groin.

As she urgently pulls and caresses, Duggin hisses through tight teeth, "Trust me, Torgus. You won't feel a thing."

51

"This may hurt."

Lola yanks out the last needle from Agnus's scalp. He doesn't flinch, even though the fast removal pulls some flesh. Blood dribbles down his face. Lola has no time to wipe it clean.

By coming back to life like this, Agnus has condemned himself. Any tolerance the warden may have had for their interference will surely cease now that he can officially put Agnus back on death row.

Lola runs her fingers through her hair. Feels her own scalp clotted with blood. Breathes deep.

I just need… to think. But there's no time.

Turns to Agnus. His eyes follow her about the room as she paces, planning her next step.

Those memories—that's who I was. But what matters now is what I am. What I must now do.

Above her she hears the clang of the doors. The echo of boots. Guards are approaching.

She bends down to the frame that suspends Agnus, her fingers flying as she unties the tethers that bind him. "I am here to protect you. But I don't know how long we have. So tell me what you know. Who is the Mosca?"

 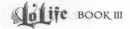

Agnus stares at her with milky eyes. His mouth slithers, "I am here to protect you."

She pauses from her task, finding his eyes. "Do you understand me? Do you know who you are?"

"Do you know who you are?" The same droning echo, then— his eyes spark. His voice sharpens. "You are Maddy Pool."

Now Lola grasps his jaw, turning the emaciated face to meet hers. "Who I am does not matter. Who is the Mosca?"

The heavy footsteps pound closer. Lola accelerates her efforts to release his limbs.

"I'm taking you from here. You come with us. And we find who the Mosca is."

"Cease now!" The roar from Agnus rips across her face like hot steam and his freed hand snares her wrist, hauling her close. "This must happen. Events must take their course. Until the time comes."

"What time?"

"You will know."

The guards burst through the door. Lola's eyes blaze, burning down the fuse of the last few seconds. "How will I know?"

Agnus's eyes close and his neck wilts. His words now slide and slur. "Not how—what. *What* you will know. That will change everything."

52

Dust rises from the back of a pew, flurried by a sigh. Grotteschi is on his knees. Beside him is Siggurson. They are in the dark arches of the prison chapel.

Grotteschi whispers, but the slate walls amplify each syllable. "So you have the Poet. Now to the Painter. But where to begin this next revelation?"

His old hands, clasped in prayer, hold a shred of paper. "Let us start with Father McDees." Grotteschi rises with a groan and slides onto the pew. "He was the chaplain at Morphic Fields when Agnus first arrived. I always liked McDees—or McSqueeze, as he was commonly known amongst the inmates. He was an ex-con… did five years for corporate blackmail, went to jail, and found God." Grotteschi grunts a laugh. "The prison system does not attract the highest caliber of churchman. And consequently we at Morphic Fields were allotted this old lag. Very few attended his confession. Would you want to open your darkest secrets to a one-time extortionist?"

A creak of wood sparks Siggurson's head upward, his training kicking in. He disguises the response by clasping his hands in prayer, mimicking the old man.

"Worms, my boy. This place is riddled." Grotteschi shifts, easing the pressure on his shins, finding a temporary comfort.

"McDees was a clever man. Most blackmailers are. And he and I enjoyed many a conversation on the topic of Agnus, at the outset, when I was sure that this new inmate was pulling a con all his own. McDees and I both admired his creative commitment. Until McDees received a personal revelation, thrust into his hand by a gibbering Agnus."

Grotteschi slides the paper from his fingers and conceals it in his palm. "I will share the note itself with you momentarily, but first let me get to the knee bone of this story. The revelation spoke of a painting—*this* painting."

Grotteschi points upward. Hanging on the church wall beside them is a heavy, framed picture. It shows three women, draped in white robes, spinning thread.

Grotteschi exhales, struggling to his feet. He puckers and puffs dust from the brass nameplate.

"This is *The Three Fates*, or, to give them their original Greek name, *The Moirai*. Painted in 1692 by the Dutch artist Emanuel de Witte. According to myth, by the spinning, pulling, and cutting of their thread, the Moirai determine our life span. Strange how that echoes Agnus's work on the human life span and telomeres."

His hand unrolls to show Siggurson the shred of paper, upon which a single sentence is scrawled.

The master Chiro Scuro Emanuel de Witte atrophied the fly of the fatal three.

Grotteschi waggles the paper, urging Siggurson to take it.

"When McDees received this revelation, I knew that the 'fatal three' must refer to *The Three Fates*. It was the only one of De Witte's works that made sense. So I persuaded McDees to order a copy of the painting so that we might study it. This is a cheap facsimile, but adequate for our purpose." He pokes in his monocle, peering at the brushstrokes. "Now I have to assume that Agnus made an error. In his haste, his misspelled *Chiaroscuro*, omitting the *a*. Chia*ro*scuro means "light and shadow" and it is an Italian style of painting. But here is the first twist of the mystery: Emanuel de Witte did not paint in the Italian style, so why would Agnus call him a master of this art? And then there is this to consider: The three Fates are women. In De Witte's work, the face of the Fate who cuts the thread and so determines death is decidedly masculine. Do you see that?"

Grotteschi's eye, made huge by the monocle, bubbles up at him. "Perhaps because De Witte knew the work was flawed in this way, he did not sign it with his real name but instead used the pseudonym *Kolibrie*."

Grotteschi's finger strokes the large, hard jaw of the deathly Fate. "McDees and I pondered over this endlessly. And oddly, I found this priest more given to fearful superstition than I. He lacked faith."

He fumbles with a chain that hangs about his distended neck, gold links that suspend a crucifix. "My mother raised me in the true faith, but when she committed the sin of suicide, I fell from the path. But now my heart has been reawakened. Whatever dark realms exist beyond this, I know that God's hand lies above them all and that He would not forsake us. But McDees, the superstitious charlatan, did not care a fig for what the message to mankind might be. He surrendered himself to dark imaginings and saw only his own future in this revelation, believing that it foretold his own death. He became obsessed with the rope in the hand of the final Fate, as if the length of it could tell him of the date of his own demise."

A shaft of light spears the gloom. The chapel door swings open. Siggurson turns to see a priest silhouetted in the arch. The long robes sweep forward.

Grotteschi nods his head. "Good evening, Father." Siggurson studies the figure as it moves through the darkness. His eyes are on a sliver of gray metal that flashes in the priest's hands.

Grotteschi sees this keen attention and waggles his head. "You think that is McDees? No, no. He's dead. Hanged himself with his own vestment belt. No easy task, the cord being only four feet long."

The priest sweeps by, hidden in a hooded robe, his hands clasped about an iron cross. He disappears into the vestry.

"That is the latest in a long line of feckless fathers who have been dispatched since the suicide of McDees. Not one has yet lasted a month before appealing to the cardinal for a transfer. It seems that Morphic Fields gives these sorry celibates the chills. But I digress. Your mind must be applied to this alone."

His old hand strokes the painting, then lowers to Siggurson's shoulder, pressing down with surprising strength. "I shall leave you now to contemplate. Let the meaning come to you."

Grotteschi crosses himself and kisses his crucifix. "Agnus is trying to show us the truth. And I know that somewhere in this painting, there is a sign of what comes."

53

HER PAINTED NAILS stab at the keypad of her phone. D'Sola picks up before she even hears it ring.

"You are extremely tense, Dr. Torgus."

She flinches, shaken. "Why do you say that?"

"I have an app that tells me how tightly you are holding your phone."

Dr. Torgus swallows, confused. Exhales at the sound of D'Sola's laughter.

"A joke, Dr. Torgus."

She tries to return the laughter but emits only a tight cough. "Mr. D'Sola, there's been a change of plan. No, not a change… a modification."

She looks in the mirror. Her fingers try to revive the drowned hairpiece that sprawls across her skull. "You should ask your driver to take you to the railway terminus behind the prison. We will be traveling with Agnus to the prison hospital. I have all the materials with me. We will have every opportunity to… take care of business."

At the other end of the line, D'Sola is silent. Dr. Torgus becomes agitated. Then: "Is this the only modification to your original proposal, Doctor?"

"Yes, absolutely. Everything else remains exactly as we

 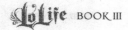

discussed."

She can almost hear the chill of D'Sola's smile.

"There's another great little app that I recommend. It gives you instant word definitions, Dr. Torgus. I suggest you look up the meaning of *exclusivity*."

✦

Ray d'Sola hangs up his phone. Slides it into his pocket. Leans back against the white leather of the seat.

The windshield wipers of his Rolls-Royce Silver Ghost silently sweep away the solid rain. The driver's voice is delivered via a walnut speaker.

"I still can't quite be sure what it is, sir." Wilson takes a hand off the wheel and tips back his chauffeur's cap. Stares hard through the downpour. Rising between the road and the distant bulk of Morphic Fields is some sort of metal structure.

"I'd say it's a music stage, sir. Because that bus"—he points to a vehicle ahead, swarming with kids who gawp against the glass—"looks to me like it's full o' fans o' some sort. But I can't read the name painted on the side, on account of all this blessed rain. So… Well, my sweet Lord!"

Wilson leans forward and points up to the heavens. "Will you look at that!" The solid black sky above Morphic Fields is splitting apart and sunlight shears through like a band saw.

Wilson shrugs, killing the wipers. "These desert storms are mighty strange."

"A detour, Wilson. Follow that bus."

The vehicle is bumping down an access road, heading

across the desert toward the structure.

Wilson yanks the wheel, churning dust. "As you please, sir."

D'Sola estimates that it will please him not at all. As the car passes the bus and nears the structure, he can now see that it is indeed a vast performance platform. Scaffold poles catch in the fresh sunlight, reflecting gold. Roadies roll drums of cable and haul generators. And above the stage, a banner rises. It bears one word:

STORK

D'Sola taps his soft chin. The name is familiar. And then the memory comes: a fat, perspiring band manager, veins bulging at his temple with desperation, pleading with D'Sola as a pleasant hour passes in his office.

He glances through the window as the car draws near to a collection of black-clad boys. They sit on the ground beneath a sunshade, surrounded by a swarm of assistants. This must be the band. Heads down, they appear disinterested in any attempt to usher them from the canopy. The only movement comes from a razor blade that flashes as it is passed from one band member to another, each taking a moment to score a fresh cut in his exposed forearm.

Walkie-talkies crackle, summoning security as shrieking fans are disgorged from the bus.

The Rolls slides between a row of metal barriers that are hurriedly hauled into place about the canopy. A pale-faced assistant, waving a clipboard, flags down the strange car.

"Here is just fine, Wilson." D'Sola ignores any attempt by

security to gain his attention. His eyes are locked upon a figure that rises from the band and walks toward the car. A long, lean boy whose face is hidden by a curtain of black hair.

The back door breathes open. D'Sola's voice rises from within, smooth as smoke.

"I think we should talk."

Hash-Tu spins the blade in his fingers as he sizes up the sleek machine, but no sound slides out from behind the shank of hair.

D'Sola smiles. "Oh, that's right. You shoe-gazing gonzos aren't much given to conversation." D'Sola leans an inch from the vehicle. His face catches in the sunlight. "Beautiful, isn't it?" He gestures to the sky, bright and clear. "I hope it holds for your performance."

A flash behind the hair shows that Hash-Tu's eyes are moving. His torso twitches a fraction closer. D'Sola smiles.

"Good. You know who I am. So can we put an end to this performance?"

"Are you here to see me?"

"Quite the opposite. I was not expecting to see anyone at all." D'Sola's hand gestures toward the massive form of Morphic Fields. "It is Agnus Day who brings you here?"

Hash-Tu nods.

"Ah, well, then, let us talk." D'Sola beckons the boy to join him in the vehicle. "Please, come. Wilson here can entertain us with another acre of desert."

From behind the barriers, fans whoop and holler as they catch sight of Hash-Tu. Two girls in the crowd stretch their necks, straining to catch a glimpse of him as he slides into the car. In a breath of dust, it bears him away across the desert.

One girl turns to her friend. Her green eyes are acid wide. "Hey, Livi, he's comin' back, right?"

"Of course, Ghost. He'll come back. He always comes back."

✦

The intercom button is flicked to private. Then D'Sola's finger rises, taps his lips. He is in no rush to speak himself. A moment of silence will allow him to gather his thoughts. Examine this emotion rising within him.

Shall I call it anger? Dr. Torgus had promised him exclusive access to the phenomenon of Agnus Day. That was one element of this venture that had attracted him, the fact that he could deny the privilege to anyone else. He had also been drawn by Dr. Torgus's knowledge of Archilochus, a poet for whom D'Sola has an unbridled passion. And of course her obvious emotional fragility was… appetizing.

But the proposal itself, to publish the convict's prophecies, seemed tenuous at best.

Still, curiosity had prevailed. The slaughter of that child-whore in Sulphur City was intriguing, and D'Sola felt a strong compulsion to be in the orbit of the one who wielded the knife.

But now that he is here, he finds some death-metal interloper has come to worship at the killer's shrine and share him with the world.

So the urge—the cold, hard longing that unfolds within him, like a many-bladed device—perhaps it is anger.

D'Sola relaxes back and moves to the more delicious

dilemma—*what to do with this anger?*

He glances at Hash-Tu, who stares out the window. D'Sola wonders if he rehearses in the mirror that tilt of his chin, high enough to elegantly stretch his neck like that of a wading bird, but not so high that his hair falls free from his face.

And then the black hair swings as Hash-Tu turns toward him. His voice has the clip of his Japanese origins. "Does the silence make you uneasy?"

D'Sola smiles.

"I think I'll stop you right there, glum-drop. You seem to be confused. Perhaps because your experience is more commonly that you are the weird one. The scary guy. The one who makes those around you… uneasy."

As he speaks, D'Sola feels his own breathing strangely accelerate. He clenches his jaw, forcing control over his lungs, determined to finish his discourse. "You don't make me feel… anything. *Nothing* makes me feel anything. But I think—in fact I know, with an awful certainty, that I can make you feel something."

Hash-Tu slides hard into the door, producing the blade from his fist. "Don't touch me, you fucking sicko."

His hand lashes and blood flies. Hash-Tu thrusts again, but slower now, unsure how it is that he draws so much blood from D'Sola when his blade does not appears to be connecting with him. And then, as he tries to raise his arm a third time, he sees it—his own hand, thrusting the blade into his own chest. Blood bubbling beneath his T-shirt as a hole opens wider.

Hash-Tu writhes, screaming, rupturing red across the white

leather. Unable to stop his own hand as it hacks and hews at his body.

D'Sola looks on, breathing hard, enraptured. The broader he smiles, the further the hole rips.

Until Hash-Tu spasms and slides from the seat.

D'Sola continues to watch for some minutes. The boy is exceptionally dead, but D'Sola feels the need for a moment's calm to examine what emotion it is that he now feels. He is an educated man, but he's not sure that there's a word for this. His finger quivers with such ferocity, he can barely secure it upon the intercom switch.

"Wilson, would you kindly stop the car."

The Rolls relaxes to a halt. The door is swept open and D'Sola exits. It is only as he stretches his arms wide and walks from the car, grinning at the vastness of the desert—that Wilson sees the bloody carcass on the car floor. The chauffeur's hand lunges inside his jacket and pulls a gun.

Turns to his boss, who smiles—utterly calm.

Swallowing hard, Wilson jerks the gun toward the corpse. "Now, Boss, you wanna tell me what's happening here?"

D'Sola inhales—then turns his eyes on Wilson.

"Wilson, I really don't know. But it is rather wonderful, don't you think?"

D'Sola seems to ripple with a strange energy. Turns his eyes on the old man.

"What do you want to do with that gun, Wilson?"

Wilson goes to speak, but something emanating from D'Sola seems to leaden his tongue, stultify his brain.

"Sir… I… I…"

 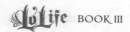

"You don't want to kill me, do you, Wilson? On a lovely day like today? With the sun so strong on the back of your neck? You want to put that ice-cold barrel against your hot head and pull the trigger, don't you Wilson?"

"Sir, I... don't."

But then Wilson feels it, the chill of the gun touching his temple. And his eyes slide to one side to see that his own hand steers the weapon.

"That's right, Wilson. Your world is a happy place."

Impossibly... irresistibly, Wilson's finger strokes the trigger and in a jolting blast... empties his brains out through his left ear.

D'Sola looks at this fresh corpse, thumping into the dust. Feels power rip through him like an execution volt.

Something is happening. He knows not what. But he knows this: It feels good. It feels right.

D'Sola bends to collect the car keys from Wilson's clenched hand. And then, before the conscious thought can find a voice inside his head, he submits to the urge to plant a hard kiss on the old man's mouth. D'Sola then twists away, drags a sleeve across his lips.

In an afternoon of first-time feelings, that last one, decides D'Sola, is definitively the most fucked up.

54

"AGAIN. SLOWER."

Bianco looks at the books spread open in front of Mo'Zart. He nods and brings his finger back toward an old art book that's open to an image of *The Three Fates*.

"This face here"—he taps the strong, masculine features of the last Fate, then sweeps his finger to a book of portraits open beside—"is this man right here."

Bianco looks from one image to the other. "And that is who… and that means what?"

Mo'Zart draws his fingertips into pincers as if conducting the most delicate part of the symphony.

"These revelations that Siggurson is gathering, every one of them is a clue to the identity of the Mosca. And Agnus was careful to ensure that each message could also be connected to the person to whom it was delivered—because that knowledge will help us to decipher it."

Mo'Zart pauses, letting each fact chime before moving on.

"What links Kon'Verse and Archilochus is that they both killed through the power of their words. McDees was a blackmailer and so was this guy." He taps the portrait of the man before them. "Jornis de Wijs."

Mo'Zart's finger rises now, moving faster, as if the music of his

 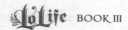

logic is gaining tempo. "Look at where the artist placed the face of De Wijs in *The Three Fates*—on the body of the Fate called Atropos, the one who cuts the thread… the Fate of Death, where the word *atrophy* comes from. And here in the revelation, it says he 'atrophied the fly.' Do you see, isn't it perfect?"

Mo'Zart is on his feet, as if ready to receive applause, but his audience of one stands with her arms folded.

"Everything. From the beginning."

Mo'Zart nods, tips up his palms. "As you want. But it begins in the seventeenth century."

He heaves across a huge art book, full of old paintings. "Back in seventeenth-century Holland, there was what I guess you could call a craze in high society. It was all about proverb paintings. They were given as gifts, simple country scenes, finely crafted. Charming and harmless, you'd think. But you'd be wrong. Every painting was intended to carry a hidden meaning, concealed in the symbols of the picture. And the message could only be cracked if you knew your proverbs well. So solving the riddle was like the equivalent of doing a crossword puzzle nowadays. People would spend hours staring at them, searching for clues. And they were motivated to solve the meaning. How else could they be sure what message the giver of the painting was sending to them. Was it a message of love, or an insult, or a threat even?"

A page falls open at a picture. It shows a serving maid pouring a pitcher of beer for a huntsman who has fallen asleep with a dead goose in his arms.

"Look at this one. Do you see that the pitcher she holds has a crack? That refers to an old proverb about a cracked pitcher not holding its beer, and it means that whoever sent this painting is saying, 'Man, you can't handle your liquor.' And the goose with the limp neck—there's a Dutch proverb that likens a man's inability to get it up to a goose that can't raise its head. I could go on, but you get the point. Whoever sent this painting was giving the message 'You can't hold your beer and it's making you impotent.' Perhaps sent by a disgruntled wife—who knows? This particular painting is clearly meant to be just a little fun. But the messages contained in some paintings were far more sinister. And none were more sinister than those sent by Jornis de Wijs."

Mo'Zart turns the book around so that the portrait of a man's sallow visage faces Bianco. "De Wijs was a blackmailer, and he hit upon the idea of sending paintings that concealed references to secrets that could defame and destroy high-society figures. All he needed for his plan was an artist willing to create the paintings, according to his instructions."

With a flick of his finger, Mo'Zart draws Bianco's eye to a book of paintings. "This is the work of Emanuel de Witte. He was perfect for ol' Jornis's plan—bankrupt, willing to do anything to save his situation. He created the paintings as Jornis proscribed. The blackmail victims were quick to read the messages hidden in the unwelcome art delivered to their doors. Some paid the price to the blackmailer, whom they knew only by the pseudonym signature in the corner of the painting, *Kolibrie*. But many—who could not pay the extortionate demand—took their own lives rather than risk exposure. In short, Jornis drove them to suicide. And De Witte, who loathed himself for the part he played, eventually took his own life. He

 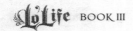

hanged himself—but not before completing a painting of his own design."

Mo'Zart now returns his hand to *The Three Fates*. "This was his final work, and in it, he left a hidden message to be found after his death. One that would expose to all society the identity of the deadly blackmailer who had been plaguing them. On the body of the Fate of Death, De Witte painted for all to see the face of Jornis de Wijs, so everyone would know that he was the mysterious Kolibrie. De Witte left the painting to be discovered on the day of his suicide. Two days later, Jornis was found stabbed through the mouth. Most assumed that the killer was one of his blackmail victims, but an eyewitness gave testimony that the knife was wielded by a man called Corbin Kraal. In normal circumstances, the master of the Burgher Guard would have pursued this villain Kraal, but none mourned the death of Jornis de Wijs, and the stranger was allowed to slip away unhindered."

Bianco says nothing, waiting for silence to signal the end of this account. She shakes her head. "The shit you know."

Mo'Zart pulls the books back toward him. "Now we gotta put it all together."

The book on Archilochus bears the poet's picture on the front. Mo'Zart adds it to his stack.

"This is what I think: Agnus is showing us that Archilochus and Jornis were both incarnations of the Mosca. Neither reached his awakening. So if we can find what links Archilochus and Jornis, then we'll know what links them to the next incarnation… the one that comes now. We look for that link—we find him."

"And kill him."

"Of course." Mo'Zart gathers the mounting pile of books to him. "Just gonna take some time."

The shriek of an alarm cuts the air, echoing from the walls, filling the prison. The door to the library suddenly thuds open. Officer Trill appears.

"Ma'am, the governor says we got trouble. Big trouble. Right now."

✦

Rum swirls in a tumbler. Duggin drains the shot and pours himself another, clamping a large telephone receiver between his neck and jowl, continuing his call.

"With all due respect, Agent Bianco, I must ask that you pay heed to my greater experience. I had no option but to order a lockdown. If we fail to take immediate action, we are sitting on a powder keg."

He swigs a second time, emptying the glass. "The reality is that Agnus Day has regained consciousness, which befits neither your objectives nor mine. Once he is back amongst the inmates, his control will return. So we have but a short window in which to remove him from the prison. Now, our means of discreetly so doing are limited. With a hundred miles of wetlands in every direction, getting anything out of Morphic Fields is a challenge."

He pauses. "Agent Bianco, would you excuse me a moment? My officers have arrived and are awaiting orders." Duggin claps a hand over the mouthpiece. "Very good, gentlemen. Very smooth. My compliments to H. Block. Those Haitians are real masters of rum. Now load it up. All of it."

Five officers nod, approaching a stack of barrels in the office, each taking one and rolling it out. Duggin smacks his lips, returns to his call.

"So this is my proposal. Each Friday night a train arrives, dedicated to Morphic Fields. It transports inmates due for trial, or those in need of advanced medical treatment, and brings in supplies—in short, a line to the outside world. It is well armed and built for this purpose, so I want you to have no qualms as to security. There will be guards and munitions aboard. Now, fortuitously, today is Friday, so I say we put Agnus on the train and defuse this situation."

He pauses, allowing Bianco to respond. His face relaxes. He is hearing what he wants. Leans back.

"I'm glad that you agree, Agent. Together we can remove a rag from a barrel o' Molotov."

55

GROTTESCHI'S MONOCLE GLITTERS as he stands tiptoe on his bunk frame. Peers out of his cell window to the floodlit desert below. A solitary rail track stretches from the dark horizon to Morphic Fields, where it thrusts between giant concrete cubes, assembled as a platform.

The surface is checkered by the pools of light, and guards in their pale buff uniforms move in and out of the shadows. Grotteschi squints, counting numbers. This is a bigger turnout than the usual bon voyage brigade. Grotteschi watches them progress across the cubed platform like chess pieces.

And then black makes its move.

Four dark suits appear. Federal agents, he's sure of it, fanning out to take up position at each corner of the platform. Grotteschi does not know what their purpose is. But he does know that Siggurson is one of them.

He watches as Siggurson turns his face up to the prison, as if sensing that one good eye is upon him. Grotteschi crinkles a smile.

He is not aggrieved by the deception. How can a fraudster such as he cast judgment? And further, he forgives them for a reason they could never understand. Their deception bears a strange truth. Siggurson is not a visionary, but without a doubt he exists beyond the norm. Life and death are no simple matters with him. Somehow, those forces coexist within his head. And what awaits him is the strangest fate, neither life nor death, but something other.

Grotteschi feels this... with all his heart. A heart now awoken to God, who speaks clearly to him. He clasps his hands together in prayer.

"Holy Mary, Mother of God, you have sent them to keep Agnus safe. So I ask that you bestow your protection, Holy Mother."

He sinks lower, burying his nose between his freshly washed hands. Breathes deep.

"Mother..."

✦

On the platform, a radio crackles.

"This is bad."

"*This is good, Lola.*"

"Good how?"

"*You think I would have agreed to this without an advantage?*"

"Which is?" Lola releases the Receive button on her radio, looks across to the far corner where Bianco stands, radio to her lips.

"*We know the Mosca is drawn to pursue the Moera. So if Agnus gets on the train, the Mosca will feel compelled to follow. And that means our search area gets smaller. In the prison, we'd be looking amongst two thousand people. On the train we're gonna have maybe fifty.*"

Lola nods. "This is good." She turns at the rattle of gurney wheels. "They're bringing Agnus now."

Two guards steer the gurney. Agnus is bound to the frame by leather straps. Bianco looks on from across the platform.

"*He can't talk?*"

"Won't talk."

"*Does he know who we are?*"

"He knows who I am."

"*What do you mean?*"

"It means I don't trust him."

Mo'Zart's voice cuts across the transmission. "*We must trust him. He's all we have.*"

From his corner, Siggurson watches. "*But look at him, he's barely alive. How can we be sure that the Moera will emerge from that? Maybe he's malfunctioning. You can wire a bomb, but it doesn't always detonate.*"

"*So with or without his help—we find the Mosca and take it down.*" Bianco raises her hand and jerks it forward, a signal for them all to board the train.

"*Lola, you stay close to Agnus. Siggurson—there's an observation car; the monitors cover the train. I've told Duggin that's ours.*"

"*Copy that. Where will you be?*"

Bianco strides toward the ironclad locomotive. "*Everywhere.*"

✦

A watch ticks. Dr. Torgus feels the whir of the second hand as if it were drilling into her wrist.

He should be here!

She paces the platform, eyes hovering on the half-lit dirt

 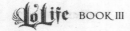

road that leads to the terminus. The train won't go until those agents are aboard, so for these few brief moments, she is glad of their presence. She watches as they walk from the far corners of the platform.

Slowly! Slowly! Just a few moments more…

Then she sees a figure mount the steps to the platform. Her eyes widen in welcome, then instantly thin. It is only the prison chaplain. What confused her was the speed of his approach. She has never known any chaplain to show an ounce of alacrity to travel with the sick. She strikes a match for her cigarette and spares herself a smile. They will actually be in need of a priest, once she has put Agnus into his endless slumber. The chaplain will no doubt be thrilled to prove himself so useful.

She sucks her smoke to life and flicks the match into a trash can. Her eyes return to their sweep of the platform and the road. As the two agents board the train, she pulls her phone, hesitant to disturb him, but desperate now. The phone does not ring before he answers.

"Yes?"

"Mr. D'Sola, the train is about to depart."

"I can see that."

Dr. Torgus swivels her head the length of the terminus. "You're here? I don't see you. Do you see me?"

"My dear Doctor, you are thoroughly conspicuous." And then she hears it. A crackle as the trash can, ignited by her discarded cigarette, shoots up a flame. She leaps to one side, hair swinging. Looks up to see Ray D'Sola is onboard the train, his shoulder casually propped against the window of the warden's private carriage.

56

THE SOUND OF a muffled scream has a special quality. The stoppered mouth means the cry is forced back down the throat, resonating in the belly. This particular body, however, is as thin as a piccolo and makes a pitiful sound.

Stripped to the waist, bound and gagged, a man is crammed beneath a wooden frame. An altar of sorts. It rocks back and forth as the train gathers speed. The altar is one of many crude fixtures that dress the carriage as a chapel of rest. It is here that the corpses are placed of those inmates who fail to survive the journey. Such is the fate of many who receive a shank to the guts and are able to do nothing but bleed for a hundred miles.

But now the chapel is splattered with blood from the many deep cuts that cover the man's body. And on his forehead, the knife arrives to bite again—once, twice—making a raw *V*.

A voice whispers.

"Now, my dear chaplain, let me be clear: I intend to carve my entire name upon your face. By the time I reach the *O*, I suspect that I shall be upon your eye. But you could end this agony. Simply take the blade and draw it across your neck. It is suitably sharp; I think we can both agree on that."

The bound man howls beneath his gag, writhes away from

 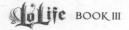

the blade. But the knife pursues him. "Your death is certain. All I ask is that you take your own life. You will, assuredly, do a kinder job than me."

A screams drenches the cloth. But still the captive does not take the knife.

✦

A thick cotton wad is shoved into an ear. Molloy grimaces and pokes the wad deeper. Turns to Officer Trill. "That done it?"

Trill looks at a streak of blood that runs down Molloy's neck and sticks to his collar. The source is the plugged ear. He nods. "Looks good."

"Damn thing jus' started today. Weeping like a wound o' Christ. I don't know what's happenin' to me."

"Maybe you can get a doc to take a look when we get to the hospital."

"I'm not hanging around for that. By the time today's batch has been processed, we'll be heading back." He jerks a thumb to the car behind. "Hell, there's gotta be more than fifteen today."

"Eighteen in total. Seven wrist-slits, two belly-shanks, four bone-snaps, five unknowns."

"You count up everything, don't ya, boy?"

Trill nods.

"I'd say there's something wrong with you."

"I'd say there's something wrong with all of us."

They turn at the sound of the train car door sliding. The black robe of the chaplain sweeps through; his hat is pulled low.

"Afternoon, Father. Can we help you?"

The chaplain pushes past the guards, brings his face against the observation slot to the inmates' car.

"I've come to see Agnus Day. I hear he is somewhat... sick."

Molloy forces himself between the window and the chaplain, irked at this intrusion.

"He's not in there. Warden said he was to be in solitary." A twitch of Molloy's head indicates the next carriage down. "Also said no one was to enter."

"Might I just have the assurity of looking in?" The chaplain wafts a hand at this simple request. But Molloy's eyes go to the fingertips. They glisten with sweat.

He adjusts the wad in his ear as he thinks. "I guess there's no harm in looking."

He leads the chaplain to the window of the second car. Taps the glass with his knuckle.

"That's Agnus. As he lives and breathes."

The chaplain's nose is all that protrudes from beneath his hat and now its pointed tip presses against the glass. "Who is that in there with him?"

"An agent—I don't know what federal flavor. Not my business."

Sweat runs down the glass and Molloy sees its source is the chaplain's chin. The collar below is drenched and sticky.

"Are you all right there, Father?" Yellow eyes swivel beneath the brim and Molloy instantly understands that this inquiry also falls beyond the bounds of his business. In a flash of black, the chaplain is gone, striding down the carriage.

Molloy ambles back alongside Trill. "Another new chaplain,

I guess." Shakes his head, ear-wad waggling. "How many we had since Agnus came, eh?"

Trill shrugs. "Ain't been counting."

+

He feels the car door slide shut behind him. Removes his hat and sweeps away a thick slick of sweat. Vassago needs span.

He hasn't fed since his last official ration from the Sinestra, and that dose is proving lamentably weak. And his accursed captive is refusing to comply. Vassago had believed the chaplain would submit readily. The way he begged and pleaded at the outset of the attack, clawing at Vassago's stolen robes, hanging about his thighs and weeping. But once bound and gagged, he became resilient. Refusing to sully his soul with suicide.

But Vassago will break him.

He must, so that the greater quest can be pursued. His fingers fumble with a fold beneath his robe, then close about the cool shaft of his clave. He has his precious tool. Now all he needs is for Scox to do its duty and blaze beside the body that bears the Mosca. Then he will act! He will plunge his clave and awaken the dark messiah.

Ah, glory so long since denied me! He can almost hear the voices ring in adulation from his brothers in the Legion.

Vassago smiles. With a hand wet with sweat, he slides open the door to the chapel carriage. And a muffled cry rises.

57

Bianco spins the chamber of her magnum shut. "I'm checking out who's on this train." She glances at the bank of monitors in the observation car. They flicker between cameras.

Looks over to Mo'Zart as her muzzle points to Siggurson. "Fill him in." She holsters her weapon. "And if something boils inside that soup you call your brain, let me know."

Siggurson gestures to her weapon. "How'd you keep hold of that? We got a heavy pat down in the warden's office."

"Maybe I got more places to hide a gun." Bianco slides it down the belt of her pants. "Or maybe I got two."

As she exits, one of the monitors captures her image. Siggurson watches her disappear into the next car.

"She thinks she can handle this alone." He turns to Mo'Zart. "She can't. So make this fast."

Mo'Zart nods. "You got it." He lifts up a book. "Once upon a double-time there was a poet. His name was Archilochus." Taps the front cover of the book that bears his picture. "Archilochus had some wicked rhymes. No doubt he was an incarnation of the Mosca, but he was silenced by the knife of a man called Corvus."

Siggurson nods and rolls his hand for Mo'Zart to continue.

"Two thousand years later, the next incarnation of the Mosca

 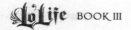

is this guy." Mo'Zart produces a copy of *The Three Fates* and points to the face on Atropos. "His name was Jornis de Wijs, but he, too, was halted before his awakening because the signature on this painting exposed him as the blackmailer Kolibrie and he was killed by Corbin Kraal, an assassin." He pauses. "That's all we have. But I believe it's enough. We find what links these two... and that will lead us to the next incarnation."

Siggurson takes the picture of *The Three Fates*, studies it. "There's no signature here."

Mo'Zart scoots closer. "That's the thing with these proverb paintings—no words. You gotta play Guess the Symbols." He jabs a finger at the corner where a signature should be. "*Kolibrie* is Dutch for 'hummingbird,' and in Dutch proverbs, it signifies blackmail. The hummingbird sucks sweetness from a flower, like an extortionist draining his victim. And Mr. Kolibrie, gotta say, he was good. After his murder, his fortune was turned over to the church. Town records show it as ninety thousand guilders. Today, we're talking about twenty million dollars."

He taps the portrait of De Wijs, a finger circling the narrow eyes. "Can you imagine if he had been awakened? The Mosca, with all that money and power behind him? And you know what? I think that dude knew that he had a destiny waiting—he was aware. More than the previous incarnation. Archilochus caused others hurt. But he was just a poet. And the urge to torment drove him insane. De Wijs was rich, with a deep reach into European society. And he relished the pain he caused. He made a business out of it. *Big* business."

Mo'Zart leans back. "If the Mosca were a serial killer, you know what the cops would say: that he's escalating. Each incarnation is richer, more powerful. And with a greater passion for the Tormenta cause. So this one that's coming, he's gonna be a natural born world-shaker."

"So we kill him in the shell." Siggurson snaps the book shut.

"But first we gotta find him." Mo'Zart takes the book back. "Which means looking for what links each incarnation. And honestly—"

Mo'Zart's radio crackles, interrupting.

"*You still talking?*"

Mo'Zart clicks the button. "Getting there, Bianco."

"*Get quicker.*"

Mo'Zart puts the handset down. Looks at Siggurson. "Who made her leader?"

"Darwin." Mo'Zart smiles. "Yeah, she's gotta lotta tooth and claw, right."

"*You wanna get your opposable thumb off the button? I can still hear ya.*"

The young agent stuffs the radio into his belt and Siggurson pushes the books back toward him. "You better crack this connection, kid, or she's gonna make you eat crow."

Mo'Zart nods. "True to her name." He rams a finger into his dreads, twists deep. And then his eyes rise. A smile ignites. "And ain't that a thing. Crow. They're both called Crow."

"Who?"

Mo'Zart leaps to his feet, hands alive. "*Corvus* is Latin for 'crow.' And *kraal* is Dutch for 'crow.'"

"So what—we have a link between the assassins. That doesn't get us any closer to the Mosca."

Mo'Zart raises a finger. "Unless of course…"

 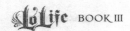

Black heels slide across the metal floor as the train lurches around a bend. Bianco's hand slams against a window as she steadies herself. She resumes her approach toward two uniformed guards who stand outside the prisoners' carriage.

Molloy stiffens, flashing the stripes on his shoulder as Bianco flashes only a smile.

"Gentlemen, how are ya?"

"Popular this afternoon."

"I'm looking for the passenger manifest."

"You mean a list of everyone onboard?"

"We can call it that."

Molloy prods the wad in his ear. "We don't have one."

"So you don't know who's on the train?"

"If it's got a gun, it's a guard. Cuffs, it's a con."

"What about civilians?"

Molloy shakes his head. "Ain't no civilians on this train."

Trill dips in. "Apart from the guy with Dr. Torgus."

Molloy stretches his neck. "Well, obviously apart from *that* guy."

"What guy?"

"Let me check with the list that we don't have and get right back to you."

Trill dips again. "He's in the Pullman, ma'am, center carriage."

Bianco nods, spins on her heel, and strides away down the corridor.

Molloy throws Trill a hot eyeball, but the young guard

shakes his head. "She's a federal agent, Wally. It ain't smart to lose it with an agent."

"I was not losin' it."

Trill waggles a finger at the ear-wad. It now oozes with fresh blood. "I think you lost a little too much brain."

✦

As Bianco walks down the corridor her radio bleeps.

She pulls it from its pouch. Mo'Zart's voice blasts. "*How good is your Greek?*"

"I can fry cheese. That's it."

"*No, no… the translation. The meaning.*"

"The point?"

"*They both mean the same thing. Kolibrie is Dutch for 'hummingbird.' And archilochus… that's 'hummingbird' in Greek. The name. The name is the destiny.*"

"So we're looking for a guy called 'Hummingbird.'"

"*Or something that means hummingbird.*"

"Fuck, I never want you on my team in Pictionary."

Siggurson's voice cuts in. "*Get serious, Bianco. Because this is all we got.*"

"Hey, I'm Missy Serious-Mysterious."

She slides the radio back, quickens her pace, and whispers to herself.

"Let's start checkin' names and shootin' brains."

 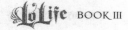

58

A FINGER TRACES the scars of a tattoo. It wraps around Lola's biceps and ripples as she flexes her fist. The original ink design has been corrupted by a knife. It once displayed her Hunter number: 101A.

But when she went rogue, she took a blade and cut the digits deep, turning them into letters to create a new name to go with her new life: LOLA.

But the scars had never healed and often still open and weep.

The blood trickles down her arm. She turns away, knowing there is no tending that will work. Her eyes go to the many drips and feeds that puncture Agnus's arms, which lie inert above the blankets.

And in the gloom of the windowless car, she contemplates again the same silent questions.

How can this be the Moera, the savior of mankind?

Everything that she knows of the Mosca tells of a fearsome force so commanding that all Tormenta will fall into his thrall.

And this pale shank of flesh is all that will stand in his path?

Then Lola inhales, stiffening. She must have faith.

Because after all, what was I? A foolish girl, too scared to live her life. And look at me now. I changed. He will change.

There must be another stage in his evolution. Perhaps it

takes the Mosca to first appear and this rising will cause him to emerge.

"I wish to rise."

The sound of his voice jolts Lola from her thoughts. Agnus is twitching a finger toward a metal plate on the bed.

"There is a mechanism."

Lola snaps into action, leaning forward, finding a panel of buttons. Stabs one. The bed slowly grinds until Agnus sits upright.

"Is that good?"

"No, my dear, it is agony, but I will endure it to set my eyes upon you." A shifting sparkle from his sockets suggests that his eyes are traveling the length of her body. "I find you most... becoming."

His blackened lips crack into a smile. "And tell me—what am I?"

Lola says nothing, her eyes hard upon him as suddenly his face sags. Then bulges and twists, as if a fist churns within his skull, stretching his features into a reptilian grin.

"I asked you a question. *What am I?*" The hissing voice does not pause to draw breath. "I will tell you what I am. I am the last and the most wretched of the three. The half-made thing!"

His hand thrashes outward, grasping at Lola's torso. "But, vile miscreant that I am, I deserve to live."

The goal of his clawing now becomes clear. He scrambles for the vial of span. Taken from Jolusa, it now hangs from Lola's belt.

"I can smell it! Give it to me!"

His body lurches upward, then snaps and spasms, arching back as if a bolt shoots through his spine, seizing his muscles.

Shrieking, he falls against the bed. His face drops. And, still gasping for breath with his mouth pressed to the pillow, his voice mumbles.

"Do you know who I am?"

Lola finds her voice. "You are the Moera. You were three—now one."

His cracked lips ease into a smile. His head nods. "Agnus was the first, the Father. Weakened by his loss. And then came the Hunter, strengthened by his training. And then came the Maniac... driven by his lusts."

He raises his hand and stares at the limb as if it were still freshly drenched in blood. His voice comes, a sorrowful whisper. "She was just a child."

Lola watches, as if mesmerized by the small, pale hand. That suddenly lashes like a viper, grasping at her belt.

"Give me life! You don't deserve it! What were you, eh? What were *you!*" He struggles for breath, overwhelmed by his fury. "You were such an ugly and despicable girl. No one liked you. No one cared for Maddy Pool. And then *he* came along and you were so stupid, oh, so monumentally stupid that you let yourself believe a boy as beautiful as he could want a creature like you. Suicide—you lacked the spine for even that! And now you dare to hold life in your hand and deny it me? Unworthy *bitch!*"

Agnus hauls himself back, roiling and writhing on the bed, his body a battleground. But his eyes are still cold and in control.

"You will obey!" Lola jolts as the muscles in her shoulder tighten. Then a searing pain comes, as if a cold steel rod is being forced into her arm, pulling her like a puppet, thrusting her hand down toward the vial. With a grunt, Lola pulls back, the heft of her resistance smashing her hand into the wall.

A voice shrills from within Agnus, "Stop! She is just a child!"

Then the same mouth contorts into a grimace, hissing. "She is just another whore for slitting…"

Lola's hand quivers as it is ripped from the wall and forced down toward the vial, fingers brushing the glass. She clasps her other hand about her own wrist, trembling with the effort of self-restraint. Until—

"Cease this!"

Her hand drops free. Lola looks up. The face before her reflects neither sorrow nor maniacal fury. What Lola recognizes is the cold resolve of a Hunter. The voice is clenched tight.

"The Father will speak and you will listen. We have little time before the other rises again."

And in that moment, the mouth drops, pale and loose. And Agnus hauls a rattling breath, then another, deeper, as if trying to blow out a fire inside him.

At last, words come.

"I am three and I am one… but I am not the Moera."

Lola leans close, measuring her words. "But the *Kata* confirmed it; you have passed through the three states. And Judas—"

"—believed what he wanted so desperately to believe."

"Your visions—"

"—were real. And with purpose. For I am nothing but the lamb, the sacrifice. My death is to pave the way for the true Moera." Agnus grimaces, as if quelling pain. Struggles for breath, and in the silence, Lola drops her head into her hands.

"But if you are not the Moera, then the Mosca... We will not find him here?"

"Oh yes, the Mosca is very close. He must be, for he is drawn to the Moera."

"But then who?"

"You! You—"

Agnus lurches forward, stiffening his lips, seeking control. But fury overwhelms him, and the bitter wretch within him completes the sentence to its own design.

"You are a stinking whore! Filthy as the one who stole from me! My life! My life!"

His hands flail wildly, clawing at the air. "But I got it back— unwittingly, perhaps. For I just stumbled on the secret—one that you already knew! But, brainless worm that you are, you wiped it from your memory!"

His eyes bulge, straining with fury. "You want to remember, don't you! You have to remember, or you will never get your span back, never pass into the third state... so think! Think! What I did to that little bitch before I ripped her belly open? I fucked her, Lola. I fucked her until she came."

And with a gasp, his throat kinks and he slumps back against the bed. His face is still twisted and sunk deep into the sheets, almost suffocating his mouth. Lola cannot tell who it is that speaks from within him.

"You know what the French call an orgasm—a *petite mort*... a little death. They say some part of you dies when you reach ecstasy. That a little of life itself slips from you and that's what makes the thrill. And they will never know how right they are. Because that is how a Hunter can redeem their lost span. Bring a Tormenta to ecstasy and when they reach release, the stolen span comes out alongside. In that moment," his fist suddenly launches upward, "it can be snatched back."

The hand hangs midair and then falls limp and tumbles back down. Agnus rolls onto his back, freed from the sheets, breathing deep, eyes wide and cold.

"To Jezebeth, I was just another trick. Neither she nor I knew the fates to which we condemned ourselves as we raged across that bed." He hauls a deep breath. "I roused Jezebeth and in her moment of release, my span was released back to me." He exhales, blood dribbling between his teeth from the exertion. "Three become one... but not in me. I am no trinity. Just a travesty. A wretched and accidental chimera."

His hand reaches out toward her. "The true Moera is aware. It has a fixed purpose. Seeking out its span, it seduces knowingly... to come... to become."

His eyes burn into hers. "What do you seek, Lola? What drove you to leave your duty to the Sinestra?"

"My span—to reclaim my span."

Agnus smiles, as if his mind, like a frail raft, has weathered the storm and pulled into its harbor.

"Yes, child."

And as his eyes stay fixed upon her, demanding more, Lola feels words rise in her throat as if pulled out by wire.

"I... I am the Moera."

Agnus nods and withdraws his hands back upon his chest, almost in prayer. "And so if the Mosca rises, you too must be ready to rise. So you must reclaim your span. If you do so knowingly—willfully—you will not suffer as I did. You will

instead pass into the third state. This is your destiny. And so, as the lamb who came to lead you, I have only one last thing to impart…"

Agnus holds out his hand, a frail finger beckoning her closer. Lola leans in. And with a roar, Agnus lashes out, snaring her wrist, pulling her closer, grinning maniacally at his subterfuge.

"I will live!"

She feels his grip weaken as a voice bellows, not from his mouth but from the chamber of his neck, which now bulges like a bullfrog's throat: "Release her or die!"

His eyes still blazing, Agnus shakes his head. "No, Hunter. I shall not!"

Lola is forced down onto the bed. His fingers claw.

But as he strains to pull Lola the last inch, the voice that comes next is that of a roused father.

"You shall not hurt her!"

Then his mouth twists again, a sliver of scorn.

"You are the weakest! You have not the courage to stop me!"

His fingertips clench against the vial, so tight a crack appears in the glass, and then something whips past Lola's face. It's a surgical tube, exploding from Agnus's neck. He howls, his grip weakening. Lola breaks free. Bolts upright to see Agnus writhing as the remaining surgical drips burst out of his body like fireworks ignited from within, spraying blood and plasma. Soaking the ceiling until finally the tube in his trachea explodes outward, blasting a gaping chasm in his neck, through which the last of him escapes in a whistling rush.

In the silence that follows, Lola stares at the flesh vessel that was once so many and which is now no one at all.

59

"My skirt's too short." Dr. Torgus twitches on a velvet stool and her hand flies to her mouth, clamping her lips. She makes sure a smile is fixed before she unmasks it.

"I don't know why I said that. I apologize; how foolish." As her hand sinks lower, it brushes her skirt, tweaking a tug.

A man's hand reaches past her, pulling a bowl of cashews closer. "My presence disturbs you."

"Mr. D'Sola, no. Please don't think that."

"I think I will."

A silence hangs.

"Martini?" The syllables tinkle down like broken glass. Torgus slides from the stool and moves behind the bar. It stretches the length of the Pullman carriage. "Let me guess how you like it." She playfully pops her eyes. "Real dirty and with olives?"

"Must you ogle so? It's awful."

Torgus blinks, feels her smile stick to her teeth. She turns toward the bottles. Trails a finger across the labels. "It seems… we have no vermouth."

"Then a whiskey."

A moustache of sweat clings to the hairs of her upper lip. She licks it away. All of the bottles are empty.

"No whiskey either—how foolish."

"Then what?"

She turns back to face D'Sola and her eyes catch on a stack of barrels concealed beneath the mahogany counter. Duggin's prison-brewed liquor.

"We have rum."

"Then you have redemption."

Torgus pulls open the cooler, tips an ice tray, and sends cubes hailing down.

"I hope this may redeem me further." She nods toward a folder on the bar. It is spilling papers. "Please take a look. I think you will find the prophecies arresting."

She turns to the cooler, replacing the ice tray. And with a subtle hand, she pulls from the shelf a small pharmaceutical vial.

With her back to D'Sola she inserts a syringe and fills the barrel of the hypodermic. She hears D'Sola flick through the papers.

The needle slips into her pocket. And D'Sola closes the file. "Intriguing, certainly."

Torgus swoops, emboldened.

"I have a campaign all planned. We tap into the online community that The Revelation Project has already grown and we launch Agnus to a new generation, looking for a prophet."

Her eyes are wide, begging for a response. "An unusual name... Torgus. Annie Torgus."

She flinches, confused by D'Sola's sudden change of subject. Gathers herself, leans back against the bar. "Annie is short for Anstice. It is Greek."

D'Sola smiles. "Now I understand your appreciation of

Archilochus." He leans in close. "For most, his vicious words hold no appeal. People find him… crushing."

Torgus forces herself to speak, to mask the weight of her breathing. "*Anstice* means 'resurrection'—that's me, you see. I cannot be crushed. I will always rise again."

D'Sola's fingers are now sliding under the cuff of her blouse, easing the silk upward. Torgus inhales, unable to move at his touch. Unable to distinguish between the pulsing sensations of fear and arousal that travel higher with each thrust of his fingers. Until the fabric rips and exposes on her forearm a tattoo. A long-beaked bird.

"And what is this?"

Through dry lips, she whispers, "A stork. That's what *torgus* means—in Greek."

D'Sola is close now, his lips almost upon her.

"So here you are, a Greek bearing gifts." His hand slams down on the file. He suddenly withdraws from her. "So you will understand that I cannot trust you."

Torgus blinks, thrown from his thrall.

D'Sola is all business once more. "I need to see some evidence that you have ownership of these papers."

Torgus smoothes her jacket, using the move to check that the syringe is securely in her pocket.

"Agnus Day will transfer the rights to me before the train arrives, Mr. D'Sola. Now I suggest you sit back and relax, peruse the writings. I shall shortly return."

Wrapping a smile across her jaw, she moves toward the carriage door, swinging her hips as if she imagines D'Sola's eyes are upon her.

Then she halts with a sudden untidy stagger. The door bursts open.

Stood in the frame is Bianco. She rips a smile. "Bon'swa, as we say in the swamps."

Torgus opens her mouth, releasing a hiss of surprise. But she is too slow to summon words as Bianco's arms thrust past, beckoning D'Sola to exit the car.

Torgus inhales, swelling her resistance. "This gentleman is my guest and you cannot just—"

Bianco addresses D'Sola over the invisible shoulder of Torgus. "I need you, sir."

✦

In the hallway outside, D'Sola sweeps forward. "That request from one as lovely as you, I can't resist."

He exits into the corridor and Bianco slides the door shut, erasing Torgus's face behind.

She turns to the dark, sleek figure who stands so very close. "I need your name."

"Marry me and it is yours."

Bianco says nothing. D'Sola smiles, nodding compliance. Passes her a thick white business card. Watches as her eyes scan the glossy print.

"And might I ask your name, Agent?"

"My name doesn't matter."

"Oh, I think you know that names matter a great deal."

He snares the card, draws it back. Bianco flinches, surprised by the move. Disturbed that she allowed it to happen. She flexes her fingers. They feel slow, reluctant.

"I suspect that my name is not what you hoped for. I have disappointed you." He pockets the card. "Men are always such a disappointment. And you, Agent Nameless…" He leans in close, dragging his nose up the curve of her neck. "You smell like a woman who has been recently… disappointed."

Bianco moves sharply away. Except that she doesn't. Her mind gives the clear command, but her body is deaf to everything save the sound of his voice, strumming the tiny hairs of her ear.

"What was it—one night and then nothing. Not even an acknowledgment that it happened. I think he is blameless. The fault is yours. You just don't have it. That thing that men want. The va-voom, the moves. *You* are a fuck to forget, Agent Gameless."

Bianco feels herself fall back against the wall. Her eyes closing. His breath caressing her lips.

"I don't think we should see each other any more." Silence, then—

She opens her eyes.

The corridor is empty.

He is gone.

60

THE TIP OF a blade circles an eye socket, sinking deep and creating a perfect O. Vassago leans back, admiring his work. The letter completes his name, now carved across the sweating face of the chaplain.

"So, I ask you again, would your merciful God want you to suffer? Is suicide a sin when it ends such anguish?"

The chaplain's eyes, sticky with blood, stare upward. Vassago shirks away. "You look at me with all your fancy faith as if I am not worthy. A lesser thing than you! Well, I have a creed. I have belief! It is my faith that forces me to wreak these wounds upon you... and my faith is strong."

The knife hovers, ready to strike again.

And then the chaplain opens his mouth a crack and whispers, "Tell me of your faith."

Vassago bends lower as the chaplain whispers again. "What do you believe?"

Vassago thins his lips, which crack and crumble with decay. "What I believe... you could never comprehend."

Blood oozes from the chaplain's mouth as he struggles to form words. "Perhaps if I understood your creed, I could find a rationale that would allow me to comply... allow me to exit by the means you wish."

Vassago is now bent double, his shriveled ear close enough to the chaplain's mouth to glean every word. He feels hope rise within him. "So you are saying that if I explain my faith, you will do as I bid?"

He feels the chaplain's head rock in his grasp—a nod!

"Then I tell you this. I believe that the Mosca will come and unite all Tormenta, show us the strength that comes from acting as one—and that once joined in combat, we will usurp humankind and bend them to our needs. This will be done when the messiah comes. And I, Vassago, shall be the one to bring forth his glory."

"His glory… or yours?"

Vassago stiffens. "A glory I deserve! Where so many have failed, I will succeed! And my place within the Legion will be restored." His fingers tighten about the chaplain's skull. "My name will be forever honored."

The chaplain's voice is now no more than a gasp. "True worship is what the soul does unseen. Faith is to forget the self."

Vassago's skinless fingers feel once more for the knife. "I do not think, churchman, that we are walking toward common ground here."

He folds the chaplain's fingers about the hilt and places the edge to his throat. "So now, do as I bid and take your life."

The chaplain twists a thin smile. "I have done… as I was bid."

The knife falls unused as finally, the chaplain's many wounds gather him to death.

Vassago throws back his head and howls in frustration. Rises up, paces about the car. His eyes catch in a mirror. His flesh is

now grizzled down to the bone. He lifts his hand, sniffing it, recoiling from the stench. More than decay, he reeks of defeat.

He has no span. He has no sign of the Mosca. And now—he has no time.

✦

Outside the chapel car, Officer Trill raps his knuckles again.

"Father? Are you in there?"

His fingers try the door. It is locked. He knocks a third time. "Officer Molloy sent me. He says that you should come. It's Agnus… He…"

Trill stops. Molloy had given him strict instructions not to say too much. All he had to do was ask the chaplain to come to Agnus's car. If for any reason he would not attend the body, then Trill was to insist he stay inside the chapel. Molloy wants the train on lockdown. So two options only. No arguments.

Trill wrinkles his lips, irked by the lack of response. The chaplain must be in there if the door is locked from the inside. He glances up at the fire axe, braced above the door. One swing and he could gain entry. But that might be beyond the bounds of Molloy's directive.

So Trill knocks a final time. "Father, either you come with me or you stay in there until we arrive. Choice is yours."

From inside the car comes a loud metallic creak. And then the thud of boots on the roof.

Sounds like the chaplain has exited through the skylight.

Trill frowns. That option, Molloy had not covered.

61

THE NIGHT WIND rips through Lola's cropped hair. She sits on the roof of the train as it hurtles through the desert. Her eyes are wide but fixed on nothing... on everything.

Beside her is the open skylight through which she climbed to find this rushing sanctuary. The bolted cover that gave so easily to the force of her fist bangs in the buffeting air. Then Lola's boot strikes out, smashing it back against its hinges again and again until, with the last furious strike, the cover shears away.

Lola watches it tumble free, spinning high.

And a thought flies upward, filling her head: how wonderful would it feel to hurl herself from this roof and fall into the roaring air. To be free for a moment. And dead forever.

An easy forever. A small life lost that was, in truth, never her own.

She was ever under the control of others. As Maddy, she lived in fear. As 101A, she lived in obedience. And now her life is to be taken once again for the purpose of another.

Her fists clench and a fury rises. A fierce refusal, finding form.

Who forces me to be the Moera? Who tries to bend me to this destiny?

She leaps to her feet. Throws her head back and a roar rips free, ricocheting against the sky.

"Who are you?"

Her body drops and wracks.

And, as if her furious sobs are rising high and chilling against the sky, a rain falls, cold and hard. Returning her words in stinging blows. Beating down, soaking her face, and mocking her rage as nothing.

✦

His boots, though heavy, move without a sound. And he is able, oh so easily, to observe her. She stands with her back to him, battered by the wind but feet firmly planted, muscles tight. So unaware, so rapt in some strange fury that Vassago knows he could—in one step, one push—joyfully remove her from the roof.

But he has another purpose. And that must take precedence over pleasure.

He slides another yard.

She is a Hunter, certainly. He knows the stance. He would even say he knows the smell. Each time his duties as Lord Chancellor forced him to visit the training arena, to feign an interest in their fitness, his nostrils burned with their stench. That residual humanity in them that ages and stinks like milk. And their new Tormenta trait that, to Vassago's nose, refreshes the air like liquid nitrogen.

He smells this now. But over and above those fumes, another fragrance comes. One that he inhales so deeply he can taste it on the back of his tongue.

The smell of span!

He knows not how or why, but he is certain that this Hunter carries a vial. So he will take her by the neck and take it from her.

He flexes his long fingers, ready to snatch, and then…

…she turns.

She is young and lacks the scars to prove experience. Vassago tilts his chin so she can see whom she opposes.

She flinches not. Her fists rise up. Vassago nods. Almost smiles.

This Hunter has some nerve.

Above the roar of the wind, he thrusts his voice: "You bait me, Hunter? Then you cannot know me."

✦

She knows him too well. She's heard Père D speak of him many times, and at the shaping of his name, her mentor's lips would thin like razor blades. With such hatred, she never understood why they defected together. But they did and now Vassago has the same illustrious pedigree as Dali—the best of the Tormenta breed, a G-Man no less, strengthened further by the skills and secrets bestowed by the Sinestra.

If she were just a Hunter she would know her grim fate this instant. But she is more. Much more. And she will prove it.

Lola grins.

You *don't know what* I *am.*

She thuds a step forward, fists bristling, inviting attack. Then her head cracks back. Her jaw jerks high. Her lips burst blood.

Punch after punch. Vassago assails her—faster, harder, keener. Stumbling and dazed, she flails her fists and falls. She cannot pierce the complex attack that travels her body, sending her this way and that but always into the cut of his knuckles. Her eyes rock in their sockets as his punches pound down the front of her face.

Then his hand stiffens to a blade and scythes into her sternum. As the blows explode through her body, blood erupts, spewing from her mouth. And amid the crimson spray something glitters blue, arcing through the air. And Vassago's hand lunges forward, clawing at Lola's body, roaring as he pulls forth a smashed and empty vial.

His jaw drops as he wails wildly. "My life! My life!"

Then his fingers close about the glass, jagged like a blade. Leering down, hot spittle flying.

"Then your death."

His hand jerks and the glass thrusts deep into Lola's belly, churning in the wound as his furious fist flings her from the roof.

62

THE TATTOO ON the back of D'Sola's hand expands as he clenches his fist. The image is a sun with rays reaching out. The jagged design is shaped by the dark blemish of dead skin that it attempts to conceal.

In his fist he holds a thin silver case, containing business cards that bear the same logo. He snaps the case shut.

"Will there be *anyone else* on this train to demand that I identify myself?"

"I apologize, Mr. D'Sola. We need tolerate these agents for just a few hours more. They are a necessary evil."

"I find unnecessary evil much more entertaining."

Dr. Torgus lets his words fly past her like arrows. She knows not where they come from, nor even if she is their target. She smoothes her jacket, checking the pocket once more, and strides into the corridor, coming to a sudden halt as Officer Molloy appears, gun raised, approaching fast.

"Gonna have to ask you to return to your carriage, Doctor."

Torgus retracts, feeling the Pullman door swing back open behind her. Gathers herself. "I need to check on Agnus. His physical condition is my responsibility until we arrive at the hospital."

Molloy gestures with his rifle for her to step back. "Then

your duties just got a whole lot lighter."

His eyes shoot up at the sound of boots on the roof of the train. "Whereas mine now…"

"What is going on?" Torgus attempts to make her tone stern. Molloy's eyes are still locked on the roof.

"Agnus Day is dead, Doc. And that agent—well, she's all gone." Torgus reels back, caught at the elbow by D'Sola's firm grip.

"Dead, you say?" From behind her, D'Sola's voice almost cracks with laughter. "This is something of a setback, is it not, Doctor?"

"I'd say. I'd say that for sure," Molloy responds, as if these recent events crush only his plans for a quiet turn of duty.

He thrusts the doctor back into the carriage with the tip of his gun. Pulls the door shut. Then moves on, prodding the cotton wad deeper into his ear.

63

THE PAIN is unbearable. But so is the beauty. Sunlight is ravaging Siggurson's retina and he wants to close his eyes. But he can't. And so he must look at what glitters before him.

No muscle is under his control. The pressure in his skull is mounting, forcing his body ever further beyond his reach. But his mind echoes, unleashed and loud.

This will pass. It always passes.

He has known these attacks since boyhood. The tingle that starts in his fingertips. Travels upward, twanging tendons, pulling his body into an agonizing rigor. And then the vibration begins at the back of his brain, as if the bullet has sprung wings and is flying against the gray, curling current of his cerebellum. Then his senses dip and distort. First sound fades away. Then his mouth moves, shaping thoughts he can't control. Siggurson knows that by the time the attack has reached this stage, he must have sought solitude.

As a child, he used to make believe that he was a superhero who must hide away as his transformation comes and goes. And in truth, he does get a power of sorts. With his senses distorting, he would see the simplest things in extraordinary detail. As if every atomic particle were becoming visible.

And now, standing hard against the wall of the train car,

 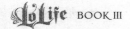

he finds it is not Mo'Zart's face ripped with confusion that holds his eye. Instead, Siggurson stares at a blowfly. It hovers midair, an inch before him. Caught in a slender ray of light that refracts from its wings in iridescent rods of red, gold, green, and blue.

Siggurson's mouth is moving. He knows this by the soft billow of air across his tongue. But he doesn't know what he says. And he hears no sound.

But he sees the fly, a ball of sunlight. A thief of color.

✦

It is a beautiful gun. Cold and smooth. Bianco watches her fingers drift down the length of the barrel.

The rifle is braced to the wall. One of many that flank the wall like iron ribs.

She knows that she is in the munitions car. What she can't remember is how she got here.

In the corridor… He was there… his voice… and then he's gone.

As if clutching at the fog of a dream, Bianco forces her mind to retrace her steps. Steps that staggered and stumbled. She saw the door to the munitions car. She wanted to enter. Was forced to enter.

And then… she remembers opening her eyes to this glory of guns.

Bianco's hand drifts toward a rack of high-velocity handguns. She wants to bring her fingers back toward her but the tips seem drawn to the Magnums, as if magnetized.

The voice in her head questioning her actions is small, a whisper. But something in Bianco tells her to breathe in, swell that voice.

Heed it!

Move your hand away from the gun.

The beautiful gun. That would feel so good against her skin. Her fingers curl about the handle, popping it from its mount. Drawing it down toward her temple.

Drop the gun.

It is cool. And hard. And it would push that bullet in fast, so far.

Drop the goddamn fucking gun!

With a roar, Bianco slams her hand against the steel floor of the car.

This is him! This is what he wants—ridiculous! You barely spoke. Barely touched. He just gave you his card.

And his name was... was...

A blast of static rips against her ear. And only now does she realize that she is lying on the floor of the car, her legs spread as if she'd dropped like a cut puppet. Her radio, sprung from her belt, lies by her ear.

From somewhere deep inside her brain, she is certain she knows this voice.

"Bianco—you read me?"

Mo'Zart. His name is Mo'Zart.

Bianco tries to move her hand toward the radio. Her fingers resist.

"Bianco, pick up. We have a situation here."

She grits, grunts, and shoves her arm as if poking it with the stick of her mind. Fingers grasp the handset, press the button.

"I hear you."

"Siggurson's down. Not down… but out. Not out. Not here."

Bianco rises up, feeling her mind shiver and shimmy, finally slipping free. She exhales through tight teeth. "Again. Slower."

"You weren't responding, so Siggurson said he was coming to find you. He got up and then—it happened."

Bianco rolls her neck, the rest of her body returning to her. "What happened… ?"

"Nothing. That's the thing. Nothing happened. He just froze. Like someone flicked a switch in his head. I don't think he can hear me and he's making no sense. Just keeps saying the same thing, again and again."

"What?"

"That the fly has stolen the colors of the sun. You think when he says 'the fly' he means—"

"I'm on my way."

Bianco rises to her feet. A hand that must be hers rubs her skull. *The bullet. Must be the bullet.*

Deep in his brain. Not deep enough to kill him… not yet. But clearly deep enough to inflict these seizures. These hallucinations.

The fly… stealing the colors of the sun.

And now Bianco feels an idea impact the back of her head, hard as a shovel.

The Fly so loved the Lily, to woo her he stole the colors of the sun.

Bianco keeps walking, thudding her fist against her temple, forcing the rest of the memory to drop into her mouth.

And so it was that the Fly became the hummingbird. And his name was…

Bianco closes her eyes. *Think! Think back!* And then she sees it. The china plaque on Fan Fan's wall. The one that the old woman told her about a thousand times. Always the same story.

And his name was…

She clenches a fist. Pounds it against her thigh. And then she remembers… smashing the plaque. And placing the pieces back together, making the words of warning from that old Taino proverb.

Beware of… of what?

"Guacariga!"

✦

Mo'Zart screws his face, listening hard. "Now you're talking crazy."

Bianco's voice is breathless, rasping from the radio. She's walking fast. *"Just do what I say. You got eyes on the Pullman?"*

Mo'Zart punches up a screen that shows Dr. Torgus with a male guest at the carriage bar. "I see a man."

He peers closer, eyes suddenly widening. "Hey, isn't that—?"

"Keep up, kid. You're gonna love this." Bianco's voice pounds from the radio. She is increasing her speed. *"Guacariga is the Taino god of death. He's always shown in the form of the hummingbird—because he was cursed for stealing his colors from the sun. And in English,* guacariga *translates as 'rays of the sun.'"*

Mo'Zart's eyes now bulge, swelling with realization.

"Ray D'Sola. The guy with the Revelation thingy and the—"

"Suicide hotline." The voice comes from behind him.

Mo'Zart spins round to see that Siggurson's eyes are now open and alert.

Mo'Zart grins and bellows into the handset. "Hey, Bianco, Elvis is back in the building."

"*Then we got ourselves a hunting party.*" Bianco's radio clicks off.

Mo'Zart drops his handset and claps his palms on Siggurson's shoulders. "Man, you had me worried!"

Blood threads heavily from Siggurson's nose. Mo'Zart averts his eyes, forces his smile wider. "Thought you were dying just then."

Siggurson staggers to his feet, breathing deep. "Not then." He raggedly drags a sleeve across his nose. "But maybe now." Turns and lurches toward the Pullman.

64

Torgus taps her watch. The second hand has stopped. Taps again, harder. But time refuses to revive. She can feel the first rays of sunrise through the metal slats of the Pullman window. There can be only another fifty miles to go.

"It is all too late, isn't it, Doctor?" D'Sola slowly unsheathes his commentary, every word a fresh inch of bared steel. "Too late for your body, so old and ugly now. Don't you feel the flesh falling away from your bones like ham?"

Torgus quivers—feeling the cut of each syllable. The pain is sharp… but thrilling.

"Too late for your reputation to be redeemed. Too late for your life to have any meaning at all…"

She finds her eyes drawn to her own hand. Seeing it in awful detail. The hairs that curl from the back of her fingers. The fatless veins that bulge, blue as ink. And, as if her arm is a snake, charmed upward by the sound of D'Sola's voice, it rises… floats.

Fascinated by her own actions, she says nothing as her fist suddenly drops and clumsily swipes the file of prophecies to the floor, the papers gathering at her feet.

"There is nothing to live for now, is there, Doctor? All that awaits you at the end of this journey is the indignity of decay.

Can you smell that sickening sweetness? Does it repulse you, Doctor? I believe it should."

Torgus begins to unbutton her own blouse, thrusting her fingers across the loose, wrinkled flesh of her breasts. Unzips her skirt. It ripples to the floor, piling upon the papers. She feels her head rolled by her own neck muscles that twist like a tourniquet. She is made to look at the tall glass of rum that stands on the counter. D'Sola is filling it to the brim. Passing it to her.

"Shall we have one last drink, Doctor, to your one last glory?"

Torgus's eyes slowly lift to meet D'Sola's. Entirely within his thrall, she brings the drink to her lips. But her mouth remains shut. And with a determined jerk, she splashes the spirits down her chin. Dribbling the rum between her breasts and down her exposed belly.

"Cigarette, Doctor?"

D'Sola strikes a match and hands it to Torgus, who—silently, obediently—grasps it. Then opens her fingers, letting the match fall onto the papers at her feet.

The flame ignites, instantly finding the fuse of alcohol down her body. Licking upward, her loins hot at last.

65

SOMETHING CRAWLS ACROSS the roof of the chapel car. It is Vassago, his chin so low it almost grazes the metal. Grunting and sniffing, he pursues a splattered trail of span.

That I should be reduced to this! Truffling like a pig!

Borne on the billowing air, the span has spread the length of the train. Vassago inches on, licking and grubbing, sucking up what dregs remain, knowing that this gives him just hours more.

Then his nose twitches, twanged by another smell.

Smoke!

His head cranks up. An acrid carpet ripples down the train, forced by the wind. He can't see where it originates until flames burst up from the farthest carriage.

And Vassago slowly rises to his feet, his eyes locked upon the fire that draws him down the train, his boots gathering speed. He breaks out into a thudding bound as he leaps from car to car, arriving at the shattered skylight, filled with fire.

Drops to his knees, forcing his face against the searing heat, staring down into the carriage.

And then he sees it. Flames rising up a woman's naked body. She writhes and wails, thrashing across the floor.

And there, on her arm—a tattoo.

 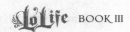

Vassago's eyes seize upon it. Inked black and tall—a stork!

Scox! The sacred stork! The blazing beacon sent to guide the Legion's search. And so...

His eyes sweep the car. And there he sees him—the man who watches unmoved this immolation.

It is he!

Vassago grasps his clave, thrusts his boots through the skylight, crashes to the floor below.

D'Sola turns. Breathing hard, aroused and so enraptured by the death of the crone doctor that at first he cannot determine what it is that interrupts his pleasure.

Then his eyes narrow, locked on the gray, gracile creature that lands, uncoiling, before him. It wields a metal shaft. D'Sola wants to step back. But his body, beyond his control, thrusts upward.

And Vassago plunges the clave down. Releasing it to stand proud in D'Sola's chest.

Vassago grins exuberantly. *It begins!*

Falling to his knees, he bows his head, bellowing an exultant welcome to the long-awaited messiah. Throws his arms high.

Feels blood splatter down.

He lifts his eyes to find that his messiah is—gone.

66

"*It has to be somewhere!*" Bianco's voice blasts from the radio. Mo'Zart responds as he runs down the corridor, his eyes flashing left and right, looking at the walls, the roof.

"I don't see one."

"*Look harder.*"

"I'm heading for the guards' car."

Mo'Zart's mind is racing. If he had built this prison train, where would he put the emergency stop?

He bursts through the connecting door to the guards' car, gaining speed and then slamming hard against the wall.

The corridor is suddenly flooded by guards. Guns drawn, they are responding to the fire alarm triggered in the Pullman. Mo'Zart can't move, flattened by the surge. Can't even lift the radio to his mouth as he hears Bianco's desperate cry.

"*Find that button and push it or what's gonna stop the train is my fucking body on the tracks!*"

✦

Her feet hang above the racing ground. Bianco has one hand clamped about D'Sola's neck. His unconscious body, impaled upon a metal shaft, hangs in her grasp. Her other hand holds

 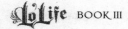

them both against the train door, which swings wide open over the whipping terrain. Mo'Zart's got ten seconds to stop this train.

Less than ten. A dark figure, glistening with sweat, has burst from the Pullman and is striding down the corridor, reaching out for D'Sola, roaring wildly. Blasting blood as something strikes him hard from behind, the figure buckles to its knees, revealing Siggurson poised with a fire axe in his fist, pulled back and ready to deliver another blow.

Siggurson's eyes go to Bianco. She wrestles D'Sola hard against her chest. He is regaining consciousness.

One word flies from Siggurson's mouth: "Go!"

Bianco doesn't look down. Holds Siggurson's eyes to the last. Lets go of the door. Clutching D'Sola, she jumps.

Vassago musters himself to his feet, mumbling, "The deed is done. I can let them go." He folds a fist and turns to face his assailant. "So let's go."

Siggurson nods, grunts. He swings the axe, but Vassago is too quick, sucking upon his Tormenta strength and snatching the axe. Thrusting it back, he clubs the blade against the side of Siggurson's skull. The agent reels back into the Pullman. Stumbling and dazed, he rises up, determined, as Vassago appears through the smoke in the doorway. Siggurson leaps through the spreading flames, dives over the charred remains of Dr. Torgus, and lands behind the bar—a space shielded from corpses and with room to fight. With a thud, Vassago is on the counter, pacing its length, swinging the axe and looking down at Siggurson. Flames ripple across the floor.

Vassago sees Siggurson's eyes glance below the bar. "No hiding place, dear boy, I fear."

But Siggurson's legs kick forward, and as Vassago hears them connect with something below, he senses danger. Too late, as the barrel of rum propelled by Siggurson rolls into the flames and ignites, spewing forth a wall of fire, blasting the axe from his hand and forcing Vassago from the bar. He lands and turns, the heat haze blurring his vision. He does not see the flash of steel as a bar stool swings and smashes down upon him.

But not upon the back of his skull. Vassago is too nimble. The edge of the stool scythes air and strikes the bar, bouncing up as Vassago snares it, twisting the momentum of the blow back on itself. And, like a sledgehammer, the stool crashes into the back of Siggurson's skull.

Knocking him down. Nailed, for the killing.

Vassago lunges, then stops at the sound of guns being primed. As he turns, a slew of guards surge into the burning car.

67

"WHAT DO YOU see?"

"I see you." The face of Agnus is above her.

Lola doesn't feel her mouth move, but still, she hears her own voice. "Which one are you, Agnus?"

"Of the three, I am the greatest. I am love. And I will not forsake you."

Lola feels cold metal against her spine. Rolls with the rock and rush of the ground below her. She is sprawled on the couplings between the cars. She tries to rise but a hand—or the shadow of a hand—moves across her eyes, plunging her into blackness. And now Agnus's voice comes not from above her, but from within.

"What do you see, Lola?"

A light flickers as if her eyes are opening, but she can feel her lashes still intertwined. The beam shines from the back of her skull and the images are projected on the reverse of her retinas—inverted, swirling, confused. Snatches of sound, crashes of color.

"I don't know what I see."

"What do you feel?"

And that answer comes instantly. "Afraid."

And suddenly the images blaze forth. She sees a torrent of red. Blood, from Siggurson's head. He is face down, eyes locked, mouth open. Above him stands a howling figure, raising a gray, skinless fist.

Vassago.

Lola hears her own whisper but feels no breath pass over her lips.

"You see clearly now. You feel it. You *know* it." Agnus's encouragement no longer comes in words. Lola feels him urging her on as if he has a hand about her heart, pumping the beat to quicken.

Lola's voice rises, panting. "Vassago needs span. He hears them coming." Her muscles twitch and tense. "They have guns. They feel strong."

She sees the first wave of guards burst into the car, weapons thrusting as Vassago spins to face them.

"They don't understand."

Vassago's jaws drop wide and in a storm of glistening limbs that sweep back and forth, up and down, he wildly conducts a chorus of carnage, ripping the guards belly to chin, mouth to ear, nostril to eyelid. The steel walls of the car run thick with blood and flesh and the screams that strike the metal rebound as though in an abattoir.

Lola feels the hand rise from her eyes. "I must stop him."

"Yes. You know what has occurred. And you know what you must do. This is the first stage of your great alteration—the nexus of knowing. But now, in this moment, you know too that you are dying."

"If I am to become the Moera, how can I die?"

"Vassago tore a hole in your belly. You are here, severed and unseen."

 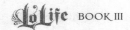

"I should have defeated him. Where is my strength? What must I do?"

"Give up, Lola."

She tries to move her body, but it is as if her flesh is made of water and the command to her muscles is like a breeze upon the surface.

"Give yourself up. Set yourself free. Because to receive the strength to win, you must first surrender."

Lola grits and grinds her muscles again. "It is my destiny! I must have the strength!"

"The power of the Moera is not from you, it is *through* you."

The heat of his hand hovers above her heart. "The plan is not yours, and the path is never of your making."

His voice dwindles, like a wick with a last drop of wax. And the light dims.

"If you are ready to surrender, declare it. Cry out, 'Take me! Use me!' Do this and the world will turn to give you victory. Surrender, and you will triumph."

Lola opens her mouth, this time feeling the muscles respond, shaping the words. At first just a whisper.

Take me.

And then her voice bursts forth. A roar. "Take me!"

"I've got you."

A hand heaves her up, dragging her beneath the arms. "I'm gonna get you somewhere safe."

It is Mo'Zart.

With strained grunts, he drags Lola backward through a car door, into the smoke-filled corridor, finally heaving her into the relative safety of the munitions car. Sets her down, gasping for breath. His face is thick with soot.

"The G-Man impaled D'Sola with the clave, and he's gone. So if Bianco survived the jump, she's out in a thousand acres of dirt with the Mosca."

Lola grabs at a rung of the gun rack on the wall, hauling herself upward. The slit across her abdomen yawns wide, exposing red gums of muscle.

Mo'Zart lowers his eyes, "Have we lost this, Lola?"

Lola grips the bar harder, pulling straighter. "I'm just beginning. And first is one who took me down."

Mo'Zart leaps to his feet. "The G-Man? Forget it, Lola. You're all busted up!"

Lola wraps her fingers about a Winchester rifle that is braced to the wall. Mo'Zart tries to grab her. "He's gonna have you on your knees!"

With one tug, the restraining bolts shear away and the gun pulls free.

Lola turns her eyes to Mo'Zart. "Have faith, kiddo." She slides the gun across her back. "The world will turn and make him kneel first."

68

WHAT DOES HE see?

Perhaps sunlight, sheering through trees. The trees shiver and twitch and then he knows that they are his lashes. His eyes are barely open. And what he feels beneath his skull is rock and dust.

He is lying where he fell, flung from the train. And something pierces him. A metal shaft, stuck deep. And the stickiness of blood across his skin.

He inhales, feeling the pain yawn between his ribs. And then he feels…

…something more.

Unfolding within him. Forcing him upward.

And D'Sola staggers to his feet. Swivels his head as words—not his words, but the utterings of others, thousands of others from thousands of years—swell his skull.

Believe and you will become!

His eyes go to the clave, cocked in his chest. The shaft is thin and square. On the upturned face is an ornate *I*, the capital to a column of engraved letters spelling INEXORABLE. And as D'Sola mouths the word, a joyous chorus of understanding explodes in his mind.

Yes! Yes! I cannot be stopped. I cannot be resisted.

He lurches forward, sensing a growing strength in his limbs. Stumbles over the motionless body of a woman, sprawled in the sawgrass. *This creature… she grabbed me, she pulled me…* a flicker of recognition that is suddenly snuffed, as if all memory of who he once was is razed.

So I can rise anew.

And his hand is compelled once more to wrench the clave, twisting it deeper, turning up another face of the shaft. Beneath an engraved *N* is NIHILATOR.

The Unmaker of Man! The Destroyer! A head, the horizon glints like a razor's edge. D'Sola staggers on, feeling his muscles pulse and push against his skin, thinning it.

His fist grasps and twists the clave again.

The *R* of REX.

Oh, how he wrecks! This coming King!

The last twist of the clave punctures the pulp of his heart. And the upturned *I* delivers… IMMORTAL.

Everlasting, unkillable.

This is I… this is I—

And the human husk that holds the last of D'Sola, walks towards the rising sun.

To steal the light.

To bring forth a new dawn of darkness.

69

A KNIFE POKES out of Molloy's ear. It doesn't plug like a cotton wad, but the blood has ceased to flow, now that he's dead.

Vassago pulls a gun from Molloy's mouth and rises up, stretching his torso. It is now healing with fresh flesh as the siphoned span begins to take effect.

He looks down at his skin with the expression of an unhappy bride. This isn't what he wanted at all. The tissue is thin and slow to grow. He ripples his lips in disappointment.

He had persuaded Molloy to end the agony of the knife's slow entry into his skull by blowing his own brains out. Vassago then fell to his knees and siphoned the span.

But something had caused the previous bleeding from Molloy's ear. Vassago would say a tumor by the taste of it. The man had only days remaining so what Vassago has siphoned is nearly useless.

He needs more. Enough to buy him time to get the Mosca back. The awakening is under way, but he needs the Mosca in his care, to glorify the moment of his great return to the Legion.

So Vassago inhales, scouts about the smoke-filled carriage to find another fix.

The flames are high now, licking at the ceiling, seeping out into the corridor. And the heat is horrible. But Vassago sets about his task with a flurry of hoisting kicks, bouncing bodies from the floor, looking for one that still lives. And then he hears it—the music made by the instrument of misery.

A pained exhalation.

And then he sees it—a body by the bar. Still moving.

Vassago strides across the car. Time is short, and so he begins his opening argument even as he approaches.

"You have a choice. You can burn to death, an excruciating exit. Or you can take the chance to end your own life with a single clean and painless shot."

A hand of the crawling victim reaches up through the smoke, grasping wildly as if searching for the gun.

"An excellent choice!" Vassago smiles and makes a mock bow, like a maître d'. Pulls a weapon from one of the nearby dead guards and empties the chamber of all but one bullet. He folds the smoldering fingers of his victim about the butt of the gun.

Then he drops to his knees, ready to feed.

The thumb of his victim peels back the priming pin. Vassago swipes his tongue, wetting his lips.

"If it makes you feel any better, your suicide will not be in vain."

The victim's finger closes about the trigger and pulls. The bullet rips through his skull. His final breaths come in short, hard jags.

Vassago twitches, listening to the dwindling gasps. And his ears are also alert to the crackle of the flames that race ever closer.

Bends down to the gaping mouth. Perhaps a breath comes; he cannot be sure. But the smoke of the fire is belching hard down the back of his neck.

He cannot wait. Vassago slams his jaw down and begins to inhale. And rising up comes a pulsing coil of span. Disappearing gulp by gulp into Vassago's gullet.

Then, bent double as he swallows, Vassago halts. Amid the heat of the fire comes something cold upon his neck. He rises to find the massive barrel of a Winchester rifle thrust against his skull.

Releasing the half-sucked span, Vassago twists round. And there she is, that strange Hunter. One hand clamped to her bleeding belly, the other holding the gun to his head.

Vassago smiles. "Will you grant the last request of a dining man?" He dabs his lips. "I should like to know your name."

"It's spelled just how it sounds."

A deafening *ba-boom* blows Vassago's head from his shoulders.

The force of the recoil thrusts Lola back, sends her staggering into Mo'Zart, who catches her from behind.

"Now can we get outta here? If those flames reach the stockpile, the whole train is gonna blow." He pulls her arm about his neck, supporting her. He gives a backward glance and then—

—wrenches to a halt. His eyes locked on the body beneath Vassago.

"Siggurson! That's Siggurson!" The blue eyes are wide and staring and a length of half-sucked span still trails from his mouth.

Mo'Zart lurches toward the body as if to gather it up. But Lola's fist flies, snaring Mo'Zart by the throat, pulling him close.

"He's gone. And we need to go."

She kicks the compartment door open. With one thrust, Lola hurls Mo'Zart into the rushing air outside as the flames explode in a fresh wave of fire.

She alone looks around to see that amid the many corpses, Siggurson's body has now gone. Leaving just a carbon ring.

And as the flames lick into the munitions car—Lola leaps from the train, blown high by the immediate blast.

70

BLACK SMOKE BELCHES from the burning train.

Bodies of prisoners and guards, blown by the blast, are strewn far from the track.

A figure moves amongst the dead, white and ghostly. It is Mo'Zart, caked in ash and coughing hard. He drags a sleeve across his eyes, clearing a band of black flesh. The explosion still hammers inside his head, a crashing confusion. But he knows this—he'd be counted amongst the corpses were it not for Lola.

And where is Lola?

He rolls another body with his shoe. What's left of the face is male and unfamiliar. Mo'Zart hobbles on, moving down the track. Halting at another corpse.

This one is strangely stripped of clothes. Mo'Zart approaches, tipping it over. Seeing now that the neck is a severed stump. He drops to his knees. The absent head is not what draws him—many of these dead are less a limb—what mystifies him is a shaft of metal, clutched in one rigored hand: a clave!

Mo'Zart wipes a cuff across the corpse, clearing ash. The torso is intricately inked with a repeating symbol: twin keys, turned back to back to form a skull. "The Chiro Scuro?" His eyes narrow, confused. "What would one of the Brotherhood be doing here? And with a clave?"

He lifts the monk's other arm upward, tracing the inked design down the forearm to the wrist as—

—a hand lands on his shoulder.

Mo'Zart jerks round. Finds a face above him. Blotted with bruises and blood but all the same—Bianco.

He exhales, rising to his feet. "I thought you were dead."

She brushes sand from her sleeve. "Yeah, well, dead ain't what it used to be." Cranks her neck, easing her shoulders. "Guess D'Sola bounced better than me." Looks past the debris and the dead to the wasteland beyond. "But we've kept him from the Legion. For now. And this is a hard place to hide."

Mo'Zart scans the empty acres. "You think we can still stop him?"

Bianco checks her holster, feels the lump of her gun. "Kid, where's your faith?"

Then turns. "Where's Lola?"

Mo'Zart points to a blood trail, freshly dripped across the dust. "Only one person I know who'd bleed that hard and still be walking."

Bianco nods, following the bloody blots. "And Siggurson?"

Mo'Zart inhales, raising his voice as her stride accelerates. "Bianco, he ain't with us, he's—"

"—with Lola. Yeah, that figures." She marches on. "He's always gotta beat me to the action. But it's me she needs." Turns to Mo'Zart. "Ain't that so? In the legend, it's the one called Crow that delivers the kill-shot."

Mo'Zart is motionless, mouth open. Mumbling now with a

new distraction of words. "Yes… yes. Corvus, Kraal. But only if you get there in time. Before the Fly… the Mosca is fully awakened."

Bianco jerks her head forward.

"Then move it, soldier. Time's flying."

71

D'SOLA'S ARMS fly upward, clawing at the air. He gasps. And he falls to his knees.

I am dying!

His head hangs.

My blood is gone!

But then he grunts, defiant. Grits his jaw, drags a ragged breath.

Mere mortal fluid! I do not die... I become!

And with a roar, he rolls his head upward, forcing his eyes open, then wider still, as he sees what walks across the wasteland toward him.

A woman, blond and bleeding.

Her left hand is balled, damning a slit at her side. Her right hand holds the severed head of a man.

Lola comes to a halt, standing before D'Sola. But only for a moment, then she buckles to the ground. And on their knees, broken and bleeding, the two silhouettes face each other.

The wind suddenly roars, like a coliseum crowd. Raising a wall of dust that swirls about them.

D'Sola stares at Lola. Something flickers like a wick behind his eyes. And a thought, not his own, commands his tongue. His voice comes low.

"So, here we are at last. Drawn together. The One, the Other. How strange that combat should commence with us both upon our knees."

Lola raises her eyes, breathing deep and slow.

"There will be no battle."

D'Sola shunts a laugh between his teeth.

"Unnecessary, I agree. For you have already failed." D'Sola wrenches himself to his feet. "The act is done and I am becoming! This human cage withers and I shall be released! And here you are but a half-made thing. You are incomplete."

"But I am not alone."

With a surging strength, Lola hikes up the head of the monk. "That he was here… that told me something. And now that I see the clave within your chest—I know. And what I know," she says on an inhale, rising to her feet to meet him, "will bring you down."

D'Sola thins a smile. "I doubt you know anything of such magnitude."

Now Lola's body uncoils, spine straightening. "You are not becoming."

D'Sola caresses the clave in his chest. "Here is the evidence, in my own hands."

Lola lifts her eyes, locked upon his now. "And that is your weakness. You trust only in what you can see… the physical world, the touchable truth. And so you are blind. You cannot *know*. And I know this: You are dying."

D'Sola clutches the clave closer and his face ripples as a wave of pain consumes him. Averts his eyes as Lola presses on. "You speak of the decay of your human cage and the birth of your greater self. But this is no release. What you feel is no more than the hapless human creep of death. And after death, you will not rise, you will not return. You will rot, as flesh. Because the clave that impales you has no power. See, I know that weapon well, inch by inch, its every nick and scratch. And I know that it is not Vassago's."

D'Sola's hands jolt from the clave, as if her words have suddenly rendered it red hot.

Lola takes a step forward. "It belongs to one who has long since abandoned all that the Legion believes in. And without belief, the clave is nothing." She lifts high the monk's head. A gold crucifix swings from one ear. "Many wear a crucifix, but without faith, a cross is nothing, a trinket. And in the same way, that heretic shaft in your heart"—she snaps her fingers—"it is powerless."

The light in D'Sola's eye gutters, shrinks. But then—

—he clasps the clave once more, twisting round the lettered shaft, shrieking wildly, "I.N.R.I."

Flesh flies as he grinds on. "Inexorable Nihilator! Rex Immortalis!"

The wind flings his screams across the wasteland, now a churning sea of sawgrass.

And like masts, governed by the gusts, two figures appear, following the screams to their source.

D'Sola watches as the silhouettes gain form. A woman, wading against the wind. A cop badge glints on her belt. And beside her, a long-haired creature, black and bowed as he forces his way forward.

The woman holds a gun, two hands braced against the gale,

training her aim on D'Sola.

"Immortal. That is I… that is I…" He bellows to Lola, beckoning. Then he gestures to the gun. "I cannot be killed. And I shall prove it."

Lola's eyes do not leave him. "Now that you seek proof, I know you doubt."

As D'Sola pulls himself to his full height he uncurls his fingers from the clave. Sweeps a hand across his mouth, erasing any evidence of agony.

Arms wide, he turns toward the woman who totes the gun. "Suicide-by-cop, were I human. But I have crossed to the other side." Flashes her a smile. "So pull! And prove my power."

Bianco tugs the trigger, just once.

And a hole blasts between D'Sola's eyes.

His smile does not flicker.

But his legs bow and with a thud, he falls dead to the dirt.

Bianco slides her magnum back into its holster. Glances about her as the wind falls silent, like a sudden gasp. She spits soot, wipes her eyes and walks over to D'Sola's body. Mo'Zart follows.

Lola is already bent over the corpse, tugging hard at the clave. It comes free in a torrent of tissue.

"And for those of us who missed the start of the movie"— Bianco looks from the monk's severed head to the clave—"what the hell just happened?"

Lola rips the sleeve from D'Sola's suit. She says nothing as she binds the cloth tight about her belly.

Mo'Zart gathers up the monk's head, examining the face. The skin, cruelly carved with a knife, bears a name: Vassago.

"This monk, he was from the Chiro Scuro, correct? So what was he doing here and how did he…"

Lola snatches the head back, slinging it into a sack swiftly made from D'Sola's shirt.

"His name was Brother Scarbo. I met him with the Primus Pater. He was sent to do what the Brothers do best, the art of the hidden hand." Lola holds up the clave. "He disguised himself as a chaplain, to lure Vassago close. And then switched Vassago's clave with this one… Dali's."

Bianco rubs her head with the heel of her hand. "You knew it was Dali's—you saw that thing every day. But how did you know it would have no power?"

"I didn't know."

"You mean you just guessed? Or what… you made it up?"

Lola shrugs. "I believed."

Mo'Zart takes a step forward, nodding now. "And your belief made D'Sola loose faith. And without faith, the clave would fail. The Mosca must believe… to become."

"So you're sayin' that my super fine shot—slap-bang between the eyes—that isn't what killed him. He died because of… doubt?"

Lola slides the clave into her belt. "Doubt is a pain too lonely to know that faith is his twin brother."

Bianco gags. "What the—?"

"It's Khalil Gilbran." Mo'Zart smiles in appreciation.

"Okay, so hold it right there." Bianco pokes a finger at Mo'Zart. "Fancy fuckin' philosophy from a Yale yahoo—that I expect. But you, Lola?" She throws her hands wide. "You're a 'Fu-fighter. A kick-ass killer. And now, outta nowhere… it's like

 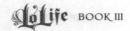

you've eaten a bowl of guru stew with a big ol' side of mystic biscuit. What the hell is happening to you?"

Lola smiles. "When I know, you'll know." Then she turns, scanning the horizon in search of a road. Sets off, heading north.

Bianco follows, shrugging. "I guess we're all coming out of this a lil' different." She feels Mo'Zart fall in step behind her. "And where the hell is Siggurson? You said he was with Lola."

The silence causes Bianco to glance back. Catches Mo'Zart's expression.

"I said... he isn't with us, Bianco. Not anymore." Mo'Zart swallows. "It was just before the blast that... it happened. Vassago was—"

A hand rises, silencing him. Bianco's eyes are strange, set hard.

"It happened. That's all I need to know."

She turns and walks on, following Lola across the swaying sawgrass.

72

SHE HAS ПО teeth, so she sucks the meat off the bone, then chucks the chicken wing to the floor of the flatbed truck.

Mo'Zart can't take his eyes off the woman. She's a hooker, for sure. And old for her trade, maybe the neck end of fifty. Looks like the madam of the bunch. There are five girls in total, and Mo'Zart skims a glance across them all: stick thin and thickly rouged, with hair whipped up by the wind into a cotton candy chaos.

They sit on one side of the flatbed truck, facing Mo'Zart, Bianco, and Lola.

The madam reaches into a grocery bag on her lap and pulls out another piece of chicken. Starts sucking, squeezing grease down her chin. Then jerks a finger at the bag on Lola's lap.

"What you got in there?"

"Human head."

She looks at Lola's bloodstained torso, Bianco's broken arm slung in a belt, and Mo'Zart's face, a shade deeper with smoke.

"I'd say chicken's better for ya."

The truck bounces high as it hits a deep rut in the road. "Not much farther now, my dears."

The voice comes from the driver's cabin. At the wheel is Sister Vermillion Rose. Her huge face turns, wimple flapping. "Five miles, no more."

 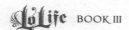

A cigarillo droops between her lips, and the hands that wrench at the wheel are covered in tattoos.

"It's a little bitty town but there's a sheriff's office. Got a phone that works and a deputy that don't. But I hope that is sufficient for your needs."

She flashes a toothy tobacco smile at her new companions.

Mo'Zart musters a smile back. He is sure that her church does wonderful work providing succor to streetwalkers, but he had felt a ripple of reservation when the truck first pulled up and offered them a lift. The mission banner painted on the side read THE WHITE LILY OF THE TRINITY.

Mo'Zart had whispered to Lola, jerking a finger at the name. "It's a sign."

"It's a truck."

And with that, Mo'Zart found himself bundled aboard by Lola's boot.

And in truth they had been walking for an hour before they hit a road, and then another hour had passed before they even heard the chug of an engine. The heat was unbearable and so was the silence. No cars. And less conversation. Neither Bianco nor Lola wanted to talk about what happened to Siggurson. But Mo'Zart did.

Maybe they're used to this kind of crazy, but I still got questions.

Like: "Why would Siggurson do that?"

Lola says nothing, just paces the roadside, eyes on the horizon.

Mo'Zart persists. "Why shoot himself?"

Lola still paces, but now she elects to speak. Slowly, as if she is piecing events together in her own mind, step by step.

"He faced death every moment of every day. The frag in his brain was like a ticking bomb. This way he could control the moment of his death—and make it count for something." Lola falls silent for a moment, as if deciding whether to say more. Finally exhales.

"He saw me in the doorway. He saw my blood. He knew that I would need Vassago to be vulnerable if I were to stand a chance. He'd already watched him siphon the other guard. So Siggurson knew how to bring Vassago to his knees."

Mo'Zart hangs his head, eyes down. "Then he sacrificed himself for us."

Bianco snaps her head round. "He's dead. We're alive. It's over."

✦

Sitting in the back of the truck, Mo'Zart glances over at the detective. She hasn't spoken since. Which he finds strange. Such a cold comment to make about Siggurson. Maybe she really never liked him. Or maybe she liked him too much.

Or maybe she hasn't spoken because there's nothing more to say.

Mo'Zart looks out at the desert. A distant column of black smoke rises above the horizon. He exhales, resting his chin in his hands.

We're alive.

And it is over.

 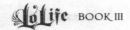

ADDENDUM

(i)

Long cuffs graze across a card table.

Dali is dealing out a game of Boo-Ray, the first time in a long time that his deck has been used for anything other than solitaire.

Sitting across from him is the Commander General. He sucks on a cigar and gathers the cards dealt to him.

The rules of Boo-Ray demand that you show to your opponent two of the three cards in your hand.

And as Dali contemplates his hand and takes a sip of the Commander General's finest Vesuvio port, he ponders the rectitude of his decision to show the Commander General only two of the three pieces of evidence that he received against Vassago.

The items had arrived neatly boxed. So tight and tidy, in fact, that the thought never occurred to Dali that the sender might be Lola. She was not one for doing things so properly. But clearly, her time as a renegade has sharpened her skills with Bubble Wrap.

Dali had first lifted out the note. It was written in her hand—he knew that instantly. He recognized the style from the dense notes she'd made in the margins of all those library books that so perversely held her attention.

And no one but Lola would begin a missive to him with the words *Cher Père D.*

He scanned the contents quickly. The letter made no mention of her leaving. No reason as to why she quit his loving care. But Dali no longer held out hope that this particular hurt would be healed by explanation.

The letter told him only that the enclosed clave belonged to Vassago.[1] And the severed head—oh yes, there was, in all its stinking glory, a severed head—that particular delight once belonged to Brother Scarbo. The name carved across his forehead was clear despite the shrinkage of his skin. A

---

[1] I do not claim this story as my own, and so to add an obelus is a prime impertinence. But this is my nature. And should I neglect to record this event, then in years to come, I may begin to doubt that it occurred at all. But it assuredly did—and just so. Primus Pater Umberto summoned me to a meeting. Without explanation (and why should I expect that courtesy?) he announced his belief that I was innocent of any involvement in the murder of Hunter 666A. And this, dear Reader, at a time when the Sinestra was quick to judge and find me wanting. The Primus Pater told me that my clave, the tool of Hunter 666A's death, was in their charge and they wanted my permission to retain it. They had reason to believe that the Mosca was rising. They knew well enough that no false clave could stop him—the Mosca is too mighty for such mundane machinations. Their only hope would be to wield a weapon of a different sort. They must cause the Legion of Gehenna to doubt whether this apparent manifestation is indeed the promised lord of legend. For if they doubt the Mosca, they will not follow him. And if they do not follow him, the Mosca fails. And so it was that the Primus Pater made his proposal: the Chiro Scuro will ensure that the clave deployed in this Awakening is mine—the clave of a traitor. This will sow seeds of suspicion amongst the Legion. I praised the Primus Pater for his plotting, but followed with my fear that this plan, in truth, amounted to a paltry opposition. I have betrayed the Legion once before. Might they not convince themselves that I—like Vassago—have all along been acting as a double agent, biding my time within the ranks of the Sinestra until the chance presents itself to act? The Primus Pater took my hand—with a grip of unsettling strength—and told me that he had one very good reason to believe his plan would succeed. "And in what do you place your faith, Eminence?" I asked. "Not in *what*, Dali," he replied. "But in whom." And with that he took his leave and I was left alone with just my curiosity as companion.

signature declaring guilt.

The letter was not signed. It finished with the words, *I miss you Père D. Ah, chère, tu es perdue…*

Dali deliberately lost the letter forever in a flame and handed over to the Commander General only the clave and severed head. Vassago's absence had already aroused suspicion, so these items easily elicited a verdict.

Dali returns his attention to the game as the Commander General sets down his cards—two jacks. Dali sets his expression to one of engaged interest.

"We owe you an apology, Dali. But in our defense, once we learned what had befallen Judas… and the considerable evidence presented by Vassago, the case for your treachery seemed strong."

"Ah, is that how it *seemed* sir… ?"

The Commander General pauses, exhales. Point taken. "We gave Vassago's testimony too much credence."

"If my reputation is restored sir, I ask for no more."

"Apart from our gracious tolerance of your… personal project. Something that you should have disclosed to your superiors much sooner."

Dali taps his nose, the length of his cuff concealing his mouth. "Perhaps I feared ridicule."

"I suggest instead you fear failure. She is lost to you."

"Sir, there is much that we don't understand, and I, for one, relish our ignorance. Because in the darkness, there may hide hope." Dali twitches a smile. "I will find her."

The Commander General bites down on his cigar to free up a throaty cough.

"Your turn, I believe." He gestures to the table and Dali obliges, making his play—two threes.

"No word on Vassago's betrayal must escape. We may have successfully thwarted the Legion of Gehenna once again, but they would draw encouragement from this breach."

"Understood, sir."

"This is the closest they have got. Chilling, indeed, that Vassago succeeded in applying the clave." The Commander General stifles a shudder. "We must increase our vigilance."

"Sir, I recommend that we begin the trainin' of a new Hunter with immediate effect. We focus him from th'outset to do nothing other than track down the Mosca, when he next rises."

The Commander General digests this thought "This is somewhat unorthodox..."

"Sir, yo' said it yourself. The Legion is gettin' faster and better informed. We must respond... adapt. I just ask that yo' consider my proposal." Dali slides a file across the table.

The Commander General fills the silence by sweeping up Dali's losing pair and sucking hard on his cigar. "First time I've played and I've won."

His hand descends upon the file, resting gently.

Dali nods and smiles, ever the grand master.

(ii)

Her belly is stretched into the bright bulge of late pregnancy. Bianco leans back into the swing on Fan Fan's porch. She is barefoot and shelling peas, a world away from being the hardened cop. But at the first ripple of a raft, she has a gun in

 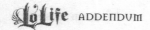

her hand, primed and pointed at the foot of the steps.

Lowers it with a smile as she sees the familiar blaze of blond hair. Lola mounts the steps, eyes on Bianco's belly.

"So, when were you gonna to tell me?"

"When I started showing. Or when you showed up. Whichever came first."

"So here I am."

"And here we are." Bianco pats the bump.

"It is Siggurson's, right?"

Bianco tosses the gun onto the porch. "You see me with one goddam guy and so you assume it must be his. Like I don't get guys. I actually get a lot of guys. I've dated two detectives at the station. I have a life outside of you, you know."

"But it's Siggurson's, right?"

Bianco shrugs and smiles. "Either that or this baby is the second coming. I ain't been swung since this swing." She pats the old cotton cushions.

Lola drops into the seat. Glances at Bianco's bump. "You gonna be all right doing this alone?"

"I'm not alone. I got Fan Fan. I got you." Now Bianco raises one hand to Lola, a finger tracing some small, fresh scars across her forehead. "You look pretty much in one piece. Guess I was worrying for nothing."

Lola smiles but she feels that Bianco's eyes are still hard upon her.

"So tell me, Lola, what's been keeping you away, if it ain't been the fighting?"

"I've been thinking."

"Shit, now I *am* worried."

Lola rolls her shoulders. Chin down. "I had to figure some things out. Make some decisions." She lifts her eyes, turns to Bianco. "I gotta tell you something that Agnus said about the Moera…"

Bianco suddenly jolts and gasps, her hand on her stomach. "Got his daddy's big feet." She shifts, easing her spine, looks back at Lola. "So… what did Agnus say?"

Lola shrugs. Smiles back at Bianco. "Ya know what—it can wait. Let's just celebrate what's inside of you." She rests a hand on the dome of Bianco's belly. "Never seen you so big."

Bianco shrugs. "I'll drop it again. You musta been over two hundred pounds when you were Maddy and look at you now."

"So you're pretty sure about all this?"

"I know it's gonna change everything, but this baby is part of me, my future." She resumes her pea shelling. "I like to fight and I can fight most anything… but destiny, that's always gonna get ya."

She jerks her head to the cabin behind. "Now go find Fan Fan. She's been keeping a barrel of Old Artemis for your return. Thinks it's her best brew yet."

✦

A rose bends as a knife strips it of thorns. They fall into Fan Fan's lap.

Her piled-high yellow hair flops back and forth as she rocks in her chair. And her voice floats.

"Ah, child, yo' been a long time comin'."

"I'm here now." Lola exhales silently, as if ridding herself of

 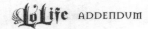

the last chance to change her mind. "Because there's something I need to do... a man I have to find."

The only sound is the creak of Fan Fan's chair. Head down, Lola continues.

"He has something that belongs to me." Lola swings off her long coat. "And so do you, Fan Fan."

She lowers herself to the floor. "You have my memories." Lola crosses her legs, back straight. "And I want them back."

The rocking chair halts sharply, mid-creak. "You sure you ready?"

"I don't have a choice."

Fan Fan heaves herself up from the chair onto her feet, turning round in lumbering half steps. And then Lola sees her face.

It is painted white, with eyes blackened into empty sockets. A rictus grin painted red across her lips. And from her hand hangs a little skin poppet. A jagged red line circles its neck and its head is spiked with thorns.

"Then let's begin."

Fan Fan lifts the doll, cradling it in her arms. She pulls a thorn from her pocket, drags it through her lips, loading it with spittle. Holds it above the doll's head.

"Close your eyes, child." The thorn is thrust down—

And Lola convulses, a bolt of yellow light blinding her. The light refracts from golden letters, embossed on the cover of a leather book. They spell *Codex Gigas*. It lies open in her lap. She is in the Archivum, slowly turning the pages. Her bare feet are propped up on the table.

The voice of Fan Fan drifts over the memory.

"This is where you spent so many hours. Poring through

the books of the Collegio Romano. You felt drawn to them. Perhaps the first sign of your destiny—the way the books called to you. And within the pages of Brother Magen's book, what did you find?"

Lola's eyes are dilated wide. And she can see the page before her, as if it is held again in her hand.

Lola recites the passage, word for word.

...and this is the unspoken truth. Hunters can reclaim their human life. To do so, they must find the Tormenta who stole their original span. And when they find this host, this is how the span must be redeemed: They must rouse that Tormenta to ecstasy and in that moment of release, as something of life is lost, the span escapes and can be snatched...

"And so you came to your dark discovery. That the Sinestra had lied to you, for their own gain. They said that you were neither dead nor alive, and so you had no other fate but to be a Hunter. But in truth, there was another path—one that would return to you your original span. In one crude act of union, you could get your life back.

"From the moment you made that discovery, you could no longer serve the Sinestra's cause. Because you had one of your own. You were going to find Kave."

Fan Fan thrusts down another thorn—

Lola jolts as her head fills with an explosion of green. A dirty green. Perhaps once a peppermint but now a putrid shade, stained by nicotine.

It is the wall of a smoky salsa club. Tables dot the edge of

the room, lit by velvet lamps, worn thin.

Young men, slicked with hair oil and sweat, heave large-boned ladies about the room to a salsa beat.

Beneath a corner table, long legs, hers, swing. Not to the music; this twitch comes at a quicker tempo. A tell-tale sign of impatient tension. But the body feigns a relaxed pose. One hand holds a drink, bombed with cherries, and the scarlet dress clings like paint. Cut low and strapless, it allows a swathe of flesh to flow free. The tattoo around the biceps reads LOLA. Another tattoo that reaches down the back of her neck is a twisting metal spike.

And at her heart, rising across the swell of her breast, is a black lily.

Lola's eyes are on the dance floor. Amid the forest of tall, waggling wigs, she finds the face she's looking for.

A man. Dark hair. Blue eyes. He wears his shirt open to the navel and lets his long hair sweep free. And feeling the diamond drill of Lola's stare, he turns.

It is Kave.

Fan Fan's voice comes like a whisper, as if she is sitting alongside Lola at the table.

"When you left the Sinestra, you devoted every waking moment to tracking Kave down. And seeing that face, those eyes—that night came back to you. At the Sewercide Club. When he took poor Maddy onto the dance floor, turned her once, twice, and then released her. Taking the hand of the beautiful Gina. Kissing her hard, as all those faces turned to Maddy, jeering, pointing, pushing, punching as she tried to escape the dance floor. Escape her skin by slashing it with razor blades."

Lola uncrosses her legs beneath the table, the twitching becoming a furious tremor. Breathes deep as she watches Kave finish the dance and kiss the heavily jeweled hand of his lady partner. He then turns and walks toward Lola, eyes set on her like lasers.

Fan Fan's voice breathes on. "Here was your chance for sweet revenge. Kave would never know the true identity of this assassin, so transformed, so beautiful. A real Cinderella Killafella. And he came to you, so willingly... so unaware."

Kave sinks into the seat beside the blonde in the red dress. His voice rings in her mind.

"This is very beautiful." A finger points to the tattoo of her name. "But it robs me of the chance to ask you your name." His eyes glitter, locked on Lola's face. "So I will have to engage you in conversation by other means." Lola feels his eyes sweep down across her body, lingering on the tattoo at her heart.

"The black lily. Highly poisonous." His fingers approach as if to connect with the soft rise of her breast.

Lola cuts him a smile. "One touch and you're dead."

Kave sweeps his fingertips closer still to her flesh. "We've all got to go sometime."

Lola's hand flashes and snares his fingers and as she twists his wrist to its snapping point, she swivels from the chair and slides away, disappearing through sequins and smoke.

Knowing that Kave will follow.

A heavy rain is falling outside. The rush of tires and splattering gutters drown the sound of footsteps. But Lola senses he is close behind.

She takes a deliberate turn into an alleyway. And then she

hears the echo of his boots.

And she turns. And Kave faces her. He reaches out, as if inviting her to dance. Lola tilts her head in assent, spinning around as if to enter his arms, but instead delivering a crashing blow to his neck with the side of her hand.

Kave rolls with the blow, exiting the spin with his fists ready, swiping her jaw, twisting her around and then snaring her waist, hooking her spine to save her from the ground. For a beat, she dangles across his arm like a tango queen until Kave jerks hard, cracking her back, forcing a cry from her throat. Then she drops as her leg swings high, kicking Kave in the side of his skull. He rocks backward, stumbling hard. Snaking around so fast that Lola is still rising from the ground as he grabs her from behind, clamping her body, his mouth to her ear.

"I did not know who you were."

Lola tenses, but her voice remains calm. "And who am I?'

"You are one of us." Kave inhales deeply, sweeping his nose up the length of her neck. "I can usually smell one of our kind. But not you."

"Must be the soap I use."

"Or perhaps you're a Hunter."

Lola doesn't move. She lets the silence hang until Kave continues, his tone still hushed.

"Hunters, I always think, have a gentler fragrance. I guess it's their residual humanity. But—if you were a Hunter, you would have killed me in the dance club. And you didn't. Well… perhaps you killed me just a little bit." She feels his lips smile against her ear. "Broken heart."

He slowly releases her.

"So let's discuss what brings you to my beat. This is a small town. No room for two, so I'm not about to toss you for the territory."

Lola flexes her fingers, arches her back. "Why would I want these dusty acres?" She kinks her hip. "And also, why would you?" Shakes her head. "Something doesn't fit. The old gigolo grift in a deadbeat town, plied by the mighty Kave?"

He runs his tongue along his teeth. "Then you've heard of me?"

"I wouldn't get too psyched. What I heard is that you've lost it."

"Things change. By choice."

He pauses, turns his head away. Then smiles. "I have been alive a *very* long time and I have done amazing things. I don't think there's a grift I haven't perfected. So I started setting my own challenges. I once even found myself wondering if I could get a girl to kill herself because she was too happy. I was making up new rules just to stay interested in a game that was becoming too easy. What we do… it used to take real skill. People were tough, tenacious, unbreakable. Now I sometimes wonder if we actually drive them to death at all. I think we could just sit right back and let the world do it for us. It's like everyone is lining up along the edge of the ravine and all we have to do is give the final shove—and what's to love in that?"

"You're saying you ducked out because you were bored?"

"Maybe I just wanted to live a little. You ever thought about that, Lola?" He raises his arms, warming to his rally. "We spend all our time conspiring and conniving, duping and demeaning… just to get more life to carry on doing the same thing. We live forever... but I don't think I ever lived at all. Until that day."

"What day?"

Kave smiles, his fingers brushing her arm. "I know your name. But I don't know who you are." He leans in, whispering. "I'd like to know. So—let's spend some time. We've plenty to spare." He releases her fully, walking away. "I'm at the Salsa Shack on Mondays and Wednesdays."

Lola calls after. "I don't dance."

"Yeah, for sure. No rhythm." He flips his collar up against the rain.

"We could just talk. That doesn't take timing."

"Unless it's comedy."

"Very funny."

And he slowly slides into the darkness.

That bursts into red.

A pain blazes through Lola's head as Fan Fan digs in another thorn.

"You went back to the Salsa Shack. You had no choice. The seduction of Kave was going to take time. You kept up the pretense that you were a Tormenta. So you could draw him closer, win his trust."

The red haze melts into her red dress as she spins and fast-steps across the floor. Kave has her by the hand. The music blares and Lola finds herself throwing back her head and singing as the band breaks out into Cuban beats.

And drifting above the music is Fan Fan's voice.

"You told yourself that seeing Kave at the club was a good thing. Dancing with him, feeling your hand in his, it would keep your fury fresh. Never let you forget what he did to Maddy."

As Lola and Kave move to the heaving rhythms, their bodies collide, wrap close, uncurl, then spin back tight.

If they fight like dancers, then they dance like lovers.

"And you told yourself that this tantalizing closeness would rouse him faster, so you could throw him to your bed and get your span back."

The music changes to a rumbling grind and Kave pulls Lola close, locking their hips, his mouth wet against her hair.

"But this was a lie. It was all a lie. The truth was a terrible thing. You were falling in love with him. Just like before."

✦

"No!" Lola's voice rings out from the walls of Fan Fan's cabin. She is up on her feet, eyes wide, grasping at the doll in Fan Fan's arms, wanting this to stop. Her words come in angry bursts.

"That's not true! It was all an act. To make him want me. I hated him!"

Fan Fan says nothing, allowing Lola's ragged breathing to relax. In the calm she asks, "Do you want to stop? We can stop. The choice is yours. Always has been."

Lola sinks back down to the floor, her head lolling forward. Fingers balling into fists of tight control.

"No. We go on."

Fan Fan pulls another thorn and nestles the doll deep into the crook of her arm. "Very well." She thrusts hard.

A blast of blue. Sunlight on water. Lola and Kave sit by a vast lake. It captures the sky like a mirror.

 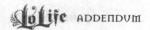

They are not talking, but the silence between them seems easy. Lola speaks first. "So this is it?"

"Yes. This is living."

"But we're not doing anything."

"Yes, we are. We're doing nothing."

Lola shrugs, not getting it.

Kave smiles and reclines back onto the bank, kicking off his shoes. "Don't underestimate it. Doing nothing is hard. You never know when you're finished."

Lola falls back to join him, staring at the sky. "But this isn't what Tormenta do."

"It's what people do."

"But we're not people."

For a moment Kave says nothing. Then he rolls onto his elbow.

"I don't expect you to understand." His mouth momentarily tightens. "Or any Tormenta. That's why I've never spoken of it before. But now, with you... I want to talk." He nudges Lola's face toward him, demanding her attention.

"A while back, I took a measure of span. From a girl. Not all of it. I fucked up. The mighty Kave fucked up. Only the second time in quite a few thousand years, but still... it happened. I don't know what became of the girl; maybe the Sinestra swept her up—who knows? But I know what happened to me."

He pauses, as if passing the last exit from this confession.

"When a span is half-taken, you know the human gets Tormenta traits. But if the Tormenta gets tainted by any human traits, they are easily crushed, squeezed out like pulp. So I didn't expect to feel anything, apart from fury that fresh span had slipped my grip. But this girl—it felt different."

He glances away, his eyes on the lake.

"I met her by a lake, just like this. She was nothing much to look at. Lonely, vulnerable… an easy siphon. And yet…" He shakes his head, eyes down. "There was something about that girl's span—it was strong. I couldn't shake the taste of it. And the high it gave me… messed me up. Made me feel things I had never felt before. Made me look at my life as a Tormenta and see that it was just an *existence*."

He sits up now. "I mean, we laugh at mankind for being so dumb and weak and persuadable. Because they love and hurt and trust. Emotions that we just don't deal in. But I'm no longer sure that makes them weak."

He turns to Lola. "One human will lay down their life for another. Without even knowing that person's name. They care. They cleave together. Tormenta can't even share one acre of ground without ripping each other to pieces. And I guess what I'm saying is, I like the way that her span made me feel. I like the fact that it lets me love."

And she knows that he is going to kiss her. The kiss that Maddy had longed for, eyes closed on the dance floor.

So now Lola closes her eyes and she waits.

And she feels it. His lips. His kiss. Where everything began. And where everything must end.

Lola opens her eyes and the sunlight burns white, blinding her.

She blinks and slowly the sun haze swirls into prisms. Balls of color that stream through a stained-glass window.

Lola is in a church confessional. Through the wooden

grille she can see the outline of a monk.

Fan Fan's voice is a whisper, as if respecting the peace of the church.

"Now you found yourself troubled... conflicted. Could you trust to your heart, when Kave had deceived you before? And what of your span? You had given up everything, turned the Sinestra against you for this one quest, and now you're thinking that you cannot go through with it. Because you love him."

Lola's head is bowed in the shadows of the confessional.

"You sought solace... wisdom. You went to the church by the old soap factory, the White Lily of the Trinity. You knew from your training that it was a safe house for the Chiro Scuro. There you found a monk who would listen to your story, advise you, perhaps. Brother Fidel was kind and patient.

"So you told him the truth. The Brotherhood has no great love for the Sinestra, so they would keep the secret of your desertion safe. And Brother Fidel was much intrigued when you told him how you studied the books of the Collegio Romano—a collection of works that the Sinestra had still failed to return to the Brotherhood, almost two centuries on."

Brother Fidel's voice seeps soft through the confessional. "You said that you have questions and seek answers."

Lola's voice comes clear. "I am aware that since the theft of Brother Magen's writing, much of your knowledge has been lost. So I am not asking what you *know*, Father, just what you believe to be so."

"Very well, my child."

The inhalation from the adjacent box is deep, held long.

"If I take back my span from the Tormenta who stole it, will he die?"

"Yes, we believe he will. But no Hunter is taught how a span is reclaimed, so it has never been proven."

"But I know, Father. I have discovered the means for myself."

"How... how did you discover it?"

"It was in the *Codex Gigas* of Brother Magen. The very last book I read. And I read them all. Every one."

"All of them? But that's... impossible. It is a library in itself!"

"I know... and reading came hard. I never had the patience before. But these books, they spoke to me. They drew me."

"As if their call lay beyond your control?"

"Yeah, I guess."

Brother Fidel's voice is barely more than a whisper. "Just as the legend says. The books are like a magnet to the chosen mind..."

A silence ensues from the monk's side of the confessional. Lola continues.

"So from what you have been taught, from what learning remains, do you believe there is a way that I can redeem my span without causing the death of the Tormenta?"

Now the monk speaks, giving a short, abrasive cough.

"No... I believe not. Death must follow. A Tormenta can release span into the body of another Tormenta, but not back to its original host."

Now it is Lola's turn to fall silent.

"Then I have no choice. I must leave. Harden my heart to him and return only when I can bear his loss."

"That is your only hope, my child."

"Will you help me?"

"Of course… but how?"

Another silence. And this one persists. Until Brother Fidel is forced to quit his box and open the door to Lola's side.

To find her gone. All that remains is a piece of paper. A note addressed to Kave and one request to Brother Fidel written on the reverse: *Please see that Kave gets this.*

The note is not sealed, written in haste on a page torn from the Bible that rests in the confessional.

> Kave,
>
> *I have to go away. If you love me, wait for me. I will return.*
>
> *Lola*

✦

"Did the brother give him the note?" Lola looks up at Fan Fan, like a child still hoping that this story might turn out well.

Fan Fan reaches out, smoothes Lola's hair with a gentle hand. "It is nearly over, child. But close your eyes."

She pulls the final thorn. "This one will hurt."

As she thrusts it between the eyes of the doll, Lola spasms back, a blackness engulfing her. This time, Fan Fan's voice comes distant and distorted, as if carried by the solar wind across the universe.

"You went to cool your heart. And nothing chills it faster than the drill of killing."

Lola's eyes stare out from a face set like stone. A splatter of blood arcs across her cheek as a blade flies in her hand.

From her grip, the slit neck of a woman slides free.

"You went on a killing spree. You slaughtered every Tormenta you could find."

As dark as her eyes, the twin barrels of her shotgun rise. Blasting smoke, and a man explodes across the dashboard of his car.

"You wanted each kill to refresh your hatred of Tormenta. Remind you of what brought you here. Teach yourself a lesson in vengeance."

A bullet shears through a young girl's neck. Lola cranks and reloads her automatic. "You were merciless."

A smart-suited guy backs away, hands up in surrender as a bullet carves out his heart.

"You had everyone looking for you. Tormenta were running scared. The Sinestra dispatched their best to bring you in. You didn't care."

Lola stands high atop a warehouse. The wind-torn factory sign behind her reads THE SOFT SOAP FACTORY. Like an eagle, Lola stares down at a church far below. White paint curls from its walls, like the petals of lilies.

"The day came for you to return. You felt ready, capable of ruthless subterfuge, to look at him with eyes of love and then drag the life—your life—from his body."

Her eyes sweep to the distant neon rooftop sign that flashes SALSA SHACK.

"Like all good Hunters, you would observe him before he knew of your return."

She pulls a set of high-powered binoculars and scouts the streets about the dance club.

"You have been long gone. Your absence may have caused his heart to cool."

A flash of black hair. Lola zooms in.

It is him. She zooms closer.

"For all his talk about believing in love—you may have fallen from his affection the moment you left. Because Kave is a liar, a deceiver, a Tormenta... a believer."

An image fills the binocular lenses. A black lily, tattooed across his heart, wrapped with a ribbon that bears the name LOLA.

Her mouth opens. Then she immediately rips the threatened smile from her lips.

She will not be diverted! She will complete her plan. Seduce him. Steal back her span.

Lola descends the rusted fire escape of the factory, arriving on the sidewalk. Scarlet heels stride toward the dance club.

"You would be just how he remembered you. That knowing smile, those diamond eyes. And now your lips will tell him that by leaving him, you proved to yourself how much you want him."

The red dress swings with every step as Lola approaches the club.

"The lily tells you that Kave's feelings for you are real. So you will assure him that you feel the same. Your heart is his. You love him."

The little red shoes hasten, suddenly breaking into a run.

"And these things that you tell yourself—you suddenly realize they are not lies intended to seduce him. They are true. You love him."

Lola is laughing, tears running down her face.

"All thoughts of vengeance are forgotten. You do not want your span back, for you know now it would be no life without him."

Lola bursts into the club. It is in darkness and empty. Her eyes search the shadows. Wanting to call out his name, but something halts her. A sound.

Breathing—hard and strained. Like that of someone dying.

Lola paces toward the back hall, eyes wide, fearful. And then she sees him.

Not him at first. At first she sees the woman. Naked, strong and beautiful, writhing on top of Kave, who is sprawled across the bare dance floor. Grasping the woman's hips, grinding her down, groaning in ecstasy.

The woman has black features but pale skin. A strip is painted across her eyes, like a honeybee. And long, albino dreadlocks ripple as she rocks and rides Kave's body. And with a roar, Kave explodes into her body and she shrieks wildly as she arches high.

Lola stands rooted, open-mouthed. Plain little Maddy, watching Kave kiss Gina on the dance floor.

Just the same.

Except Maddy had run to cut her own throat.

Lola sinks back into the shadows and pulls her blade. From the covering darkness, she watches as the albino woman gathers her clothes, throwing them about her as she exits the club.

Kave heaves for breath on the wooden floor, his body dripping with sweat. He rises and turns at the sound of footsteps. And as he sees Lola's face, he smiles, barely feeling the chill of her blade. Only the warmth of his blood lets him know that she has cut his throat. And as he falls, the blood pools fast from his neck, running behind Lola as she walks away, as if her red dress is melting like a Popsicle.

"You don't look back. Looking back is what hurt you in the first place. Those memories of Maddy—those are what made you fall in love with him again. Now the past is done with. Kave has deceived you for the last time."

Lola's face is set hard, denying the tears that fall. They are lost in the rain that now pours as she walks through the streets.

Ripping off her scarlet shoes, she feels the sidewalk splash beneath her feet. Hurls the shoes to the flooding gutter. Wipes the knife blade clean against her dress as she walks. Feels the wet satin cling to her thighs. She looks up to see the church of the White Lily of the Trinity. Bursts through the doors, her skin cold, her fury burning. Spins round with her blade up, thrusting it against a throat.

Forcing to the wall a man who yelps in fear. It is a young monk.

He burbles, finally finding his voice. "I know who you are."

Lola lowers the knife, her hot eyes unblinking. The brother blusters on. "Brother Fidel said that you would return one day. He told me to watch, to wait faithfully. He had not long to live, so he knew he might not be here when you returned... to give you this."

He pulls a letter from within his robes, holds it before his face, like a thin shield. "This letter tells of something wonderful. That's what Brother Fidel said. I haven't read it—that would be a sin of transgression. He said that only you must see..."

"I saw enough."

The young brother shrieks as the knife flashes past his face. And the letter, speared on its tip, is gone.

Gone, too, is Lola.

✦

"You never read Brother Fidel's letter." Fan Fan sets down the doll and strokes Lola's eyes, forcing them to open.

"You came back here to me and I had never seen you so crazed with grief... with anger. The pain was jus' too much for you to bear. You had fallen in love, to find it as sharp as a Romeo spike. You told me everything and then begged me, right here in this very room, to burn the letter and to remove every memory, every thought of Kave. You told me to leave you with just enough of your past for you to know who you are now... and what you must do. Enough for you to function in your duty as a Hunter... but, child, not enough to *live*."

Lola looks up at the old mambo. "Did you burn the letter?"

"No, child. Because I knew this day would come."

Fan Fan's eyes go to the row of poppets, hung on the wall. "Each one o' them holds a little of what I took from you. But this one..." She looks down to the doll in her arms. "This one holds the truth."

She takes a knife and slits the throat of the doll, along the jagged red line that circles its neck, now revealed as stitching. Its thorny head falls away, and rolled within its body, like a spine, is a letter. Fan Fan pulls it out, smoothes it flat against her lap. Then offers it to Lola.

"Might you read it aloud, child?"

She pushes a candle closer as Lola unfolds the papers. Inhales... finding her voice.

Lola,

My time is short. So I leave you this letter, so you may know the truth.

Let us begin by returning to the night of our first meeting. You believed that your only goal was to redeem your span. You knew nothing of the Moera. But I did.

Years before, the Fuga di Spino came into my hands. This book had been brought to the Brotherhood by Judas. He was engaged in his own lonely search for the Hunter who would pass into the third state.

When you confessed that you felt drawn to the works of Brother Magen, my suspicions were aroused. Could it be that you were destined to be the Moera? Then, when you further confessed that you felt compelled to reclaim your span, I was utterly convinced. But you slipped through my fingers, disappearing into the night, leaving only the note addressed to Kave. But I could not stand idle—I had to do all within my power to ensure that, upon your return, you would see your calling through to its completion.

The sole obstacle to this event was Kave. That is to say, your love for him. So I prayed for guidance. I asked God, "What should I do?" And the answer came: Do as she bids you. Deliver the letter. And so it was that I went to Kave. I must confess that I was fearful... to be in the presence of something so ungodly. But as I observed him read the words that told of your leaving, I witnessed what I believe to be a miracle. In his eyes—the eyes of a

Tormenta—I saw real hurt. And emboldened by this, I risked my life. I asked him if he wanted salvation.

And he met my eyes and he said yes.

What followed was a strange exchange. I told him all that I knew of you, of what you are. Of what you must become. Of the Moera.

And despite my fear of his hurt becoming fury, I told him that what stood in the way of your destiny was him. Because for you to enter the third state, he must give up his life. And you loved him too much for that.

But there was hope. If he were to release your span into another Tormenta—one for whom you had no affection—then you would reclaim your span from that Tormenta without hesitation. And your transformation into the Moera would be complete.

He told me that he would comply. His only wish was to see you fulfilled.

Then I told him of the sacrifice that he must make. He must renounce all his Tormenta ways. This would be the price of his soul's salvation. He must live as a human, take no more span... die as a human.

He agreed to this covenant. We told no one, and in secret we strove to find the perfect vessel into which he would decant your span. We needed a Tormenta who would succumb to both his seduction and yours.

We found the one. Her name is Bee-Bee. All the information you need is on the reverse of this letter. A Hunter of your caliber will have no trouble tracking her down.

Kave will complete his task before your return. Then he must leave. And you and he must never meet again. As succor to your

hurt, I offer you this from the gospel of John 4:18: Perfect love
casts out fear, because fear is torment.

Kave loves you. So know that what he does, he does for love.

And so my heart goes with you, Lola, heart of the world.

Forever,
Fidel

The letter falls and Fan Fan reaches down, pulling Lola upward, forcing her to stand.

Black eyes meet blue. "So what you gonna do, child? Choice is yours. Always has been."

Lola says nothing. But her heart answers.

Find Bee-Bee. Take back my span. Become three... and so become one.

(iii)

A needle pierces tense flesh. Black ink spurts. The needle sinks again, faster now, the metal flashing as it gains speed.

The machine is forging a tattoo. As the design takes shape, it becomes clear that it is a number. It arches across the curve of a huge muscle.

Dali peers closely as the ink and blood bubble and set. Then inhales to project his voice above the jabber of the machine.

"I have been accused of favoritism in the past, and to that I plead guilty. But the way you came to me, how could I not adore you?" He pulls a handkerchief, dabbing at the blood that dribbles down the arm. "The most fundamental error... and yet still Vassago still commits it. He could not wait until the life had left your body. You practically tricked him into making you this!"

Dali tuts as he tucks the handkerchief away. "Your training has taken longer than usual, because your duty as a Hunter is unique. Unlike your associates, you will not be hunting Tormenta. You will seek out only the Mosca."

His last word rings loud as the machine stops, the number complete.

Dali gently dabs the arm, blowing on the flesh to cool the sting. "You step into some big shoes. The last Hunter to bear this number was amongst the greatest to ever serve the Sinestra."

He takes a stride back to admire his new protégé. The quiver of his cuffs suggests a huge satisfaction.

"I have been permitted to train you for this one task because the Legion's last attempt demands that we raise our game. And in addition to a dedicated Hunter, we have installed a new security measure into the Helix Vivat."

Dali taps a shiny, giant oscilloscope that is plugged into the dash of the machine. "In exchange for the High Command's gracious toleration of a particular pastime of mine, I have applied my private research to the design of this device."

He leans low, huffs upon the glass, and buffs it with his cuff. "This scope is tuned to the frequency of the Mosca's span. It is still somewhat rudimentary, as my memories of meeting him are fleeting. Yo' have to consider, it was more than a century ago and I barely glimpsed the boy. There was a fire, yo' see. And he was shrouded in smoke with just that little wooden bird in his hand. And in all honesty, my mind was much in flux, so filled with my beloved that—"

Dali halts mid-sentence, a careful hand rising to his lips. "I digress. Suffice to say I saw the boy." He now clasps his hands together in moderated joy. "And even with this scant information, our new scope has succeeded at last in issuing us a reading."

He slides over a sheaf of papers. "If we have deciphered it correctly, it indicates that the Mosca arrived five years ago into the body of a male child."

His fingers tap the file. "This contains the full report. It will enable you to locate the target."

Dali looks up. "Any questions, 101B?"

The Hunter steps forward, a taut body wrapped in black, moving like a shaft of midnight. The face is harder, the eyes colder. He says nothing.

But it is unmistakably Siggurson.

Dali grins. "Then let the hunt commence."

(İV)

The little boy has eyes only for the fly. He sits in the corner of a noisy nursery. He has been excluded from the game at play, but he seems not to care. His dark eyes follow the insect as it creeps up the wall. With a flash of his small hand, he snares it, wrapping his fingers tight. Pulling his fist toward him and then opening it, finger by finger. The fly remains on his palm, washing its bulbous head, twitching its wings that catch in the sunlight, twinkling with a rainbow of colors.

Even when a teacher smoothes her skirt and kneels down

beside him, the boy doesn't turn.

She inhales, gathering patience. "You know that what you did was wrong, don't you?"

The boy says nothing, his eyes still set on the fly. The teacher perseveres. "You may not have pushed Beatrice from the monkey bars, but those nasty words you said about her weight, you really upset her. And then she fell."

The little boy turns, his eyes unblinking. "She jumped."

The teacher thins her mouth, attempting to hold her smile. "Your mommy told me that your daddy used to be bullied at school. They called him an unkind name because he didn't have a mother. So you don't want to hurt other children like your daddy was hurt, do you?"

"I don't have a daddy."

The teacher inhales, realizing that this was perhaps a bad tactic. She turns at the sound of footsteps behind her.

"Ah… I'm glad you're here." Appearing at her side is Bianco. "He's been doing it again, I'm afraid."

The teacher pauses, then feels compelled to continue. "What concerns me is that upsetting the other children clearly gives your son so much… pleasure."

Bianco stiffens, instinctively rising to her son's defense. She grasps his hand. "It is very hard for him."

The teacher nods, trying to sympathize.

"I appreciate that. Every boy needs a father to look up to. But his behavior is entirely inappropriate. So perhaps it would be best if you found another nursery. Somewhere better able to assist such a… challenged little boy."

Bianco spins on her heel, exiting with her son in tow.

As she walks out into the sunshine, she forces a smile. Hoists her son up onto her hip.

"You don't listen to her. You do have a father, and he is someone you can look up to." She tips her head toward the sky. "Because he is up there. And he is looking down on you."

She squeezes his little body tight. "No matter what you do, he will be watching, my darling. And no matter where you go, he will find you."

ACKNOWLEDGMENTS

To ALL THOSE who recognized that my antisocial and obsessive habits would be best suited to the solitary life of a writer—thank you for your encouragement. Among them, I must single out for special mention Howard Reay and Peter Lukas.

To Edward Fitzpatrick, who saved me the cost of a stamp by passing the manuscript to the publisher, my ongoing gratitude.

And to Andrew Goth, my everlasting thanks for your insight and vision. I could not have done this without you.

ABOUT THE AUTHOR

FIRST-TIME AUTHOR Joanne Reay began as a documentary maker for The Discovery Channel, where her films focused on the mysteries of brain function and the human mind. She then moved to the BBC, creating the acclaimed detective series *The Murder Rooms*. As a film writer/producer, her credits include *Bring Me the Head of Mavis Davis*, *Cold & Dark* and *Gallowwalker*.

COMING SOON FROM TITAN BOOKS

JOANNE REAY'S

Lo'Life Trilogy continues!

BOOK TWO
BLACK
ANTLERS

AVAILABLE IN 2013

TITANBOOKS.COM